PRAISE FOR *BITTE*

A Young Adult Libra[...]
Best Ficti[...]

A *Kirkus* Be[...] [...]

An Indie Next Pick

★ "This multifaceted book successfully manages to be many things: a satisfying paranormal mystery, a family narrative examining the damage of secrets kept and the ways in which silence allows violence to grow, and a paean to the immense Appalachian forest and the small communities nestled between the trees."

—*Kirkus Reviews*, starred review

★ "Pearsall pulls on elements of Appalachian lore around Mothman but makes the creature and its origin uniquely her own, setting up Faustian deals and fateful tragedies that build tension and surely break hearts (both of characters and readers alike)." —*The Bulletin of the Center for Children's Books*, starred review

★ "The writing is tense and suspenseful with each new discovery bringing more questions. VERDICT: A compelling story as the James women struggle to deal with their own secrets and, in the process, reveal some [of] the darkest ones in town." —*School Library Journal*, starred review

"Debut author Pearsall balances paranormal thrills and the horrors of the central mystery to craft a cottage-core-infused world replete with cozy domestic enchantments, a close-knit female cast, and a captivating romance."

—*Publishers Weekly*

"The details and the lyrical yet accessible writing are what set this debut apart from other small town murder mystery YA novels." —*NPR*

"Haunted golden boys, deeply nuanced, magical girls, and the threat of something lurking in the woods kept me turning the page long after dark. Pearsall's debut is positively spellbinding."
—Sasha Peyton Smith, *New York Times* bestselling author of *The Witch Haven*

"A story rich in tradition and lore. Let the James sisters lead you deep into a world where beauty and evil hold hands in the shadows."

—Ginny Myers Sain, *New York Times* bestselling author of *Secrets So Deep*

"A captivating debut that blends a palpable atmosphere, visceral magic, and the depths of sisterly love to create a concoction even more enticing than the Harvest Moon's famous tomato pie."

—Andrea Hannah, author of *Where Darkness Blooms*

BITTERSWEET

IN THE

HOLLOW

Also by Kate Pearsall

Lies on the Serpent's Tongue

BITTERSWEET
IN THE
HOLLOW

Kate Pearsall

G. P. PUTNAM'S SONS

G. P. PUTNAM'S SONS

An imprint of Penguin Random House LLC
1745 Broadway, New York, New York 10019

First published in the United States of America by G. P. Putnam's Sons,
an imprint of Penguin Random House LLC, 2023
First paperback edition published 2024

Copyright © 2023 by Kate Pearsall

Lies on the Serpent's Tongue excerpt copyright © 2024 by Kate Pearsall

G. P. Putnam's Sons is a registered trademark of Penguin Random House LLC.
The Penguin colophon is a registered trademark of Penguin Books Limited.

Visit us online at PenguinRandomHouse.com.

THE LIBRARY OF CONGRESS HAS CATALOGED THE HARDCOVER EDITION AS FOLLOWS:
Names: Pearsall, Kate, author.
Title: Bittersweet in the hollow / Kate Pearsall.
Description: New York: G. P. Putnam's Sons, 2023. | Series: Bittersweet in the hollow
Summary: When a girl goes missing in her secluded Appalachian town, seventeen-year-old Linden, who can taste other people's emotions, recovers haunting memories of her own disappearance and explores the legend of the Moth-Winged Man, leading her to wonder if there are some secrets best left buried.
Identifiers: LCCN 2023009516 (print) | LCCN 2023009517 (ebook)
ISBN 9780593531020 (hardcover) | ISBN 9780593531037 (kindle edition)
Subjects: CYAC: Ability—Fiction. | Emotions—Fiction. | Missing persons—Fiction.
Mothman—Fiction. | Fantasy. | LCGFT: Fantasy fiction. | Novels.
Classification: LCC PZ7.1.P4345 Bi 2023 (print) | LCC PZ7.1.P4345 (ebook)
DDC [Fic]—dc23
LC record available at https://lccn.loc.gov/2023009516
LC ebook record available at https://lccn.loc.gov/2023009517

ISBN 9780593531044

1st Printing

Printed in the United States of America

LSCC

Design by Nicole Rheingans
Text set in Perrywood MT Std

For Ava

And for anyone ever made to believe
they felt too much or too deeply.

June

➤➤ Strawberry Moon ◄◄

June's full moon peaks as wild strawberries blush to ripening. Emotions run high on full moon nights, and summer heat brings with it a restless energy that heightens our intuition. Beware of fiery tempers, unnecessary risks, igniting passions, and well-concealed deception. An ideal time for working charms of protection, decisiveness, strength, love, and fertility.

➤➤ In Season ◄◄

Garden: asparagus, beets, broccoli, cabbage, carrots, cherries, greens,
        green onions, herbs, peas, radishes, rhubarb, strawberries,
        and sweet peppers
Forage: wild strawberries, sarvisberries (gather from the trees on top
        of the mountain to avoid worms), stinging nettles,
        dandelion greens, chicken of the woods mushrooms,
        wild carrot, arrow leaf, and cow lily root

➤➤ Stinging Nettle Rope for Protection ◄◄

Spin the long fibers from stinging nettle into yarn under the full moon and braid three strands into a rope. Knot the rope around the doorknob to protect a place, or around the wrist to protect a person. When the threat has passed, burn the rope or invite new trouble.

A bowl of beer in the garden will get rid of snails and slugs, but of late has proven to attract the eldest son of the family on the hill. Placing a slug in the bowl before setting it out seems to work, judging from the gagging and spitting sounds last night.

—*Elora James, 1935*

CHAPTER ONE

HERE'S WHAT I know for sure: A cast iron skillet must be seasoned with lard. Pickling and preserving are best done during a waning moon. And secrets buried deep never stay that way.

I plant myself in front of the box fan wedged into the window and lift the hem of my shirt so the air can move across my skin. The Harvest Moon was once a gristmill, and its thick old limestone walls help cool the inside. But we serve breakfast and lunch six days a week, and there's no escaping the heat once it really gets cooking.

Gran eyes me from the opposite side of the small kitchen, where she's prepping food for tomorrow night's festival. She runs the blade of her knife between the ribs of a side of pork she was given for curing the Thompson baby of colic. Breaking through the bone, dismantling it piece by piece, her hands never pause, never falter, even with her gaze on me. She tosses strips of meat into a bowl of spicy marinade, her own secret recipe, and the bones into a roasting pan for broth. Nothing ever wasted.

My sisters and I grew up in this kitchen with its stainless steel tables, white walls, and faint scent of bleach. We've been rolling out biscuit dough, scrubbing salt into cast iron, and sneaking spoonfuls of strawberry moonshine jam from the time we could barely see over the counter. So I know what Gran is thinking: Standing here next to the fan could be construed as idleness, something she cannot abide, even if it's only June and already ninety degrees in the shade.

A bead of sweat slides down the back of my neck, drawn out by the humidity that's been hunkered down around the base of the mountains for weeks now. I once read that there's a correlation between an increase in temperature and in brutality. That hotter summers are violent ones. I don't know if that's true, but with the way the air sits now, thick and heavy, everyone's temper seems set to boil.

At the back of the kitchen, Rowan, my older sister by eleven months, lifts the metal handle of the commercial dishwasher, releasing a cloud of steam that plasters her dark hair against her pretty face. All four of us sisters have long dark hair, bright blue eyes, and rosy full lips, but Rowan has the darkest and the bluest and the fullest. Yet she wears her beauty like armor to keep others from getting too close. A rose with sharpened thorns.

Her shirt lifts as she reaches up to put some glasses away on a high shelf, just enough to expose a few lines of the black ink that slithers and curls along her hip. It was Mama's discovery of the snake tattoo that relegated Rowan to dish duty all summer. And much as I'd like to avoid the dining room, I don't envy her. It's the hottest job in the kitchen.

Sorrel, our eldest sister, shoves through the swinging door, a tray piled high with dirty dishes on one shoulder. She rushes past me toward the dishwashing station as Rowan turns, likely unable to hear Sorrel's approach over the rattle of the high-pressure wash cycle. They collide with a clatter, and the entire tray tips backward. Plates and glasses clang against each other, and all I can do is watch, waiting for everything to come crashing down. Yet somehow, at the last possible second, Sorrel manages to right it.

She lets out a slow breath of relief just as a single steak knife, teetering on the edge, topples over the side. It lands on its point with a sharp thunk, quivering as it sticks straight up from the floorboards.

"Knife fell," Mama warns from her station, pausing in drawing her own serrated blade through the green skin of a tomato.

"Trouble's comin'." Gran finishes the old bit of folk wisdom with a glance toward the window. The skies have gone a sickly shade of green as storm clouds gather strength over the mountains.

It may sound like superstitious nonsense, but this is the true James family legacy. For as long as I can remember, in the evenings, long after the last customer had gone home, we'd write our wishes in white ink on bay leaves, crushing them between our fingers and releasing them to the wind over and over until all the air around us was scented with their bitter green bite. We learned special words, never to be written down, that must be said in one whispered breath. We watched as burns from hot pans disappeared clean off the skin with little more than Gran's gentle murmur of a few of those words.

"Watch yourself," Sorrel snaps at Rowan as she bends to slide the tray off her shoulder and onto the counter. Then she spins to glare at me. "And thanks for just standing there, Linden. As usual." It's snakebite quick, and by the time I feel the sting, she's already turning away.

We've always been close; four sisters born in as many years meant we had to be. But now that Sorrel is back from college, everything feels different. The first James girl ever to go, it's like she doesn't quite fit in the same space she left behind.

Mama wipes her hands on the dish towel tucked into the apron strings around her waist, then sets two final plates on a large tray. "Order's up," she tells me with a nod toward the dining room.

No amount of wishing on bay leaves will get me out of work. I glance once more at the knife in the floor before pushing past Sorrel and out of the kitchen.

When I reach my table, I set the tray on a stand, then slide each plate in front of the proper customer. Fried green tomato BLT for the man with the beard, buttermilk biscuits and sausage gravy for the younger one with a tiny hole in his collar, skillet-fried chicken drizzled with honey and a side of soup beans for the woman with the glasses, and a slaw dog with thick-cut homemade potato chips for the little boy who keeps wiping his nose on his sleeve.

"Let me know if y'all need anything else," I say, dropping an extra stack of paper napkins next to the boy as they tuck into their lunches.

I move to pick up the empty tray, and a taste like the candied jalapeños Gran makes at the end of the summer, sweet and hot, lights up my tongue. My head jerks in surprise, catching the younger man gazing toward the woman when the bearded man isn't looking.

I turn toward the kitchen, eager to avoid secrets I shouldn't know, only to collide with someone. Hard. The edge of the tray smashes into my chin and drives my teeth into my tongue. I stumble backward, tripping over my feet. Just as I'm about to end up ass over teakettle in front of everyone, a hand shoots out to grab my shoulder. When my gaze travels up the strong arm to an all-too-perfect face, it's only my stomach that plummets to the floor.

Cole Spencer. The town's golden boy, at least according to the gossip that fills the diner day in and day out. Class president, valedictorian, star quarterback, basically God's blessed gift to Caball Hollow all wrapped up in a six-foot package of muscles and glowing skin. His sun-kissed hair might as well be a goddamn halo.

He drops my arm and slides his hands into his pockets. "Watch where you're going, James."

James, like he can't tell me apart from my sisters. Like we'd never been close. Like none of it had ever happened.

He hasn't been in here much since last year, but I heard he's helping with football training camp this summer, and it's tradition to come to the Harvest Moon after. A tradition Cole started back when his dad and mine still used to camp out at the corner table between shifts. Back when things were different.

"Sorry." I nod slowly, sucking the sting out of my tongue. "Not all of us can float above the earth on angel wings."

The corners of his eyes narrow, and his body tenses up underneath his worn gray T-shirt. A reaction so subtle, I might have missed it if I hadn't been watching for it. While the entire town may revere the Spencer family, Cole has never been comfortable with the adoration or the pressure of keeping up appearances. Not when the Spencers have secrets of their own.

But my petty victory is short-lived, as a taste like raw ramps slides under my tongue, pungent and sharp with fear and disgust. My nose wrinkles reflexively, and I swallow hard against the invasion, struggling to push away any feelings that aren't my own. The kind that seep in whenever I'm not careful, until I'm heavy and bloated with them.

It's bad enough to be unwillingly privy to someone's innermost feelings, but it's gutting to have such a potent reminder of how differently Cole sees me now. And that he's right to.

"So can we sit here, or . . . ?" Bryson Ivers, the kicker for the football team and Cole's frequent shadow, slings an arm around Cole's shoulders and gestures toward an empty table near the door. I startle at his sudden appearance. "Whoa, sorry, didn't mean to interrupt . . ." He waves his hand between Cole and me. "Whatever this is."

My fingers tighten against the tray and my cheeks warm as Cole's honey-colored eyes come back into focus. There's something in his expression, gone too quick for me to name. A self-satisfied grin spreads across his lips in its place, and it dawns on me just how long I've been staring at him. I blink and look away.

"What was that all about?" Bryson asks as he pulls Cole toward the open table, not realizing or not caring that I'm still close enough to hear.

"You know how she is," Cole says with a half shrug. His voice drops lower, and I can't make out the rest of his words, but Bryson throws back his head and laughs.

I push through the swinging door to the kitchen, a bitter taste like chicory root in my mouth. I'm sure Cole will have forgotten all about me by the time he finishes his lunch, but I'll be replaying this moment for a good long while and kicking myself for letting him get under my skin.

"What's wrong?" Rowan asks when I scramble to the back of the kitchen.

"I can't take the new table," I urgently whisper with a glance toward Mama and Gran. "Sorrel, will you do it?"

"My section is chock-full, Linden." Sorrel doesn't even look up as she checks over a tray, waiting for the rest of the order. "I have enough of my own tables to worry about."

"Who jerked a knot in your tail?" Rowan leans a hip against the counter next to Sorrel and crosses her arms. "You know Linden would do it for you."

Sorrel huffs and turns back to me. "There's not always going to be someone here to fight your battles, Linden. The sooner you learn that, the better." She shoots a dark look at Rowan. "That's how I'm helping her." As she shoves her order pad into the front pocket of her apron, she leans in and murmurs low so only I can hear her, "Good lord, quit being such a baby."

I look down and study my hands. "It's Cole," I say softly, the words sticking in my throat like gristle. I hate that he can still get to me after all this time.

With a pointed sigh in Sorrel's direction, Rowan pushes away from the counter and pulls off her dirty kitchen apron, the kind that's plain white and easy to bleach, exchanging it for the pretty embroidered one on the hook by the door.

Sorrel is already shaking her head. "Mama said you're pearl diving all month—no tables and no tips," she tells Rowan. "She'll be madder'n fire if you're not back here washing dishes."

I glance over to where Mama stands with her back to us, scribbling on a notepad with the phone squeezed between her ear and shoulder. She's probably taking an order or placing one with a supplier. Either way, she won't be distracted long.

Before I can muster the courage to stop her, Rowan squeezes past Sorrel and pushes through the swinging door. "Be back directly," she tosses over her shoulder.

Sorrel watches her go, mouth set in a hard line. I hesitate for a moment more, then follow Rowan out of the kitchen, pausing behind the front counter. She's already made it to the long table where Cole sits surrounded by his friends and is scribbling their orders down on her pad, flatly denying Bryson's substitution request. As she passes me on her way back to the kitchen, she slides me the ticket with a wink. I'll hang it on the order rail, and Mama will be none the wiser.

Just as I start to let myself relax, the Harvest Moon is plunged into darkness. A hush falls over the dining room as the sky outside turns black. I look toward the big front window as the long-distance bus turns on its headlights and pulls away from the stop at the corner. Summer storms can be sudden and powerful in Caball Hollow, but this one is blowing up especially quick.

In a burst of wind, the front door blows open so hard it bangs into the wall. I lift a hand to protect against the onslaught of dust and debris that gusts in on the draft, scented faintly with sweet asphodel blossoms and peppercorns, until the wind shifts again and the door swings shut.

When I open my eyes, a face I haven't seen in a long while is looking back at me from the other side of the counter.

"Dahlia," I force out as my mouth goes dry. "I didn't know you were back in town."

Dahlia Calhoun graduated with Sorrel, went off to college in the city, and never looked back. We'd been friends once, an unexpected pair perhaps, as she was outspoken and well-liked, and I was quiet and strange. I nearly didn't recognize her because her hair, which had been the color of mouse fur, is now an improbable shade of red, like it's been poured directly out of a Cheerwine bottle.

"Hi, Linden." She leans across the laminate countertop to pull me into a quick hug, and the brightness of lemon bursts against the roof of my mouth. "You know how it goes. The reigning Moth Queen has to crown the new one, so here I am." She shrugs, but then something sparks in her eyes. "You're going to try for queen next year, right?"

Each year during the Moth Festival, senior girls complete projects that honor the history of Caball Hollow in the hopes of being crowned Moth Queen and earning a college scholarship. Dahlia's project was a podcast about the legend of the Moth-Winged Man that inspired the festival. Now she's majoring in broadcast journalism, which is no surprise, considering her voice, all smoky and buttery like sourwood honey, and her habit of never running out of questions. But the idea of me ever being the Moth Queen is laughable for all manner of reasons.

"I'm not sure that's a good idea," I hedge.

"Are you kidding? With your recipe collection project, you'd be a sure thing. You know my mamaw was so pleased when you wanted to learn her old recipes. She used to love to talk about the time she spent with you before she passed."

Asking elderly neighbors to share their old family recipes was plain natural curiosity at first. I'd always liked to bake, but so often favorite dishes come with as many memories as ingredients, and I could tell it made folks happy to share their knowledge with someone who was keen to listen.

Dahlia's grandmother, Parlee Wilkerson, agreed to teach me how to make her famous salt-rising bread. It had once been a tradition in Caball Hollow with nearly as many variations as there were families, but these days few have the time or inclination for such labor-intensive baking. Dahlia lived with her grandmother then, and we'd gotten to know each other during the two-day process. Afterward, Mrs. Wilkerson kept inviting me back to share more: the vinegar pie her great-aunt had perfected, the blackberry dumplings made from leftover biscuit dough that were a favorite of her mother's, and the cinnamon apple cake that had a splash of her husband's homemade moonshine. Through it all, Dahlia and I became closer, our friendship spilling out of the kitchen to school and beyond.

But all that was before. Salt-rising bread is notoriously finicky dough, and tradition says a failed loaf is a sign of ill fortune. That day in the kitchen with Dahlia and her grand-mother, the recipe worked, but it never has for me since.

"I'm not really doing that anymore." My neck goes hot, but my fingertips feel cold. How is it possible to both long for something and dread it at the same time? My eyes slide away from Dahlia to the table where Cole sits with his friends. "Not since last summer."

"Oh." Her eyebrows draw together in sympathy, and I watch as she comes to the wrong conclusion. "If you're worried the judges will hold what happened last year against you, don't be. Everyone knows it was a terrible accident."

"An accident, right." I shrug and glance away. More like a scandal.

When I meet her eyes again, she gives me a sympathetic smile and leans closer. "You really can't remember anything?"

A chill goes through my body like my blood has been switched for ice water, and I squeeze my eyes shut. This is why I avoid everyone who was there the night I went missing. I've spent the last twelve months trying to forget what little I remember, and now, with just a few words, I'm back in those woods. The darkness pressing in on me with an unnatural weight, unseen branches pulling at my hair and tearing at my skin as I run fast. Faster. Fast as I can. My chest heaves, the memory fragment stealing my breath even now. Dahlia doesn't seem to notice.

"Only bits and pieces," I finally answer. My hand trembles as I press it to my brow. "Nothing that makes any kinda sense. The doctors call it post-traumatic amnesia."

A horn honks out front, and Dahlia turns to look. "I've got to go, but there's something I want to talk to you about. You'll be at the festival tomorrow, right?"

I swallow the tang of hot fear and manage a nod. She smiles wide and squeezes my hand, then hustles toward the door, pausing a moment to pat Cole's shoulder and wave to Bryson across the table. A man I don't recognize, in a Caball Hollow High School Athletics polo shirt, holds the door open for her, and then she's gone.

When I can't see her anymore, I let my mind press around the edges of that night last summer, like mapping the shape of a bruise. But all I have is the tattered edges of moth-eaten fabric.

The Appalachians are among the oldest mountains in the world, once connected to the same ancient range as the Scottish Highlands. These hills and hollows are where legends and lore thrive, alive and well. Mine is a story of being lost for a night in the vastness of the National Forest, of fearing the unknown and what may be hiding in shadows of the deepest dark. But make no mistake, it's far from the only mystery held beneath these ancient peaks.

And as much as I want to forget, I know that sometimes secrets are seeds, just waiting for the right conditions to sprout. The deeper you bury them, the stronger they grow.

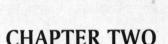

CHAPTER TWO

SOMEWHERE WAY up in the middle of the night, I kick off the last stretch of tangled sheets and stare at the whorls and knots in the tongue-and-groove ceiling. The storm clouds never did deliver on their threat of rain, and now the humidity is so thick that the air feels heavy with it. The farmhouse itself seems to sag under the weight.

Bittersweet Farm doesn't have air-conditioning. Gran claims the house is too old and temperamental to retrofit with central air, but I have my suspicions she just doesn't want to give us any excuse to sleep in on summer mornings and shirk our chores.

I roll over, searching for a cool spot on my pillow, when a sound reverberates in the distance. Church bells. Not the dutiful call to Sunday service or the joyful chime of a wedding celebration. No, these bells mean something else entirely. Mournfully deep and slow, they toll death.

As the quiet starts to close back in, leaving only the even sound of my younger sister Juniper's sleeping breath in the bed next to mine, a knock at the front door startles me back from the edge of sleep. Late-night visitors aren't all that unusual at Bittersweet Farm. At the end of the day, long after the one streetlight in town switches to blinking yellow, those in need of our special skills seek us out.

They come when the sky is inky purple and moonlight limns the gravel path down to the old summer kitchen behind the farmhouse. Some have been up for hours, rocking babies with earaches or children with fevers, and are too fretful to wait for morning. They're willing, at last, to try the old ways they look down their noses at us for practicing. So embarrassingly backward, they snicker, until it's them that need our help. Then they hope the rumors might be true, that somehow our homemade remedies and whispered words can do more than should be possible.

Others wait longer still, until the deepest part of night, before they summon the courage to ask for what they want. Those are usually the ones desperate for something, love or money, though they sometimes ask for other things too, dark things like revenge or harm. Things we won't do. Gran always says we mustn't ever use our abilities to unduly influence the lives of others. It's our most important rule.

I crawl out of bed and creep down the front stairs, skipping over the one that creaks and stopping just before the turn that opens up to the first floor.

"Odette, get the candles and the salt bowl," Gran murmurs as she pulls open the front door.

The man on the porch is standing just out of sight, and I lean forward as much as I dare to catch a glimpse. "Sorry to disturb y'all at this time of night." His voice is like an old gravel road, dry and worn. "She was betwixt this place and the next most of the afternoon, but she's passed on now."

"I'm so sorry for your loss, Amos." Gran reaches out to briefly clasp the man's hand.

"If'n it weren't too much trouble, ma'am, would you come sit up with her?" he asks. "I know most people don't bother anymore, but Nora found comfort in the old ways."

Even people who don't believe in anything tend to get superstitious around death, and when they do, they come to Gran. With flame and salt, she'll bless the body and protect the spirit on its journey, like her mother and grandmother and all those who came before her did. Saining is an old practice, brought over by Scots-Irish ancestors, then altered and adapted and now, like so many other things, mostly forgotten.

Mama steps into the foyer from the kitchen and hands Gran her bag of supplies. "Better get a chicken ready to fry," Gran tells her as she steps out the door. Leave it to Gran to think of people's stomachs as much as their souls.

Out front, a car engine fires up, and the glow of headlights traces a path across the wallpaper, then disappears.

Mama turns from where she's been watching out the window. "Tea?" she asks softly. I make my way down the rest of the stairs, and she wraps an arm around my shoulders, leading me toward the kitchen. Her thick chestnut hair is swept up in a loose ponytail, and she smells like the violet soap she makes every spring.

"Bad dream?" Mama lights the stove and moves the kettle onto the burner.

"Mm-hmm," I murmur, sliding into a chair at the table.

She reaches up to open the cupboard and takes out a mug, her back to me, then stills, cradling it in her hands. It's a chipped old brown one she made years ago. My father's favorite. It's been months since he moved out. I should be used to it by now, but it all happened so fast, and seeing the things he left behind still feels disorienting, like a glimpse into a different life.

"It's been a while since the last one, hasn't it?" Mama asks as she exchanges the brown mug for a green one.

"A good while, yeah." *No.* The dreams still come nearly every night until I wake up gasping for breath. I rest my elbows on the table and trace a finger across its worn surface. "Dahlia stopped by the diner today. She's home for the festival."

"Ah." Mama turns to face me, leaning against the counter. I can feel her eyes, but I don't look up. "She wants to talk."

"Maybe that's a good idea," she says gently. "I know you want to put it all behind you, but it might help to talk to someone who was there that night—"

"Mama, stop!" I jerk my head up, pressing my hands against the table, and catch her startled expression. "There is nothing she can say that will change what happened. What good could come from remembering the worst day of my life?"

"I don't mean to push, sweet girl, but I've seen how you've pulled away from everyone." The kettle starts to whistle, and she turns to move it off the heat. "I'm worried about you, that's all."

"Sorry." I drop my head into my hands and blow out a breath. "I just wish . . ." I trail off. There's so many things I wish were different that I don't even know where to begin. My eyelids are heavy, but every time I close them, I'm back in those woods, panicked, running. Lost.

When the search party found me early the next morning, only steps from where I'd disappeared the night before, I had a concussion and no memory of what had happened. The official report concluded that I'd fallen—there's no shortage of hazards up in the mountains—and gotten disoriented, then lost in the dark. But that doesn't explain the nightmares. It doesn't explain the way my pulse speeds up when the moon casts shadows of tree branches against my bedroom wall or the cold dread that fills my stomach every time I venture too close to the Forest.

Maybe our bodies hold memories, too, written in the bone, woven between sinew, hidden beneath the skin. My fingers trace the scar across my neck, the only reminder of what happened that still remains. That and the guilt, sitting heavy in my chest. "I wish none of it had happened," I whisper.

I was reckless and foolish in more ways than one, and now

everyone around me is paying a price. Mama most of all. For a long time after, she wouldn't let me out of her sight. She slept on the floor next to my bed for weeks, reaching for me in her sleep. Even now, she peeks in my room late some nights. I don't think I'm the only one with bad dreams.

Mama pulls the jar of Gran's special sleep-easy tea from its perch on the back of the stove. She's quiet as she makes the tea, but when she slides the cup in front of me, she rubs a hand across my shoulders. "Linden, maybe you should consider talking to Dahlia, not because of that night but because of all the ones that came before it. That was one page of a much longer story."

I wrap my hands around the mug, swallowing back the emotion that bubbles up inside of me.

"Do you know why I named you Linden?" Mama asks. I nod, this story is a well-trod path, but she keeps going. "The linden tree is known for its power of protection, for luck, and for love. I named you after it to bless you with those same characteristics. And you have them, Linden. There is no one else like you. And there is nothing wrong with being exactly and completely who you are."

Mama gives my shoulder one last squeeze before she heads back to bed. She may believe that, but there are plenty of people in this town who would disagree. I pull the mug closer, staring down into the pinkish liquid as the steam dampens my cheeks.

And as I lift it to take a sip, I dare to hope that maybe, if I can't wish it away, I can somehow make it up to those I hurt.

When the first sherbet shades tint the tops of the mountains, I give up on sleep. I don't really mind early mornings. Lately, it's the only time when it doesn't feel like living inside a dog's mouth. Even now, with the sun barely cresting the hills, steam rises to meet it as the morning dew cooks right out of the grass.

I slap open the screen door with one hand as I pull on a pair of worn sneakers with the other, not bothering to untie them, then tripping and nearly wiping out on the back steps of the wraparound porch.

This rambling old farmhouse has been home to James women for generations, the fieldstone wing tacked on to the clapboard extension of what remains of the original eighteenth-century log cabin, the structure itself growing right along with the family at Bittersweet Farm. It's said that the protective bittersweet vines sprung up at the fence line of their own accord, surrounding the land and giving it its name.

There has always been something of the unexplainable here, an air of strangeness around us James women that keeps others at a distance. The old story goes that way back when Caball Hollow was little more than a handful of neighboring homesteads, the first James woman walked out of the Forest all alone. No one knew where she'd come from. She was said to be a bit peculiar and kept to herself. But that was nothing unusual for West Virginia, and she had a special knack for getting anything to grow even in the most inhospitable soil.

I don't know if any of it is true or not, but I do know that James women are born with certain talents. Sorrel, as nocturnal as a brown bat, can charm bees to make honey that will bind any promise or strengthen any spell. Rowan can smell a lie on the teller's breath and talk sour milk sweet. Juniper has one eye between this world and the next, like Great-Granny Sudie before her.

But we never talk about our abilities outside of the family. People fear what they don't understand, and fear can make them dangerous. It's a lesson we've learned well enough through the generations, and one the scorch marks on the wall of the old log cabin won't let us ever forget.

With my shoes securely on, I trudge along the dirt path from the back porch to the barn. When we were little, we never wore shoes in the summer. We'd race over the crab-grass and run down the rocky mountain paths, thickening up the soles of our feet as we searched for crawdad holes in the creek behind the farm or plucked sun-warmed rasp-berries from where the vines grew wild. In the barn, we'd swing from a rope high up in the hayloft and drop onto the pile of fresh sawdust meant for the livestock stalls, until the day Rowan tried to do a flip in midair and missed the pile entirely. She might have broken an arm, but we're lucky we didn't all break our fool necks.

Today, I bypass the ladder to the hayloft and pull out the old bike that has faded to the mottled pink of an unripe strawberry. It was secondhand before it belonged to Sorrel, then it went to Rowan, and now Juniper and I share it. Sorrel and Rowan can drive, so they have little use for it, but I don't have my license yet, even though I've been old enough for more than a year.

As I push the bike out of the barn, a clod of dirt whizzes past my head and explodes against the wall behind me.

"If you can't be bothered to tell the truth, at least keep your stinking lies from spoiling my breakfast," Rowan yells from the porch, one hand covered in dirt and hovering over the flower box, the other pointing at a dumbfounded Hadrian Fitch where he stands at the gate to the sheep pen.

The lone masculine presence on Bittersweet Farm, Hadrian showed up just in time for the harvest last year, looking for work in mirrored aviator sunglasses, jeans with holes ripped in both knees, and a fiddle case tucked under one arm.

He's no one's idea of a farmer. Black tattoos trail across his skin, down his arms, across both hands, along his fingers, even crawling out from under his collar and up his neck, getting lost in the ever-present scruff on his face that leads up to his unruly swath of dark hair.

He told us he'd run out of money up near Rawbone while searching for his brother after aging out of the system a couple years ago. It didn't take long for Rowan to pronounce him a liar, but there are a million reasons people lie, not all of them malicious, and to her all lies smell the same. We were desperate for the help, and he was willing to work for little more than room and board and the freedom to take on other odd jobs in the area. In the months since, he's proven himself to be a hard worker who doesn't say much, which means Gran will never let him go, no matter how much Rowan protests.

He lifts a single dark brow at her. "What are you on about now?"

"You told Gran you needed the truck today so you could go to the feed store," Rowan grinds out between clenched teeth. She chucks another dirt clod at Hadrian's head that misses him by inches and peppers his hair, then stalks down the steps toward him. "But you and I both know that's not true. So where are you really going?"

"Rowan, stop." I drop the bike and move to intercept her. "You know what Gran said." I lower my voice as I catch her around the wrist.

She looks at me, her eyes still flashing, but a voice interrupts us before she can speak. "Rowan Persephone," Gran calls as she steps out onto the porch. "I told you to leave that boy alone and let him do his work. Come in here now, please. I have a job for you."

Rowan lets out a tiny growl of frustration and sends a dark glare in Hadrian's direction. "This isn't over," she threatens low, then turns to stomp back up the porch steps toward what is sure to be an unpleasant task as she wipes the dirt from her hands onto the side of her jeans.

"It never is." Hadrian's voice is quiet behind me.

I glance over my shoulder, but he's already gone. Instead, a woman stands in the driveway. She's wearing black boots and a motorcycle jacket that makes me sweat just to look at it but doesn't seem to bother her in the least. Tossing back her long dark hair, she slides off her sunglasses, revealing sparkling eyes the color of wood smoke, framed by perfectly winged liner. A slow smile works its way across cherry-red lips like sticky-sweet sorghum syrup.

An amused snort comes from the porch, and I look to see Gran holding the door open. "Land sakes alive, trouble indeed. Hurricane Salome just blew into town."

"Hey there, Mama. You miss me?" Aunt Salome walks toward the house but stops in front of me and puts her hands on my shoulders, holding me at arm's length. "And this can't be my sweet little Linden. You've gone and grown up while I was away."

"You wouldn't miss so much if you came home more often," Gran chides.

Caball Hollow has never been big enough for fiddle-footed Aunt Sissy. She lit out of here as soon as she could. Off hither, thither, and yon, yet always returning to this little scooped-out tablespoon of a town about two hours from anywhere. The only way in or out is a switchback that washes out a few times a year. It's so far off the beaten path that Gran says electricity didn't even find its way to Caball Hollow until she was in the fourth grade.

It's been almost a year since Salome rushed home at the news of my disappearance, the longest stretch between visits that I can remember, though Mama and Gran say there's been longer. "Welcome home, Aunt Sissy," I tell her, my voice thick with emotion. We do love our nicknames in Caball Hollow, the way they're a shorthand for shared history or a shortcut back to another time.

She leans in to press a quick kiss to my cheek, but for a brief moment, it looks like all the shine's gone out of her. A furrow between her brows replaces her easy smile and the oily taste of sardines coats my tongue. Guilt. For a moment I'm not sure if it's hers or mine, then a wash of shame prickles under my skin.

I pull away as Gran reaches to give Sissy a hug of her own, rushing to pick up the bike and be anywhere but here. "I better get to the diner or Mama will have my hide," I call, already standing up on the pedals to push hard up the hill and out onto the dirt road without a backward glance.

The shortest route from Bittersweet Farm to the Harvest Moon goes directly past the Caball Hollow cemetery. Back in our loft-jumping days, Rowan used to tell us that if we didn't hold our breath as we passed, the spirits would steal it and we'd be the next to die. Until Gran caught wind of it and told us it was pure and utter foolishness. What would haints be hanging around a cemetery of all places for, anyhow?

But sometimes, on days like today—right before the solstice, when the air feels thick and close—I still take a big gulp of air and hold my breath, just in case. I'm fixin' to speed past the cemetery as fast as I can when a dirty white pickup truck shoots out of the gates without stopping, nearly putting me in need of a plot myself.

Pulling the bike to the right, I brake with all my strength. It wobbles hard, and I barely have time to jump off before it crashes into one of the ornamental pear trees that line the street.

I push myself off the ground and kick some loose gravel in the direction the truck sped off in. When I reach down to pick up the bike, a sting blazes across the skin of my elbow. As I twist to inspect the injury, something else catches my eye. Near the river, in the shade of the big sweet gum tree beside the Spencer family mausoleum, a backhoe rests beside the gaping hole of a freshly dug grave.

The loamy, sunbaked smell of dirt floats to me across the still morning air. Two men in coveralls stand solemnly near the machinery. One holds a shovel; the other clasps his hat in front of him. But it's the man standing next to the open earth that draws my attention. He's hunched in on himself, his white hair unkempt as if he's been running his hands through it, and though he wears a suit, it's a bit snug around the middle, faded and moth-eaten like it hasn't been worn in years. He digs a handkerchief out of his pocket and holds it up to his face. His shoulders shake, but he doesn't make a sound.

The man drops a handful of dirt into the open earth, and as my gaze follows it down, a noise like the buzz of a cicada or a power line zips through the air and along my spine. I should give him his privacy, but there's a pull low in my stomach now that urges me closer. He looks familiar some-how, and as I draw nearer, I realize it's the man who came to the house last night.

There's something strange about this. After all, what kind of burial has only one mourner and takes place so soon after death? But as I reach the mausoleum, a taste like Mama's pickled beets fills my mouth, and I realize I've let my curiosity override my common sense. Not suppressing my ability is an especially foolish mistake after what just happened with Aunt Sissy. And this time it's so much worse. I brace myself as the flavors overwhelm me. It would be obvious to anyone that he's heartbroken, but it's more than that—the oily brine of guilt, the vinegary bite of anger, the pungent whiff of despair.

Violating this man's innermost feelings at a time like this makes my stomach twist. It's like eavesdropping on a private conversation or reading someone's diary. It's wrong to know these things about someone without their permission. I stumble backward, away from the power of his emotions, blinking against the press of my own tears as I make my way back to my bike as quietly as I can. It's not until I'm halfway to the Harvest Moon that I realize I forgot to hold my breath.

CHAPTER THREE

TODAY IS exactly one year from the day I went missing. By the time Mama flips the sign on the door of the diner to CLOSED, I've already reached the limit of my antiperspirant and my nerves are fully fried. The whispers and the curious stares cast my way throughout the day prove no one has forgotten what happened, but work isn't even close to over. It's the biggest night of the year in Caball Hollow.

The Moth Festival is a celebration born in part from one of the town's oldest fears. The legend of the Moth-Winged Man is whispered over campfires and into the ears of children up past their bedtimes. Set to the creak of a porch swing or the tap of rain against a metal roof, it's the tale of a mysterious creature—the sight of which is a sure sign of impending death—that haunts the Forest and travels on moonlight.

The festival itself is so old no one remembers exactly how it began, but it's always held on the summer solstice, the day with the longest period of light. A date chosen as a precaution against the nocturnal Moth-Winged Man, maybe. Or is it something else? The old ways teach that the solstice is liminal, a time between time, as we shift from days growing longer to shorter. A time when magic weighs heavy in the air and the line between the known world and the unknown blurs.

According to legend, the white moths that appear on the night of the solstice are the spirits of our lost loved ones, come to say hello. But there's an old rhyme we learn as children: *Moth of white, loved one in flight; moth of red, you'll soon be dead.* The Moth-Winged Man appears sometimes as a red moth that flies in through an open window and lands on the person marked for death. And other times—worse times—he comes as a man with the wings of a moth. He comes as a warning of a violent and tragic death. Maybe that's why we still celebrate, year after year, like an offering to a vengeful god.

Mama catches hold of my hand before I can follow the others out the Harvest Moon's back door. When I look at her, I know what she's going to say from the tightness around her mouth. "You can go home if you want. You don't have to work the festival. Everyone will understand."

I stare back at her bleakly. That everyone will note my absence and pity me is exactly why I can't skip out tonight. "No, I want to go. I should try to talk to Dahlia, like you said."

She studies me a moment more, just long enough that I start to worry she'll insist I go home where it's safe. Finally, she squeezes my hand. "If you're sure."

Our festival booth is set up in the center of town, a small white tent above folding tables covered in white cloth with a garland of cedar boughs and eucalyptus swagged across the front to keep the bugs away. It's one of many booths that line the sides of the street with café-style lights strung in between, leading to the stage where a handful of middling local bands will take turns playing later in the evening.

"Hey, where are the porta potties?" a man wearing a headband with giant, feathery moth antennae asks, and I point him toward the school parking lot at the other end of town.

Caball Hollow isn't big enough to attract many tourists, but those we do get come tonight. All because twenty years ago, reported sightings of the Moth-Winged Man made the local news and suddenly the town's oldest fear became its biggest claim to fame. It still draws in those who want to believe there's something more than their everyday lives, despite the fact that saying you'd seen the Moth-Winged Man now would be like declaring you'd spotted Bigfoot— likely to be met with laughter at your expense.

Beyond the stage, where the lone road into Caball Hollow dead-ends, is the National Forest. But it isn't only there. At nearly one million acres, it surrounds us, pushing in on all sides like a beast cornering its prey. The Appalachian mountain range forms its spine. Its muscle and sinew are rocky crevices, steep passes, dense woods, and thick underbrush.

And at its center, its very heart is mystery, massive, shifting, and unknowable.

It's there, deep inside the hidden places, where the Moth-Winged Man is said to make his home. When we were little, tales of the monster terrified me, but they thrilled Rowan. Maybe it's innate in some of us to be drawn to the unknown, to both fear and desire it in equal parts. She'd tease me relentlessly, hiding dead moths under my pillow and tickling a blade of switchgrass against my skin like the brush of a wing, all while filling my head with the most lurid tales she could imagine until I'd run crying to Mama.

I glance over at her now and find her already watching me, a crease between her brows. "Why don't you stay here and help ring up orders tonight?" she suggests. There won't be any jokes about the Moth-Winged Man this year.

"Sure," I agree, with a small smile that feels as uneasy as it must look. My gaze slides over her shoulder toward the Forest, straining to see as far into the dense woods as I can. When the crisscrossing branches and shadows trick my eyes into seeing movement that makes my heartbeat falter, I turn away.

Spread out on the table in front of me are infusions, tonics, tinctures, teas, and balms, the recipes of which have been passed down through the women in our family for generations, just like those for green tomato preserves and chowchow relish. Each bottle is labeled with its purpose and key ingredients. Gran still uses the old folk names for the plants to keep our traditions alive. Or maybe it's just good marketing. Rattleweed for black cohosh (to relieve menstrual cramps), serpent's tongue for trout lily (to clear up skin ailments), cranesbill for wild geranium (to reduce inflammation), and newt's eye for black mustard (to soothe a cold) certainly sound magical compared to their more mundane counterparts.

Across the tent, Gran works the little portable grill while Mama dishes up slaw dogs, pork sandwiches, and tiny golden solstice cakes. I baked them before the diner opened this morning with lemon zest, a little ginger, and some of Sorrel's honey. Underneath the table, Gran has a stash of her secret merchandise for special customers: dandelion wine, known to help wishes come true, and apple pie moonshine, which can grant clarity in small doses yet completely obliterate it in larger ones.

After a few hours and a steady stream of customers, Juniper drops a crown made of cedar onto my head before she and Rowan set off toward the stage, their arms lined with more to sell. The Moth-Winged Man may be nothing but a folktale, but it's still our protection charms that sell out first, the cedar crowns and the yarrow sachets, black tourmaline crystals, and tiger's-eye bracelets. After all, why tempt fate?

From across the street, Wavelene Edgar approaches the booth like it's against her will. "Do y'all have some of that willow bark cream?" Her face, which always looks a bit like uncooked biscuit dough, twists in distaste. "I don't know how y'all do it, but it's the only thing that works on my joints." Her words are pleasant enough, but underneath there's a hint of something rancid and acidic, like sour milk.

"Sure thing." Sorrel plucks a jar from the display on the table and wraps it in paper as I ring up the order on the tablet.

Wavelene is careful not to accidentally brush Sorrel's hand as she takes the package. Once she moves on to a booth selling T-shirts down the street, I can no longer hold my tongue.

"If she thinks we're so awful, why doesn't she take her business to the corner drugstore?"

Sorrel and Mama exchange a look, and I know immediately that I'm overreacting, but it only serves to make me angrier.

"She seemed fine to me," Sorrel says with a shrug.

I untie my apron and pull it off, getting even more frustrated when the strap catches on my hair. "That was our last jar of willow bark cream. I'll go grab another box from the truck."

Mama looks like she wants to stop me, but she nods. "Don't be long."

It's not just Wavelene; she's not even the worst. But no one else seems to see it, the strange sort of way people look at us from the corner of their eyes sometimes. Or when they come to us for a tonic or tincture, something to help them, and buried deep down underneath the surface, where maybe they're not even aware of it, is a little kernel of fear and disgust. People like her are the reason we keep the full truth of our abilities a secret.

How strange it is to be born and live somewhere our whole lives, to have roots here, and yet be made to feel we don't belong. To be outsiders in the only home we've ever known. Could that be the true story of the first James woman all those generations ago: not someone who closed herself off from others, but someone who was shut out? Maybe that's our family legacy.

I used to dream of owning my own bakery, starting out with a little counter at the diner to sell my baked goods. But that was before I realized people may be right to feel the way they do about me. Before I realized how much of a violation my ability can be.

I'm only halfway back to where the truck is parked by the diner when two older ladies hurriedly cut across the street in front of me, both glancing over their shoulders and whispering to each other. "That's Amos McCoy. Can you believe he'd come here of all places?" the first woman says. "Him walking around free all these years doesn't mean we forgot."

"Murderer," the second one spits in a tone clearly meant to carry. "He has a lot of gall, showing his face in town, mixing with good, normal folks."

When they pass by, I see it's the man from the cemetery, still in his funeral suit, still hunched in on himself, turning down the alley toward the Pub and Grub. I'm thrown for a moment by the vitriol before I connect the dots. McCoy was the last name of the little boy who disappeared without a trace about twenty years ago or so. The reason those sightings of the Moth-Winged Man became newsworthy.

Those who had claimed to see the Moth-Winged Man probably would have been dismissed as tippling fools back then too, if not for Elam McCoy's disappearance during a family fishing trip on the Teays River inside the National Forest. The story has been retold and altered and embellished among the young and foolish of Caball Hollow so many times, it's become something of an urban legend. No trace of him was ever found, and the case remains unsolved. Except for in the court of public opinion, which has clearly tried and convicted the boy's father based on, from what I can tell, merely the fact that he was the last one to see the boy alive. But lord, does this town love to gossip.

"Caball Hollow is a town that honors its history." A voice crackles through a speaker as I near the stage. "Like the very first families who founded this town, we come together to celebrate the Moth-Winged Man festival today. This scholarship was created to ensure our younger generations remember that history. And while the projects were all exemplary, one stood out as the very best. So without further ado . . ." The school superintendent, a man with a shiny bald spot and a thick mustache, signals to the band setting up behind him to play a drumroll. "This year's Moth Queen is Maude Parrish!"

Dahlia stands above the crowd in a diaphanous white dress. Maude bends her knees slightly so Dahlia can place the crown on her head and I hesitate. I told Mama I'd talk to Dahlia, but now I'm not so sure. What's the point in rekindling a friendship when it's best for everyone if I keep my distance?

When Maude smiles widely toward the audience, I spot Cole standing head and shoulders above the other familiar faces in the crowd. All the people I once considered friends. He sticks two fingers in his mouth and lets out a shrill whistle as the others applaud. It's strange to see everyone together like this, so much like last summer, yet irrevocably altered. It's the fun-house mirror version of what we once were, stretched and distorted until I'm not sure what was ever real in the first place.

Behind Dahlia and Maude, the other Moth Queen nominees clap politely, their heavy gowns and a glaze of sweat shimmering in the stage lights. Dahlia shines like moonlight and beams at Maude. Then the members of the scholarship board surround them, offering smiles and handshakes. Cole and Bryson make their way to Maude and Dahlia, all of them laughing as Cole pulls Maude into a congratulatory hug. I turn away.

After I grab the box of willow bark cream from the truck, it's slow going back through the crowd. Even more people have gathered around the stage as a band gets ready to perform, testing equipment in random bursts of sound. I only make it a few feet before a hand catches my elbow.

"There you are." Dahlia presses closer, glancing over her shoulder, then pulls me back, away from the crush of people. There's something frenetic about her. Maybe it's the excitement of the festival, but she's a flurry of motion. Crossing her arms, uncrossing them, dragging the charm of the necklace she always wears back and forth along the ribbon it hangs from. She can't be still. "I've been looking for you. Did you see the Moth Queen ceremony?"

I shift the box, balancing the edge on my hip. "A bit."

"Maude Parrish was a surprise," she continues. "I mean, don't get me wrong, she's great, but about as exciting as a glass of warm milk."

A disbelieving huff of laughter escapes me. I forgot she was like this, saying whatever she thinks as though it's something everyone does.

"I really hope you reconsider applying next year," she continues without pause. "That scholarship money was the only reason I made it out of this town, and you have so much potential. Remember when you and Mamaw were making her cinnamon apple moonshine cake and she told us about how mad she got when Granddad built that hidey-hole in her kitchen to stash the moonshine he was runnin'?"

I smile at the memory of Dahlia's grandmother telling us that story in the cozy warmth of her small kitchen, the air scented with cinnamon and apple peel. "She invited the sheriff and his wife over for dinner and served them that cake just to make her husband sweat."

"See? That's what I mean." She leans closer. "Those kinds of stories have meaning. They should be remembered." For a moment, it almost looks like her eyes glisten with tears in the glow of the lights above us before she looks away.

"Yeah, they should, but, Dahlia, I don't know if I even want to leave Caball Hollow," I say. As hard as it can be to live here sometimes, it's still home. These mountains are as much a part of me as my own reflection. "There's a lot here worth staying for."

Dahlia considers, gently shakes her head. "You're lucky, then. Not everyone has that." She steps closer and reaches out to squeeze my arm.

When she touches my skin, I'm hit by a wave of emotion. I look down to where her fingers clutch at me and see a deep red bruise across her forearm. There's something familiar about the shape, but her feelings are a confusing mix of sadness, anticipation, and apprehension so strong I can feel it crawling up my throat, and I can't focus.

"I need to ask you something." Dahlia drops her voice to a whisper. "What if there was someone else there that night last summer?"

"Linden James!" a loud voice calls from behind me before I can process Dahlia's words. I turn, searching the crowd until my eyes land on Malcolm Spencer, Cole's father and the current mayor of Caball Hollow, as he lifts a hand to wave.

"I was hoping to see you here." He's smiling broadly when he reaches me, and it makes him look boyish somehow, though he must be fifty if he's a day. "How are you?" He doesn't wait for me to answer but draws his eyebrows together in concern. "Listen, I've been thinking a lot about what happened last summer, and I owe you an apology. It was only a matter of time before that foolhardy tradition the kids have of camping out in the Forest ended in disaster. I should have put a stop to it instead of suggesting Cole invite you to join them. It was just so adorable the way you tagged along behind him when you were little, and when you started to do it again . . ." He gives me a sheepish look and shakes his head. "Well, obviously, I had no idea what would happen, but still. It was an error in judgment for me to encourage such a thing. I hope you can forgive me. I've requested added patrols this year to make sure nothing like that happens again."

My face feels wrong, like the muscles are pulling in opposite directions. I can only imagine the grotesque expression I must be making, but I manage a shaky nod.

"I . . . um . . ." Before I can fumble a reply, an older couple approaches to shake hands with the mayor and pull him away to speak with the rest of their group.

I turn back to Dahlia, rattled, only to find she's gone. Scanning the crowd, I look as far as I can in each direction, but it's starting to get dark, and the trees cast long shadows over the crowd. I let out a long, slow breath and press a hand to my forehead, not sure if I'm more embarrassed over the fact that I'm clearly so pathetic even Cole's dad noticed, or that Cole didn't even invite me that night. He told me to stay away, but I didn't listen.

On the night of the Moth Festival, graduating seniors and their friends go to the place in the Forest where Elam McCoy is said to have disappeared and call out to the Moth-Winged Man three times. If he appears, he might grant you your deepest desire. Or he might mark you for death. It's become more than a tradition; it's a rite of passage. Everyone dares each other to do it, but last year I was the only one foolish enough to try.

The Moth Festival is my favorite night of the year. The lights, the sounds, the magic. The smells of deep-fried food and freshly squeezed lemonade floating through laughter-filled air.

Daddy and Juniper return to the booth, sticky and triumphant, with plates of enormous elephant ears, crisp dough tossed in cinnamon and sugar. Rowan, wearing moth wings made of gossamer white, hands Mrs. Boggs her change and a bag of elderflower soothers.

"Lyon, will you take that box back to the truck?" Mama asks Daddy, pointing to a crate of supplies under the table as she starts to pack up the booth.

Daddy holds out a piece of his elephant ear, dipped in strawberry jam, offering it to her. She opens her mouth, and he drops it in, a sticky red dollop landing on her lip. He takes Mama's face in his hands and kisses the jam from her skin. "Delicious," he proclaims as she laughs.

"Ew," Rowan objects, averting her eyes.

Juniper giggles as Daddy drops kisses all over Mama's face.

"You two are so embarrassing." Sorrel shakes her head, scanning the crowd to make sure no one she knows is watching.

"Linden," a voice whispers next to my ear as a hand slides into mine. "Can I steal you for a minute?" Cole asks, pulling me away from the booth.

I haven't seen him for days. He just got back from a visit to Georgetown, where he'll go after he graduates next year. Tonight, we'll venture out into the Forest with our friends, like others before us have done for as far back as we can remember.

No one really believes that calling the Moth-Winged Man can grant your deepest wish, but somehow, under the twinkling lights, with all the promise of summer spread out before us, it feels like anything is possible.

CHAPTER FOUR

THE NIGHTMARES are getting worse. Maybe I should have listened to Mama and stayed home tonight. I don't know if it's because of the strange conversation with Dahlia or just the nature of the summer solstice, but it feels as if my missing memories are a sliver under my skin now, a word on the tip of my tongue, an itch I can't quite scratch.

I set the kettle on the stove and strike the long match to light the flame under the burner. The house is quiet in that middle-of-the-night sort of way when the crickets are long asleep and the birds hours from waking. The ticking of the clock on the wall and the hum of the refrigerator seem unduly loud. It's said that the last sound heard before the clock strikes midnight on the solstice will be a sign of what is to come in the months ahead. With only a half hour to go, everything but my mind is calm.

As I wait for the water to heat, absently tapping the spoon against my lips, I let myself slip back to the few memories I have of last summer. I remember venturing into the Forest alone. I remember saying the words three times. *Moth-Winged Man. Moth-Winged Man. Moth-Winged Man.* I remember that by the end, my voice had faded to barely a whisper, the skin on the back of my neck tingling as I imagined all manner of horrors that might be hiding in the shadows. I twisted around, searching for the eyes I felt on me. A flash of light and my memory skitters out, then the shock of cold water. Another blank, and I'm running, panicked, through the Forest. Something drips down my forehead, into my eyes, tinting my vision red.

I jump when the kettle whistles, nearly burning myself on the hot metal, and scramble to yank it off the heat before it wakes the others. After I add the water to my tea, I stir in a spoonful of honey. This batch is thyme, for courage and strength.

As I move to the table, the back door bangs open and Aunt Salome glides in. "Well, hello, my sweet Linden. You didn't need to wait up for me," she teases.

"You scared the livin' daylights out of me." I press my hand to my chest. "Where have you been all night, any-how?" I ask.

"Oh, here and there." Sissy drops into the chair across from me. "I hiked out to the Bone Tree for the sunset."

I jerk hard enough to slosh tea onto the table. The Bone Tree is liminal too, like the solstice, only it's a space between spaces. Stretching from one side of the creek to the other, it's bare of any leaves, with bark bleached so white it seems to glow in the moonlight. Yet somehow it lives, its five thick branches reaching out of the earth and grasping for the opposite shore, like a giant skeletal hand deep within the National Forest.

For generations, we've gone to the Bone Tree for divination rituals, meditation, and even spirit work. And when one of Gran's potions needs a little extra something, we go to gather ingredients because she believes the plants that grow nearby are more potent. Its location has been a closely guarded secret passed down from mother to daughter for more than two centuries.

I haven't been in more than a year, unable to set foot into the Forest after last summer. But my skin still prickles at the idea of the place. The Bone Tree is neither here nor there, a place where seen meets unseen, known meets unknown. And it feels that way, almost like reality shifts and time itself moves differently. But a place where the veil is already thin on a day when it becomes even thinner could be dangerous. After all, if we can reach through, what's to stop those on the other side from reaching back?

"Why'd you go and do a thing like that?" I ask as I dab up the spill with a napkin.

Sissy lifts one shoulder in a shrug that looks more cunning than carefree. "To meditate, pull some cards, seek a little guidance." She leans forward to take my hand. "And how are you, darling girl? Today couldn't have been easy."

She's being evasive, but it doesn't necessarily mean she's hiding something. That's just Sissy. Mama says she's always been this way. I let it slide, too tired to worry about what she might be up to.

"I'm glad it's almost over. And I'll be even happier when everyone forgets what happened last summer altogether." I take a sip of tea.

"I'm sorry to be the one to tell you this, but Caball Hollow never forgets." She gives me a sympathetic grimace.

Her words remind me of the women at the festival and the vitriol they hurled at Amos McCoy. Maybe it's because the legend of Elam McCoy's disappearance and that of the Moth-Winged Man have become so conflated, but it wasn't until tonight that it struck me that what happened to him wasn't all that long ago. "Hey, can I ask you something?"

"Of course," she answers absently as her phone chimes and she glances at it.

"You were still living here when Elam McCoy went missing, weren't you?"

"Oh." Sissy leans back in her chair, clearly not expecting the change of topic. "Yeah. Why do you ask?"

"Do you believe what people say, that his father killed him?"

"Well," Sissy says on a long exhale. "I think if there were any evidence, he would have been arrested." She shrugs, then leans forward. "Is that tea? Perfect, I'll read your leaves." Sissy puts a finger to the bottom of my mug as I drink, pouring hot tea down my throat. "Bottoms up."

I gulp it down and come up sputtering. "Sis! Good lord, you nearly drowned me," I manage to rasp out between coughs.

Sissy takes the cup out of my hand and jumps up to snag a saucer from the drying rack next to the sink, unconcerned by my grumbling. She covers the mug with the plate and flips it upside down, then right side up again. Peering inside, she starts at the handle of the cup, then slowly works her way in a clockwise spiral, searching for symbolic images from the present near the rim toward the future at the bottom.

I study her as she focuses, her eyes even darker in the dim light. As long as I can remember, people would comment on how unique she looked or ask about her heritage as if they hadn't watched her grow up here. Sissy would roll her eyes behind their backs, then disappear again for months at a time. But she never stays gone too long. She's Caball Hollow through and through, just like the rest of us.

"I see you in turmoil," she begins, her gaze focused on the cup, her voice barely above a whisper. "An unexpected discovery will put you in a perilous position."

She meets my eyes over the rim. "I fear your struggles aren't over, little one. There is more trouble ahead." She casts her eyes back into the cup. "Be wary of who you trust. Some who seem like friends may be powerful enemies, yet unexpected allies will be watching out for you. I see conflict. But I also see you coming into your own, finding your strength and owning your power."

She's quiet for a moment as she turns the cup again. Her eyes narrow. With a gasp, she leaps out of her chair so forcefully it tips over, then throws the cup and saucer into the sink hard enough that the delicate ceramic snaps.

"What the hell, Sis!" I push up from the table, then pause for a moment, listening, to make sure the racket hasn't woken the whole house.

She ignores me, turning the water on full blast, washing all the tea dregs down the drain and carelessly scooping the ceramic shards into the trash. When she turns back to me, sagging against the sink, her eyes are wide and her breathing heavy.

"What was it?" I demand, fingers curled tight around the back of the chair. Less afraid now that we might have woken the others and more just plain afraid. I've never seen her react this strongly to a reading before. The sharp acidic taste of fear, hers and mine, sticks in my throat. "What did you see?"

She shakes her head, either refusing to tell or refusing to accept what she read in the leaves. "It doesn't matter. Your future is within your power to change, Linden." She rushes forward and grabs my shoulders, looking deep into my eyes. "Never forget that."

"Wait, tell me what you saw," I plead, reaching out to grab her arm, but she's already striding toward the back door.

"Don't wait up, I need to take care of something." She turns the knob but pauses to make one last parting statement over her shoulder. "Just—please stay out of the woods, Linden. And stay away from Cole Spencer."

The door bangs shut behind her, but I'm across the room pulling it back open in a blink. "Wait!" I call out, but the engine of the farm truck turns over with a growl and I'm forced to shut my eyes against the glare of the headlights. When I open them, she's already gone.

If the sleep-easy tea had any chance of working before, it certainly doesn't now. What does Cole Spencer have to do with her cryptic predictions? He certainly couldn't be the enemy who seemed like a friend. We haven't been friends for a good long while.

I glance at the clock on the wall. It's nearly midnight. "Five, four, three, two . . ." I count down the final seconds. "One," I whisper.

A woman's scream cuts through the night.

My heart stutters in my chest and my breathing stops in the seconds it takes for another scream to echo outside and my brain to catch up. Not a woman, a fox. But probably not a good omen, neither.

I wake up to a finger tapping against my forehead in the familiar rhythm of an old nursery rhyme. "Is that 'Frère Jacques'?" I ask groggily, grabbing the offending hand and slowly cracking open my eyelids. Juniper's face is upside down over mine, so close I can only see her unusual eyes. I was finally able to fall asleep as the sun was coming up, but my body still feels wrung out. The aftereffects of last night and trying to block out the feelings of so many people. Not to mention Sissy's concerning tea reading.

"Are you sleeping? Are you sleeping?" Juniper singsongs, breaking into a grin. I bite her finger and she squeals, yanking her hand away. Her face disappears as she topples off the bed with a thud. "And here I thought you were the nice sister." She pulls the pillow out from under my head, then smacks me in the face with it.

Juniper was born during the worst blizzard Caball Hollow has ever seen. It's the storm folks still call The Big One, even though it happened sixteen years ago. The wind was so strong it blew the sign clean off the Piggly Wiggly and drove folks to seek shelter in their root cellars amongst the sweet potatoes and jars of pickled ramps and sour corn.

Mama says it might have been the rare winter thunder that shook the baby right out of her. Or maybe something in the storm called to something in Juniper. Either way, Juniper arrived in this world, more than a full month early and barely the size of a kitten, in the worn back seat of a police cruiser stuck in the snow halfway up the driveway.

Despite the frigid temperatures, she was born with eyes the brightest blue of a summer sky but for one stripe of darkest brown down the center of her left iris, reinforcing the feline resemblance. Gran took one look at her and immediately predicted that Juniper would be able to see things that others couldn't. But we didn't realize until later that the things she saw might be able to see her too. That the dead are often hungry for any taste of life.

"Mama says up and at 'em. The lunch rush waits for no witch."

"You know Gran hates that word." I push up on one elbow and rub the sleep from my eyes just in time to see Juniper roll hers. "Wait, did you say lunch?"

"Mama thought you could use the extra sleep, so Sissy took your morning shift." She pushes up off the floor and heads for the door, but not before tossing the pillow in my face. "You best get a move on, though."

Junie doesn't work at the Harvest Moon in the days around the summer solstice. Too many customers no one else can see have led to bless-her-heart comments from busybodies about her imaginary friends. At least any spirits she encounters at the farm would be familiar ones.

I scramble to get ready, then pedal as fast as I can toward the diner. Heat and humidity hang low in the hollows, steeping the honeysuckle, wild carrot, and dandelion like a kettle until the air tastes floral and earthy and bitter.

When I arrive, I lean my bike against the side of the old stone building and push open the back door. "Mornin', y'all," I call as I step into the sweltering kitchen.

"Well, would you look at that, Sleeping Beauty has finally decided to grace us with her presence," Gran teases as she dices an onion with decisive strokes.

"Oh, thank the lord. I'm officially off duty." Sissy tosses me her order pad and plucks a warm biscuit off the cooling rack, pulls it apart with her fingers, then reaches for a jar of apple butter.

Mama squeezes my shoulder as I put on my apron and flip through the pad before tucking it into the front pocket. But there's no time to stand around because the bell on the front door is already chiming the arrival of a new customer.

I understand Sissy's relief when I step into the dining room. Every single table and most of the stools at the counter are taken. We're always busy around the festival, but not like this. This is as crowded as I've ever seen it, and the number of eyes that turn toward me as the kitchen door swings shut makes my cheeks heat up.

Hillard Been sits at his usual table next to the front window. He retired from the post office last month, but he still meets his last trainee, Buck Garland, for lunch every day, arriving as soon as we open to stake out his table, read the paper, and drink us out of coffee. It's Buck that's just walked in.

"What's doing?" Hillard greets him as he heads toward their table.

"Oh, 'bout the same," Buck answers as he takes his seat, and I fetch him his usual glass of sweet tea.

"What's good today?" Hillard turns his attention to me, tapping the paper menu with one gnarled finger.

"The tomato pie is delicious. I made the crust myself." Behind me, a whisper starts at one end of the dining room, gaining volume and speed. I steal a glance over my shoulder, but there's nothing out of the ordinary that I can see.

Hillard sucks a tooth and eyes me warily, like he thinks there might be something a little wrong with me. "Lemme get that tomato pie," he finally says.

"Me too," Buck agrees. "But bring mine with a side of fried okra."

I nod and scribble their orders on my pad, then hurry back toward the kitchen.

"Linden, sugar," a voice to my right calls. I turn to see Mrs. Hinkle, Dahlia's aunt. Nettie Hinkle was the lunch lady when I was in elementary school and always knew the name of every single child who went through her line. "Sorry to bother you when y'all are so busy, but have you spoken to Dahlia today?"

"No, sorry," I blurt out quickly, instead of explaining why Dahlia and I aren't close anymore.

"Oh, all right." Mrs. Hinkle smiles and waves a hand as if to brush aside any concern. She starts to turn away, then pauses, pursing her lips. "It's just she didn't come home last night, and I haven't been able to reach her all morning. Mr. Hinkle said not to worry on account of she usually stays out all night after the festival, but if you do see her, could you ask her to give me a call?"

"Sure, of course, Mrs. Hinkle," I agree.

"I heard she's been seeing some boy over in Rawbone," Lorena Boggs tells the other two women sitting at her table as soon as the door closes behind Mrs. Hinkle. "Hopefully she's not following in her mother's footsteps."

"I saw you talking to her at the festival," Beulah Fordham Hayes from the school board says when she catches me looking in their direction, a disapproving pinch to her mouth. "She wouldn't have been so foolish as to go out to the Forest last night, would she? I thought the sheriff would be keeping a closer eye on things after what happened last year."

"I . . . I don't . . ." My thoughts scatter at the biting reference. It's all still too close to the surface after last night, and I struggle to push away the images from my nightmares of branches pulling at my hair and thorns ripping at my skin.

"Oh, leave the girl be, Beulah. No need to get worked up," Dreama Kinnaird, an old classmate of Gran's, asserts, pulling me back to the present. "Dahlia is in college now. She's used to her freedom. No doubt she'll be home by supper."

She's probably right; there's no way Dahlia would have gone out into the Forest after last summer, but an uneasy feeling has tied a knot in my stomach that I can't loosen. While they continue to gossip, I slip into the kitchen. I have to try twice to get my ticket onto the rack.

Mama slides the paper over to read the order. "I've got two more tomato pies. That's six slices all day," she says.

"That's it for the pie, then," Gran replies, erasing it from the whiteboard behind her. "Eighty-six the tomato pie, girls."

I cross it off the list of specials in my notepad, then splash cold water on my cheeks at the hand-washing sink and press my fingers against the back of my neck.

"What's wrong with you?" Rowan asks, squirting the dish sprayer in my general direction. "Is Cole Spencer back?"

"No, it's nothing," I lie, and this time when she sprays, water hits me between my shoulder blades.

"Fine, don't tell me. But if you want to switch, I'm sure we could convince Mama to allow it for today," Rowan offers as she slides a rack of clean glasses out of the dish-washer and dries her hands on her apron.

"Thanks, but I'm fine." I'm not entirely sure if she's offering because I look rattled or if she's doing whatever she can to get out of washing dishes. But it doesn't matter, because if there is any news about Dahlia, I want to be out there to hear it.

I head back to the front of the house, and I pour myself a mug of coffee from the wait station. Despite sleeping late this morning, I'm still only running on a few hours of rest over the past several days, and after that jolt of adrenaline, I can feel myself crashing.

The bell over the door chimes again. Hadrian steps into the dining room and makes his way to the counter, tucking his sunglasses into the collar of his shirt as he takes the last empty stool.

"Hey, there." I set a menu down in front of him. "I didn't expect to see you on your day off."

Before he can respond, Rowan comes out of the kitchen with a tray of clean glasses. "Nope." She sets the tray on the counter and grabs the menu out of his hand, using it to point toward the door. "Pub and Grub is about a half mile up the road."

"Rowan!" I'm used to the verbal sparring between the two of them, but it's been getting progressively worse as he's resisted her every attempt to drive him off. And now she's being rude in front of customers. Already those sitting closest are starting to stare.

But Hadrian just leans back, bracing a foot against the bottom of the counter, and crosses his heavily tattooed arms. "My shampoo bottle was filled with sour cream this morning. Know anything about that?"

My eyes go wide, but Rowan turns from putting the glasses away, casts a long look up and down his body, then wrinkles her nose. "No, but now that you mention it, you do look a bit . . . curdled."

"Can I get you something to drink?" I try to defuse the situation.

Hadrian turns to me, the mossy green of his eyes flashing like polished serpentine. "Water?"

"Is that a question?" Rowan takes the last glass from her tray and fills it with ice. "Yes, we do have running water in Caball Hollow." She sets the glass in front of him, then picks up the pitcher and pours.

"Yeah, I do know that, actually. I used quite a lot of it rinsing dairy products out of my hair." He leans forward, resting his arms on the counter in front of him. "I've been working at Bittersweet for months now. Any idea when I might expect this little feud to be over?"

"You know what, you're right." Rowan nods with a glint in her eye I know not to trust. "Let's start over. Welcome to the Hollow." She reaches out like she's going to shake his hand, knocking the glass she just filled into his lap. He leaps backward off the stool, but not fast enough.

"Rowan!" I toss a towel to Hadrian and grab another to mop up the water on the counter as a sizzle of charred anger hits the roof of my mouth.

"Oops." Rowan spins toward the kitchen, but before she pushes through the swinging door, she looks back over her shoulder, a furrow between her brows.

"Sorry," I say to Hadrian. "I don't know how you put up with her."

"Easy, I need the work." He shrugs, then looks down, taking in the thorough soaking of his jeans. "She doesn't do things halfway, I'll give her that."

I cringe in sympathy. "Lunch is on the house."

Hadrian tosses the wet towel back to me. "Thanks, but I think I'll take a rain check, as it were." He pulls the sunglasses from his shirt and heads for the exit as the kitchen bell dings, announcing an order is up.

When I step through the swinging door, Mama nods toward a loaded tray before turning her attention to the next ticket. I move to pick it up, but Rowan grabs my arm and pulls me to the back of the kitchen.

"I know you think I should be nicer to him," she starts, her hands on her hips. "But he's lying about something, and I'm going to figure out what it is."

I don't try to hide my annoyance, and she leans back against the counter. "I should have cut my finger on his glass instead of knocking it into his lap," she grumbles.

Learning Rowan's blood was something of a truth serum was my fault. I was too young to have any real memory of it, but the story has been retold enough it feels as if I do. When I was three and she was four, we were fighting over some toy. I bit her hard enough to draw blood, then immediately tattled on myself when Mama asked what happened. Rowan still has a tiny scar, the mark of my baby tooth, on her right index finger. But it isn't a gift that should be used lightly, especially when it would be a direct violation of Gran's most important rule.

I shake my head in frustration. "Don't you think people are entitled to keep some secrets?"

"No, especially not when it might put my family at risk," she snaps back.

"That's pretty hypocritical, considering how many secrets this family keeps. Do you really think Mama and Gran would ignore your warnings if they didn't have reason to trust him?" I ask.

She looks ready to argue back, but then her shoulders slump. "No, of course not," she murmurs, letting out a long breath before she continues. "It's just, I don't know what your talent feels like, but for me it's like an itch underneath my skin every time he opens his smug, deceiving mouth. And it will stay there until he goes away or I find out the truth."

I stare back at her, thrown off-kilter for a moment. How could I not know it was like this for her? My gift has always felt like a burden, but maybe I'm not the only one who feels the weight.

"Linden, there's an order dying on the counter while you flap your gums," Gran calls out from the other end of the kitchen.

I squeeze Rowan's hand, then hustle over to retrieve my tray and head for table three.

"And just how much 'shine had they poured down their gullets before they claim to have seen this thing?" Hillard asks Buck as I approach their table, his bushy white mustache quivering with incredulity.

"Well, fine. But you know they weren't the first to see it, neither. Vern's son and them were out camping at the National Forest, and it flew right over their car. Two, three nights past," Buck insists. "He said it was as big as a man with a double set of wings, like a moth, but with a wing-span maybe six, seven foot across." Buck spreads his arms to demonstrate and nearly knocks his plate out of my hand. "Oh, sorry. Didn't see you there." Buck reaches out as if to help steady the plate, but I freeze.

"You okay there, girlie?" Hillard gives me a look like now he's sure I must be touched in the head. But it's as if I hear him through a long tunnel. Air seems to rush past my ears, taking his words with it. Carefully, I set down the plates, then turn and head for the front door.

"See?" Buck says. "Something strange going on. And I tell you what, my ol' hound dog was baying his fool head off at something last night right when my cable went all whompyjawed."

"Your cable goes squiggly nearabouts every night because you hooked yourself to your neighbor's line." I hear Hillard guffaw as the door shuts behind me.

It's like walking into an oven. Hot air presses against me, heavy and unrelenting. I lean against the ledge of a long-ago bricked-in window on the side of the building and try to settle my racing heart.

I finally figured it out. It was the talk about supposed sightings of the Moth-Winged Man, like right before Elam McCoy vanished all those years ago, that made it click. Maybe it's nothing, but the weight in my stomach feels a lot like dread. Because now I know what was familiar about the shape of that red bruise on Dahlia's arm. It was a moth.

CHAPTER FIVE

THE HOUSE feels close and airless and a little frenetic, like Bittersweet Farm itself is uneasy. All evening, doors have been shutting with a bang, then slowly creaking back open.

"Remind me to ask Hadrian to oil those hinges," Mama sighs as she pulls a plate from the cupboard.

"When do I get to meet this mysterious farmhand?" Sissy asks from where she's scouring dinner dishes in the sink.

"You haven't?" Mama replies absently, sucking sticky juice from her finger as she slices into the pie on the counter.

Sissy shrugs one shoulder without turning from the sink. "I guess y'all are keeping him busy."

"Well, it won't be today, either. He took the tractor down to the farm mechanic." Mama slides a slice of strawberry rhubarb pie in front of me, the fruit plucked from our own garden, maybe even by my own hand, but I'm not sure if I can stomach a bite.

"Want to talk about it?" she asks gently.

The trick to a good crust is cold butter and not to fuss with it too much. This one flakes beneath my fork as I cut into it and bring a bite to my mouth. The strawberries are sweet with the taste of the sun, and the rhubarb sparks bright and tart across my tongue. Yet that puckery tang is the same flavor as worry. I press the tines of the fork against the crumbs left on the plate and watch as they melt back together.

After we closed the diner, I called Mrs. Hinkle. She still hadn't heard from Dahlia and was growing ever more concerned. "She's always been independent," she told me. "But she knows I worry. Mr. Hinkle said to leave her be, but if I don't hear from her by nightfall, I'm calling the sheriff."

My own instincts are screaming at me that there's something wrong, but I don't know if I can trust them. What are the chances of another girl going missing exactly a year after I did? Maybe my own fears are clouding my judgment. But I keep thinking of that question Dahlia asked me at the festival. *What if there was someone else there that night last summer?* I don't know what she could have meant. Most of the senior class and many of their friends had been there with us.

Yet, maybe for the first time, I find myself wishing I could remember what really happened out there in the Forest.

"Don't pick at her, Odette," Sissy chides when I don't answer Mama. "She'll talk when she's good and ready." Sissy winks at me over her shoulder as she stacks plates in the dish drainer.

"You know, Sis, you never mentioned what brought you home. We weren't expecting you." Mama gives her an appraising glance from across the kitchen.

"Oh, you know how it is, Odette," Sissy says as she dries her hands on a dish towel. "The salt calls to me."

It's a Sissy sort of answer if ever there was one. She means the salt under our mountains. Long before coal, it was salt that was pulled from beneath them. Salt from an ancient ocean that was pushed underground when the Appalachians rose up. The soil here in Caball Hollow is still rich with its protective brine, and as all James girls know, evil cannot cross a line of salt. But what if the evil is already inside the circle—does all the salt only serve to keep it from getting out?

When Mama turns to swat Sissy with her dish towel, I push the plate away and slip out through the screen door. As I make my way along the wraparound porch, Gran pokes her head out of the summer kitchen's open door.

"Linden," she calls, beckoning with the sweep of an arm.

I move down the steps and up the path toward the squat old stone building that was first used by James women more than a hundred years ago, back when cooking and canning were done out here over a wood-burning stove to keep the house cooler during the hottest months and protect it from the risk of fire in the driest season. Now it's a workshop where Gran and Mama make and store all the infusions, tinctures, and balms we sell.

As I step inside, the fragrance of the drying lavender, sage, and other simples tacked along the walls washes over me. It takes a moment for my eyes to adjust to the dim interior after the brightness of the summer sun outside, even though it's long past dinner. With her reading glasses perched on the end of her nose, Gran stands at an old wooden table, marked and marred from years of use and cluttered with various bottles and herbs spread out across the work surface. Just then, a book from the shelf above Gran's head tumbles off, landing on the tabletop and falling open to a recipe for elderberry syrup.

"Ah, yes," Gran murmurs as she runs a finger down the page. "The youngest Boggs girl was feeling poorly today. I'll whip up a quick bottle."

This is how it is here at the farm. We live surrounded by those who've come before. Some of them through the wisdom they've left in the books that line these shelves, but others in more tangible ways. Walking into a room and smelling a hint of Granny Sudie's favorite perfume, seeing the rocking chair that was a wedding gift Gran's great-aunt Philomena never got to use suddenly swaying on its own, or waking to find the dirty clothes dropped on the floor the night before somehow already in the hamper.

Gran looks at me, then follows my gaze to the numerous volumes. "We've had a lot of sisters on this farm over the years."

She turns her attention back to the work of her hands, seemingly dropping the subject. But I know her, so I wait.

"Even when you plant seeds at the same time, they sprout at their own pace, they bloom when they're ready. That doesn't mean one is better than the other. All it means is that you can't expect a cornstalk to become a squash plant or a bean vine. But we plant them together because they grow better that way. A vine can climb the stalk while the leaves of the squash shade the roots and prevent weeds.

"Sometimes sisters grow apart, they argue, they disagree. But we need each other, maybe more than most. It's been a difficult year, I don't need to tell you that." She pulls the cork out of a bottle of dark liquid, then uses a funnel to decant some into a smaller bottle. "With everything that happened last summer, then Sorrel going off to college, and now Rowan and her ridiculous feud. But there are growing pains in every family. What's important is to not let the disagreements fester. I'd hate for what happened with me and Zephyrine to ever happen with you girls." She meets my eyes above the frame of her glasses, making sure I understand.

And I do. Great-Aunt Zephyrine is Gran's younger sister. Sometime before I was born, they had a falling-out, and she ran off. My eyes slide down to the locked drawer in the center of the cabinet, the drawer that holds the book I suspect of being at least partially to blame.

The diablerie is filled with a different sort of James magic, a dangerous sort that has been the source of more than a few family disagreements over the generations, which is why Gran keeps it safely locked away. I've never set eyes on what's inside, but the way she explains it is that the magic in the family books is all about pushing intentions. It's a gentle request of the universe. But the diablerie magic is different. It's a hard shove, a forceful demand. And it comes at a price. Zephyrine thought all James women should have access to the book and decide for themselves if the magic was worth the cost. But Gran says the temptation would be too great, that this type of magic is a dangerous step toward undue influence.

She pauses to scribble a note on the scratch paper she's using as a checklist, then turns back to me. "I need you to run this sleeping tonic up to Vivian Spencer." She gestures with her pen to the small glass bottle. Gran has the uncanny ability of knowing exactly when someone is in desperate need of one of her potions. It's often inconvenient for those of us required to serve as delivery girls.

"It's for Cole's mom?" I twist a loose thread from the hem of my shirt around my finger as apprehension makes a similar knot in my stomach. "There's no one else who can do it?"

Gran gives me a look that brooks no argument and hands me the bottle. "Shoo, hurry now so you can get home before dark."

She turns back to her work, but when I move to pull the door closed behind me, she calls out once more. "Straight there and straight back, you hear?"

"I will," I promise, very much in agreement with getting this particular errand over and done with as quickly as possible. There's a shortcut—out back, past Sorrel's night-blooming garden and her beehives, then through the orchard—and I make my way toward it.

The Spencers live in one of the biggest houses in Caball Hollow's exclusive Heights neighborhood, high up in the hills, quite literally looking down on the rest of the town. The imposing limestone estate, built back in 1798 by Bowen Spencer, the most well-known of the original town founders, is one of the oldest structures, too.

By the time I reach their porch, my shirt sticks damply against my skin. I press the doorbell next to the stately front door, which is crowned with an enormous fanlight that is inset with a clover, likely a nod to their Scots-Irish heritage.

"Hey, there. Come on in," a woman's voice, liquid around the edges, floats down from an upstairs window.

I breathe a sigh of relief that Cole wasn't the one to answer as I push open the heavy wooden door. "Hello?" I call as I step onto the polished wood floor of the foyer, but there's no answer.

We used to come here for summer cookouts, back when Daddy and Malcolm Spencer worked together at the sheriff's department, before he was elected mayor. Even then, Mrs. Spencer didn't leave the house much. Mama once told me that she hadn't always been such a homebody, but she changed after Cole was born. She became more withdrawn, more anxious. I guess it happens sometimes with new mothers. No one was all that surprised, given Cole's poor health, that she kept him home until he was nearly a year old. But while Cole got older and stronger, Vivian Spencer only got more reclusive.

In front of me, a wide staircase with a prominent newel post hugs the right wall, then curves left to the second story. When we were kids, Cole and I would race through the house playing hide-and-seek. But going upstairs now, even though his mother doesn't seem to be in any hurry to come down, feels wrong. Instead, I follow the main hall toward the kitchen at the rear of the house, hoping she might be on the back stair.

My footsteps slow outside of the study with its built-in bookcases filled with antique books. Last year, I brought over a pie from the diner, forgetting Cole had practice. His mom let me in to wait, then disappeared. I'd wandered in to peruse the shelves, when Mr. Spencer walked into the room, clearly surprised to see me. It didn't occur to me until that moment that I shouldn't be in the home office of the new mayor. This wasn't the place we played hide-and-seek anymore.

A loud thud comes from somewhere above me.

"Hello?" I call out again.

No one answers, but there's another sound like scratching against wood. Then another thud, louder than the first, followed by the sound of breaking glass. A frisson of fear runs down the back of my neck, and I wrap my arms tight around me.

As I step into the gleaming marble kitchen, footsteps skitter down the back staircase, and a petite woman stumbles the last couple steps but finds her footing. Tossing gleaming flaxen hair out of her face, red lipstick slightly smudged and mascara tracks under one eye, she startles when she looks at me. I haven't seen Cole's mom in a good long while, but she still has the same sort of timeless golden beauty as her son, even under the fuddled haze and with the astringent tang of alcohol wafting off of her.

"Oh, Linden. I thought you were someone else." She stops short, then spots the bottle in my hand and rushes toward me. "I broke my last bottle, this week of all weeks." Her voice wobbles, and she stops. A faint taste like buttermilk, sour and potent, rolls over my tongue. Then she covers with another bright smile. "I don't know how your granny does it, but I'm so glad she does."

She reaches for the bottle, and when I place it in her hands, she yanks out the cork and gulps down several mouthfuls. "You can see yourself out, right?" She covers a yawn with her hand and starts back up the staircase.

I tried Gran's sleeping tonic once, last summer, when I first got home from the hospital, but it worked a little too well. I slept so deeply that when the nightmares came, they felt real and I couldn't escape.

"Wait," I call to her, uneasy about leaving her in this big old house all alone in her present condition. When she turns, I have to force the words out, and my voice goes softer. "Um, is Cole home?"

One corner of her mouth tips up, but the smile is pitying. "No, hun, he's not."

"Oh, no." I feel my cheeks heat. "No, I'm not . . ." I stumble in the rush to deny her misconception, then let out a breath and try again. "It's just, I don't like to leave you alone while you're feeling poorly, is all."

"That's sweet." A small smile flashes across her mouth so fast it's more like an involuntary muscle twitch, an after-image. "But I'll be asleep as soon as my head touches the pillow." She holds up the bottle, then yawns again so wide I can see her back molars, before heading upstairs.

I scurry toward the front door, walking as fast as I can while still convincing myself it's in any way dignified. That it doesn't look exactly like what it is: running away.

When I close the heavy door behind me, I lean against it and let my head fall back. "What is wrong with me?" I whisper harshly to myself. The last thing I need is for Cole to think I'm pining away after him because of this.

But there's no time to wallow in self-pity. The sun is already sitting low over the mountains. If I don't hurry, I'll get caught in the dark.

CHAPTER SIX

THE PATH is packed earth, grown chalky from lack of rain, and the stale smell of it stirs up with every step I take until I can taste it. If the word *terrestrial* had a flavor, this would be it. Shadows grow and stretch out in front of me, longer and longer as each minute ticks away. Once the sun begins to set, darkness comes quickly here in the valleys and hollows.

The rhythmic song of the katydids is the only sound louder than my footsteps. I don't realize how much I've increased my pace until I'm winded, the sound of my breath so loud I almost miss the roar of an engine in the distance. But that can't be right because this isn't any kind of road. Except it's getting louder, heading this way, and fast.

I'm walking down the center of the path, far from the brush that encroaches along each side, but it twists and turns too much to see very far in front of me. I turn onto the smaller trail that cuts back to the road and slow my steps. It'll take longer to get home this way, but it's better than facing off with some joyrider looking for trouble.

Only, I've miscalculated the echo off the mountain because as I come around the bend where a half-toppled old shed stands, a motorcycle flies toward me. I jump out of the way to let it go past, but it slows to a stop.

The rider wears a full-face helmet of shiny black. Long, jean-clad legs stretch out until dusty boots hit the ground to hold the bike in place. I back up a few steps and the worn wood of the shed snags the fabric of my shirt.

This bike is different from those I've seen out in front of the Pub and Grub. Those are all wide hips and shiny chrome. This one looks scrappy, with one big headlight on the front. The chop of the engine cuts off, and the rider gives a slow, disbelieving shake of the head before yanking off their helmet.

Cole.

For a moment, I'm not sure if this is better or worse than a random stranger cornering me alone in the hills.

"You're bound and determined not to let me have any secrets, aren't you?" He climbs off the bike and walks it toward the shed. I slide out of the way as he rolls it inside and pulls a heavy-duty cover over top.

Worse. It's definitely worse.

"Oh, sorry, is your fancy clubhouse no girls allowed?" I demand as soon as he steps out of the crumbling shack. I don't like the idea that he thinks I'm intentionally out to snoop on him. When I uncover his secrets, it's almost always completely by accident.

He puffs out a breath and rubs a hand over his hair. It should be messy from the helmet, but annoyingly it's not. It's burnished bronze by the last rays of the setting sun. A buzzing near my ear startles me and I wave a hand at the mosquito.

"Since when do you have a motorcycle, anyway?" I ask, keeping my eyes on the horizon instead of him as the sun sinks lower, sending ribbons of pinks and oranges across the sky.

"It was my great-uncle's. I found it under a tarp in his barn after he died, and fixed it up." He leans back against the shed, crossing his arms and kicking a boot up against the wall behind him. "It's a 1978 Triumph Bonneville." He shrugs a shoulder, but there's pride in his voice. "And, James, I can't stress this enough. No one can know about it."

"And you think, what? I'm going to race down this mountain, screaming it at the top of my lungs like some sort of rabid town crier?" I spin around to face him. "Spencer, I can't stress this enough, I don't care about your secrets."

"And yet you seem to collect them." He pushes off the wall and moves closer.

I resent the implication. "Your daddy would spit nails if he knew you were riding that thing." Malcolm Spencer was in a near-fatal motorcycle accident in his younger years and ever since has been very outspoken about the dangers. And, yeah, it might be a low blow, but a few minutes in Cole Spencer's company, and I'm already fit to be tied.

"Why do you think I'm riding up here on these old trails instead of the road?"

"Because you're a damn fool. Why risk it all?"

"Come on, you should know the answer to that." The words are so quiet, I'm not sure I'm meant to hear them. When it's clear I have, he crosses his arms and his expression goes wry. "Oh, right, you don't care about my secrets."

I roll my eyes, but I think I do know the reason, and it irks me that I can't say it now. Cole is still the mayor's son. It's important for him to keep up appearances, to be the perfect golden boy and pick up the slack for his reclusive mother. The motorcycle must offer a bit of escape from it all for him. I take a breath and muster the will to steer the conversation back to safer ground. "You fixed it up all by yourself?"

He shrugs. "Read some manuals. Watched a bit of YouTube. Made a lot of mistakes." A small, self-deprecating smile flashes so fast I might have imagined it. "I like to work with my hands."

"Yeah, I remember." I say it without thinking as I swipe at another mosquito, then immediately could kick myself. So many months of pretending none of it mattered, gone with one slip of the tongue. My fingers stray to the small scar on my throat, all that's left of the necklace Cole gave me the day I went missing. The first and last day I ever wore it. I glance up at him from the corner of my eye, and I'm almost sure I see him flinch.

"What are you doing up here, anyhow?" he asks, and it feels like an accusation. I've strayed into his territory uninvited.

"Gran asked me to deliver something to your mom." I struggle not to sound defensive.

"You were at the house?" This time I know I'm not imagining the sharpness in his voice. "Did you talk to my mom?"

It's not a leap to figure out why he wouldn't want me, in particular, around his mom, which gets my blood even hotter. "I didn't . . ." All the things I want to say get tangled on my tongue, and I'm not sure if it's fear or frustration, but I swallow them instead. "I dropped off a sleeping tonic. I barely saw her."

He lets out a breath and focuses on the horizon somewhere above my head before he responds. "She hasn't been doing well lately, especially at night." He looks down to meet my gaze. "The tonic is better than the pills that knock her out for full days at a time and a lot better than her other methods. So, thank you."

"Sure, glad to help." I nod. "See you around." I need to get home before Gran starts to worry, and I've about reached my limit of Cole Spencer.

"Let me walk you back."

I ignore him and stride off down the path, but another buzzing sound catches my attention, and this time it's too loud to confuse with a mosquito. "Did you hear that?" A taste like brine fills my mouth.

I glance back in time to see Cole's head jerk like I've startled him. "Hear what?"

The noise comes again, and I follow it, straying off the path. It's like a string pulls my spine up tight. Something isn't right, I can feel it. My feet are moving faster now.

"No, wait . . ."

But his words barely register as I pick my way through the trees. I pause, listening. It's a sound that feels like the crook of a finger, like a push against the small of my back. It's like that morning at the cemetery, but so much stronger.

The buzzing is getting louder as darkness settles into the valley. I think the sound is coming from somewhere over the next hill, maybe near the football field through the woods to my left. I slip my hand into my pocket to squeeze my tiger's-eye stone for courage. White moths flutter at the edge of my vision and I hesitate, but the buzz is growing louder. It feels like my skull is full of bees. I can't stop, beckoned by something I can't name.

I take another step, and my stomach cramps. I go staggery as the taste of metal fills my mouth. Like copper. Like blood. And I can't catch my breath. Anyone raised in these hills knows they can be dangerous. Bears, mountain lions, coyotes are all native predators. Not to mention the venomous snakes: rattler, copperhead—and the two-legged variety. These remote hills are ideal for hiding all kinds of nefarious activity.

I pull my cell phone out of my pocket and see several missed calls from home as I switch on the flashlight and move deeper into the woods, down the dip of a small hill toward where the creek runs.

"James."

I whirl toward the sound of my name, pinning the speaker with the light in my hand.

Cole throws a hand up to block the beam, squinting at me. I'd forgotten all about him.

"What are you doing?" he demands.

I don't have an answer, so I ignore the question. All I know is that I'm close now. I take two more steps toward the creek, and it's like walking into a wall of panic and terror. My throat feels like it's squeezing shut. I fight for air, dropping my phone as I claw at my neck, coughing and gasping.

Cole grabs me, pulling my nails away from my skin and lifting me onto my toes. "Stop it," he roars into my face. "What's happening? What's wrong?"

But the emotions in this place are so strong, I struggle to hold on to myself as they wash over me, through me, pulling me under like waves. My breath comes in sharp bursts, loud in the unnatural quiet. I struggle to get out of Cole's hold, and my foot connects with my phone, sending it sliding partway down the hill. The beam of the flashlight catches on something along the bank of the creek.

A woman. Her cheek is pressed against the algae-covered root of a weeping willow tree. The fabric of her white dress wraps damply around her body like a shroud. She's too still, her eyes open and unblinking.

And there, trailing out among the rocks behind her, flows hair the color of Cheerwine soda. I found Dahlia Calhoun.

CHAPTER SEVEN

I PULL out of Cole's grasp and run to the edge of the creek. Dropping to my knees in the mud, I press my fingers to Dahlia's neck, even though it's clear she's beyond help, her body cold, her eyes coated in a milky film. When I stretch to push harder, desperate to feel a flutter of a pulse, she rolls in the shallow water, exposing the back of her head. Rust-colored ribbons trail from the dark, sticky mass of matted hair.

"Goddammit." Cole catches me around the waist. My feet slip in the mud as he hauls me up, half carrying me back the way we came.

I cover my mouth, pressing hard until the pain of my teeth cutting into my lips reassures me that I am still alive. That even though I somehow picked up the echo of her panic and terror, final emotions so strong they linger like a ghost, they were hers. Not mine.

"Come on, there's nothing we can do for her now." Cole shakes me like he's trying to wake me from a bad dream. "We need to go."

I look up at him, and his jaw flexes tight, eyes scanning the woods around us. But my body is freezing solid in the summer heat, muscles going stiff.

Cole must feel it. "You're in shock." He wraps an arm tightly around my shoulders, tucking me into his side and propelling me toward the high school parking lot. He pauses halfway up the hill to pick up my cell phone, shining the beam of light out in front of us.

A branch snaps like a gunshot. I jerk and risk a glance back over my shoulder, but I can't make out anything in the dark. And then I taste it, the sharp tang of Cole's fear, and with it comes the realization that whoever killed Dahlia might still be out here. My teeth start to chatter, and Cole tightens his hold as he quickens his pace away from the sound. But the crawling sensation of eyes watching from the shadows doesn't leave me.

When we break through the trees, the bright lights of the parking lot hurt my eyes, and I flinch, pressing my face into Cole's shirt without thinking. He smells faintly of cloves and the Forest: cedar, clean air, and fresh earth. I realize how close I'm pressed against him just as Cole steps away.

"Hey!" he calls out. "Can we get some help?"

But there are no cars here this late on a summer evening and no one around. Then I see what Cole must have. Someone stands in the open doorway of the field house on the edge of the lot, outlined by the light behind him.

He rushes toward us, his Caball Hollow Devils Football staff polo shirt bright white like a beacon. "Cole? What are you doing out there in the dark? Are you hurt?"

"Coach Hammond, it's Dahlia Calhoun," Cole tells him. "She's dead."

At the sheriff's station, Mama's arm around my shoulders is like a vise. She squeezes as close to me as she can in the uncomfortable molded plastic chairs. The glare of the fluorescent lights is so harsh no lies could hide here, and a headache has settled deep behind my eyes.

After deputies had locked down the crime scene, they took Cole's statement and drove him home. But once the ambulance crew had cleared me, I was brought here.

Deputy Ethan Miranda rolls a stained chair closer to the desk between us with a squeak. The newest deputy, he graduated from Caball Hollow High School three years before Sorrel and doesn't look old enough to be an Eagle Scout with his coal-black curls and deep dimples. His gaze strays toward the meeting room where the rest of the department is in what looks to be an intense discussion.

Ethan taps his pen against his notepad as his eyes, the color of the bottom of a magnolia leaf, focus back on me. "So tell me again how you found the body?"

The shock seems to be wearing off—at least my teeth have stopped chattering—but I'm going from numb to raw fast.

Every time I blink, I see her too-pale skin, her sightless stare, that trail of blood in the river. I let out a long, shaky breath and rub my sweaty palms against my thighs. I've explained everything several times now, but this is the part he keeps going over.

"Ethan, she's already told you everything she knows, and it's nearly midnight. Can I please take her home?" Mama interjects.

"Ma'am, with all due respect, I'm just trying to do my job. And I'll thank you to remember that when I'm in uniform, it's Deputy Miranda."

Mama raises her eyebrows and leans in. "Well, when I used to babysit you—"

"It's fine," I interrupt. She's got the look of a bear defending her cub, and that never tends to end well for the person on the receiving end. "Like I said before, I was making my way back home when I felt a . . . a sort of pull that led me to where she was. I don't know how else to explain it."

"Yeah, I know what you said, but you don't really expect me to believe that, do you?" He clenches his jaw. "I can't write a feeling pulled you to the body in an official police report." And there it is. The strong, sharp black walnut taste of suspicion that rolls off him in waves every time we go through this.

"Miranda," a deep voice cuts in from behind him.

My head jerks up, and Ethan scrambles to his feet as the sheriff makes his way across the open office toward us. I feel Mama tense beside me. Sheriff Chapman is an imposing figure with his wiry strength, ginger hair peppered with gray, and the stern expression he wears more often than not these days. He's also my father.

"Could you give us a minute?" He claps Ethan amiably on the shoulder, but his words are clearly not a request. Ethan gathers his papers and throws one more frustrated look at me as he makes his way to the break room. "Linden."

"Hey, Daddy." My voice wavers, and he reaches for me, pulling me to my feet and into his arms. He's still got a long night ahead of him, and he's loaded down with a radio, flashlight, pepper spray, handcuffs, and service weapon on his duty belt.

He drops a kiss on the top of my head, then lets out a heavy sigh. "I just came from the scene. We won't know all the particulars until we get the report from the county coroner, but it seems pretty clear that foul play was involved. I'm sorry you had to see your friend that way. How're you doin'?"

"Um, not great." I shake my head to dislodge the images that seem to have seared themselves into my brain. "I saw her at the festival last night. And then her aunt came into the diner this morning looking for her, but there was a rumor she might be staying with her boyfriend nearby."

Daddy pulls his little notebook out of his pocket, flipping it open. "Dahlia Calhoun had a restraining order against an ex-boyfriend whose permanent residence isn't too far from Caball Hollow."

"Why would she meet up with someone she had a restraining order against?"

Daddy lets out a slow breath like he's weighing out his words. "We see it more than you'd think. When you love someone, it gives them a sort of power over you." Mama shifts in her chair, and Daddy seems to carefully avoid looking at her. "That's not necessarily a bad thing, but some people use that power to hurt and manipulate the ones who love them." He squeezes my shoulder, then turns to Mama.

"Odette, can I speak with you for a moment?" he asks, gesturing toward a quiet corner, and Mama stands to follow him.

They've been separated for a while now, though they never actually got around to getting legally married during the nineteen years they were together. The way the story goes is that he'd newly arrived in town after being hired as a deputy, and one day after a long shift, he walked into the diner and spotted Mama. He says she was a vision, like a glass of ice water when you're dying of thirst. She says she was sweaty and tired, and probably smelled of bacon grease. He asked her what her favorite thing on the menu was, and she told him it was the blueberry buttermilk pie, so he came in and ordered a slice every day for a month before working up the courage to ask her out. He didn't tell her he was lactose intolerant until after they moved in together.

Sissy, for all her romantic notions, says we James women only fall in love in one of two ways: doomed or unrequited. She may have a point, as Mama's father died suddenly when she was barely two years old, and Sissy's father is a man she's never met. Doomed and unrequited.

But when it comes to my parents, the truth is simpler than all that. It's my fault.

Last year, on the night of the Moth Festival, I begged to go to the Forest with my friends. I wanted to be normal for once, to do what everyone else was doing, but Mama and Daddy refused. It was the biggest argument we'd ever had and over something so meaningless. In the heat of the moment, spitting nails, I told them I hated them both.

I'd long suspected my abilities might be even more terrible than I knew. At times when I felt something especially strong, those nearby seemed to develop the same emotion. I was afraid to admit it, so I brushed it off, telling myself it was normal for others to get excited with me when I shared good news or for my sisters to cry with me when I was hurt. But what if my own anger and heartache were so strong that I made Mama and Daddy feel that way too? They were happy before, and then, after that night, they were just . . . over.

They've never spoken about what exactly caused their split, and I've never admitted my suspicions to anyone either. How could I look in my sisters' eyes and tell them I'm to blame for unraveling our family? But when Mama and Daddy are in the same room like this, I can almost taste the ghost of what was, bittersweet like the skin of a plum.

Before I can overthink it, I push out of my chair and slide closer until I can just barely hear their words.

"I'll be blunt. Linden finding the crime scene won't be good, Odette," Daddy says in a low voice. "Some are already saying how *peculiar* it was. Not to mention the timing of the Calhoun girl's disappearance. I've warned everyone here in the department not to speak about active cases, but you know how it is in this town. It's only a matter of time before people start talking."

A rush of dizzying warmth spirals through my body. I've spent the last twelve months trying to be as invisible as possible to quell the insatiable rumor mill in this town. I don't want to be the topic of gossip again.

"Listen, I need you to know something."

I jump at the sudden interruption. Ethan Miranda makes his way toward me carrying a stack of folders.

He drops them on his desk and crosses his arms. "I want to say up front that I'm going to make sure we do everything by the book this time."

"I'm sorry, I don't know what you mean."

He leans closer, his expression determined. "I covered for your dad last summer when you disappeared for twenty-four hours and then showed up under a rhododendron bush mere feet from where you'd last been seen. But this is serious. A girl is dead. And I'll follow the investigation wherever it leads. No one is above the law."

I glance over to where my parents whisper to each other, concerned looks on both their faces, and my mouth goes dry. "I don't know what happened last summer, and I know even less about what happened to Dahlia, but she was my *friend*, Ethan."

And that's when it finally hits me. After the shock of finding her body and the tumult of the investigation and all the questions tonight, it's only now in this moment that I truly grasp the fact that Dahlia is dead.

Once when I was little and my sisters and I were playing hide-and-seek, I tripped over a tree root running full tilt and hit the ground so hard it knocked the wind out of me. I couldn't force my lungs to fill with air for what felt like an eternity, and it was like drowning on dry land. That's what this feels like.

My eyes go wide, and my heartbeat kicks into overdrive. I press my palms onto the metal surface of the nearest desk and lean over, trying to suck in as much air as I can, but it's like breathing through a straw.

"Hey, are you all right?" Ethan puts a hand on my shoulder. "Let me get your parents."

"No." I catch his sleeve before he can move away, my voice a rasp. The last thing I need to do is create any more of a scene. "I'm fine." I will the words to be true.

"Linden, I'm going to pull the car around," Mama calls from the other side of the room. She's already holding open the door that leads into the lobby. But Ethan is standing between us, blocking her view of me.

Daddy watches her leave, brow furrowed. He carefully relaxes his face and smiles when he realizes I'm looking at him. His wide gait eats up the space between us, and he pulls me into a quick hug. "Take care, you hear? No more walks in the woods at night. Promise."

"Promise," I whisper, and my voice is almost normal as he drops a kiss on the top of my head.

"Sheriff Chapman?" Daddy turns toward the deputy standing in the doorway of the meeting room. "We have that information you requested."

"Thanks, I'll be right there," he tells the woman.

"Will you let me know what you find out?" I ask.

"Go home and get some sleep. We'll talk more tomorrow." He squeezes my arm, then disappears into the bustle of the next room.

When I step outside, the night is so quiet it's jarring. Few have heard the news about Dahlia yet, and standing here is unsettling, like in those moments right before a dream turns into a nightmare. I mourn the loss of peace that those who awake to the news will suffer. Because if the past year has taught me anything, it's that nightmares don't end just because the sun comes up.

July

➤➤ Buck Moon ◄◄

As summer heats up, deer scrape the velvet from their antlers, sharpening them to hard points for the feverish rut. This is a period of wild, intense energy. Exercise caution and agency. True feelings and buried secrets will rise to the surface, for better or worse. Now is the time for works of healing, intuition, and manifestation.

➤➤ In Season ◄◄

Garden: apricots, beans, beets, cabbage, carrots, cherries, cucumbers, eggplant, greens, nectarines, peppers, plums, potatoes, radishes, raspberries, summer squash, tomatoes, zucchini

Forage: black raspberries, blackberries, elderflowers, gooseberries, mulberries, currants, milkweed, cattails, catmint, oyster and chanterelle mushrooms (find these in the mossy areas of coniferous forests)

➤➤ Calming Oatmeal and Honey Soap ◄◄ for Healing and Protection

Combine oatmeal to soothe irritation and shed what no longer serves you, honey to disinfect and add stability, goat's milk for nourishment and strength. Under the waning moon, heat oils, add lye solution, and stir with a wooden spoon. Insert small stones of jet to ward off evil and protect against hostility. Once set, wash away all manner of trouble.

When soap is not enough, a more ancient magic may be required. Under the full moon, bring a bowl of mountain salt, a knife, and sprigs of comfrey, cedar, and honeysuckle to the Bone Tree (see diablerie, p. 43).

—*Beatrix James, 1883*

CHAPTER EIGHT

THE OLD gristmill that houses the Harvest Moon has creaky, wide-plank floorboards, worn smooth by generations of hard work, with cracks between them just wide enough for secrets to fall through. But for every truth whispered over a pitcher of sweet tea, a dozen rumors are spread faster and thicker than Duke's mayo on a fried green tomato BLT.

It's been more than a week since I found Dahlia's body, and the speed at which gossip can travel through a town with limited internet access and nearly nonexistent cell service is shocking. The whole town is in a frenzy. Not since Elam McCoy's disappearance has such a scandal hit Caball Hollow. This time might even be worse, because no one seems inclined to wait for the official ruling before calling it what it is: Dahlia Calhoun was murdered.

The morning after, a line of people stretched down the block waiting to get in. When I stepped into the packed dining room to take orders, a hush fell and everyone turned to stare. But even that was preferable to when they started talking, with their intrusive questions and baseless theories. For every person who was genuinely concerned, there were three more who said all the right platitudes but had eyes hungry for scandal. Almost gleefully so, as if their morbid curiosity gave them the right to every gruesome detail. As if the life of a girl they watched grow up was worth nothing more than entertainment value.

I walked out and haven't been back. But today my fingers are desperate for the comfort of mixing up some dough. I'm never more at peace than when I'm in this kitchen, rolling out piecrust or testing a new recipe. And the Harvest Moon is closed on Mondays, so I'm determined to use this time alone to stir, whip, and chop until my hands are busy enough to quiet my mind.

Dahlia's funeral is tomorrow, and I want to bring something I've made myself for the repast. I flip on the radio and pull a clean white apron out of the stack in the supply closet. From the pantry, I fill my arms with ingredients, then line the glass jars up on the prep table. Salty, sour, bitter, sweet— all my strongest memories are steeped in flavor. Maybe it's because of my strange ability, or maybe it's a part of growing up here at the diner, where Mama and Gran believe that a good meal is the cure for just about anything.

The James family book isn't like normal cookbooks. It's been passed down through the ages, an inheritance more valuable than all the boxes of old heirloom silver. A birthright that, along with the diablerie, will one day be entrusted to my sisters and me, until we pass it down to the next generation to inhabit Bittersweet Farm.

I take it off the shelf now and flip through it. Amongst the recipes for buttermilk biscuits and fried chicken drizzled with honey are charms for soothing bees and coaxing cows to produce more milk. Next to the recipe for Great-Granny Sudie's famous berry pandowdy is scrawled a note in her own hand: *Berry picking done by the light of the full moon is sure to yield double the amount and will in turn bless those who eat the cobbler with abundance.* So much knowledge, yet no clues as to where or how our more uncanny abilities began.

I slide the book back where it belongs. As familiar and comforting as the words shared in those pages are, there's an itch of restlessness under my skin. I want to make something new. Maybe a shortbread, rich and buttery, with some lavender from the farm, a hint of vanilla, the zest of a lemon.

I'm singing along absentmindedly with the radio for a while as I measure out ingredients before the song registers. It's one of my favorites, Emmylou Harris, "A Love That Will Never Grow Old." But this time I can't help thinking about what Daddy said about love having power over us.

Is it ever worth the risk? What if Sissy is right and we James women are destined to only fall in love if it's doomed or unrequited? Or if it turns dangerous, like it did for Dahlia.

Emotions are complicated things. Sometimes a strong flavor, like anger or sadness, hides a whole host of others underneath—guilt, fear, hurt, nostalgia. Yet other times they enhance each other, like salt to caramel or coffee to chocolate, like grief bringing into sharper focus the shame of letting a friendship fade away. A tear slides down my cheek and drops into the bowl.

I add the softened butter and sugar to the big mixer. Mama and Sissy once told us that they'd put flower blossoms under their pillows on the summer solstice when they were kids so they would dream of their one true love. But I wish I knew an anti-love spell. Something to protect my heart from being vulnerable. After all, what has love ever brought any of us but heartache?

My fingertips trace along the thin white line on the side of my throat, and my thoughts go to Cole. I shake my head as if it will erase the memories, cracking each egg one-handed against the counter and adding them to the bowl. No, no dreams of true love for me. Instead, I ruthlessly zest the lemon, then cut it in half and squeeze the juice into a measuring cup.

A good while later, I'm pulling the last sheet pan out of the oven with a towel, still singing softly along with the radio, when a throat clears behind me. I jump and the pan slides out of the towel and slams into the edge of the prep table, teetering over the far side. I reach for it, but another hand comes up from behind me, pushing the hot metal back onto the table.

I spin around and come face-to-face with Cole Spencer.

Gran doesn't believe in charging someone more for our special brand of help than they can afford, but the people of Caball Hollow don't take charity. Instead, those she helps give what they can—vegetables, chickens, freshly ground cornmeal grits, tomato jam and hot pepper jelly, wild ramps and dandelion greens still wet with dew. So I had expected a previous client, not Cole Spencer, standing right in front of me as if I've conjured him up out of thin air.

My face heats instantly as I recall my earlier thoughts, as if somehow he might have heard them. Or maybe he can see them now, written on my skin. He just might with how warm my cheeks feel. Oh, good lord, how long have I been staring at him this time?

"We're not open today," I blurt out, and immediately wish I could shove the words back into my mouth and swallow them.

"I do know that," he says, one side of his mouth quirking up.

This makes my stomach drop, mostly because I'm pretty sure he's trying not to laugh at me, but partly for reasons about that smile I don't want to admit. I pull open a drawer at random and move around the utensils inside so I don't have to look at him.

"I knocked. Must not have heard me on account of the kitchen karaoke."

I pause my search for nothing to cut my eyes at him. "Why, Cole Spencer, that was almost a joke. I hope you stretched first. Don't want to pull something."

When he doesn't say anything, I close the drawer with a sigh and turn to face him. "What are you doing here, Cole?"

"I saw your bike out back," he says. "You haven't been around lately, and I wanted to see how you're doing."

"You lose my number?" The question is sharp enough to cut us both.

"More like I didn't know if you'd want me to use it." He hesitates, looking more uncomfortable than I've seen in a while. "So how are you?"

I swallow against the emotion that rises up again, already so close to the surface, and shrug. "About how you'd expect after something like that, I reckon. You?"

"I can't believe she's really gone." He looks down at his hands, and I watch his jaw clench. I have to look away. "That day, it was like you were being led straight to her."

"Oh, please, not you too." I shake my head in frustration. "That's all anyone wants to talk about. I don't know how, and I don't know why." I yank open another drawer.

"Has something like that ever happened before?"

"No!" I grab a spatula and start moving cookies from the pan to the cooling rack, even though it's too soon. I need something to do with my hands that doesn't involve throttling Cole Spencer. But then I remember the cemetery.

I thought the pull I'd felt then had been on account of Amos McCoy's strong emotions, but the pull to Dahlia was even stronger. Was it the echo of the intensity of Dahlia's final moments that drew me closer? Or was it something else entirely?

"You were acting so strangely before we found her," Cole says, voice soft. "At first, I thought maybe you were the one who was sick or hurt."

"What?" I ask, distracted by my own thoughts. It's an unusually intimate admission, not the guarded and taciturn responses I'm used to from him lately. I glance up, but he's not even looking at me. He's inspecting his hand, eyes pained, mouth tight.

"Oh, lord! I'm sorry." I drop the spatula and wipe my hands. He must have burned himself when he grabbed the hot pan. "I didn't even ask if you were all right. Here, let me see."

"It's fine. It's nothing," he protests as I gingerly pull his arm toward me.

An angry red welt marks the place where the edge of the metal touched his flesh, and it's already starting to blister. It must hurt something fierce. I suck a breath in through my teeth. "Nothing? You seared yourself medium rare."

"I guess sometimes my physical reflexes are faster than my mental ones."

"Lucky for you, we're prepared for burns in this kitchen." I turn to the small hand-washing sink near the back door and open the cupboard above it. I can see the edge of the first aid kit, but someone tall has inconsiderately put it on the top shelf, probably Rowan. I curse her for being blessed with those extra three inches as I stretch up on my tiptoes and reach as far back as I can, but my fingertips only brush against the cold metal of the box.

The air shifts as Cole steps close enough behind me that I can feel the heat coming off his body. Close enough that I can smell his cedar-and-clove scent. He reaches over my head with his uninjured hand and plucks the box from the shelf.

"Here." His breath tangles in my hair.

I turn to take the first aid kit and realize immediately it's a mistake. He's looking down at me, so close I could chart the constellations of tiny freckles that dust the tops of his cheeks and trail across the bridge of his nose. It's disorienting, both familiar and foreign. Despite how we feel about each other now, I still recall in exact detail what it would feel like to lean forward and erase the last bit of distance between us.

"Show-off." My voice is rough, and I snap my mouth shut. "Being tall isn't really a skill."

"Spoken like someone who's never been short."

"Fair enough." The corner of his mouth tips up again as he passes me the box.

I spin around to set it on the counter and put some space between us. Rummaging through the contents of the box without really seeing them, I try to get myself back under control amidst the disorienting and contrary feelings whirling through me. I need to stop being completely ridiculous.

I grab the small jar of pale yellow balm that looks a bit like freshly churned butter and reach for his hand, avoiding his eyes as I scoop out some of the salve with my finger and spread it lightly over the angry skin of his palm. Once the burn is coated, I lean in to gently blow air across it to dry the balm while I push healing intention through my breath. I don't have anywhere near Gran's skill, but with the salve, it should at least soothe the pain and speed the healing.

"What is that?" he murmurs, lowering his head for a closer look, and suddenly I feel too exposed. I drop his hand and pack up the first aid kit in sharp, precise movements.

"Secret family recipe." I mean the words to be breezy, but they sound breathless, and I clear my throat. "But mostly lavender oil with a little apple cider vinegar and honey."

"That's incredible, it feels better already," he says, mostly to himself, as he stretches his hand, testing for hidden sensitivity. He looks over at me as I slide the metal box back onto the shelf. "Are those for Dahlia's funeral?" He nods toward the table where the lavender shortbread is cooling. "They smell amazing."

"No, that's for the funeral." I point to the stainless steel prep counter by the far window where a blackberry jam cake topped with meringue sits. "These are because I needed more time in the kitchen."

"You always did tend to bake your feelings." He leans back, bracing his hands against the counter behind him in a way that pulls the soft-worn gray T-shirt taut across his chest.

Him being here like this, talking—for a moment it feels like before, and the sharp pang of loss I feel knocks me back. How did I manage to lose so much in one night?

"I should go." Cole pushes off the counter and moves toward the door, then hesitates. "If you ever do want to talk about Dahlia, or about finding her, I'm around," he says.

"Sure." It's such a Spencer thing to say. At least seven generations have served this town in one capacity or another, from a founding father all the way to his dad, a former sheriff's deputy and now the mayor. Being a pillar of the community is Cole's birthright. And I appreciate the olive branch, but a call from me to talk about feelings has got to be pretty much the last thing he would ever truly want.

When the door closes behind him, my fingers stray once again to the scar on my neck.

That night, I lie awake, staring at the ceiling in my room and dreading closing my eyes. Every time I try, I see Dahlia's face. Not the smiling, vibrant person she was in life, but the way she looked lying in that creek. Empty. Death does not look like peaceful slumber; it looks cold and lonely. After seeing Cole this morning, last summer feels even closer, lurking just beneath the surface.

Dahlia was killed exactly one year after my own disappearance. It feels like too much of a coincidence to be chance, yet the only suspect in her murder is an ex-boyfriend I've never met. So what is the connection, and why did I get to come home and she didn't? If I had tried harder to remember what happened to me, could I have saved her? Because now they're not just lost memories—they could be clues.

I give up on the pretext of sleep and tiptoe down the back staircase to the kitchen, making my way to the stove for the kettle and the jar of tea. The small light over the stove is on, but it's dark enough that I almost run smack into a shadowy figure.

"Gah!" I raise the kettle up in front of me like a shield, even though I can see now that it's Sorrel. "You scared the livin' daylights out of me," I hiss.

"Sorry." She shrugs, her arms full of one of the black cats that prowl the farm at night for mice and other critters. She rubs a cheek against the cat's head and scratches her under the chin before setting her down. "Good girl, get to work." Sorrel opens the back door a crack, filling the kitchen with the lullaby of mountain chorus frogs and crickets. The cat slips out, and I watch until it melts into the darkness.

"Can't sleep?" Sorrel asks as she rummages around in the refrigerator for a minute, finally emerging with a jar of last summer's dilly beans. She grabs a fork from the silverware drawer and hops up on the counter.

I shake my head, stealing the fork out of her hand to spear one of the beans from the jar, then letting the tangy brine roll over my tongue. The salty, vinegary taste matches the flavor of the melancholy that seems to permeate everything lately.

"Me neither," she says, lowering her eyes as she fishes another bean out of the jar. "I always thought the first ceremony I attended in honor of a classmate would be a wedding, not a funeral."

"Did you have classes together?" I ask as I light the stove and set the kettle over the flame. Sorrel and Dahlia weren't close, but they graduated together, and in a town as small as Caball Hollow, everyone knows everyone at least a little.

I pull a mug from the cupboard and hold it out to her. She shakes her head at the offer of sleep-easy tea. I'm pretty sure Sorrel prefers to be nocturnal.

"Some." She smiles around a mouthful of green beans, her eyes lighting up with memory. "We had math together junior year, and it was so boring, we used to pass silly notes to each other on our calculators."

"How do you mean?" I steal her fork and another bean, half-heartedly hoping the weird midnight snack mixed with the tea might at least give me different nightmares.

"You never did that? When you put in certain numbers or equations, then turn the calculator upside down, you can spell out words." She scoots off the counter and twists the lid back on the jar. "It was mostly a lot of 'hello' and 'lol.'"

We both laugh, but when the quiet closes back in around us, it feels heavier somehow. I stir honey into my tea, replaying all the same memories of Dahlia in my mind that I've had on repeat this week to try to avoid thinking of that final one.

"The funeral will be hard for you, won't it?" Sorrel ventures into the quiet, leaning back against the refrigerator after putting the beans away. "Not only because she was your friend. A lot of emotions are going to be packed into that one little room."

I nod, focusing on the swirling liquid in my teacup instead of the swirling thoughts in my head. It's another worry that's been keeping me up at night. But not going to Dahlia's funeral is unthinkable, so I just shrug. "What's the worst that could happen?"

I think I may have always been a little bit in love with Cole Spencer. Or at least since I was six years old, parched after a spirited game of tag. The garden hose was too unwieldy for me, and he cupped his hands so I could drink from them. I hadn't even had to ask; he'd just done it. But I'd long since realized that everyone in Caball Hollow was in love with him for the same reason. He went out of his way to see people.

Yet sometimes I'd catch the taste of angst like dandelion greens, earthy and bitter and sharp, wafting off of him when he'd offer to do something for someone. After a while, I realized it was because he was always sacrificing what he wanted to help everyone else.

When I close my eyes, the sounds of the festival seem louder. Every summer, a traveling carnival company trucks amusements on flatbeds up the mountain and into the high school parking lot, unfolding the Tilt-A-Whirl and the Orbiter and the narrow little fun-house trailer like rusted bindweed petals. I can hear the music of the midway games, the laughter of little kids as they chase each other through the park, hopped up on way too much sugar. I can even hear Dahlia Calhoun's name announced as the new Moth Queen all the way down at the stage. But here, it's all muted, removed.

"How was Georgetown?" I ask.

"Hmm." He hesitates. "My father is disappointed I won't be on the football team. It would have been good publicity for the town." I feel him move behind me.

"I'm glad," I tell him, surprising a chuckle out of him that tickles my skin.

"Why's that?" His fingertips brush the back of my neck, and a shiver runs down my spine before cool metal touches my skin. "Open your eyes," he murmurs, pressing his lips briefly to the same spot before taking a step back.

"Because you hate football." It's another thing he does for the good of the town. And maybe secretly I like that I'm the only one who knows this about him. I look down and see a necklace with a tiny bluebird holding an envelope in its beak. "It's beautiful," I breathe, reaching up to trace the delicate shape of the bird's wing.

I swallow, summoning the courage to open up to Cole more than I have to anyone else. "You don't have to pretend with me," I tell him. "You never need to hide how you really feel, because I know anyway."

"Cole!" someone shouts, and I spot Bryson Ivers by the midway games. He taps the person next to him and gestures toward us. I only have a few moments to explain myself.

Cole moves the strap of my tank back into place. "That's the new assistant coach." When his breath catches, I glance up in time to see his expression go from open and happy to guarded and wary.

"What's wrong?" I ask, squeezing the pendant in my hand.

"Nothing." He rubs the back of his neck and looks away, jaw clenching. "Nothing." But his words don't match the strong feelings pouring off of him in choking waves of shock, disbelief, and stark metallic fear.

"Cole." I try again, turning to study his face. I lean closer, wanting him to confide in me. "I know something is wrong. That's what I'm trying to tell you." I swallow hard, hesitating now that the moment is here. And then I leap. "In my family, everyone is born with a special gift. Mine is that I can taste what others are feeling." I reach out to touch his arm, and he recoils. His eyes slide away from me to somewhere near my shoulder and then over to where Bryson and the other man approach. He takes a step back.

"You can do what?" His voice is low, but the careful mask that had settled over his features slips just long enough to show stark horror. He swallows, hard, and my mouth fills with the taste of revulsion, bitter and sour. "Do you have any idea how violating that is?" His jaw is clenched so tight he can barely get the words out.

They hit me in the center of my chest, and I don't know how I manage to stay on my feet. How did I misjudge this so badly? I'd been working so hard to muster the courage to tell him my deep, dark secret that I'd never stopped to think about it from his perspective. In exposing my most hidden self, I'd also exposed his.

"You should go home, Linden." He shoves his hands in his pockets, and I notice they're shaking. "Go home and stay there. Don't go out to the Forest. Everyone going there tonight deserves their privacy. And so do I."

He walks away, and he doesn't look back.

CHAPTER NINE

ON THE day of Dahlia's funeral, the air itself feels charged with some strange sort of agita. Daylilies open under the light of the moon, nightingales sing at midday, and all the ice cream in the freezer at the Harvest Moon melts.

I sit at the desk in my bedroom as Juniper curls my hair into loose waves. Rowan lies draped across my bed, flipping through an old magazine she found underneath it. Both of them seem bound and determined to stick close by me today, but my stomach is already tied up in knots.

"You might need something stronger than concealer for her dark circles," Rowan tells Juniper, then raises her eyebrows at me above the magazine.

"Like spackle," Juniper murmurs as she releases a curl, then twists another around the iron's hot barrel.

I shrug, careful not to burn myself. "I don't think I closed my eyes for more than a minute or two last night."

"How about this one?" Sorrel sweeps into the room holding up a vintage black dress with lace sleeves and a full skirt. I'd only realized this morning that I didn't own a black dress suitable for a funeral. Sorrel has been scouring the house looking for something that might suit.

"Pretty! Try it on, Linden," Juniper urges, releasing me from her curling iron.

"It's beautiful." I take the dress from Sorrel and run my fingers over the fabric. "Where'd you find it?"

"Up in the secret cupboard, where else," Sorrel says as she drops down onto the edge of Juniper's bed.

In the attic, across from Sissy's bedroom, is a wardrobe filled with all manner of elegant gowns, party dresses in every style, floral silk robes, boxes full of sparkling jewelry, shelves of hatboxes, and even a drawer filled with nothing but gloves and embroidered handkerchiefs. When we were little, we called it the secret cupboard and spent hours unearthing its treasures to play dress up. It wasn't until we were older that we learned they were all things that had once belonged to Zephyrine.

"You don't think Gran will mind?" I ask as I shuck off my shorts and tank top to pull on the dress.

"I don't think you have much of a choice," Sorrel says. "I searched the entire house, and it's either this or leggings."

"People would really be surprised we don't own more black," Rowan deadpans.

Juniper helps do up the tiny fabric-covered buttons along the back, and I push the bedroom door closed so I can look in the full-length mirror that hangs on it. I run my hands along the sides of the dress. It fits like it was made for me, but it still feels strange somehow, like I'm someone else.

"Well, hot damn," Rowan says as she sits up and piles her mass of thick, dark hair on top of her head. "Speaking of which, you could boil water up here without even trying. Can we go now?"

We tramp down the stairs in a single-file line to the kitchen, where Gran is frying up some chicken for the meal after the funeral. "I've got five more minutes on this and then we can head over." Gran turns from the stovetop to look at us and her face goes white. "Oh!"

"What happened?" Mama rushes over to the stove as Gran folds up the bottom of the apron that's protecting her church clothes and presses her face into the fabric. "Did you burn yourself?"

"I'm fine." Gran waves Mama off and dabs her eyes. "Linden, you look so much like Zephyrine in that old dress of hers."

"Gran, I'm so sorry! I'll go take it off." My own voice is watery at the sight of Gran's tears. She isn't one to cry, especially not with the intensity of this sudden outburst.

"No, no, honey." She wipes at her eyes. "It's fine, really. Those things don't do anyone any good sitting up in the attic. I miss her, is all."

I run a hand down the fabric of the skirt, feeling un-moored yet weighted down by the sense of loss that hangs heavy in the air. Lost sisters, lost daughters, lost sons, lost memories. Loss can't be all there is, can it?

Heck Funeral Home is filled to capacity. People mill around outside the stout brick building, and a news crew out of Charleston films live shots from across the street. I duck my head as we pass, and Gran clucks her tongue, making it clear she finds the spectacle tasteless.

"Really, it's one thing to report the news, but buzzing around outside the poor girl's funeral like a flock of vultures is completely uncalled-for," she grumbles.

In the reception room, white paper tablecloths are spread over large round tables, each surrounded by folding chairs, ready for the repast. I set my cake on the long buffet table, in between Gran's fried chicken and Mama's pickled water-melon rind salad.

"How's this for irony, a group of feasting vultures is called a wake," Rowan whispers in my ear.

But of course Gran hears it. "Hush your mouth, Rowan Persephone," she declares from the other side of the table, shaking her head. "Honestly, it's like you've got no fetchin' up, child. Now is neither the time nor the place. Go and find somewhere to sit." She shoos us toward the chapel across the hall.

I squeeze Rowan's hand in gratitude for her attempt to distract me as we slide onto the polished hardwood of a pew near the back where Juniper, Sorrel, and Sissy have saved space. Mama and Gran join us a few minutes later, right before Pastor Crawley Boggs steps up to the lectern.

He begins with a prayer, then settles in for a long soliloquy about a life cut short, peppered with Bible verses and hymns led by Mrs. Boggs, the choir director. I only half listen, because I can't take my eyes off the small brass urn sitting on a pedestal next to an enlarged copy of Dahlia's senior class portrait, all wide smile and wild mane of hair, the limitless future spread out in front of her like a promise.

Pastor Boggs finally takes a seat, and a tall man in the front row moves toward the lectern. When he turns to face the congregation, I realize it's Mayor Spencer, Cole's father.

"Nice of Malcolm to say a few words," Mama whispers to Gran. Sissy grunts, though I'm not sure if she means it as agreement.

"Hello, everyone," he begins. "I'm Malcolm Spencer, mayor of Caball Hollow, yes, but first and foremost, a neighbor. My family has made this place our home for generations, and the circumstances surrounding the death of this young woman trouble me just as they do you. I've expressed my condolences privately to the family of young Dahlia Calhoun, but I also asked that they give me this opportunity to address all of you.

"Dahlia was a shining star, a bright light extinguished much too soon. And I want to make a pledge to all the members of this community that I am taking a personal interest in ensuring that the person responsible for her death is brought to justice swiftly and absolutely. Caball Hollow has always been a safe place to live, and I will ensure it remains that way, especially for our young people."

I glance toward the rear of the chapel, where Daddy and several deputies stand. He gives me what I'm sure is supposed to be a reassuring smile, but there is a tightness around his mouth that I find troublesome.

Dahlia's aunt, Nettie Hinkle, makes her way to the podium, her eyes red-rimmed and face puffy, with a tissue and a folded paper clutched in one hand. Solemnly, Mr. Spencer takes her other hand in his, then leans in to murmur something before retaking his seat.

She sniffles, and the taste of grief like bitter blackstrap molasses hits the back of my throat. I shift in my seat, wary. I'm not sure I can block out the strong emotions of this many people, especially when they're combined with my own.

"Most of you know Dahlia didn't have an easy life. Her mother, my sister, God rest her soul, struggled with her own particular demons and died when the poor girl was still in diapers," Mrs. Hinkle begins, her voice thin. "Her father was gone long before that. Dahlia was real close with my mother, her mamaw, and took it hard when we lost her last winter. Through it all, Dahlia was a beautiful, thoughtful girl. She had a quick smile and an even quicker wit. But most of all, she had plans.

"She worked hard so she'd be able to follow her dream of attending college and becoming a journalist. She is . . . was . . ." Mrs. Hinkle starts to cry, tears sliding slowly down her cheeks. The taste of grief intensifies, inky, salty, and bitter. "I'm sorry." She purses her lips and carefully folds the paper back up. "But what do you say about someone whose life hasn't even really begun yet? How do you memorialize a person when everything was still ahead of her?"

Mrs. Boggs comes forward to wrap an arm around Mrs. Hinkle's shoulders, leading her back to her seat in the front row. I cough as the pungent essence of blackstrap molasses trickles down my throat.

Juniper leans over and presses a tissue into my palm. "Are you all right?" she whispers. I nod but cough again.

Pastor Boggs invites people who were close to Dahlia to come up and say a few words, and as each of them stands, the potent, viscous grief thickens until it makes me choke. After the third person, I press a hand over my mouth and shoot to my feet, rushing toward the exit and feeling the curious stares of everyone I pass.

I burst out of the chapel, gagging as I stumble down the hall with no direction in mind other than away from the overwhelming amount of grief so I can breathe. There's a sharp ringing in my ears. My vision starts to tunnel as my feet take me down the long hall, past the lobby and the bathrooms, until I reach a door marked STAFF ONLY that feels cool to the touch. I press my forehead against it, ears buzzing and stomach roiling; something within me needs to get to whatever is on the other side. My hand finds the knob, but it's locked.

A throat clears behind me. "Miss, is everything all right?"

I turn, pressing my back up against the door. The man is

in his early twenties, with hair the color of wheat like all the members of the Heck family. I've seen him before in the diner with his many siblings and their parents. He might be one of the twins, Boyd or Boone.

"I'm fine, I just needed a minute," I tell him, swallowing hard against the lingering aftertaste of grief. It finally registers that he's caught me trying to open a door clearly marked off-limits. "Sorry." I clear my throat. "The air felt a bit cooler here." I try to explain, even though I'm confused myself by what I've done.

The concerned expression drawing together his eyebrows smooths away, and he offers a small smile instead. "That's the door to the basement. I'd let you down, but that's where the preparation rooms are for embalming, and we have a, um . . ." He tugs at the collar of his cream-colored dress shirt and shakes his head. "A recent occupant from over in Rawbone. You can have a seat in the office if you'd like." He gestures toward another door across the hall.

"Linden?" My head jerks up, and I see Cole striding down the hall toward me in a dark suit, a bottle of water in one hand.

"Ah, Cole." The man pats Cole on the shoulder. "Good to see you again."

"Hello, Boyd," Cole says, without looking at him, as he opens the bottle and hands it to me.

Boyd waits for a moment, but when it becomes clear no one is going to say anything else, he excuses himself. "Well, I need to finish getting the reception room ready for the repast, so I'll leave you in Cole's capable hands." He nods at me and pats Cole again, then heads briskly for the front of the funeral home.

"Are you all right?" Cole asks, voice low. "What happened?"

"I knew it would be difficult." I draw in a shaky breath after taking a long drink. "But I could barely breathe in there." I brace myself for the taste of disgust I'm sure will come after such a bald acknowledgment of my talent, but it doesn't. Cole's gaze stays steady.

"So you wanted to hide?" He tilts his head toward the basement door.

"I don't know, Cole, I . . ." I'm about to say that I needed to get away from the crowd, but that's not exactly true. I left the chapel for that reason, but then it had felt like I was pulled here, a much slighter echo of the night we found Dahlia. But when I'd felt the pull then, it was toward intense emotions. This time, I'd been pushed in the opposite direction entirely, away from the funeral service and all its grief.

I look up at him, surprised by the realization, but before I can say anything else, the doors of the chapel at the other end of the hall open up and people flow out. Cole gives a low grunt of frustration as his father spots him and heads directly for us.

"Hello, son." Mr. Spencer turns to nod politely in my direction, then does a surprised double take. "Linden James, my goodness. I almost didn't recognize you." He shakes his head slightly. "You are the spitting image of your great-aunt."

"You knew Aunt Zephyrine?" I'm not sure why this surprises me so much, as they both grew up here in Caball

Hollow, but because she left town so long ago, she's always seemed more like family lore to me than an actual person.

"I did, yes." He nods and clears his throat. The rosemary taste of nostalgia pings against the roof of my mouth, bright and piney. "Pretty well, actually. When I was up at Georgetown and she was working at the library here, I'd plan all my study time at home for her shifts. Her answers were always better than mine." He chuckles, then winces and presses a hand to his stomach. "Anyway, I hope you don't mind, but I need to drag my son away. I find I'm feeling a bit poorly and need to get home. It's nice to see you again, Linden. I only wish it wasn't under such sad circumstances."

Mr. Spencer moves away toward the exit on the other side of the room, and Cole follows, giving me one last long look, like I'm a puzzle he can't quite figure out.

"How are you feeling, kiddo?" Daddy asks as he crosses the space between us from the chapel, reaching out to set a reassuring hand on my shoulder.

"Better now," I answer, not liking the dry, stale taste of weariness coming from him. "The mayor seems confident that Dahlia's killer will be caught soon," I offer.

"Mayor Spencer may have gotten a bit zealous." Daddy blows out a breath and glances over his shoulder to make sure no one is close enough to overhear. "He was the deputy assigned to her case when she came in to file the restraining order, and I think he feels like he let her down. But we found the ex-boyfriend. He's been working on an oil rig down off the coast of Florida for the past three weeks.

There's no way he could have done this, which means we're back to square one."

"So then, the killer could be anyone." My mind spins at the idea that someone I might know could have done this. But, of course, monsters live in small towns too.

"The last thing anyone in this town wants is a long, drawn-out investigation, but it's looking like that's what it'll be," Daddy says with a sigh. "Unless we find a lead soon."

I'm quiet while I work up the courage to ask the question I've been afraid to all week. "Did she suffer?"

I count the seconds, holding my breath before Daddy finally answers. "I'm not going to lie to you. We can't know for certain what her last moments were like. But what we do know is that she was killed from behind and most likely never saw it coming. It was over quickly."

I shut my eyes against the pressure building up behind them, but I can't stop one shaky breath from escaping.

"Listen, I don't want you to worry. I'm handling this." Daddy pulls me into a hug, and a taste like Gran's biscuits, buttery and warm, lands on my tongue. Sympathy. He pushes me back so he can look me in the eyes, while I try to muster a reassuring smile before I have to face everyone at the repast.

Inside the reception hall, people mill around, taking turns offering their condolences to Dahlia's family and making small talk amongst themselves as they fill their plates. The taste of grief isn't so overwhelming now, but I've heard more than a few whispered theories and questions about why it's taking the sheriff so long to arrest the person responsible for Dahlia's death.

"The last time anyone saw the Moth-Winged Man was when Elam McCoy went missing," says one woman loudly enough to cut through the low hum of conversation.

"You know what I think," starts up the woman next to her, whose perennial state of displeasure has etched itself on her face. When she glances in my direction and finds me watching her, she shuts her mouth and pulls her friend away to gossip in a more private corner.

I look away only to see another person quickly turn when our eyes meet. I've been getting quite a few measured glances.

"Is this a new recipe?" Rowan asks, standing next to me as she eats an enormous slice of blackberry jam cake and ignores everyone else in the room.

I shrug. "No, not really. I added a bit of clove and did a meringue buttercream instead of the usual cream cheese frosting."

"It tastes different." She takes another bite, chewing slowly, brow furrowed. "More complex, or deeper somehow."

"Hello, girls, so nice to see you again." Mrs. Boggs puts an arm around my shoulders and gives me a quick little squeeze.

Rowan lifts her plate closer to her face, hiding the way her nose wrinkles slightly. A lie, then, from Mrs. Boggs.

"I was just talking to Sorrel about how much she enjoyed her freshman year at that school in Kentucky. Rowan, what are your plans now that you've graduated?" she asks.

"You're lookin' at 'em," Rowan says as she scoops another big bite of cake into her mouth.

Mrs. Boggs chuckles lightly, but her eyes are the slightest bit alarmed. She's clearly not sure if Rowan is kidding or not. To be honest, neither am I. With Rowan, it could go either way.

"Are you all right, dear?" Mrs. Boggs asks suddenly, concern sharpening her voice.

I turn to see tears rolling down Rowan's cheeks. "It's all so sad." She sniffles. "So much loss."

I'm surprised. Rowan isn't one to show her feelings so publicly, even at a funeral. I move closer to block curious stares as a woman near the dessert table bursts into sobs. Then, behind us, a man sniffs loudly, and when I glance over, he's crying silent tears directly into his own plate of blackberry jam cake.

An awful suspicion makes my stomach drop as my mouth floods with a nauseating mix of powerful flavors—the whiff of shame, the burn of anger, the bite of fear. The blackstrap molasses taste of grief, the sharp onion tang of loss, caramelizing into something deeper, bitter and sweet. All the things I felt so strongly when I baked the cake are now manifesting in anyone who ate it. I've influenced the emotions of an entire room of people.

I barely miss Mrs. Boggs's sensible heels when I bend over and throw up what little I had managed to eat today.

CHAPTER TEN

I'M WALKING the same path I took the night I discovered Dahlia's body, but I try not to think about that right now.

"This might be a terrible idea," Rowan observes as we cut across the valley, the beam of the flashlight in her hand leading the way.

"Yeah, you're probably right," I agree. Gran and Mama think I'm still sleeping off a sour stomach. But when Sorrel told me she'd heard Dahlia's friends were planning to hold a vigil for her tonight, I knew I had to be there.

After what happened at the funeral, it doesn't feel like I've properly said goodbye to Dahlia. But it's more than that. With her ex-boyfriend ruled out as a suspect, the similarities between her death and my disappearance are impossible to ignore. We both went missing on the night of the Moth Festival. I came home with a concussion; she died of a head injury. And then there's her strange question the last time I saw her. Had she known something about the night I went missing? Maybe if I hadn't been so determined to forget, I could have done something to prevent her death. And maybe if I hadn't pushed everyone away, I would have some idea of where to start looking for answers.

"Hey, listen." Rowan grabs my wrist and pulls me to a stop. "I know you like to keep everything bottled up tight, but it's actually pretty selfish to act like you never need help."

"You think I *like* keeping everything bottled up?" I look at her in disbelief. "Remember when you told me it feels like an itch that won't go away when someone lies?"

Rowan nods, impatiently urging me to go on.

"I've always been afraid to talk about it because I thought everyone else had good, useful abilities and mine was the only one that was invasive and troublesome. I'm sorry that I let that get in the way of being there for you." I look away, ashamed. "But I think this . . . this thing I can do— it's getting worse. You know what happened with the cake at the funeral. It's dangerous if I don't keep it locked up."

Rowan doesn't say anything for a long moment, and my stomach drops. But when I risk a glance at her, she looks pensive. "Linden, I think we've all wished we could return our gifts a time or two," she finally says.

"Gran's most important rule is not to interfere with the lives of others. I don't think I can stand to have her disappointed in me," I tell her as we start walking again.

When we reach the field by the old bridge over Stillhouse Creek, dozens of people I recognize from school are already milling around. The road that passes over the water here isn't used much anymore since the coal mine it leads to closed forty years ago. It's not far as the crow flies from where I found Dahlia's body, or from the Forest, a fact that already has me feeling anxious.

"What's the plan?" Rowan asks.

"We need to find out whatever we can about Dahlia's life these last few months," I answer, eyes scanning the crowd for people who might have kept in touch with Dahlia while she was at college. But there are so many people here. "Divide and conquer?"

Rowan crosses her arms and gives me a dubious look. "Fine, but we meet back here in exactly one hour." When I nod, she melts into the crowd.

I step out onto the bridge, where sporadic clumps of candles are lit. A small fire burns on the opposite shore, and I scan the faces surrounding it. Harper Farrow, who was co-editor of the yearbook with Dahlia last year, stands at the outskirts of the group.

"Harper!" I move to intercept her.

She turns, spotting me, then glances away. "Linden, I didn't think you'd be here." The taste of her discomfort makes my still-sensitive stomach start to ache.

"Oh, why's that?" I ask, trying to keep my voice sweet and not sharp.

"Just with everything, you know." She waves a hand as if to clear the air, but her eyes search the crowd over my shoulder.

Sensing she's not going to stick around long enough for a deep conversation, I cut right to it. "Hey, do you know if Dahlia came back to Caball Hollow at all in the past few months? The last time I saw her was for her grandmother's funeral."

She shrugs. "I doubt it. All she ever seemed to talk about was how much she couldn't wait to leave town. I'm probably not the best person to ask, though. We didn't really keep in touch after graduation." Her eyes light up as she waves a hand at someone in the distance. "I've gotta go. See you around."

She takes off before I can say another word, and I watch as she joins a small group on the other side of the fire. Maude Parrish turns at her approach and pulls her into a quick hug, then dabs prettily at her eyes with a tissue. She smiles up at someone behind her, and as he moves into the light of the fire, I realize it's Cole. Something hot sparks in my chest, and I look away.

There must be more than just cheap beer in the cooler next to Bryson Ivers's beat-up truck, because after only an hour, people are getting rowdy. Every person I've spoken with has said pretty much the same thing as Harper. No one seems to know anything about Dahlia's final months, and I'm no closer to finding any answers. I puff out a frustrated breath.

"To Dahlia!" someone shouts from across the bridge. Others echo the sentiment, red plastic cups lifted up, reflecting the glow of the bonfire in the gathering darkness. Some people are crying, but others are laughing, sharing stories, remembering.

I find Rowan on the bridge as she waves off a whiskey bottle someone holds out, but I take a quick slug to dull the headache that's settled between my eyes.

"So, be honest. What really happened to Dahlia?" Bryson asks with a boozy exhale, leaning close like he's telling a secret instead of asking for one.

I jerk back, noticing for the first time how closely the others have filled in around us and how many eyes are on me waiting for an answer. The fire on the bank flares, grotesquely stretching the shadows and pulling up a flash of memory from last summer of another bonfire in the woods surrounded by these same faces.

"We deserve to know the truth," says Lydia Rucker, a senior who was on student council with Dahlia, eyes red-rimmed.

"I don't know any more than you do." I mean for the words to be firm, but they come out soft and wobble in the middle.

"But you *are* a witch," Bryson insists, as if this revelation will remind me that I do, somehow, know all. "Aren't you?"

"They used to test if someone was a witch by throwing them in the water to see if they would float," Lydia says, something calculating in her tone that makes me look back at her sharply.

"Let's see if it works!" Bryson crows, all the words sliding together as he lifts his hands and moves even closer.

I'm not sure if it's supposed to be a joke or if he really means to push me, but before I can react, my mouth floods with the taste of hatred, bitter and powerful, as someone starts shoving at the back of the crowd, and a fight breaks out behind Bryson. Like dominoes, someone knocks him into me. I reach out as I fly backward, fingers clutching at thin air. Rowan shouts something I can't make out and rushes forward as if she could catch me. I see her hand grasping for mine, but it's too late. As the cold water closes over me, my last clear thought is a flare of panic: This is the creek where Dahlia died.

LAST SUMMER Solstice, 11:40 p.m.

The water closes over my head, so cold it drives the last of the air from my lungs. I'm trapped. Something is keeping me pinned beneath the rushing river. I scrabble for purchase on the slippery rocks below me, becoming more and more frantic until I finally manage to get my hands underneath me. Curling my fingers into the mud of the riverbank, I push back as hard as I can.

My head breaks the surface, and I come up sputtering, coughing up water and gulping down as much oxygen as I can in great heaving drags. The darkness, both under the water and out of it, is disorienting and heavy, almost like a presence. Someone, or something, just out of sight. I struggle to stand, panicked. Something hard strikes the back of my head and everything goes hazy.

I slip under the water.

CHAPTER ELEVEN

MY HEAD breaks the surface of the water, and I suck in air as my heart pounds hard against my ribs, just above where a strong arm is banded around me. The fragment of memory is still so vivid and overwhelming that I struggle to get away before the sight of a bridge full of people, instead of a wilderness of trees, pulls me back to the present.

I wipe my eyes, and slowly the world comes into focus. Faces peer over the railing, cast in shadow by the bonfire behind them. I look over my shoulder at the person who pulled me from under the dark water.

Cole's jaw is tight with carefully controlled anger, the spicy flavor cutting through the silty and metallic taste of the creek filling my sinuses. "I've got you." His chest is pressed against my back, and I feel the rumble of his voice as my muscles slowly unclench. He adjusts his grip, pulling me more tightly against him and leaning back so he can swim for both of us.

When we reach the water's edge, he lifts me onto the bank and I drop to my knees, coughing up muddy water. Rowan rushes over to help me stand, putting an arm around me to keep me on my feet.

"You're all right," she insists, pushing wet hair off my face, before she turns to yell, "What the hell is wrong with you?"

I follow her line of sight to Bryson Ivers, blood streaming from his nose and dripping down his chin. "Oh, relax, it's not like I meant to do it." His voice is defensive, as if I brought this on myself.

Behind me, Cole pushes out of the water, and Bryson holds up his hands. "It was an accident, man!"

Cole is still wearing his shoes, and his clothes are soaked through, his shirt molded to him and dripping. He pulls the wet fabric over his head, the faint light of dusk casting its glow on the faded scar that zippers down the middle of his chest.

"Can we please go?" I ask Rowan, my voice shredded and raw. I don't want to make any more of a scene than we already have, and I keep my head down as she helps me move away from the crowd.

Something vibrates against my leg. I flinch, then realize it's my cell phone and wrestle it out of the pocket of my waterlogged shorts. "Hello?" I answer without thinking. "Hello? Is anyone there?" A faraway buzzing sound is the only response.

The line cuts off. I pull the phone away from my ear to look at the number. The screen says *unknown*, but there are only six digits: 531734. Before I can make sense of it, the display goes wavy, then stripes of neon colors cut through it before it flashes white and dies.

"Shit," I whisper, squeezing my eyes shut. This is the last thing I need tonight. When I stumble, Cole's hand finds my elbow.

"Are you hurt?" he asks.

"No, just embarrassed." My legs choose that moment to turn to jelly, and Rowan hugs me tighter, rubbing a hand up and down my arm.

"Will you quit being so stubborn and let me help you," Cole rumbles, pulling me to a stop.

I want to argue. I want to tell him I can do it on my own, but the truth is I'm utterly exhausted, and as embarrassing as it will be to let Cole carry me, it would be so much worse to collapse in a heap on the ground. When I nod, he scoops me up in one fluid motion.

"I'm parked over here," Cole tells Rowan, indicating a line of cars along the side of the road.

"Why'd you go and jump in after me, anyhow?" I demand as my teeth begin to chatter, burning off the excess adrenaline, and a foul temper settles in. The last time I caught sight of Cole tonight, he was clear on the other side of the bonfire, and I'd gotten the impression he was intentionally putting space between us.

"You think I should have let you drown? Another scandal is the last thing this town needs," he answers flatly.

I've almost forgotten my question entirely by the time Cole leans down to settle me in the passenger seat. "Besides, I've been jumping in after you my whole life, James. Why stop now?" His voice is low, and I catch a hint of that spicy, simmering anger. "And I think what you meant to say was thank you."

I jerk up to see his face, but he's already turned away, the door closing between us with a resolute thud as he makes his way to the driver's side.

Later, as I'm pulling my pajamas on after washing off the creek, a voice calls softly from the bottom of the back staircase.

"Linden?"

I twist my wet hair into a quick knot and make my way down to the kitchen. Sissy is peering out the window next to the back door, then drops the curtain and flips the lock. She turns when she hears me and tosses her purse onto the table.

"I thought I heard you moving around up there. Quite a day you've had. I'm starting to think you're after my crown as the most scandal-prone James woman." She curls up in a chair like a cat, crisscrossing her legs underneath her. "Did you really puke all over Mrs. Boggs?"

"No, I did not." I open the refrigerator, savoring the cool air for a moment before I take out the pitcher of water. "Well, almost," I admit as I pour a glass.

"Too bad," Sissy says. "She kicked me out of Sunday school once for questioning why all the disciples were men."

I sit in the chair across from her, and she steals my water glass. "Can I ask you something?" I say, thinking back to the last night we sat alone in this kitchen. She gestures for me to continue as she takes several long gulps.

"When you read my tea leaves the other night and told me to stay out of the woods, did you know what I'd find there?" I ask.

"No, of course not." She slides the glass back across the table. "You know it's never as cut-and-dry as that. It's all symbols and suggestions."

"What about Cole Spencer, then?" I press, leaning forward. "Did you see his face in the shape of the leaves or something?"

She smirks and crosses her arms. "No, smartass, that is wisdom born of experience. The Spencers are nothing if not beautiful heartache."

I wait for her to continue, but in typical Sissy fashion, she doesn't. "That's it? What does that even mean?"

"Ah, so it's the long version you want," Sissy says. She blows out a breath and settles into her chair. "To tell that story, I have to start at the beginning, way back when I was your age and Vivian was the most beautiful girl in Caball

Hollow. She was a few years older, and she seemed so different from everyone else, sophisticated and elegant in a way I'd never seen before.

"She went up to Charleston three times a week to study at the ballet academy. Sometimes we'd be walking down the sidewalk or standing in line for a movie, and she'd start to dance. I was completely in love with her. But she was in love with someone else."

"Malcolm Spencer." I draw the obvious conclusion.

"Yes, Malcolm Spencer, who once had his own star-crossed love affair with a James woman."

"Wait, not Great-Aunt Zephyrine?" I jump in, remembering Mayor Spencer's comments at the funeral. "He said they'd known each other."

"Oh, I'd say." She nods. "Zephyrine was completely in love with him, and I suspect their breakup had more to do with her leaving town than any argument she might have had with your gran."

I shake my head. "Sometimes this town feels entirely too small."

"The good news is, you don't have to stay here," Sissy says. "There's a whole great big world out there, baby girl."

"Dahlia said something similar at the festival." I lapse into silence, puzzling through the strange events of the past few days. But I keep returning to the tea leaf reading; I can't get Sissy's strong reaction to what she saw in that cup out of my head. She may have a Scorpio's natural inclination to keep secrets, but this is too important to let go.

"Sis, you taught me that the leaves are like the cards, some symbols have universal meanings, but some hold a personal connection." I meet her eyes across the table. "If you saw something bad in those leaves, I need to know what it was."

Sissy swallows and looks down at the table, running a finger along the surface. "What we can see of the future are glimpses of possibilities that shift with every choice someone makes. Sometimes just knowing your own potential future is what brings it into being."

"Sissy, please," I say softly.

She takes a deep breath and lets it out slowly. "All I know is that what is happening in this town is far from over, and whatever comes next, you'll be tied up tighter than a fiddle string right in the middle of it." She gives me a small smile to soften her words, but it's the tang of fear behind them that sticks in my throat.

Sissy reaches across the table to squeeze my hand, then unfolds herself from her chair to head up to bed. I cross my arms on the table and lay my head on top of them, so tired even my bones feel heavy.

A dull tapping sound comes from the window. It couldn't possibly be someone looking for a tonic or tincture tonight of all nights, right? I move to investigate, pushing aside the gauzy curtain to find two eyes staring at me. I stumble back, nearly falling, before I realize it's not eyes but eyespots on the hindwings of an Io moth. It flutters against the pane, closer and closer to the open gap.

I rush forward and slam the window shut, but as I do something moves outside. It's a shadow just past the barn. I squint and press closer as a tall figure appears at the edge of the property line. My breath fogs the glass, and when I wipe it away and look again, there's no one there. Was it Hadrian or some figment of my exhausted mind?

I drop the curtain and puff out a breath. After everything that happened today, I'm letting my imagination run away with me. I head upstairs to finish getting ready for bed, but when I reach the bathroom, the door is locked.

"Occupied," Juniper calls when I rap my knuckles softly against the solid wood. A dull splash from the other side of the door punctuates her words.

"Juniper James, are you taking a *bath*? It's the middle of the night."

"It's the only time the bathroom is free long enough for a bath worth taking," she answers, and I can't disagree with her logic. One bathroom shared by four teenage girls is busier than a moth in a mitten.

"Well, cover up what you want to keep private, 'cause I'm coming in." I twist the knob hard to the right and pull up. When I hear the lock pop, I push open the door.

"Can't sleep?" Juniper asks. She's lying back in the claw-foot tub that's older than Gran, the enamel all but worn off the bottom, with bubbles up to her neck, dark hair piled on top of her head, and a deep-purple crystal balanced right between her eyebrows.

Amethyst can be useful for a great many things—concentration, memory, serenity—but where Juniper is concerned, it's most likely spiritual protection.

"What about you?" I raise my eyebrows at her in the mirror as I pull my toothbrush from the cup mounted to the wall above the sink.

"You can talk to me, you know. I want to help." She plucks the stone from her head and sits up.

"I know," I tell her. And I do, but she's my little sister. I'm not sure how I can ask for her help with all this and still keep her safe.

She sighs and slides deeper into the water, splashing a little over the edge of the too-full tub. "This house is haunted by secrets." Juniper's voice is strange behind me. When I turn to look at her, light glints off the amethyst in her hand.

Without warning, a flash of memory from another night like this overtakes me. I sat in bathwater tinged pink as Sorrel knelt beside the edge, her eyebrows knit together in concern. She scrubbed my shoulders with a bar of oatmeal honey soap as tears traced salty tracks down my cheeks. A pile of clothes, muddy and bloodied, lay on the floor next to the tub.

I brace my hands on the edge of the porcelain sink, letting my head hang down as my heartbeat pounds in my throat like the flutter of wings.

The last twenty-four hours don't feel real. Already, large chunks of time are missing, but it's getting harder and harder to recall the rest, too, like something from a dream.

I asked the counselor at the hospital about it. She told me it was a trauma response, my mind distancing itself from what happened. My body, however, feels like an illustrated guide to what I'd experienced, each bruise a landmark, each gash a wrong turn. When we finally make it home, Sorrel practically carries me up the stairs and into the bathtub.

"Where should I put this?" She holds up the bag from the hospital filled with the clothes I'd worn and everything I had with me yesterday. She opens it and looks inside. "Most of these are probably ruined. What is this shiny thing—something you won at the festival?"

My mind immediately goes to the memory of Cole putting that necklace around my throat. "Throw it all away," I tell her, my voice raw.

She hesitates. "I'll put it in your closet for now, in case you change your mind."

Outside of the bathroom, Mama's and Daddy's sharp whispers, like hissing snakes, echo down the hallway, and I can't help but listen.

"What did you do?" Daddy demands.

"What I had to," Mama growls back.

"It wasn't your decision to make." His voice breaks at the end.

It's summer, but I can't stop shaking, hot tears rolling down my frozen cheeks.

"Hush now, you're safe," Sorrel whispers from beside the tub as she kneels on the floor next to me, washing blood down the drain.

CHAPTER TWELVE

THE NIGHTMARE starts the way it always does. Branches and brambles pull at my hair and rip open my skin, but the thrum of terror racing through my veins numbs me to the pain. I skid to a stop, flip-flops barely staying on my feet, frantic to find a place to hide. Footsteps echo behind me, hitting the ground in the same rapid rhythm as my racing heart.

Closer. Closer. Closer.

I move as fast as I dare. It's dark as pitch, except when the clouds shift enough to let the light of the moon break through the forest canopy. I see it in one of these moments. A shape in the distance, seeming to ripple and shiver in the moonlight. The whisper of secrets I can't quite hear brushes across my skin.

This is new.

I step closer and realize what appeared to be one solid form is actually thousands of moths. The oculiform spots of the polyphemus moth with its golden, navy, and lavender colors; robin moths with their wide wings of iridescent black and orange; and even luna moths, their bright green bodies seeming to glow in the moonlight.

My hand lifts slowly, though I don't recall moving it, and somehow I get closer still without taking a step. When my outstretched fingers can almost brush the closest set of powdery wings, the moths take flight as one before scattering in all directions. And I finally see what they were hiding all along. Dahlia Calhoun.

My eyes fly open, and I bolt upright, gasping for air like I'm once again surfacing from underwater. I press a hand to my chest, trying to will the rapid beat of my heart to slow down as I kick the sheets from my sweat-slicked body.

Even this early in the morning, the air is hot and humid. The lavender in the garden is at its peak, and the warm breeze that gusts in, fluttering the gauzy curtains, is full of its fragrance. But underneath, I can still smell the creek and the metallic stench of fear on my skin.

Juniper makes sleeping noises in her bed next to mine as I blink against the brightness of the rising sun streaming through the window. I turn toward the bowl on the nightstand, where my phone sits under a mountain of dry rice, and take a moment to cross my fingers.

As I think of that strange call just before it died, a cool finger cuts through the stale air of the room and runs down my neck. I cross the room to pull open the top drawer of the desk, rummaging around until I find what I'm looking for: an old calculator, like the ones we use at school.

I fish out the phone and hold down the power button, whispering a breath of thanks when it boots up. Opening the recent calls list, I pull up the strange number I'd dismissed as a glitch and type it into the calculator instead: 531734. I flip the calculator around to look at the numbers upside down, like Sorrel said she used to do with Dahlia.

My vision blurs around the edges as my focus narrows to the dimensions of the tiny screen. The numbers have been transformed into six little letters: hELlES.

It slips from my fingers and falls to the floor with a clatter.

Juniper rolls over and blinks up at me from her bed. "Are you going to tell me what's going on yet?"

I pick up the calculator and hand it to her as I sink down onto my bed. After glancing at the screen, she pushes up on an elbow and blinks at me. "I don't understand. What is this?"

"I think it's a message from Dahlia."

"Dahlia sent you a message . . . on your calculator?" she asks slowly, with a look of concern.

I roll my eyes and explain about the strange phone call last night and the game Dahlia and Sorrel used to play in math class. "That's the message: He lies."

"But if it really is a message from Dahlia, who is *he*?" Sorrel asks from where she leans against the doorway. I'm not sure how long she's been there, but clearly long enough.

"I don't know. Her ex-boyfriend has an alibi, and no one at the vigil would tell me anything. It could be anyone."

My skin feels buzzy as one perfect golden face in particular comes to mind with the echo of Sissy's warning to stay away.

"What's going on?" Rowan asks through a yawn, rubbing sleep from her right eye as she walks into the room. "I can hear y'all clear across the hall."

"But why now, a week after her death?" Sorrel ignores Rowan and sits down next to me on the bed. "Did something else happen?"

"Maybe." I stretch out the word. "My nightmare tonight was different. Dahlia was in it, covered with moths. And right before I went to bed, I thought I saw someone outside, behind the barn, but it was probably just Hadrian or maybe my eyes playing tricks on me."

"Well, there you go, that's who lies." Rowan picks up the calculator and gestures toward the window with it. "I've been saying that since he showed up here."

"Yeah, we know." Sorrel rolls her eyes, her voice flat. "But you never seem to have a clear idea of what, exactly, he's lying about."

"The reason he's here, for starters," Rowan retorts. "Randomly looking for work here, in Caball Hollow, a town too small to show up on any map. Please," she scoffs.

"There's a flaw in your theory, though," Sorrel says. "Dahlia and Hadrian never crossed paths. She's been away at school the entire time he's been in town, so how could she possibly know whether or not he's a liar?"

"Rowan doesn't like him because he reminds her too much of herself." Juniper tosses a pillow at Rowan. Speaking of

139

too much alike. With their fiery tempers and strong wills, Rowan and Juniper are always either best friends or worst enemies.

"That's just plain hurtful." Rowan sticks her tongue out at Juniper, then sits on her pillow.

"Besides," Juniper continues, "I don't know if we can assume any message from the other side would be so straightforward."

"Sure, but it's not like we can call her back. There aren't even enough numbers to dial, so what do we do now?" I ask. Everyone falls silent, considering.

"There is one thing we could try," Juniper offers hesitantly. "I've been working on some of Granny Sudie's old spells, but I've never done it before, so it might not work."

"What would we need to do?" I ask.

"We'll need salt and a candle that's been charged in the light of the full moon." Juniper pauses for a moment, looking uncomfortable. "Plus something personal that belonged to the departed. And I think we should do it near the creek where you found her body, Linden."

"We can't, Junie." Sorrel stands, crossing her arms. "It's a crime scene. Besides, we don't need to be stirring up any more gossip. Daddy would want us all to stay far away from this."

"It's really our best chance. Dahlia's presence there was so strong that Linden could feel her emotions even after she'd been killed. And that call came through right after Linden fell into the creek last night. But the parking lot of the high school should be close enough, and plenty of kids go there at night for all sorts of reasons," Juniper says.

"Junie! How do you even know that?" I demand.

"And how exactly would any of those other reasons not lead to gossip?" Rowan asks at the same time.

Juniper presses her lips into a flat line. "I'm only a year younger than you, Linden, not some naive baby. Besides, Dahlia wouldn't be reaching out to you from beyond the grave if it wasn't important."

Rowan and Sorrel exchange a glance, then look to me. They're letting it be my decision. But Juniper is right. And with what Aunt Sissy told me last night, I'm not sure I can afford not to listen. I nod, just once. "If we can somehow manage to get something of Dahlia's, then I think we should try."

"We need to act quickly," Juniper says. "The ritual can only work under the dark moon. Once the new moon rises, she'll have moved beyond our reach."

"Juniper, that's in two days," Sorrel protests as she checks the lunar phase app on her phone.

"Then we better hope an opportunity arises quickly."

Juniper and Rowan head down to breakfast, but I grab Sorrel's arm to hold her back. "Something weird happened last night." I pause. "I mean, another something weird. I had this flash of memory from last summer of you helping me scrub off blood. Did that really happen?"

"Yeah," she answers softly. "When we got home from the hospital, your hands were still shaking so badly you couldn't hold the soap. Are you starting to remember?"

"Mostly it comes in flashes and feelings, nothing substantial. Everything is all chopped up, like pieces are missing or in the wrong order, and I can't seem to straighten it all out."

"You fell and hit your head, not to mention being lost and afraid that night. Trauma can do strange things to memory."

"Mama and Daddy were arguing," I press.

"Yeah," she agrees. A faint taste of sadness, sour and potent as buttermilk, brushes against my tongue, but just as quickly it retreats when Sorrel sets her jaw.

"Was it what happened that night that caused them to split?" I ask it fast, not really wanting to know the answer.

"Maybe," she says with a sigh and a shrug. "But probably not the way you're thinking. I've read that sometimes traumatic events can lead to life-changing decisions. It's like it makes people reevaluate. But they made their own choices, and you can't blame yourself." She reaches out and squeezes my hand before stepping through the doorway.

I want to tell Sorrel the truth. I want to tell her about the awful things I said to Mama and Daddy that night. That it really might be my fault. But instead, I let her walk away.

When we get home from the festival, I lock myself in the bath-room and turn on the shower so I can cry in peace, clutching at the bluebird necklace I can't bring myself to take off. I'd shared a part of myself that I never had before, and the rejection feels like a gaping hole in my chest.

But at the thought of putting on my pajamas and going to bed, my grief twists into anger. Why should I have to miss out on all the fun? I don't have to stay home because Cole Spencer told me to. I shouldn't for that very reason.

I pull on a clean pair of shorts and a tank top, taking extra care with my hair and putting on makeup, even though my hand shakes as I apply mascara. Holding my sneakers, I tiptoe down the back stairs to the kitchen.

My hand is on the doorknob when I hear Mama clear her throat. "And where do you think you're going in the middle of the night?"

I turn to find her standing in the doorway between the kitchen and the hall, the bluish light of the television flashing in the den behind her.

"Lyon, could you come in here, please," she calls over her shoulder.

I lean my head against the back door, a miasma of heartbreak and hurt and anger and self-loathing and a million other feelings swirling deep inside of me, pressing against my skin. It's too much to hold.

Daddy comes up behind Mama, resting a hand on her shoulder as she crosses her arms. "What's going on?"

"Nothing. I'm meeting up with friends," I tell them. My voice sounds defensive even to my own ears.

"Oh, no you're not," Mama says. "I know what those kids are up to tonight, and no daughter of mine is going out into the Forest in the middle of the night on the solstice. You know the dangers of liminal times."

The frustration would be a minor thing on a normal day, but right now, on top of everything else, it's too much for me. I need a release valve, and I'm all out of tears, so I yell instead.

"Why can't I be like everyone else for once?" I spin around, anger burbling up stronger than sadness. The bitter burn of hate singes my tongue. Hate of this strange part of me that has kept me an outsider, that makes me unlovable. That came from her. "I hate you! Why can't you let me be normal?" I'm yelling now, my volume increasing right along with the emotion inside of me.

"Linden Tallulah James, don't you speak to your mother that way," Daddy says sternly. "What's gotten into you? This isn't like you."

I spin around and race up to my bedroom, slamming the door behind me. Throwing myself down onto my bed, I grab my pillow and scream into it until my throat is raw and I'm left feeling empty.

And then, once I'm quiet, I hear Mama and Daddy's voices, angry and arguing, coming up through the floorboards.

CHAPTER THIRTEEN

IN THE end, it doesn't take long to create an opportunity. That afternoon, I ask Gran if I can take another meal over to Dahlia's aunt and uncle. Since they were her last living relatives, Dahlia had been staying with the Hinkles while she was in Caball Hollow.

They live in a small white clapboard house in town, a couple blocks from Heck Funeral Home. When I arrive, balancing the big casserole dish on my hip, I pull open the screen door to knock on the metal one behind it. A dog starts to yap from somewhere inside.

As I wait, two girls from the grade below me step out of the Piggly Wiggly at the end of the street. One stops when she catches sight of me, then grabs the arm of the other and whispers something in her ear. They hurriedly cut across the street, and as they pass, they cross their index fingers into the shape of an X as if they're warding off evil. When they reach the corner, they take off at a run.

I stand there, stunned by the overtness of their reaction. I'm used to the insidious way so many can be wary of us, but this was different. Their disgust and fear strong enough that the stomach-turning taste of rotting fish reaches me even from this distance. And I can't help but be reminded of the night of the festival when those women did the same thing to Amos McCoy.

"Oh, Linden," Mrs. Hinkle says as she opens the door. "Hello, dear."

I swallow back the bad taste in my mouth and give her a small smile. "Gran sent some of her roast chicken and dumplings over."

"Well, that's too kind of y'all," Mrs. Hinkle says, stepping back to open the door further. "Come in, come in."

I follow her inside and through the front room to the small kitchen at the back. She takes the dish from me and puts it in the refrigerator, then pulls out a pitcher. "Can I get you some sweet tea?"

"Sure, I'd love some," I tell her.

Mrs. Hinkle pours two glasses and brings them over to the round wooden table in the center of the room. "Come sit a spell." She passes me a glass and adjusts her floral housecoat as she takes a seat.

"How are you holding up?" I ask gently as I move to the chair across from hers.

"Oh, about as well as can be expected, I suppose," she says, then takes a sip of her tea. "I don't know how we'll recover, to be honest. She was the best of us, with so much ahead of her." She stops talking when tears gather in her eyes and pulls a handkerchief out of her sleeve to dab them away.

I reach out to squeeze her hand.

"It's hard, the not knowing," she continues. "And when I went to pick up her things from the sheriff's department, her four-leaf clover was missing."

"The one she always wore around her neck?" I ask. The image of Dahlia fiddling with her charm the last time I saw her is vivid in my mind. "She had it at the festival."

"I've never known her to be without it. My sister, Dahlia's mother, found that clover the day she went into labor and pressed it between glass. After she passed, Dahlia took to wearing it on a piece of ribbon. It was no bigger than a button. It isn't a valuable thing, but it means a lot." She wrings her hands anxiously.

"I'm so sorry, Mrs. Hinkle. Maybe it will turn up in the course of the investigation," I offer, but I don't really believe it. The clover is probably long gone, washed away downstream.

"I hope so," she replies. "We appreciate everything your dad and his deputies are doing, but I know mistakes happen sometimes. There was someone else's necklace packed up with her things. Maybe the clover got put in the wrong box, is all."

"Are you sure the other necklace wasn't hers?" I ask, surprised. With the amount of attention on this case, a mistake that sloppy doesn't seem possible.

"Oh, I'm sure," Mrs. Hinkle insists. "Not with her gold allergy. If she'd tried to wear that one, she woulda broken out in hives instantly." She shakes her head and lets out a long sigh. "So many questions. I don't think we'll be able to rest easy until we have some answers."

"When I last saw Dahlia, she seemed a little tense." I scoot to the edge of my chair, unsure how to even ask the question. "I didn't think much of it at the time, but now . . . Do you know if there was anyone she might have been upset with? Maybe someone she thought was dishonest?" I cringe, feeling silly for my ham-handed attempt at sleuthing.

She sniffs and runs a hand over the tablecloth in front of her, waiting long enough that I'm about to tell her to forget the whole thing when at last she answers. "Well, to be honest, I had my suspicions that she'd been in touch with her father lately." The heavy, bitter taste of worry flavors her words.

I hadn't really expected any answer, but definitely not this one. "I didn't think she knew her father." Dahlia had certainly never mentioned him to me. "She told me he left when she was a baby."

"He'd come around once in a while when she was growing up. My mother tried to limit his contact with Dahlia as much as she could on account of him being the one who introduced my sister to the drugs that took her life. Dahlia was with her that day, you know. Barely three years old." Mrs. Hinkle shakes her head and sniffs. "But we haven't seen hide nor hair of him in years. I thought that was the way Dahlia wanted it."

"So then, if you don't mind my asking, what makes you think she'd been in contact with him?"

"She was acting squirrely lately," Mrs. Hinkle explains. "She'd get a phone call or a text and go into another room. That wasn't like her. She might have been feisty, but she wasn't secretive."

"Did she ever mention her father specifically?" I ask.

She shakes her head as she takes a sip of her tea. "At first I thought it might be that business with her school loans falling through, but she told me she'd straightened all that out." She shrugs and lets her shoulders droop. "I can't think of anything else she'd have wanted to hide from me."

I consider her words. I don't know why Dahlia would send me a cryptic message about a man I've never met, but I can puzzle over that question later. Right now, something else has snagged my attention.

"Dahlia was worried about paying for school?" I ask. Anyone who knew Dahlia knew there wasn't anything more important to her than going away to college.

"Well, her first year, anything not covered by financial aid, the Moth Queen scholarship and what little my mother could afford made up for. This year, she would have had to make up the difference all on her own." Mrs. Hinkle trails off for a moment, her eyes getting the faraway look of memory. "She was so desperate she even asked if there was anything we could do to help, though she knew we're barely making ends meet as it is with Mr. Hinkle's illness. They got into a bit of a tiff about it, actually. He told her she should be grateful for what she got, because if he hadn't set her right about that project, she wouldn't have won Moth Queen at all."

"Mr. Hinkle helped Dahlia win the scholarship?" I ask. "How?"

She slides a glance toward the door at the far end of the hall, where the thrum of a snore rumbles rhythmically. "All her research for the podcast that won her the Moth Queen crown," Mrs. Hinkle tells me, her voice almost a whisper, "was originally about Elam McCoy's disappearance."

I lower my voice to match hers. "Oh, but—I thought her podcast was about the folklore of the Moth-Winged Man?"

"Mr. Hinkle convinced her that the scholarship commit-tee would be more likely to select her if her project cast the town in a positive light, but originally it was about the sightings before the McCoy boy went missing." Mrs. Hinkle pushes up from her chair and bustles around the kitchen, cleaning up the iced tea glasses and wiping down the vinyl tablecloth. She pauses as another thought occurs to her. "You know, it's strange, all the reports of people seeing the Moth-Winged Man lately. Fitting almost."

"How so?" I ask.

"She'd started back up again, looking into what happened, I mean," Mrs. Hinkle tells me. "I think maybe she thought it would make a good research project for her journalism classes or something."

"Did anyone else know what she was doing?" I ask, an icy tingle down my neck making me sit up straighter. Could she have figured out something about the case even when trained investigators couldn't? And if she had, would someone kill to keep it secret?

"I don't think she ever told anyone else, but you know how she was. That girl was never afraid to ask questions." Her attention turns toward the bedroom again when the snoring becomes a wet cough. "Oh, Mr. Hinkle is awake. I'll need to go help him get up. Thank your gran for the meal."

"I will." I hesitate. I'd been planning to ask her outright for something that belonged to Dahlia, but after seeing those girls outside, the words get stuck in my throat. I keep imagining kind Mrs. Hinkle looking at me in disgust at the idea of me communicating with her dead niece. "Do you mind if I use your powder room before I leave?"

"Of course, sugar," she says as she starts toward the bedroom door. "Go ahead and let yourself out when you're done, and don't be a stranger, now."

I wait for the door to close behind her before turning toward the only other bedroom in the small house, the one where Dahlia would have stayed. As soon as my fingers curl around the doorknob, furious yapping erupts from inside. I stumble back a few steps.

"Fidget?" Mrs. Hinkle calls, the sound of her footsteps changing direction.

Frantic, I spin into the bathroom on the other side of the hall. Mrs. Hinkle's footsteps patter across the floor outside just as the door latches behind me.

"Fidget, hush," she tells the dog. "That's my good girl."

I press my back against the door and drop my face into my hands. There's no way I'll be able to get into that room now, and I have no idea where else I might find something personal that belonged to Dahlia in time for the ritual. With a frustrated breath, I lean against the sink. And right there, sitting on the countertop, like it's meant for me, is a hair-brush threaded with the bright burgundy strands that could only belong to one person.

I pull the hair free from the bristles and shove it into my pocket before pressing my ear against the door. Mrs. Hinkle sighs from the other side as she moves past the bathroom and toward her bedroom. When I hear the click of the door closing behind her, I rush back through the kitchen. But as I turn to leave, my eye catches on the sheriff's department logo printed on a large manila envelope sitting on the counter.

I pause, listening closely for any sound, then grab the en-velope and undo the red string. Inside are several random items: Dahlia's driver's license, some cash, a hair tie, and there, at the bottom, is a small plastic evidence bag with a tangled necklace balled up in the corner. I pull the bag out, shaking it slightly to straighten the necklace, then lay it flat against my palm. The writing on the bag notes that Dahlia was wearing it when she was found, but the words go blurry as I stare down at what's in my hand. On a golden chain is a tiny bluebird holding an envelope in its beak.

All the blood drains to my feet, and my fingertips brush the small scar on my neck. Mrs. Hinkle may not recognize the necklace, but I do. It's mine.

I stumble out of the Hinkles' house, reeling. The first and last time I laid eyes on that necklace was the day Cole gave it to me, right before everything went sideways. Now, a year later, it's reappeared in the most unlikely and disturbing way possible: on the body of my murdered friend.

I rush toward home, cutting across the orchard on the back of our property where black raspberries grow along the side of the hill. Maybe it's seeing the necklace again after so long, but my thoughts are immediately pulled to last spring when I was here with Cole. When things first started to feel like they were changing between us, so different from how they feel now.

"Race you," I told him, kicking off my sandals and running toward my favorite tree, the heirloom black apple that grew fruit the color of shadow and made the most delicious pies.

I jumped to grab the lowest branch but missed. Cole laughed, tall enough that he didn't even need to jump. He pulled himself up, then reached down a hand and pulled me up beside him, our arms pressed together from shoulder to wrist.

His father was hosting a fundraiser for the Caball Hollow historical society at their house, and he'd snuck away as soon as he could; his tie and suit jacket hung on the branch of another tree. "Do you think they've noticed you left?" I asked him.

"I don't think I care, to be honest." He pulled a leaf from a branch above us, then slowly ripped it to shreds. "I'm sure my father will have something to say about it," he said on a long breath. "But sometimes it feels like my entire life was planned out before I was even born, and the weight of it all can be suffocating."

"So what would you do, then, if you didn't have any expectations to live up to?"

He was quiet for so long I thought he wasn't going to answer, and my cheeks started to heat.

"No one's ever really asked me that before," he said at last. "I'm not sure what I would do." He went quiet and I watched a bee buzz among the branches while I waited. "I like to work with my hands: build things, fix things." He cleared his throat and shrugged. "But mostly, I want to see what's on the other side of those mountains."

"I'm pretty sure it's just Virginia."

"Smartass." He bumped his shoulder against mine, but then the grin dropped from his face. "It doesn't matter, anyway."

"Of course it does," I started to argue, but a bluebird landed on a branch, inches from where we sat, and I grabbed Cole's hand to still him. "Look," I whispered. Neither of us moved—I don't think I even breathed—as the bird trilled a few notes, then took flight. "Gran says bluebirds are good luck. They mean something good is heading your way."

Cole squeezed my fingers, and I looked down, surprised to see my hand still holding his. When I met his gaze, he smiled at me. "Yeah, I think it might already be here."

Maybe it's this memory that turns my feet, not toward the farmhouse but to the old shed, where I find Cole hunched over his motorcycle, tools spread out across the ground and hands covered in grease. I don't say anything, pausing to let my whirling thoughts settle.

"Engine trouble?" I ask at last.

He jolts up and whacks his head on the handlebar. "Dammit, James."

"Sorry." I wince in sympathy, biting my cheek to hide a smirk.

"Just so I'm prepared—is this going to become a regular thing now? You dropping by?" He crunches down on one of the hard candies he's always eating and releases the scent of cloves. I spot the bag of the pink lozenges, each with a red stripe through the center, sitting on an old folding table nearby.

"Don't flatter yourself," I tell him.

He turns to look at me, ready to say something, then changes his mind. "Don't take this the wrong way, but you look like shit." He wipes his face against the shoulder of his shirt.

"No wonder everyone thinks you're so charming."

"Trouble sleeping lately?"

"Only if by lately you mean the past twelve months." I lean against the side of the shed. "Hey, did you keep in touch with Dahlia while she was away at school?"

"Some." He shrugs, but his focus is back on whatever he's doing to the bike.

"Did she ever mention her dad? Or maybe someone she was upset with . . . for lying, maybe?"

"What's this about?" he asks instead of answering the question.

I bite my lip, unsure how much I want to tell him. How much I want to remind him of my *peculiarity*. Or if I want to examine too closely why I still care what he thinks of me at all.

"Dahlia said something strange to me at the festival, about what happened last summer." I shake my head, not sure how to say the rest of it. "Look, I need to tell you something, it's about the necklace."

A series of emotions flickers across his face, too fast to catch, before he schools his features into a detached mask. "I thought you didn't remember anything from that night." His eyes go to my neck.

An unexpected lick of flame shoots up my spine at his words. He's barely spoken to me since then; he doesn't get to care about my scars. "Yeah, well, it was easier to let you think I forgot the entire night instead of only the last bit." I press a hand to my forehead and blow out a breath. "Sorry, that was hateful. I didn't mean that."

"Yes, you did." The side of his mouth quirks up, but there's no joy in it.

"Well, when I woke up in the hospital, this was all that was left of the necklace." I run my fingers along the scar as I try to get the conversation back on track. "It must have caught on a branch or something in the woods. But, Cole, they found it on Dahlia's body. She was wearing it when she was killed."

Cole's face pales a little beneath its summer glow, and now, as I look down into those amber eyes, I see something I never expected. Guilt. Coiled up so tight and deep that I can only taste a hint of its fishy, oily flavor, like what lingers in the mouth hours after biting into a sardine.

He clears his throat before he speaks. "The Forest is the size of Rhode Island. How could she possibly have found it?"

"I don't know, but she was allergic to gold. She never would have worn it even if she had." I shrug and shake my head, at a loss. "None of it makes any sense, but I think somehow what happened to me is connected to what happened to her. And I need to figure out how."

He stares up at me, not moving at all, but every muscle tensed. "Is that so?" he drawls. Turning back to the bike, he tightens down a bolt a little harder than seems necessary, but I'm no mechanic.

"Remind me, wasn't it you I fished out of a creek? I seem to remember something about half the senior class fixin' to drown you for a witch. And now you want to go diggin' around in a murder investigation while the killer is still out there somewhere." He stands and sets the socket wrench on the table, then grabs a rag to wipe his hands.

"No, Cole, I don't want to, I *need* to," I insist.

"What are you thinking?" He throws the rag back on the table. "Why are you so bound and determined to rush headlong into danger? This is just like last year—you won't listen to sense."

My blood runs hot. "Last year? You made it perfectly clear what you thought of me last year."

"What the hell is that supposed to mean?"

I let out a humorless laugh. "You really want to have this conversation? Fine, let's finally have it. After the worst day of my life, every single friend I had happily moved on without me, you most of all."

"Don't put that all on me," he argues back. "You didn't want anything to do with the rest of us after that night. And I get why you did it with me, but you didn't have to cut off everyone else too."

"Look, I'm sorry for what I did to you last summer. That was wrong of me, and I wish I could stop it from ever happening again. I understand why you hate me—most of the time I hate that part of me, too. But we were friends once, Cole, before we were anything else, and you just . . ." I swallow back the tears that threaten to choke me, but the words sound as lonely as they feel. "You just left me."

His jaw goes slack, then clenches so tight his words are strained. "God, Linden, is that what you think?"

"You didn't speak to me again after that night. And I get it. I get it now that this awful ability I have is a huge violation, but . . . I needed you." My voice softens until it all but disappears.

Cole's head drops, and he rubs a hand over his hair, all the fight seeming to drain out of him in an instant. "That wasn't . . . I don't hate you. I never hated you." He tilts his head to look up at me from under his arm, his eyes almost pained. "You shouldn't want me to speak to you. The things I said to you . . . I was scared, and you got hurt because of it. I didn't protect you when you needed me most."

I open my mouth to respond, but I'm stunned. It's not what I ever expected him to say. "I never asked you to protect me, Cole," I say at last. "You can't blame yourself for my mistakes."

He drops his arms and turns to face me. "Maybe not, but I can't forgive myself for mine, either." He looks away, up toward his house on the ridge. It feels like a door slamming in my face. Like he's carefully and methodically rebuilding the wall we just started taking down, brick by brick. "Can I walk you home?" he asks, ever the gentleman.

I shake my head at him, slowly, disbelieving. "I never knew you for a coward, Cole Spencer." My throat is so tight it comes out like a whisper, and I spin on my heel, striding down the path as fast as I can, hoping he doesn't follow.

And if my eyes sting a little, it's probably just the pollen in the air. And maybe, if I run fast enough, I can tamp down all the feelings from last summer that threaten, once again, to overtake me.

CHAPTER FOURTEEN

SNEAKING OUT is easier than I expected. After we're sure Mama and Gran are asleep, we duck through Rowan and Sorrel's bedroom window and out onto the porch roof, one by one, then reach out and grab the branch of the big hemlock. My stomach drops when I step off the roof, trusting the tree and my own strength to hold me. When I'm steady, I climb down, dropping the last few feet to the ground with a muffled grunt.

Sorrel hops into the front seat of the Bronco and flips down the visor so the keys fall into her lap. She puts it into gear and steers while Rowan, Juniper, and I push it up the driveway. We don't dare start it until we reach the road, or we risk Mama and Gran hearing. It's only a couple of miles to the school, but Juniper attempting to contact the other side means chances are good she'll be done in after, and we'll need the truck to get her home.

"I never really think about the holler being downhill until I have to do something like this," Rowan grunts as we finally shove the Bronco onto the road and Sorrel fires up the engine.

I cast a worried glance back toward the farmhouse, watching for a light to come on and signal we're caught. "How often do you do something like this?" I ask, and she winks in response as she wipes the sheen of sweat from her brow with the back of her arm.

Sorrel idles the car, and we run to jump in. It's not nearly long enough before we're pulling into the parking lot above the football field. I cast a glance toward the far end, past the track, to the woods near the field house where Cole and I stumbled out that fateful night, and my pulse kicks up a notch. A few lampposts near the edges of the lot keep it from being completely dark. The light from one catches the trailing end of crime scene tape caught in the branches of a tree, but here in the center, the dark is thick enough to be tangible, like a fifth presence.

"Remind me again why we had to come here in the middle of the night," Rowan whispers as we pile out of the truck. "This place is giving me the jibblies."

"We need darkness, remember?" Juniper says as she takes the salt out of her bag. "Plus the whole not-getting-caught thing." She pours a careful line onto the asphalt as she walks in a large circle three times. This is local salt, pulled from right here beneath these mountains, a connection to the earth, to those who came before.

"Let's get this over with." Sorrel blows out a breath and steps into the salt circle as a flash of heat lightning streaks high across the sky.

Rowan raises an eyebrow. "That wasn't ominous at all," she mutters as she follows Sorrel into the circle.

We sit, side by side. Juniper takes the candle, the lock of Dahlia's hair, and a small vial of oil out of her bag. She uncorks the oil and uses a single finger to anoint the candle, then her own forehead. The scent wafts toward me on the warm air. It smells like mugwort and myrrh, woody and earthy. Then she places Dahlia's hair in her left palm and closes her fingers tightly over it.

"The way this works is, we get one question. And the answer can't be more than a word or two, so think hard about what you want to ask," Juniper explains.

"We need to know who killed her," Rowan says.

"But Daddy said she most likely never saw her killer," I object. "If we ask and she doesn't know, then we've wasted our question."

"True, death doesn't make people omniscient," Juniper agrees.

"Then we should ask her who lies," Rowan suggests. "That's the message she sent you the night of her vigil."

"Yeah," Sorrel agrees, her eyes on me, heavy with concern. "There must be a reason she reached out to you."

I nod as I work through my thoughts. Why *did* Dahlia come to me? We were friends once, sure, but we had barely spoken since last summer. Did she know there was a connection between what happened to me and what happened to her? Was she trying to warn me of danger, like Aunt Sissy and her tea leaves, or was it something more? And with a warning about someone who lies, who can I trust to tell the truth?

Juniper closes her eyes, takes a deep breath, and slowly exhales. "Dahlia Calhoun. If you're here with us tonight, we have a question for you." She pauses, her eyes moving beneath their lids as though she's searching for something. Her breathing gets heavier, until her expression changes, relaxing a bit. She opens her mouth to continue.

"Wait." I reach out to touch her arm. Dahlia was researching the Elam McCoy case and talking to someone in secret, and somehow, against all odds, she had my necklace. Maybe she had discovered something, some connection, between us. Something that might have gotten her killed. Maybe whoever she'd been talking to knew what it was. "Ask her who knows the truth."

Juniper nods in acknowledgment. "Dahlia Calhoun, who knows the truth?" She keeps her eyes closed for several long minutes. When she opens them, the glow of the candle flame makes the dark line through her left iris an even more striking contrast to the brightness of the blue. She leans forward and slowly blows out the candle. The flame sputters for a moment, then dies.

In the soft glow of the parking lot lights, we watch, barely breathing, as a trail of smoke streams out from the wick. Somewhere down near the creek, a bullfrog drones mournfully, punctuating the song of the crickets. A coyote cries up on the mountain, followed by an answering yip farther away. A cool breeze whispers through the valley, and behind it falls an unnatural hush.

Slowly, so slowly, the smoke turns in on itself, stretching and twisting until it curls into letters: *L, I, N, D, E,* then finally *N,* each one curving into the next like cursive dancing in the air, before it swirls away and dissipates into nothing. Juniper slumps forward, wrung out. Rowan grabs her by the arm to hold her upright.

"*Linden?*" Sorrel asks, perplexed. "How could you know the truth about what happened to Dahlia?"

"I think we must have lost something in translation," Rowan says.

"Sorry, maybe I did it wrong." Juniper's voice wavers.

"No, it's my fault. It was a stupid question." I blow out a breath. But before I can even consider what Dahlia's answer could mean, a branch snaps in the woods behind me like a crack of lightning. I whip around toward the sound.

My eyes haven't adjusted to the dark after the brightness of the candle flame, but I make out a shape in the shadows, beyond the football field, right at the edge of the trees—a man, maybe the same one I saw out the window last night.

I suck in a sharp breath and grab Sorrel's arm, pulling her closer. "There's someone out there," I whisper, voice tight, then scramble to my feet for a better look.

The shape moves slowly between the trees, but it's too dark to tell if he's moving in this direction or toward the creek. I step forward to get a better look without thinking, and the candle flares back to life.

"Stay in the circle," Sorrel hisses. She grabs my arm and pulls me back into the protective ring of salt while Rowan helps Juniper to her feet.

An engine roars to life out on the road in a sudden, sharp burst, and I nearly jump out of my skin. In the darkness over my shoulder, I can make out the shape of a pickup truck as it peels out. The headlights flash on as it passes, and I squeeze my eyes shut. I blink away spots, turning to where I'd seen the figure in the woods, and for a moment, I see two glowing red eyes staring back at me. I blink again, and they're gone.

"Hurry, let's go!" Sorrel grabs Juniper's bag, then blows out the candle and breaks the salt circle with her foot.

She runs to start the truck, and Rowan and I help Juniper climb into the back seat. Sorrel speeds out of the parking lot before I've even buckled my seat belt.

"What the hell was that?" Rowan demands.

"Did you see it? Was it a man, or was it . . . something else?" I lean forward over Juniper, who is stretched across the seat with her head in my lap.

"It was a shadow," Rowan answers. "That's all I could tell for sure."

"With your luck, it was probably a killer," Sorrel adds, jaw clenched. "I knew this was a terrible idea. You already walked directly into those woods and straight to the crime scene. They're probably real curious about how you knew she was there. And what else you might know."

"I'm sorry." I brush the hair out of Junie's face. She's already sound asleep, worn out from the effort of connecting to the other side. "I put you all in danger for nothing."

"What if it isn't nothing, though," Rowan suggests, glancing at me in the rearview mirror. "Maybe what it means is that you already know the truth, you just don't *remember* it."

"You think the key is something that happened last summer?" I ask, watching the trees blur around us as we speed past. "Like whatever Dahlia was trying to tell me at the festival."

But if the answer is locked away in my mind somewhere, I don't know how to access it. And if it was what got Dahlia killed, I've now put my sisters right in the middle of this mess and in the sights of who- or whatever had been out there watching us tonight.

A few minutes later, we roll slowly down the driveway of the farm and slide the Bronco into its parking spot. I help Junie to bed, then creep down to Gran's tiny office under the stairs and boot up her old computer. If Dahlia had reopened her investigation into Elam McCoy's disappearance, could it have been something that happened the night I went missing that gave her some new insight? As legendary as the tales of the Moth-Winged Man sightings have become in Caball Hollow, I know little of the actual details of the case.

After nearly twenty years, there's not much information about what happened to Elam McCoy online. Our tiny local paper doesn't have a digital archive, but a few pages deep on an internet search, I find a brief mention on a website about cold cases.

Elam McCoy, 4, disappeared during a family fishing trip in the National Forest near Caball Hollow, West Virginia. As soon as he was reported missing, local law enforcement scrabbled together a search team of nearly 125 volunteer firefighters, forest rangers, experienced hikers, and neighbors searching on foot, horseback, and ATV. From the start, rescuers were hampered by the vastness of the area. At nearly 1 million acres, the Forest is one of the most biologically diverse pieces of public land in the entire United States, from 4,863 feet above sea level at its highest peak to nearly a mile down into deep wilderness at its depths. It was too vast, thick, and overgrown for infrared imaging. And at barely 4 feet tall and less than 50 pounds, Elam McCoy was a small needle in a massive haystack. Thirteen search dogs were brought in to assist, then later three cadaver dogs, but none could pick up a trail.

I keep digging, but the handful of other sites that mention Elam all seem to reiterate the same limited information. Could this really be all that's known? The last record of an entire life, someone's child, reduced to a short paragraph of text and a cold case file. I shut down the computer with a sigh. That could have been me. I won't let it be Dahlia.

CHAPTER FIFTEEN

I'M STANDING in the middle of the front yard, wet, dew-coated grass pushing up between my toes, when I wake up. Gasping for air as if I've been underwater, I desperately look for some sign as to how I got here. My head feels like it rolled down a mountain and hit every rock along the way. My palms and knees are dirty, the hem of the shirt I fell asleep in, damp. Did I sleepwalk?

"You're up with the sun this morning." I spin around at the sound of Mama's voice. She's loading a basket of produce from the garden into the back of the farm truck.

We grow most of what we serve at the Harvest Moon. Maybe the soil at Bittersweet Farm still bears the memory of the original James family matriarch. The ground is so fertile that, once, watermelon seeds carelessly spat from the porch became a patch of the sweetest melons overnight.

Tangled vines, curling up along the railings and posts, deposited fruit into the bedrooms on the second floor.

Her expression turns to concern as she watches me. "You feelin' poorly?"

I shake my head, not in disagreement but in an attempt to clear the confusion clouding my thoughts.

Mama closes the tailgate carefully. Years ago, the original one rusted clean off, and she replaced it with a wooden one she built out of two-by-fours and painted with a landscape of Bittersweet Farm. Mama is always doing stuff like that: fixing, mending, making the broken more beautiful than it had ever been before.

Crossing the distance between us, she puts a warm hand to my forehead. She smells like the garden: fresh dirt and sun-warmed tomato vines. "Hmm. You are a bit clammy," she murmurs. "Come on in, and let's get you some breakfast."

I follow Mama around the stone side of the house, climb the stairs of the wraparound porch, and pull open the old screen door to the kitchen. She toes off her garden boots as I wipe the dew from my toes on the rag rug that covers the slate floor. I don't have much of an appetite, but with her eyes on me, I grab a piece of cornbread from last night's supper and break it up in a mason jar with a little sweet milk and a drizzle of Sorrel's sourwood honey for calming.

"Mornin', sugar," Gran says as she buzzes around the kitchen.

"Those black raspberries up on the hill will be ready to pick once the dew burns off," Mama says from the sink, washing the dirt from her hands.

"Maybe a cobbler tomorrow for the dessert special?" Gran suggests as she wipes down the cast iron skillet and hangs it back on its hook. "What do you think, Linden?"

I swallow a bite of cornbread, and it feels like a sodden lump of cement in my throat. On a normal day, my mind would be whirling with possible flavor combinations and new recipes to try with the wild berries we only get for a month or so each summer. But today I can't seem to even pretend everything is normal. "Cobbler would be good. Maybe some muffins, too. Or . . . scones?" I manage to get out.

"We'll have to see how many we can get today." Mama leans a hip against the butcher-block counter after she dries her hands. "With this heat, they might could crumble, and then we'll be lucky if they make but a pint or two."

Gran watches me, suspicion clouding her face. "What's got you lookin' more skittish than a long-tailed cat in a room full of rocking chairs?"

I stop mashing the cornbread with my spoon and set the jar on the table. Since last night, I've been trying to weave together any common threads that might connect Elam McCoy's disappearance and Dahlia's murder to the night I went missing. But with how little I know, it feels like all I have are loose ends.

"What do you remember about that little boy that went missing, Elam McCoy?" I ask.

Gran and Mama look at each other across the kitchen. "What's brought this on all of a sudden?" Mama asks.

"I'm not sure, exactly, but all this talk of new Moth-Winged Man sightings lately makes me wonder if there might be some connection to what happened to Dahlia." I scratch a nail against a nonexistent smudge on the table, feeling deceitful about not telling them the whole truth.

"Well, that sounds like one more reason to let sleeping dogs lie." Gran picks up her coffee mug and heads to the stove, where something delicious is simmering away in her favorite pot. She grabs a jar of dried herbs from the shelf and shakes some into her palm before tossing it in and giving it a stir. Gran doesn't measure or set timers. She cooks by sight, feel, taste, and smell, and there's comfort in the familiarity of her movements even now.

"I just want to understand," I murmur.

I'm not sure if they've even heard me until Mama slides into the chair across from mine. She studies my face for a moment, as if she doesn't know where to start. "It was the year I was expecting Rowan. I remember because I was sick all the time."

It's strange to hear about this story in relation to my own family. It's always felt more like a campfire tale of a time long ago, not something so nearly within my own lifetime.

"She's always been mulish, that one," Gran chimes in over her shoulder.

"The little boy, Elam, was out fishing with his family and then he was just gone," Mama continues, lifting her palms helplessly. "Search parties were sent out and special investigators called in, but there was no sign of him. And when people are upset and don't have any real answers, rumors start."

"What kind of rumors?" I ask, leaning forward.

"Oh, all sorts. Anything people thought might could've happened to him. That's the thing, Linden, after the worst, people have a tendency to look for reasons why the same thing could never happen to them. They blame the victim, they accuse the family, but the truth is sometimes terrible things just happen." Her eyes on mine go liquid, and I know she's thinking about last summer. About the terrible things that happened to our family.

I blink a few times, refusing to be sidetracked by the sick feeling in my stomach. I was only lost for one night; Elam McCoy has been missing for eighteen years. And Dahlia, she'll never come home again.

"So they didn't have any leads about what happened?" I press.

"It was so long ago, Linden," Mama prevaricates. "He was, what, four?" She looks to Gran for verification.

"Thereabouts," Gran agrees. She puts the heavy lid on the pot and wipes her hands with her apron. "And small for his age. It was as if the boy disappeared into thin air. It was the strangeness of it all that got people talking more than anything. Everybody had their own pet theory, each one more outlandish than the last. It got to be where you couldn't walk down to the mailbox without hearing a new one. It was a bear, it was a kidnapper, it was his own family. His daddy got the worst of it, poor man. It got so bad, his wife left and went back to her people up the river.

"Course those damned rumors about the Moth-Winged Man did nobody any good. It's taken one family's worst tragedy, mixed it up with an old folktale, and turned it into Caball Hollow's claim to fame," Gran says.

"People sure like to toot their own horns about knowing tragedy was coming once it's already too late to be useful." Sorrel walks into the kitchen and lifts the lid off the pot on the stove, leaning over to take a big whiff.

Gran swats at her with the dish towel. "Leave that lid on, or the roast won't braise," she admonishes. "A steady simmer will break down even the toughest meat."

It's a slow morning at the Harvest Moon, with customers few and far between. I've already scrubbed every chair, stool, and table in the dining room, washed the windows, baked a batch of lemon thyme bars, and refilled Hillard Been's coffee cup enough times to scandalize his heart doctor. When the bell over the door finally rings again, it's been so long that I startle, spilling decaf coffee grounds all over the counter.

"Go ahead and sit anywhere," I say, cleaning up the mess, then look up to see Bryson Ivers walking toward me.

He's red and a little sweaty, like he just stepped off the field from morning football practice. His nose is swollen, the skin underneath one eye bruised red and purple. But it's the potency of everything churning in him that gives me pause: the pungent taste of disgust, the metallic tang of fear, and other things too, all muddled and fluctuating so much they're impossible to parse.

He startles when Rowan lets out a low whistle from the opposite end of the counter, where she's doing inventory. "Quite the shiner you've got there. Maybe you should take your business elsewhere. Wouldn't want you scaring off all the customers."

Bryson lifts his chin. "I wasn't planning to stay. I'd just like to apologize for my involvement in what happened at the creek the other night."

"Well, by all means." Rowan sweeps an arm toward me like she's giving him the floor. "But unless you'd like a matching set, make it snappy."

Bryson jerks back in surprise. "I don't . . ." he stammers, then frustration flames up inside of him like burnt bacon as he turns to me. "Look, I'm sorry. I was joking around, pretending to shove you. I didn't know that other guy would run into me," he says, crossing his arms over his chest.

This is not strictly true. He may well have been teasing, but there was an edge of meanness to it, an element of eagerness and cruelty in what he did.

"So anyway, I'm sorry," he presses on. "Can you please remove the curse now?"

My body feels the words before they register, a frisson of electricity hot under my skin. Murmurs spark and catch among the few tables of customers. I pick out accusations in the whispers about how strangely I acted at Dahlia's funeral and how memory loss is a convenient excuse I can probably only get away with since my father is the sheriff. My face goes hot.

I glance over at Rowan, and she gives a small shake of her head. He's not lying. He truly believes what he's saying.

"Bryson, I didn't curse you," I say in disbelief. The words even feel absurd. "We don't do that."

"Fine, call it whatever you want. All I know is that I woke up this morning with a . . ." He pinks and lowers his voice, shifting uncomfortably. "A rash. And every time I touch something electronic, it shorts out. I blew the bulb in my bedroom turning on the light this morning."

"Sounds like a case of bad luck," I tell him.

"And maybe some irresponsible life choices," Rowan mutters. "Bless your heart."

"But, Bryson, I promise you I had nothing to do with it."

He nods, and his temper boils over into anger. "Okay, I get it. There's some antidote I need to buy or something, right?"

"You've said your piece," Rowan interrupts. "I think it's time for you leave now."

Bryson slaps his hands on the counter and leans closer. His face inches from mine, he practically spits the words. "You might have people convinced you're all benevolent now or whatever, but my granny knew the old stories. Your people certainly used to hex. And Dahlia knew it too." His eyes blaze as he sets his jaw and spins on his heel, leaving without another word. Once the bell quiets, an uncomfortable hush falls over the dining room.

"Are you all right?" Rowan asks softly.

I swallow, then nod. "Yeah, fine. What do I care what Bryson Ivers thinks?" And I don't, but I'm also not deluding myself into believing he's the only one. "What was he even talking about?"

Rowan shrugs and shakes her head. "I think that boy might be a bubble off plumb," she says, ducking back down behind the counter to shuffle ketchup bottles. "And now I've lost my place."

I turn to the coffee maker and grab a rag to wipe down the counter around it, mostly to hide from the customers in the dining room for a minute while I get my bearings. Bryson's grandmother told him that my family used to curse people. Is that the kind of rumor everyone believes about us?

Taking my phone out of my apron pocket, I pull up Cole's number for the first time in nearly a year. I've thought about deleting it a thousand different times, but I could never quite bring myself to do it. Now I type out a text and send it before I can overthink it too much:

Can we talk?

After another two hours with only a handful of customers and no response from Cole, I convince Mama to let me take lunch over to Daddy at the station. I tell her it's because I want to make sure he's eating, but that's only part of it. What better place to learn the facts of the Elam McCoy case than the office of the people who investigated it?

I lean my bike up against the side of the squat, vaguely sphinxlike brick building at the center of town. One arm serves as headquarters for the Eldritch County Sheriff's Department, the other as the local library. At the center is a clock tower that has miraculously never managed to keep correct time in all the years I've been alive.

A wall of cold hits me as soon as I step through the door. The air-conditioning is turned up full blast to counter the thick press of humidity that has taken up permanent residence in the valley.

"Hey, there, sweet pea." Sergeant Glenna Markin greets me from behind the window in the wall that separates the lobby from the open workspace on the other side. She's in her late sixties, and a force of nature at nearly six feet tall, with warm brown skin and steel-gray hair cropped short. As sergeant, she has ruled the sheriff's department for as long as I can remember, but she always keeps her desk drawer well-stocked with butterscotch candies.

"Hello, Sergeant Markin." I lay my arms on the window ledge and lean in closer. "Can I ask you about something?"

"Course, darlin'." She turns away from her computer and pulls off her reading glasses so she can focus her full attention on me. "What's on your mind?"

"I was hoping you could tell me about the disappearance of Elam McCoy."

"Oh. Sure, sure. Are you working on a project for next year's Moth Festival scholarship?" she asks, lowering her voice. "Your daddy told me you weren't sure about college."

"I'm exploring my options," I hedge. "But I'm having a hard time finding any actual information about what happened that night."

"Well, if you're asking about the Moth-Winged Man sightings earlier that day, I can't help you. And if you're asking about what really happened to Elam McCoy, I'm afraid I don't know that either. That's sort of the nature of cold cases." She pauses, tapping her fingers against the desk as she thinks back. "But what we do know is because your daddy is the best tracker I've ever seen. He was only a deputy then with a couple of years on the force, but he could follow clues like a map.

"It rained that first night. Rain erases footsteps and covers clues like bent branches and turned leaves. And it increases the risk of hypothermia, especially for young children who don't conserve body heat as well as adults. There's a lot of places in the Forest where a boy that small could hide. And it *is* common for lost children to hide, even from searchers, because when you're terrified, everything looks like a threat."

She shakes her head and takes a sip of coffee. "The cases involving kids are the worst ones. He took it real hard, your daddy. I think it's good to talk about the hard ones sometimes." She gives me a sad sort of smile, and a taste like loss, dulled but long-lasting, seasons her words. The phone on her desk rings, and she turns to answer it. "I'll let your daddy know you're here," she says, buzzing the door open for me.

I thank her, considering her words as it clicks shut behind me.

"Hey, kiddo," Daddy says, dropping a kiss on the top of my head when he opens the door to his office. I catch a whiff of stale coffee and note the wrinkled uniform shirt and the dark circles shadowing his eyes.

He ushers me in, then scrubs a hand over his face. "I hope whatever you have in that bag is for me, because I'm starving."

I set the food on his desk, next to an unopened tin of anchovies and a sleeve of saltines. "Is this all you've been eating?" I scold.

He shrugs, gesturing for me to take a seat while he shifts several piles of papers, including one he has to remove from his own chair before he can sit down. "It's hard to justify stopping for a full meal these days."

I frown a little, not sure if he means because of the murder case or because he lives alone now. Guilt bubbles up in my stomach.

For Father's Day last month, we stayed with Daddy at the little house he's renting down the street from the station. When he dropped us back off at the farm, I realized I'd forgotten my book and ran back to his truck to get it. But when I opened the door, he was wiping tears from his cheeks.

"What's wrong?" I asked, startled. Daddy has always been a gentle giant, but I've rarely seen him cry. An earthy, bitter taste like biting into a pickled beet filled my mouth.

"I can't remember it, when we were all together and happy, not really." He brushed at his eyes again and sniffed, trying to regain control. "I know all the facts and figures about you girls growing up and my relationship with your mom, but it feels abstract now, like a dream almost, all those years encased in amber. A whole life I can't quite touch."

I hadn't known what to say then, and I don't any better now, so I take care of him in the way I know best, with food.

"Well, I made you a fried chicken and hot honey sandwich on a biscuit with some green tomato chowchow relish, and a little three-bean salad. Oh, and a cherry hand pie for dessert."

"Have I ever told you that you're my favorite child?" He tucks the paper napkin I hand him into his uniform collar.

"Now, you see, that's funny, because I seem to remember you saying the same thing to Juniper just the other day."

"You're all my favorite, so it's always true." He opens the bag and smiles at me. "But thank you for this, truly. I don't recall the last time I ate a meal that didn't come from a gas station counter or a drive-thru window. We're stretched thin as it is, but this heat wave is making people hateful mean. And with everybody and their brother thinking they've seen the Moth-Winged Man now, we've got calls up all over the place. I tell you what." He points his fork at me, a wax bean speared on its tines. "If I find out someone is pulling some sort of social media prank, I'm throwing the book at 'em."

"You don't think it could be related? Dahlia's death and the sightings?" I ask.

He chews for a moment before answering. "Probably is, but not in the way people think. When you have a local legend like this one or the Wampus Cat—hell, probably even Bigfoot up north—it becomes a sort of self-fulfilling prophecy. Now that something terrible has happened, people will convince themselves the sightings were real and then every large-winged bird or strange sound in the night becomes the Moth-Winged Man."

"So you don't believe the legends even a little, with all the strangeness in our own family tree? Gran says all folklore starts with a seed of truth." I realize I'm absentmindedly rubbing at the same spot on my arm where I saw the strange red moth-shaped bruise on Dahlia's skin and force myself to stop.

"I believe we have enough real monsters in this world without having to make up any supernatural ones." He takes a bite of his sandwich, and I bite the inside of my cheek, trying to figure out how best to broach the topic I came here to ask about.

My eyes catch on a map of Caball Hollow that's spread out over part of the desk. I tap a finger against a spot on the map I know well: the one where Elam McCoy was last seen and the scene of my own disappearance seventeen years later.

"Do you think places can be cursed?" I ask. "Destined to be the stage of misfortune again and again?"

He sets aside his lunch and lets out a long sigh. "Why don't you tell me what this is really about?"

"I'm looking into what happened to Elam McCoy." I confess a small piece of the truth, avoiding any mention that it might be connected to Dahlia's murder.

"Linden Tallulah James, did I hire you as a deputy while sleep-deprived and forget?" Daddy's voice goes stern.

"How can someone disappear so completely that they leave no trace?" I pick at an imaginary spot on my shorts, not wanting to meet his eyes. I can feel him watching me for a moment, probably with his unreadable cop face on, but the warm biscuit taste of sympathy hits the back of my tongue, and I know what it means.

"Linden, it was almost twenty years ago."

"It's not the kind of thing you forget."

"No, I don't guess it is." He glances at his watch, then shakes his head. "Do you remember what I taught you about tracking?"

When we were little, Daddy would take us for long walks in the woods, passing on the knowledge that his grandmother taught him when he was a boy. Once, we were tracking a deer that had run through the orchard and back up the mountain. I couldn't figure out how he knew which way it had gone when there weren't even footprints in the hard ground. Until I saw him reach over to a bush and pull off a piece of broken twig about the size of a matchstick. It was the mushroom-gray color of bark, except for a dot of white at the broken end, like the period at the end of a sentence. He'd been following those tiny dots all the way up the mountain.

"I could see where he'd left the creek and gone up toward the woods." He points on the map, showing the direction Elam had taken. "He'd left signs, clear as day. Until right about here." He taps his finger against the map between the river and the Forest. "He stood there a while. He'd been barefoot, and I could see where he'd curled the ends of his little toes into the dirt." He's speaking slowly, pulling his words up from where they've been locked deep in the past. Earthy and raw like root-cellar turnips.

"What do you think happened to him?" I whisper. It seems wrong, somehow, to speak any louder.

"A bear, a big cat, even the rare wolf up here, they'd all leave signs. There's only one predator who covers his tracks." He's silent for a long moment, then he swallows hard, throat clenching. "You know that old abandoned coal town in the Forest?"

I nod. Everyone knows it.

"People were still living there a generation ago, and now it's completely overgrown. That happens to people, too. The earth claims them even if they were never buried. Every year that passes, more soil covers what remains. I can't prove anything, but my gut tells me if Elam McCoy is still in Caball Hollow, he's under several inches of dirt or he's at the bottom of that creek."

His phone rings, shattering the spell. He answers, exchanges a few quick words with the person on the other end of the line, then hangs up. "Mayor Spencer is here." He always calls Cole's father by his title now. I suspect it's to help everyone here remember that he's not another deputy anymore. Probably to help himself remember most of all. "Come on, I'll have Miranda walk you out."

"Why did the case go cold?" I rush to ask before my time with him is up.

"There were no leads. No suspects." He shakes his head, the frustration obvious even after all these years. "Nothing more we could do."

He opens his office door and waves a hand toward Ethan, who is standing between an annoyed Beulah Fordham Hayes and an oblivious Pastor Boggs, as Mayor Spencer approaches.

"We always remember you in our prayers, Mayor Spencer," Pastor Boggs says, patting the other man's shoulder as he passes by on the way to Daddy's office. "You're a credit to this town."

Mr. Spencer smiles and nods to the others in the room, but when his eyes meet Daddy's, his face turns serious.

"Oh, and, Linden, we're still praying for you too, young lady," Pastor Boggs says when he notices me. "Lord willing, one day you'll be fully healed and your memories will return."

"Uh, thank you, Pastor Boggs." I stumble for a response as Mayor Spencer and Daddy shake hands. "I am starting to remember a few little things."

"Well, heaven works in mysterious ways," he says.

Daddy squeezes my shoulder before he and Mayor Spencer step into the office, closing the door behind them.

"You should be praying for her immortal soul," Mrs. Fordham Hayes mutters from behind the pastor. "Or, better yet, to deliver this town from evil."

"Nice to see you again, Mrs. Fordham Hayes," I say as Ethan gestures that he'll be a minute, then turns back to some paperwork he's filling out. "What brings y'all here today?"

"Oh, uh." Pastor Boggs gets a little flustered and pink around the collar. "Just a minor fender bender."

"Minor? You tore my bumper clean off," Mrs. Fordham Hayes objects, her carefully coifed hair quivering with indignation.

"Ma'am," Ethan interrupts, clearly having heard all this before. "I'm going to need you to sign this."

As she moves to the desk, Pastor Boggs approaches me with a sheepish smile. "You know." He taps a finger against his chin. "The Spencer family is a great example of the healing power of prayer. I can't betray a confidence, but suffice it to say that they've faced impossible odds and they're still surviving. You could get your miracle yet."

I assume he's alluding to Mayor Spencer's motorcycle accident. Or to how Cole's heart didn't develop properly when he was born. The doctors told his parents he wouldn't survive more than a few days. Yet somehow the hole closed enough on its own that it could be repaired. Neither of those things are a secret by any means, but I only smile. Having my memories back might help me find Dahlia's killer, but from what I've been able to recall so far, I'm not sure they'd exactly be what I'd consider a blessing.

"Mr. Boggs," Ethan calls from across the room. "I need your signature on this form, too, sir."

When he finally gets the two of them under control, Ethan scans his ID to unlock the exit door for me. "Stay out of trouble, kid," he says, shoulders slumping slightly as he turns back to join the others.

I give a half-hearted wave to Sergeant Markin in the lobby, then push through the exterior door. It's like standing at the gates of hell after the icy chill of the climate-controlled building, and I'm wilting like spinach on the boil, but the cold sweat has more to do with what Daddy told me than the weather. Sometimes, no matter how hard you try to avoid it, trouble finds you.

That night, I wake up in my room with the moon shining through the open window and the taste of blood in my mouth. With a weary sigh, I kick off the sheets and grab my phone from the nightstand. Cole still hasn't replied.

I drag the fingers of one hand along the faded floral wallpaper of the upstairs hall, each familiar bump and tear a comfort. A warm glow flows up the back staircase from the kitchen below, and I make my way toward it. Someone else must still be awake.

When my foot touches the first step, a raised voice echoes from down below. "Odette, you don't believe in my abilities, and you never have. I am just as capable as you or anyone else. Trust me when I tell you I know what I'm talking about."

I move closer, light on my feet and avoiding the creaky seventh step, to find Sorrel sitting at the curve of the narrow staircase before it turns toward the kitchen.

"Salome, I already said my piece, and I won't chew my cabbage twice. It's got nothing to do with your abilities and everything to do with your *inability* to see reason when it comes to certain things and certain people," Mama responds, voice low.

"What's going on?" I whisper to Sorrel.

"I'm not sure." Sorrel has her elbows on her knees and her chin in her hands. "Apparently, Sissy didn't just come back to the Hollow because of a strong hankering for Gran's home cooking. There's some situation that Mama thinks is best to let lie, but they haven't said exactly what or why. It's almost like they know the walls have ears in this house." She scoots over to make room for me.

"So why did Sissy come home?" I sit next to her.

"No idea, but one thing I do know is that where Sissy goes, trouble follows." She turns her head to look at me more fully. "Rowan told me about what happened with Bryson. How are you feeling?"

I shrug and lean back against the step behind me. "It's not the strangest thing that's happened lately, but I can't stop thinking about what he said and who else might believe it." My eyes slide down to my phone, and Sorrel notices, catching the open text conversation on my screen before I think to hide it.

A sly smile twists her mouth. "You and Cole Spencer talking again?"

"That would require more than one active participant." I gesture to the empty text thread.

"Give it time, little sister," Sorrel tells me. "After all, he dove into that dirty creek water for you. In fact, I'd say he's on his way to becoming your very own knight in shining armor. That's at least twice now, by my count, that he's come to your rescue."

My cheeks heat up with embarrassment and then her words register. "Wait, what do you mean twice?"

"The creek and last summer when he came here to raise the alarm the night you were missing. If he hadn't shown up at midnight, banging our door down, we might not have known for hours." She shakes her head, remembering. "When Daddy and his deputies got there, most of the kids didn't even know you were gone yet."

"Right." I draw out the word, thinking back over the few memories I have from that night. How could Cole have been the first to know I was gone? He wasn't even there. I rub a hand over my face in frustration. "I wish I could remember what happened without having to relive it in fits and starts."

"About that . . ." Sorrel hesitates. "I've been working on something." She reaches down between her hip and the wall and picks up a small jar of amber liquid. "I got the idea last summer and thought maybe someday you'd be ready to try. I wasn't planning to harvest it for a few more months, so there isn't much, but after the candle message, I'm not sure it can wait."

"What is it?"

She hands me the jar, and I lift it into the diffused light from the kitchen, turning it slowly to watch the honey inside glow like molten gold. Sorrel likes to experiment, and because of her talent, she's able to train certain hives to pollinate different plants and make different honeys.

"This one is rosemary," she says. "For recovering lost memories."

My eyes flick up from the jar to meet hers.

"Do me a favor and promise you'll be careful. After what happened at the creek, we know those lost memories are potent and can have some very real side effects." She ruffles a hand through my hair as she stands. "See you in the morning," she says as she turns to go upstairs.

I listen for a moment more, waiting in case Mama and Sissy let loose any secrets, but it's quiet now. When I tiptoe the rest of the way down the stairs, the kitchen is empty. The kettle is still warm, so I make a cup of tea and stir in a bit of the rosemary honey.

As I sip, I consider Sorrel's words. How could Cole have known I was lost in the Forest from his house across town? Had someone from the party realized I was missing and called him instead of the police? Could it have been Dahlia?

When I head back to my room, I trip in the darkness. Juniper's shirt lies crumpled on the floor next to the closet and smelling of fried food and sweat after a day at the diner. Sighing, I scoop it up and pull open the closet door to toss it in the hamper.

The black dress I wore to the funeral is still hanging inside, the full skirt riotous among my more humble wardrobe. I need to put it back where it belongs in the attic cupboard, but as ridiculous as it is, I almost feel sorry for it being locked away up there. Reaching out, I run a hand down the side of beautiful fabric, pulling the skirt out so I can see all of it. Then I hear something crinkle.

I feel around until I discover a pocket, so well disguised I hadn't even realized it was there. Inside is a small piece of folded paper, soft with age. Carefully, I open it and read what's scrawled across the page:

> *Nora,*
> *The more I learn, the more I wonder if the right*
> *question isn't who am I, but rather what are we. 216.3*
> *I'm sorry,*
> *Z*

Maybe it's the lingering effects of Bryson's hateful comments earlier today, but the note feels downright ominous. What exactly was Zephyrine researching that had given her such concerns? Was it a philosophical question or one more specific to our family? Something else is scratching at the back of my mind, too. *Nora.* Could it be Nora McCoy? How did Zephyrine know her, and why was she apologizing?

CHAPTER SIXTEEN

WHEN I step into the kitchen the next morning, I find Gran alone, sitting at the table with a pail on the floor between her feet. Two bowls sit in front of her, one full of freshly picked sugar pea pods, the other of shelled peas. She slides her thumb along the seam of each pod to split it open, then down along the inside in one smooth motion, each perfect little round pea falling into the bowl before she drops the empty pod into the bucket on the floor.

I slip into the chair next to hers and grab a pea pod from the pail at her feet, crunching into the chewy skin. I've always preferred the sweetness of the pods to the mushy texture of the peas themselves, except in the spring when Gran mixes them in her big pot with new potatoes and fresh cream.

"It don't cost nothing to help," Gran chides gently.

I reach into one bowl for a pea pod and shell it into the other, my motions not nearly as smooth and practiced as hers. "Gran, can I ask you about Aunt Zephyrine?"

"I saw that you put away her dress. Thank you for that." She shells two peas for every one of mine, even though she's barely paying attention to the work her hands are doing.

"I'm sorry it made you sad when I wore it." I consider mentioning the note I found in the pocket, but I don't want to upset her again when it doesn't really change anything. It won't bring Aunt Zephyrine back.

Gran sighs as she tosses another empty pod into the bucket on the floor. "It's not your fault, honey. You looked beautiful in that dress, and it's plain foolish of me to keep those things tucked away up there doing no good for anyone."

"Why do you, then?"

"Because of guilt, I reckon," she admits. Her eyes go distant, and I can tell she's thinking about her sister. "Zephyrine always did things her own way. Her and Sissy are like two peas in a pod in that." She gestures with the pea pod in her hand. "And so curious, always learning something new. That's why she went to work at the library."

Gran shifts in her chair, settling in, and her fingers slow a bit. "She was quite a few years younger than I was, so we weren't close in the way you and your sisters are. I think she always felt like I was trying to boss her, which I probably was. And I always felt like she was too much of a dreamer, refusing to see sense sometimes. So when she fancied herself in love with Malcolm Spencer, I didn't approve."

I nod, swiping another pea pod. "Sissy mentioned that they'd had a relationship."

Gran makes a humming sound in the back of her throat. "Oh, Zephyrine was over the moon for him. But back then, half the town was in love with Malcolm Spencer and the other half wished they were him. And Zephyrine . . ." She hesitates. "She was a bit lost, like a lot of young people are at that age. I think that may be why she became so wrapped up in the diablerie, too, but I didn't realize it then.

"She was searching for something. Trying to figure out who she was, but you can't find that answer in someone else. When it all came to a head, we had a huge falling-out about it. She said I was bitter because I'd been so unlucky in love. I do think Malcolm probably cared for her, but not in the same way she did for him." Gran lets out a long, slow breath, seeming to steel herself before she continues.

"When Malcolm had his accident, thankfully she wasn't riding with him. But, well, something like that can put things into perspective for people. For her, it made her realize she wanted to marry him. But for him, it was the opposite. I don't think she meant it as an ultimatum, but maybe that's how it came across." Gran shrugs and shakes her head.

I run a finger along the grain of the table. Her words bring to mind Sorrel's about how traumatic events lead to life-changing decisions.

"I should have stayed out of it, I know that now. You have to let people make their own choices, even if you think they're wrong. If I had, maybe she could have turned to me when she needed someone. As it was, I think she couldn't stand to look at me. It wasn't long after they split that she took off. I came home one day to a note on the table that said, in no uncertain terms, that her life was hers to do with as she pleased and I should never try to contact her again." Gran shakes her head, her salt-and-pepper hair curling thickly around her shoulders. "That was the last I ever heard from her."

"Do you think she'll ever come home?" I ask quietly.

"It's been decades since I've seen her, Linden, but I still go to bed every night hoping she'll be home by morning." Gran pats my hand, and I can taste the wistfulness as her smile droops and her breath hitches.

I turn my hand to hold hers. It's the most Gran has ever told me about her sister. I can't take away her pain, but I can sit here with her in her grief, and I can carry some of it for her.

Yet I'm left with one question I'm not quite sure how to ask. "Gran, the woman who died last month, Nora McCoy—she was Elam McCoy's mother, wasn't she? Did Aunt Zephyrine know her?"

"Oh, not this again, Linden." Gran leans back in her chair and lets out an exasperated sigh. "I don't know what you expect to find, child, digging up all that heartbreak." But she gets that faraway expression that I know means she's going way back into her memories. "They would have been around the same age, so they probably at least knew of each other. I can't say as I remember her mentioning Nora by name, but she wasn't confiding in me much anymore in the months before she left."

A quick rap sounds on the back door before it swings open and Hadrian steps in.

"Mornin'." He pulls his hat off and wipes his forehead with his arm, smearing a line of dirt across his brow.

"Good morning. Looks like it's going to be another hot one today. Can I get you some breakfast?" Gran asks. "Come on in and sit a spell."

"No, ma'am, I'm filthy." He's got a layer of garden dirt sticking to the sweat on his arms, and his boots are coated in mud.

"Did you get the irrigation system working?" Gran asks, handing him a glass of cold water.

"Yes, ma'am." He has the water down in two big swallows. "Had to replace some of the tubing, and it took longer than expected. It's been so hot lately the lettuce in the back field is already starting to bolt. I'll need to get that harvested today before it all turns bitter."

"Don't overwork yourself in this heat." Gran takes his glass and refills it, patting him on the shoulder and releasing a cloud of dust. "I know we've given you a lot to do, but you're no help to anyone if you get heatstroke."

"Yes, ma'am," Hadrian agrees. "You ever find what you were looking for out there?"

After a long beat of silence, I look up to find his eyes on me. "Uh . . . I'm sorry?"

Now Hadrian looks as confused as I feel. "Early yesterday morning, out in the back field? You said you were looking for something."

I glance down at my hands, remembering the dirt that caked them when I woke up on the front lawn with no memory of how I'd gotten there. Had I really sleepwalked all the way to the edge of the farm and even spoken to Hadrian? My body feels like a stranger I can't trust.

"Oh, um." I can feel Gran's and Hadrian's eyes on me, the taste of curiosity with an edge of concern heavy in my mouth. "Not yet." I scramble to my feet and scoop up the bucket of pea pods. "Gran, I'll take these to the chickens and check on the black raspberries out back."

I squeeze past Hadrian and out the door before anyone can respond, because I have no idea what I could have been looking for. The only thing I've lost recently is my memory, and I doubt I'll find it out in the garden.

But I've barely reached the berry patch when my phone vibrates in my pocket. I almost drop it when I see Cole's name. Underneath is a one-word reply to my text asking if we could talk.

Shed

No punctuation. No other details. And my stomach flip-flops in a way it hasn't even through everything else that's happened this morning.

By the time I get to the old shed after my shift at the Harvest Moon and my farm chores, I'm already tired and cranky, so when I spot the Triumph under its thick cover and no sign of Cole anywhere, I'm fit to be tied.

"And this is why people who want to meet arrange specific times. Would it kill him to send a calendar invite?" I grumble as I pull out my phone to text him.

A low whistle sounds from the opposite corner of the shed, and I turn, squinting into the shadows. I step farther inside, out of the sun, and see him leaning against a beat-up old cabinet. He watches me as he wipes his hands on a rag, the corner of his mouth hitched up with the hint of a suppressed smirk.

I point a finger at him. "Don't you dare laugh at me, Cole Spencer."

He tosses the rag onto the cabinet behind him and rubs a thumb across his mouth. "I would never." He moves toward me, soft white shirt like a beacon in the dark, smelling like cedar and cloves and fresh sawdust. "I value my life too much."

"What are you doing back there?" I nod toward the old broken furniture, crates, and other clutter stacked in the far corner of the shed.

He shrugs the question away. "Is that what you wanted to talk about when you texted me?"

I narrow my eyes. "Here's something we can talk about: Bryson Ivers showed up at the Harvest Moon yesterday with a half-assed apology for what happened at the creek, then accused me of cursing him. Know anything about that?"

"Bryson Ivers wouldn't know beans with the sack open. Why would you want to waste your time talking about him?"

I catch his right hand and lift it up to display the bruises across his knuckles. "I don't know, Cole, you tell me. What'd you do, try to punch the apology directly into his head?"

He shrugs. "He got in my way when I was trying to save your life."

"Yeah, well, I think you broke his nose."

"He's lucky that's all it was," he growls, then bites his bottom lip, like he wants to say something but won't. "Look, James, I don't want to fight with you," he finally says instead, his voice weary and carefully neutral.

It hits me like a bucket of ice water when I realize what he's doing, tamping down his feelings so I don't pick up on them. I drop his hand and look away. This was a bad idea. Cole Spencer is never going to open up to me again, let alone spill any secrets he might be holding on to about last summer. Whatever we had once is well and truly over, and that realization feels like a brick in my gut.

I look up at him. A crease has settled between his eyes. "I'm sorry." My voice is strained. "I shouldn't have come." I turn away, heading for the path that leads home. What do I care about the town gossip? It's never going to stop anyway. The James women will never be more than a necessary evil to Caball Hollow.

I've only gone five steps when he calls out. "Ask me your question."

I stop and turn back, squinting against the bright sun, then putting a hand up to block it. "What?"

"Ask me your question, Linden." He moves, closing the distance and blocking the glare with his broad shoulders. "What did you really come here to talk about?"

I swallow, suddenly nervous, because I realize the question I want to ask right now has nothing to do with the rumors going around town about my family. And he knows it too, standing there, too still and tense, like he's braced to take a hit. "How did you know?" I whisper. "How did you know I was in danger last summer in the Forest when you weren't even there?"

The pulse in his throat flutters, and he responds, in a low voice, with his own question. "How did you know where to find Dahlia's body?"

"I already told you. I don't know." I shake my head, confused. "What does that have to do with this?"

"Because I'm pretty sure it's the same reason, Linden." He leans closer, his golden gaze intense. "All my life, I've known when someone is about to die—my grandparents, my great-uncle—" He cuts himself off, turning away, as if he can't believe he spoke the words out loud.

When he turns back, he watches me closely, looking for a reaction. I hold myself carefully still, even as my heart starts to race.

"You've seen it, haven't you? The red mark that appears on their skin. No one else has ever been able to."

I draw in a breath, but my chest feels tight. "There was a red moth on Dahlia's arm the night of the festival."

He nods, his face stoic. "That pull in your stomach, the murmur in your ear that led you to Dahlia's body, that brought you toward the basement in the funeral home—I feel it too. I always have."

"But how?" I demand.

"I never knew the answer to that until I started to suspect it was happening to you too." He gestures toward his chest where his shirt hides the scar. "I wasn't meant to survive the hole in my heart. And last summer, at the festival, I saw a red moth on your shoulder. I think that's why it happened. Because we both nearly died."

"Wait, what?" My throat goes dry, and my knees feel loose, like they might slip right out from under me. "I was supposed to die that night?" The words are barely a whisper, but I hear the truth in them. It fits like a key in the places where my body remembers.

"I said some awful things that night to try to get you to stay home." He shoves his hands into his hair. The disgust he feels is so strong that the sharp, pungent taste even cuts through the fog of shock. "I thought if anyone could protect you, it would be your family. But I should have told you plainly about the danger. Maybe then you would have been safe."

"I thought you hated me because of what I can do, because of the strangeness of who I am." Tears slide down my face, and I don't try to stop them. All this time, that disgust he felt around me was for himself. It had never been about me.

Cole freezes for a second, then reaches for me, pulling me into him. "I'm sorry. I'm so sorry," he says fiercely against my hair. He tightens his hold for a brief moment before stepping away. "I was too afraid to tell you the truth, and that fear almost got you killed. I can never forgive myself for that, Linden. You're better off without me."

I shake my head, but I don't know what to say. It's too much at once, a confusing rush of flavor I can't put into words. Not every feeling has a name. I look away, and my eyes settle somewhere in the middle distance to the right of his elbow, where a bag of his ever-present pink candies sits on the table, the telling fragrance of cloves emanating from it so strongly that I can smell them from here.

He clears his throat. "My mom got me hooked on them when I was little. She always had a bag in her purse, and she'd use them to bribe me to behave."

He shifts a little, obviously uncomfortable, but there's clearly more he wants to say. "I didn't realize until I was older that the reason she always had them was because they covered the smell of alcohol on her breath. It's gotten worse lately. Now she barely leaves the house. It's because of me." His jaw tightens. "One of my earliest memories is of the look of abject terror on her face when she discovered what I could do. She forbade me from ever telling anyone. And I haven't, until now."

My heart squeezes in my chest for that little boy, and I want to tell him I'm sorry, but I don't think that's what he wants to hear right now. "We all think we're trying to protect each other, but really we're just keeping secrets." I shake my head. "And the secrets Dahlia kept got her killed."

He nods and runs a hand down his face, letting out a long breath before he speaks. "I know it, and I don't want to do that anymore. What you're doing, looking into Dahlia's murder, it's dangerous."

"Don't you start, I've already heard it from my dad."

"Let me help you," he insists. "Maude's mom is the library director now that Mrs. Rowsey retired. She said all the winning scholarship entry materials are archived there. If Dahlia started looking into Elam McCoy's disappearance again, maybe we can find out why in her old research."

"You don't have to do that," I object.

"Linden, I'll be there." Cole's voice is gruff, frustration peppering his words. "I'll even send you a damn calendar invite."

It's enough to surprise a laugh out of me. "Fine, have it your way."

A smile flashes across his face, almost too fast for me to catch it. "Tomorrow, then."

It's not more than a half mile home, but the sky is already going orange around the edges as evening closes in. Unease crawls across my skin like footsteps over a grave. Maybe it's that walking this path again feels all too much like the night I found Dahlia's body, but I slow my pace and glance over my shoulder. When I can no longer see the shed behind me, I feel conspicuously alone on the rough dirt track.

As the light begins to fade, a flash of something in the trees has my neck tingling, and I twist around, searching for movement. "Cole?" I whisper, so strong is the sense that someone is watching me. But there's no one there. I take out my phone, switching on the flashlight.

A branch snaps somewhere behind me, and I fight the urge to freeze and listen. It's most likely an animal. And if it's not, stopping will do me no good. I shine the light into the trees and the underbrush running up alongside the hill next to me, the phone already hot in my hand. When I hear footsteps, I tell myself it's only the echo of my own. But the cadence doesn't match up with my gait.

I spin around and the light in my hand catches what looks like the glow of two red eyes at the edge of the woods right before my flashlight shuts off. The disorienting shadows of dusk rush in, shifting and stretching the landscape into something ominous.

My eyes start to water with fear. Frantically, I tap my phone to get the light to come back on, but instead it flickers. Green and purple lines streak across the screen before it goes completely black. When something rustles nearby, the back of my neck starts to tingle with dread, and I bolt.

But I'm not fast enough. Not to escape the past. As I run through the gathering dark, a memory washes over me like the cold mountain water of the Teays.

My shirt is wet and sticky, and my thoughts feel sluggish. I need to catch my breath, so I crouch down into the protection of a small copse of trees. Against the full dark of the night sky, clouds roil over the face of the moon. It's an unusual quiet, a full sort of quiet like a pot near to boil.

I scan the Forest in front of me, the sudden hoot of an owl startling me so badly my heart stutters in my chest. Legend has it that owls are the messengers of witches. But even if I could understand her warning, it's already too late.

A sense of movement at the edge of my vision snags my gaze. I spin to look, but the darkness is too thick to make out anything. A crack of lightning zips across the sky, nearly scaring me to death and sending up a lick of brightness. The sudden flare of light illuminates a pair of glowing red eyes between the trees. My muscles tense almost painfully with fear as my brain seems to switch over to static and I freeze.

But when more lightning flashes, there's nothing there but tree bark. As relief starts to settle into my aching bones, the trees blow apart with a sound like ripping paper. I rise slowly to my feet, using the trunk of the oak behind me to steady myself. What I thought was the bark of a tall tree unfurls into a set of cleverly camouflaged wings, like a moth, revealing the shadowed form of a man beneath, hidden in darkness that seems to shift and slither unnaturally around him.

He blinks open those red eyes. And when he narrows them at me, I do the one thing you're never supposed to do when face-to-face with a predator. I run.

CHAPTER SEVENTEEN

WHEN THE farm comes into view, I race toward it, past the bittersweet bushes and where the old farm truck sits nestled between the house and the barn. I collapse onto the grass, sucking in great gulps of air. My face is damp, and I don't know if it's from sweat or tears.

"Where have you been?"

I look up to find Sorrel standing above me with her arms crossed.

"I went to see Cole," I pant, desperate to catch my breath.

"Did you run all the way home?" Sorrel gives me a disbelieving look.

"Part of the way I was chased." I flop over onto my back. The sky has that summer haziness that settles in, just before full dark.

"By what? Wavelene Edgar's dogs get out again?" Sorrel reaches down a hand to help me to my feet.

The truth is, now that I'm home, I'm not sure if it was anything more than my own overactive imagination and sleep deprivation out there in the woods. But what about that strange memory? It felt as real as the other memory fragments I've recovered. That mark on Dahlia's arm had certainly looked like a red moth, and Cole had seen them too, so is it possible that one of our oldest folktales is real? Or am I succumbing to the paranoia that has seemingly taken over much of the town?

I blow out a breath and dive in. "There's no way the Moth-Winged Man could be real, right?" I follow Sorrel through the back door and into the kitchen. She stops walking so suddenly I almost run into her. I jerk my head up to find her staring at me in concern. "I know it sounds absurd, but—"

"What sounds absurd?"

We both turn to see Juniper holding a glass of water and standing by the sink in what we call her flamingo pose, one leg bent out at an angle with the foot pressed against the inside of her opposite knee.

"I saw something out in the woods on the way home, and it triggered another memory, but this time . . ." I trail off, squeezing my eyes shut at how ridiculous it feels to say these words out loud. "I think I might have seen the Moth-Winged Man."

No one says anything, and when I open my eyes, Sorrel and Juniper are exchanging measured glances. "What is it?"

"You said something similar right after they found you," Juniper says. "You were sort of delirious, though, and not making a lot of sense."

"The counselor at the hospital said it was probably a trauma-induced hallucination," Sorrel explains. "You were always so afraid of the Moth-Winged Man as a kid that when you were alone and scared in the Forest with a head injury, you imagined you'd really seen him. Maybe what you remembered today was that hallucination."

I sit heavily in one of the mismatched wooden chairs at the table, once painted white but now faded and worn from use like everything else. Elbows on the table, I drop my head into my hands and blow out a long breath. Hallucinations, nightmares, and sleepwalking. I'm not sure if I can trust myself anymore. "I woke up in the front yard yesterday morning with no memory of how I got there," I confess. "Hadrian told me he saw me out in the back field."

Sorrel pulls my hand away from my face as she slides into the chair next to me. "Linden, that's really dangerous."

I swallow and nod. "He said I told him I was looking for something."

"When we sleep, we're more open than when we're awake," Juniper chimes in as she refills her glass and sets it on the table in front of me. "Dreams, intuition, and messages from the spirit world can be easier to receive. Maybe Dahlia is still trying to communicate with you." Juniper pats my shoulder. "Good night."

"Why does she say that like it's supposed to be reassuring?" Sorrel asks, and raises her eyebrows at me before she heads to her room.

I gulp down water as I walk around the house, checking the windows for any sign of movement out by the trees and making sure all the doors are locked—something we didn't use to worry about.

When my heart rate finally feels normal enough to attempt sleep, I head upstairs.

"Linden, is that you?" Sissy's voice floats down to me from above when my feet hit the second-floor landing.

I climb the rest of the steps and trudge across the chipped, white-painted floor of the attic to Sissy's room. She's sitting in the exact center of her bed, tarot cards spread out all around her. "What's all this?" I ask.

"Oh, you know me. Always looking for a little direction." Sissy slides all the thick cards into a pile, then pats the now-empty space on the bed across from her. I drop down, then flop onto my back and stare up at the ceiling.

During her junior year of high school, in what she claims was a protest against the administration cutting the budget for the arts, Sissy skipped six weeks of school and painted an exact representation of the night sky over Caball Hollow on her bedroom ceiling. The stars are so realistic that at night, looking up at it like this, it's like there's no ceiling at all.

"What's got you looking so pensive?" Sissy asks.

"What doesn't?" I hold up a hand and start counting off. "I can still only remember bits and pieces of what happened last summer, yet it's becoming increasingly clear that it was something truly awful. My friend was murdered, and I'm pretty sure the entire town thinks I had something to do with it. And, oh yeah, as of tonight, I'm not sure if I can even trust the few memories I do have."

She doesn't say anything, and I roll my head to look at her, sure I'll see the same pitying expression I'm used to from

Mama lately. Instead, she looks hesitant, biting her lip like maybe there's something she wants to tell me.

"What is it?" I push myself up on my elbows. "Salome James, what do you know?"

"I heard you downstairs, talking to your sisters, and I think there's something you should see." She lays a hand over mine in the space between us. "But, Linden, what I'm about to show you can be very dangerous. I need you to promise me that you won't use it without proper supervision."

"You know Daddy taught us all weapon safety when I was, like, ten, right?"

"No, smartass." Sissy hops off the bed and starts toward the hall, pausing in the doorway long enough to wave a hand, beckoning me to follow.

She leads me to the storage room and opens the cupboard that holds Zephyrine's clothes. "You're right," I say, skeptical. "This seems very dangerous." I run my fingers over the riot of colors, shapes, and textures that hang there side by side.

"Shh, just wait." She pulls out the small drawer that holds scarves and gloves, removing it completely and setting it aside, then reaches in and presses something at the back of the empty space.

A section of decorative molding pops open, revealing a tiny hidden drawer. Inside, against faded red velvet, is an antique key with an embellished *J* entwined with a sprig of bittersweet worked into the top of it.

Sissy takes the key and leads me down the stairs, holding a finger up to her lips as she gestures for me to slip on my shoes.

"Wait." I grab her arm to stop her before she can open the door, pulling back the curtain and straining my eyes to see through the darkness. Something moves in the distance, and my heart stutters to a stop until I realize it's a tree branch.

I slowly pull open the door and follow Sissy out onto the porch. When she heads for the summer kitchen, I realize what the key must unlock, and my stomach drops in a potent mix of nerves and anticipation.

Sissy switches on the lamp; only bright enough to light the worktable, it casts sharp shadows in the corners of the room. Then she reaches for the cabinet's locked center drawer.

"Maybe we shouldn't—" I start to object as the key slips into the lock, and with a gentle snick, it's open.

Sissy lifts out a silk-wrapped bundle and sets it on the worn wooden worktable, slowly unwrapping the floral fabric to reveal what looks like an old journal with a leather cover. The diablerie. She waves me closer, and I step into the light.

Tiny words in gold ink rim the edge of the first page:

To those who chance upon this book
Though inside you may take a look
Each and every scrawl and scribble
Will be naught but worthless drivel
And if ever this book is taken
A hateful curse you will awaken
Pity this hex will have no cure
For strong magic is an enticing lure
But each spell written here within
Will work for only James blood kin

"It's an incantation," I breathe. My eyes snap up to Sissy's. "To keep the spells hidden from anyone who isn't a James."

"This book is the oldest one we have," Sissy says. "Your gran doesn't believe we should practice this kind of work, but for a long time, this is what James women did. They collected secrets, dark secrets, and needed to protect them. I meant it when I said it could be dangerous." Her eyes are wide in the lamplight as she watches me, making sure I understand.

"Then why would anyone want to practice it?"

"Just because it's dangerous doesn't mean it's bad. A lot of good has been done with this book, and many James women have contributed to it, starting with the first, Caorunn James. And Aunt Zephyrine, for one, believed we should all be able to study it and use it."

I glance down at the book with a new interest. It could be where she'd learned whatever had made her begin to question what we are. "She knew Gran would never use it, so why didn't she take it with her when she left?"

Sissy shrugs. "She likely felt it belonged here for future generations. But she did take the matching key with her." She lifts up the one in her hand to show me. "Maybe that means she really does plan to return someday."

Sissy picks up the book and flips through a few pages. "This is what I wanted to show you." She turns it back toward me.

I glance down, and electricity snaps through the nerve endings of my arms and legs until my fingers and toes tingle. Right there on the page is an illustration of the Moth-Winged Man. Not the cartoonish depictions from the old books of folktales or the drawings accompanying first-person accounts in the newspaper, with glowing red eyes in the center of his chest, but the way he is in my memory. The way he looked that night in the Forest, with the body of a man and two enormous sets of gossamer wings splayed out behind him, like the cape of some fearsome ancient warrior.

But the drawing isn't even what takes my breath away, it's what's written beside it in bold letters: *Summoning Spell*.

"The Moth-Winged Man really can be summoned? That's not some urban legend the kids at school made up?" I ask. "Wait, did I bring him here? Is all of this my fault?"

"The Moth-Winged Man is most definitely real, but you didn't summon him," Sissy tells me. "Did you really think it would be as simple as calling his name three times at midnight?" She rolls her eyes.

I barely hear her because I'm so focused on trying to take in every impossible bit of information in front of me.

"The women who wrote these pages believed he was some sort of personification of death or minor deity. Variations of the legend appear in Breton, Celtic, and even Welsh folklore; some have characteristics of owls, some ravens, others are described as skeletons with long capes," Sissy continues, pointing to different sections of the notes. "They're called the graveyard watch, and each one is responsible for protecting the souls of those who have met a tragic end on their sacred procession between death and the hereafter."

"'One of the good folk who walk among the hills, the graveyard watch is considered an omen of death and tragedy, as seeing one meant he had work to do nearby, collecting the souls of those gone too soon,'" I read, my finger tracing the words, as if that might help me better absorb their meaning. "'For each of them was once a member of the local community whose life was cut unfairly short, serving their term, before passing on his knowledge to the next.'"

I turn from where we're huddled over the book to look more fully at Sissy. "Assuming any of this is true, if the Moth-Winged Man is an omen that someone is about to die in some especially tragic way, why would anyone want to summon it?" I tap a finger against the frightening illustration.

"Because that's not what it is, or at least not all it is. Have you ever heard the expression 'make a deal with the devil'?" she asks.

"Yeah, of course."

Sissy holds up the book so I'm face-to-face with the illustration of the Moth-Winged Man. "Meet the devil." I stare at her, incredulous.

"Well, one of them at least," she amends as she turns the page. "Think of the legend. Teens have been calling to the Moth-Winged Man for generations because they think he can grant them their deepest desire."

"And like Gran always says, every tale starts with a grain of truth," I say, catching on.

"Exactly. If there was something you wanted deeply enough you'd pay any price, you could make a deal with the Moth-Winged Man, and he would grant your desire. But if he only appears when he's needed to shepherd a soul, those aren't very convenient office hours. That is, unless you're a James and have this spell." She points to the book.

"The Moth-Winged Man can be summoned with a sacrifice of our blood at the burial place of our community's first graveyard watch."

"And how exactly is anyone supposed to know where that is?"

"Ah, because it's a place of strong energy." She flips a few more pages to show me another illustration, this one of a white tree with a short trunk that splits into five massive branches like a skeleton hand bursting through the ground to claw at the sky.

This, too, I recognize. "The Bone Tree," I whisper.

Sissy nods. "So you see, the Moth-Winged Man can be summoned, but not like in that silly urban legend."

"The sightings, then, were because the Moth-Winged Man was here to guide Dahlia from this life to the next?"

"Could be." She gives me a sad smile and carefully folds the book back into its silk shroud, then gently tucks it into the drawer. "Assuming, of course, that they were real sightings and not some side effect of too many beers and too few brain cells."

After she locks up the diablerie and slips the key into her pocket, we make our way back to the house, my mind spinning. Sissy must notice, because once we're in the kitchen, she reaches out to give me a hug.

"This doesn't change anything. Everything is still the way it's always been, only now you know why." She pulls back but keeps hold of my arms. "It's like in grade school when you learn clouds are made of water vapor. It doesn't actually change anything except your own understanding."

"Yeah, except that makes clouds seem less magical, and this is decidedly . . . more." I rub at my eyes, exhaustion pulling at me.

"You've had a long day. Get some sleep, and we can talk again later. Only, Linden, let's keep this between us. Gran would just as soon keep the diablerie locked up forever, and I don't need to give your mama any more reason to argue." She pulls me in for another hug, and in the soft glow from the light above the sink, I catch the silvery flash of an inch-long, razor-thin scar on the inside of her forearm that I've never seen before. But she's up the stairs and gone before I can say another word.

I make my way to my room and crawl into bed, but I can't stop replaying that memory from last summer. If everything in the diablerie is true and the Moth-Winged Man is some sort of guide for the dead, not the monster I'd always believed him to be nor a hallucination, why was he chasing me through the Forest? And what was watching me from the woods on the way home tonight?

CHAPTER EIGHTEEN

IT'S THE loud creak of the seventh step on the back staircase that wakes me. I roll over with a yawn to check the time on my phone, and when I see it's already nine, I realize two things simultaneously: Someone shut off my alarm, and I'm late for my shift. Mama did this last year sometimes when the insomnia got really bad. I thought I'd gotten better at hiding it, but this is the second time in a handful of weeks.

I pad down the hall to the bathroom for a quick shower, then return to get dressed. Two of my dresser drawers are open, a shirt hanging out of one. I silently fume at Juniper for borrowing my clothes again without asking, but I don't have the energy to get good and mad about it. Instead, I pull the shirt out and put it on.

As I head down to the kitchen, a door hinge squeaks from somewhere upstairs. "Hello?" I call, but no one answers. "Sissy?"

There's a note on the fridge from Mama. I read it as I stir a spoonful of rosemary honey into a cup of tea.

Sissy is covering your shift this morning.
Try to get some sleep and I'll pick you up for
the lunch rush after my errands.

The faint sound of a footstep crosses the floor in the up-stairs hall above my head. I miss the saucer, and my spoon clatters onto the table. If everyone is at the Harvest Moon, then who is in the house?

"Juniper?" I try half-heartedly, slowly standing when I remember the creak of the step that woke me, a sound no one who lives here would make if they knew I was asleep.

Again, there's no answer, but I'm already out the back door, not even slowing down to put on shoes. I run toward the carriage house with Hadrian's tiny apartment above it. But movement in the summer kitchen catches my eye, and I skid to a stop, kicking up a cloud of dirt.

Hadrian steps out, sliding something shiny into his pocket. "What's wrong?" he asks. One look at my face, and he's immediately on high alert.

"Were you in the house?" I pant for breath. Logically, I know there's no way he could have beaten me here if it had been him upstairs, but I'm desperate for it not to be what I fear.

"Linden, is someone in the house?" His voice is carefully neutral.

"I . . . I heard something. The step squeaked. And I think there were footsteps." It sounds silly now when I hear it out loud. With the strain of everything lately and my lack of sleep, it's possible I imagined it all.

Hadrian reaches back and grabs a long piece of birch, about two inches thick, from the woodpile stacked against the summer kitchen. "Stay here," he tells me as he strides toward the house.

I follow him despite his instruction, far enough behind to avoid the backswing. I'd rather face a threat than have it sneak up on me.

When we step into the kitchen, he looks to me, and I point toward the ceiling. On light feet, we make our way up the back stairs, both of us avoiding the seventh step. I try to will my racing heart to slow down as we methodically check each room.

"There's no one here," Hadrian declares at last, resting the branch on his shoulder. "Is anything missing or disturbed?"

I glance around. "Seven people live here; everything is missing or disturbed."

It surprises a chuckle out of him. "Fair point. The front door is unlocked, but if there was someone here, they're gone now."

"Well, thanks for checking, anyhow." I massage an ache that's settled in behind my temple, feeling a little foolish. Yet I know I locked the doors last night, and everyone would have left through the kitchen this morning.

After Hadrian heads back out to work and I'm alone in the house, I can't shake the uneasy feeling. Even though we searched everywhere, it stills feels like an intruder could be lurking around every corner, and I hold my breath at each creak or groan the old house makes. When I catch my own reflection in the bathroom mirror and nearly scream, it's the last straw. I text Cole to meet me at the library now instead of this afternoon.

I lean my bike up against the side of the library arm of the old municipal building, dabbing at the sweat that's gathered along my hairline. Cole is already in the reference room in the back corner, the box containing Dahlia's research for her scholarship-winning project sitting on the table in front of him.

I'd tried to listen to her podcast earlier, still posted on her SoundCloud, but I had to shut it off and read the transcripts instead. The rich tone of her voice, soothing as ever, is too jarring now. After.

And it's not even the grief that's the hardest. It's the guilt. She may have been the one who went away to college, but I was all too happy to let our friendship drift apart, so ashamed of my strange ability that I didn't want anyone else to see it. How cowardly, how positively shameful, to lose those last months with her because of my own insecurities. The flavor of salt-rising bread—pungent, strong, and familiar—is the taste of missing Dahlia.

"Hey." Cole stands when I step into the tiny space. He came straight from football practice, and his hair is still damp from the locker room shower. It reminds me too much of that night at the creek and the way his skin felt under my fingertips when he carried me to the Jeep. I feel my neck go warm as the corner of his mouth tugs up in a little half smile.

"Should we get started?" I busy myself emptying the box so I don't have to meet his eyes. "We don't have a lot of time. We're only allowed to check out research materials for an hour."

But after reading through pages of notes, copies of newspaper articles, and transcripts from interviews, it becomes pretty clear that the answers we need aren't in this box. Elam McCoy's disappearance is barely mentioned and only in relation to the Moth-Winged Man sightings beforehand. Dahlia's focus on the case was clearly the folklore, not the facts.

"There's nothing here." I lean back in frustration. "If she really was investigating what happened, none of it made it in here."

"Our time is almost up." Cole stretches, lifting his arms above his head. I try to ignore the strip of golden skin that's exposed when his T-shirt rides up.

Instead, I turn my attention to gathering up the papers that we've spread out across the table until something strange catches my eye. "Wait, look at this."

Cole moves closer, that clove-and-cedar smell drifting over me as I slide the list of contents toward him and point to the discrepancy. "It says there should be a transcript from an interview with someone named Wyatt McCoy, but there isn't one here."

"Let's check again. Maybe it was mislabeled," he suggests.

But after we comb through everything a second time, there's still no sign of it. "Elam's father is Amos McCoy, so who is Wyatt and how is he connected?" I ask.

Cole shrugs and drops back into his chair. "Maybe it's a typo. The only McCoy on her list of interview subjects is Amos."

"Maybe," I concede. "But the list of contents has a separate item for the Amos McCoy transcript." That interview had been surprisingly brief. Yet even it had managed to focus on the Moth-Winged Man and how Amos didn't believe in him. I tap my pen against the notepad on the table in front of me. "If it's not a typo, what happened to the missing transcript?" Could there be something in that interview that someone wants to keep hidden?

"It's also possible that it was never in the box," Cole says, resting his arms on the table between us. It's a small table in a small room that suddenly seems full of him. "You said Dahlia changed the focus of her project. Maybe she left it out because it didn't fit the new direction and then forgot to delete it from the index."

"But if it *was* here and someone took it, they would have first had to request the box from the reference librarian like anyone else, right?" I push my chair away from the table, and it screeches against the floor loud enough to make me cringe. "I'm going to ask if we can see the list of people who've accessed it over the past few months."

"Linden, wait, I'll come with you." Cole rises from his chair, but I'm already out the door.

I move quickly until the reference desk comes into view, and I spot who's working there today: Opal Parrish, Maude's mother.

"Hello, Linden," she greets me, her white hair perfectly smooth and cut precisely at her chin. "It's good to see you again. Cole mentioned you were working on something together."

"Yes, thank you, ma'am." I hesitate. "About that, we noticed one of the items on the list of contents for that box is missing. Are the archive boxes checked over after each time they're requested?"

"Oh, dear." She pulls a sticky note from a pad and scribbles something down on it. "I wish we could check each time they're accessed, but we just don't have the staff. There's always a lot of interest this time of year, right after the new Moth Queen is crowned, when the next crop of girls get ready to begin their own scholarship projects. We've had so many people digging through them lately, something may have been accidentally misplaced."

"Would it be possible to see the names of people who have requested that particular project?"

"No, sorry." She smiles apologetically and adjusts her cat-eye glasses, making the golden chain attached to them jangle. "We have really strict rules about privacy. We can't even release that information to law enforcement unless they have a warrant."

My excitement at being onto something that could lead to answers about Dahlia's murder evaporates, and Ms. Parrish must see it on my face, because she rushes to reassure me.

"But I'll see if I can't track down the missing item. If you leave your phone number, I can let you know if it turns up." She gives me a small, conciliatory smile, but her eyes light up at something over my shoulder as the scent of cedar and cloves surrounds me. "Or I can let Cole know. He's in here often enough." She doesn't say that it's with Maude, but I hear it anyway. After seeing Cole and Maude together at the festival and again at Dahlia's vigil, I wonder just how close they've gotten lately.

Cole leans forward to slide the archival box onto the counter, close enough I can feel the warmth of his body. She thanks him and checks it back into the system, then excuses herself to file it on the reference shelves.

"Sorry this was a bust," Cole says, leaning an arm against the counter next to me so he can see my face. "Can I at least give you a ride home?"

"I'm not headed home." I hitch my bag up on my shoulder and move away, out of the distracting haze of warmth and scent that is Cole Spencer. "Thanks, though, for your help today." Before I can take another step, he catches my arm and pulls me into the nonfiction section.

"Are we good?" Cole asks, looking down at me intently, the subtle taste of doubt flavoring his words. "Because you're being weird."

I open my mouth to tell him everything is fine. "Are you and Maude a thing?" I blurt out instead, and my eyes go wide with surprise.

He looks up at the ceiling and shakes his head, the flavor of doubt morphing into something smoky and complex. "No, Linden," he says. "We aren't." Then he braces a hand against the bookcase next to my head and leans in close, golden eyes gone molten and intense. "Do you really need me to tell you that?"

My cell phone vibrates in my pocket with a text, and I jump, breaking the spell. "That's my mom. She's going to pick me up on her way back to the diner if we're done here."

Cole steps away and lets out a slow breath. "I guess we are. If you think of anything else, text me." His words are a blend of subtle flavors, frustration and confusion, and something else, something deep and intense and harder to define.

He starts to walk away, and I reach out, catching the hem of his shirt. "Hey, Cole." I wait for his eyes to meet mine. "We're good." A slow smile hitches up the corner of his mouth, beautiful and dangerous.

When he's gone, I lean my head back against the bookcase and stare up at the ceiling, taking a deep breath and letting it out slowly, before refocusing my eyes on the wall of nonfiction books across the aisle.

Something prickles at the back of my mind. I step closer, running my finger along the edge of the shelf in front of me. Little white stickers line the bottoms of all the book spines, a different number printed on each one. Aunt Zephyrine worked at the library before she took off. She would have been very familiar with the Dewey decimal system.

I open my bag and pull the note I found in Zephyrine's dress pocket out of my wallet, where it's been for safe-keeping since I found it. Unfolding it, I reread those numbers scribbled at the bottom: *216.3*.

"Ms. Parrish?" I retrace my steps to the circulation desk. "Could you help me find a book?" I tell her the number, and she types it into her computer.

"Ah, yes, we do have it. It's quite old and pretty obscure, though, so it's shelved down in the basement stacks." She scrolls down the page, studying something on the screen. "Huh."

"What is it?"

"Oh, nothing, it just hasn't been checked out in quite some time." She reaches up to adjust her glasses, and I lean forward far enough to sneak a glance at her computer screen.

She has the checkout history pulled up, and there's only one name on it: Zephyrine James. My heartbeat kicks up a notch. I'm onto something.

"Did you work here when my aunt Zephyrine did?" I ask.

"Oh, um, no, actually. I was hired once her position be-came available," she answers carefully.

I thank her and take the stairs down to the basement, where the lights are motion-activated, flicking on and off as I pass through different sections. All the books down here are on special shelving units that move on tracks in the floor to save space. In order to access one, I'll have to spin the wheel on the side to move it away from the others. I scan the numbers posted on the sides of each unit until I find the range where mine falls and open the section.

When I step between the moving shelves, the light overhead flickers and goes out. I glance up, and it flickers again in rapid succession, on then off, on then off, so quickly it takes a beat for me to realize what I'm seeing. There, trapped inside the glass of the light, two moths flutter as if in slow motion. My blood starts to feel fizzy and it makes my skin tingle, but I will myself to calm down, taking a couple of deep breaths and blowing them out slowly. Sometimes a moth is just a moth.

When the light finally stabilizes, I quickly scan the shelves, counting out the numbers until I find the book I'm looking for: *The Philosophy of Good and Evil.* I pull it off the shelf and flip it open, but inside the dust jacket isn't the dense theoretical text I'm expecting. It's a journal, filled with handwriting that matches the note in my hand. Why would Zephyrine hide this here? I glance around quickly, then slide it into my bag before rushing out to meet Mama.

A restaurant kitchen is a noisy place during service: the clatter of food being plated; the whoosh of the commercial dishwasher; the whir of the vent hood; the sizzle of the grill and clang of spatulas; the voices of the wait staff calling out orders and the expeditor, usually Mama or Gran, calling back; even the sound of soups and sauces simmering away on the stove. When Mama and I arrive at the Harvest Moon for the lunch rush, it's practically silent.

"Hello?" Mama calls as she sets a box of clean aprons from the laundry service on the stainless steel prep counter.

We exchange a look and make our way through the kitchen to the dining room. Gran and Salome are playing cards at the corner table by the big front window, a pitcher of sun tea beside them that looks to be just about done brewing. No doubt due to Gran's uncanny timing. The only customer is Hillard Been, sitting at the counter with a cup of coffee and a plate of biscuits and gravy. His former trainee, Buck Garland, is nowhere in sight.

"How's business?" Mama asks, folding her arms across her chest. The cuffs of her favorite shirt hang loose from her wrists, and the skin under her eyes looks bruised like she hasn't been sleeping. Maybe it's been that way for a while now.

"Nonexistent," Sissy answers without looking up from her cards.

"What do you mean?" Mama turns to Gran for an answer, concern flavoring her tone.

"Salome is exaggerating, as usual." Gran lays several cards on the table in front of her. "Gin."

"Only slightly," Sissy clarifies. "We've had maybe a handful of customers all morning. One of them being Wavelene Edgar, who came in to share some unsettling news."

"Are you pausing for dramatic effect?" Gran asks wryly.

"Lord, Mama, can't a girl take a breath?" Sissy fires back.

"Well, don't keep us in suspense, what was the news?" Mama presses.

"Apparently, her dogs spotted something out behind her house the other night and gave chase. Never came home. She hung up a flyer, then ordered the dandelion fritters."

"What'd they take off after this time?" Mama sighs.

I meet Sorrel's eyes from across the room, and she raises her eyebrows at me.

"Oh, Wavelene gave us the whole sordid tale," Gran says as she settles back in her chair. "The dogs went wild, and before she could get out there, they'd jumped the fence and taken off after some shadowy figure. She's convinced someone took them."

My ears perk up at the mention of a shadowy figure. Maybe it wasn't the Moth-Winged Man who'd followed me home last night, but the same person who'd been watching us at the school parking lot. And maybe they'd even become brazen enough to enter the house this morning. A chill burns through me and leaves behind a jittery sort of resolve. If someone is trying to scare me off, they've had the opposite effect.

"Ain't nobody in Caball Hollow fool enough to take Wavelene Edgar's dogs. And it weren't no Moth-Winged Man that done it, neither," Hillard chimes in from the counter without turning around. "Those dogs will turn up when they get hungry enough, like they always do." He pulls his wallet out and drops some money on top of the check sitting next to his now empty plate. "See y'all tomorrow."

An idea occurs to me as Hillard leaves, and I pull a few chocolate-dipped almond crescent cookies, a known favorite of his notorious sweet tooth, out of the jar on the counter and drop them into a bakery bag.

I rush out onto the sidewalk, scanning both directions until I see Hillard half a block away in front of the corner drugstore. "Mr. Been!" I call, waving a hand. When I reach him, I give him the cookies. "On the house for being our best customer."

"Well, now," he draws out gleefully. "That's mighty kind of you."

Dahlia's interview notes may be missing, but there's no reason I can't retrace her steps. And who better to talk to than the only other person who was with Elam McCoy when he disappeared.

"Mr. Been," I ask Hillard. "Do you happen to know where Amos McCoy lives?"

His chest puffs up with pleased self-importance. "I delivered his mail for near on thirty years, didn't I?"

That night after supper, it's my turn to wash the dishes. Rowan is sulkily drying them next to me. She'd argued that being relegated to dish duty at the diner should exempt her from it at home, but Mama just rolled her eyes and left the room. While my hands are busy, I stare absently out the window, trying to make sense of everything.

I read some of Zephyrine's journal after work today, but I still don't understand why she'd felt the need to hide it. Her notes were mostly about family history, like the legend of the first James woman, and notes on folklore, like how knocking on wood began as a way to invoke the spirits that lived inside trees for protection. One section even examined the founding of Caball Hollow itself and how, of the half dozen or so founding families who petitioned for the original town charter more than a hundred years ago, some remained prominent, like the Spencers, but most had long faded into obscurity or died out.

I pass Rowan a wet glass without turning my attention from the view outside. She nudges me with her elbow as she dries and puts it in the cupboard. "What's up with you tonight?" she asks.

I blink, looking away from the window. "I found an old journal of Aunt Zephyrine's at the library. She hid it in a philosophy book."

"Why?" Rowan asks, tossing the dishcloth over her shoulder and leaning a hip against the counter.

"That's what I can't figure out. She and Gran were arguing a lot then. Maybe she just didn't want her to find it." I shrug. "But I can't stop thinking there's got to be more to it than that. And that's not even the weirdest thing that happened today."

"What else happened?" Juniper chimes in from where she's working on a puzzle at the table behind us.

"Maybe nothing, but that's the strange part." I fill them in on the possible intruder I'm still not sure was real.

"Breaking in here would be a waste of time. The only heirlooms on this farm are tomatoes," Rowan says.

"The spirits have been especially active lately," Juniper offers, thoughtful. "And creaking doors, footsteps, a squeaking stair, those are all noises associated with hauntings."

"That's not necessarily less frightening, Juniper," Rowan tells her as she closes the cupboard door. "But what was Hadrian doing in the summer kitchen?"

I look at her, surprised. "That's so not the point of this story."

"But there's no reason for him to be there," she argues. "There's nothing in there he'd need for the farm."

"Maybe Gran asked him to fix something," Juniper suggests.

I point to her in agreement. "Besides, it's not like he could have been upstairs and outside in the summer kitchen at the same time."

"Maybe not, but that doesn't mean he's not up to something," Rowan argues.

Long after I've crawled into bed, when the first fingers of dawn are scrabbling their way over the mountains, my mind still won't rest. I keep thinking about what Rowan said, and while I don't share her distrust of Hadrian, I also know there's only one thing we keep locked up in the summer kitchen: the diablerie.

CHAPTER NINETEEN

THE NEXT morning, Rowan is in the herb garden when I find her, but instead of pulling weeds, she's standing with her hands on her hips, looking out toward the barn.

"What are you doing?" I ask, turning to follow her line of sight. "Ah." Hadrian is working on the tractor's engine, shirt off and muscles glistening in the hot sun. "Maybe it's not his lies that have you so fascinated, sister."

She scoffs and turns her back on the scene. "Mark my words: I'm going to figure out what it is he's hiding."

"Not much of anything right now." I gesture toward the full display of tattoos across his chest.

She purses her lips. "Did you need something?"

"Yes, actually, I need your help and a ride out to Amos McCoy's place." I explain my plan to ask him about the day Elam went missing, and her expression grows increasingly dark.

"Linden, half this town thinks he's a murderer," she objects. "Hell, maybe he is. He could have killed Elam and then Dahlia when she came around asking too many questions."

"I don't put a lot of stock in the accuracy of town gossip," I argue. "Especially because I'm the topic of most of it lately. Besides, you'll know if he's lying."

We fall quiet as Hadrian stalks closer, making his way toward the spigot next to the herb garden. He nods at us as he turns on the water, washing his hands and splashing the cool liquid over his head.

Rowan pulls off her gardening gloves and stomps away. "Fine, let's go. But you're finishing the weeding after."

When we pull up in front of the address Hillard Been gave me, it looks like it's been abandoned for the last couple decades. A dirt track leads up to the front door, and two cars in various states of disrepair are up on blocks in the front yard.

What was once a small clapboard farmhouse with good bones is now a skeleton, heavy trailing vines hanging from it like sagging skin. Some of the front windows are broken out, and the remaining jagged glass gapes like the mouth of a corpse missing half its teeth.

An old garage in the back looks to be more rust than metal and several half-dissected machines speckle the tall grass in front of it—a lawn mower deck, a rusty chain saw motor, even a dirt bike without either tire.

"Are you sure he still lives here?" Rowan asks, sliding her sunglasses down her nose for a better view.

"Only one way to find out," I answer with more confidence than I feel as I reach for the door handle.

Despite the oppressive heat, a shiver runs through me as we climb out of the truck. Rowan looks at me, wary. She feels it too. I may not be able to see spirits like Juniper, but I can still feel that this place is haunted. Whether it's the actual ghost of little Elam McCoy or the lingering impression of the terrors this family went through remains to be seen.

I lead the way up the cement blocks that serve as steps for the half-rotted porch. The peeling paint from the clapboard eddies around a small clover someone carved above the door for luck, which feels cruelly ironic. Why do some families seem to get it all and others only get misfortune? I knock quickly before I can talk myself out of it. We wait a few minutes, but there's no sign of movement from inside. I look at Rowan, and she shrugs.

But I didn't come this far to turn back now. I raise my fist and pound on the worn door as hard as I can, half afraid that my fist will go right through the dry rot, or the vibrations will shake loose the cobwebs that seem to be all that's holding the house together.

The distinct sound of two boots hitting the floor echoes through the quiet, and then rapid, heavy footfalls head right for the door. Rowan must hear it too, because she grabs me by my belt loop, pulling me clear before the door flies open and smacks into the side of the house, nearly coming off its hinges.

"What the hell do you want?" barks the skinny and sallow man standing at the threshold. He's missing a couple teeth, and his cheeks are angry and red. Stringy gray hair hangs in lank strands past his collar, and he's wearing what looks like it might have started life as a white undershirt but has become a dingy, sweat-stained second skin.

"Well, aren't you saltier than a country ham," Rowan drawls from behind me. Her bored tone is at odds with the hands clenched into fists at her sides and the taste of both fear and resolve rolling off her.

The man gives us a hard look for a moment, then seems to come to a decision. "My apologies, girls, I didn't mean no offense."

"None taken," I reply quickly, before Rowan can get a word in. "We're looking for Mr. McCoy. Does he live here?"

"You're lookin' at 'im."

I glance at Rowan in confusion. I've only caught glimpses of Amos McCoy before, when he came to the farm and then at the cemetery, plus once on the street. But he looks like he's aged years in the span of a few weeks. He looks like a man waiting to die.

"Mr. Amos McCoy?" I clarify.

"Only McCoy left 'round here," he answers, getting annoyed again. "You girls sellin' cookies or somethin'?"

"We were hoping to ask you a few questions," I hurry on before he can decide to slam the door in our faces. "About Elam," I add softly.

The change in his disposition is immediate, and his face almost seems to crumble. "Whew." He blows out a surprised breath. "I haven't heard that name in a while." The words taste like sadness turned in on itself, like brine. After a moment, he steps back into the house.

"Come on in." He waves a hand, gesturing inside. "I won't bite." He chuckles at his own joke, but it's more habit than anything; there's no real humor in it.

I take a step forward to follow him, and Rowan pulls me back by the belt loop she still has a hold of, pushing past me to go in first. She casts a strange look back at me over her shoulder. I don't understand until I step into the small, enclosed space behind her, and a wave of body odor, stale cigarettes, and something that smells sickly sweet like decay hits me. My stomach twists, and I try not to gag.

Amos McCoy clears off a couple of chairs at the kitchen table, shuffling around stacks of old mail, some in brightly colored envelopes with FINAL NOTICE stamped across the front, and greasy old take-out bags from the Pub & Grub. He crumples the entire mess and shoves it in a corner of the kitchen along with an overflowing ashtray. He finally sits and gestures for us to do the same.

"I'm sorry to bring up such a painful subject, but we were hoping you could tell us a little about Elam. What was he like?" I try to approach the day his son went missing carefully, to ask about the boy himself first in hopes of putting the father more at ease.

"He was such a cute little thing." The fact that Amos doesn't even want to know why we're asking questions makes me think it's something he wants to talk about. That maybe it's good to talk about even the most painful things sometimes. "Just the spit of his mama, same bright eyes and big smile. Unlike his brother, who took after me."

"Elam has a brother?" I blurt out in surprise.

"Yeah, Wyatt, my older son. He left with his mama after . . . Well, anyhow." Amos McCoy looks down at his hands where they lie on the table, palms up.

That answers one question. The missing interview from Dahlia's research was with the brother of the lost boy. One I'd never heard mentioned until now.

Amos McCoy sighs deeply. "Well, I reckon if we're goin' do it, we ought to do it right. Start all the way at the beginning."

He glances around, looking for something. When he spots a beer can on the window ledge next to the table, he grabs it and jiggles it, then casts it aside.

"Here." Rowan lifts a cardboard case from the floor and pulls out the last can. She catches my eye as she pops open the top, asking a question with her gaze. I nod and she surreptitiously runs her thumb along the sharp edge of the can's open mouth. She barely winces as she squeezes her thumb hard enough to spill one tiny drop of her truth-serum blood into the warm beer before she passes the can to Amos.

"Thank you kindly." He drinks it down fast, like medicine.

"This house didn't look like this then," Amos says once his can is empty. "I was working as a mechanic, and my wife, Nora, she was a teacher up at the high school. We were happy. Least I thought we were." He starts bouncing his leg so hard that the table shakes. I reach across the old enamel surface, painted with what looks like it might once have been cheerful flowers, and cover his hand with my own. He looks up at me, and the loneliness and heartache in his eyes is so clear that I can feel it in my own chest as the taste of lemon and salt floods my mouth.

"Can you tell me about the day it happened?" I ask gently.

He clears his throat. "It was a Saturday, one of the few I had off, so I was going to go up to my fishing spot over on Stillhouse Creek, right at the break from the river. I'd had some success catching walleye up there. Wyatt wanted to come, and so then, of course, little Elam did, too.

"The boys got bored pretty quickly and went to play up on the bank a bit. I told them to stay away from the water and not to wander off. But when I was ready to head home, only Wyatt was there.

"I ran along the river, shouting for Elam, but he wasn't in the water, he wasn't anywhere I could see. Weren't no sign of 'im." He blows out a breath. "I shouted myself hoarse. It was starting to get dark, and little Elam, he didn't like the dark. I didn't think he'd go too far into the woods, but I checked anyway just in case."

I glance over at Rowan. Her eyes are wide, but she gives me a little shake of her head. Every heartbreaking thing he's said so far is the truth, yet I'm not sure how any of it will help us figure out what really happened to Elam McCoy or how it can lead us to Dahlia's killer.

"What did you do when you couldn't find him?" I ask, squeezing his hand as his emotions roil.

"Didn't have no cell phone back then, so I ran down to that little gas station right before the turnoff to call for help. I tell you what, leaving that creek without Elam was about the hardest thing I've ever done." He shakes his head and blows out a breath. "After that, it's all sorta a blur, I couldn't even tell you for sure how I made it back up to the creek later."

He's quiet for a second, sucking a tooth while he thinks. "The sheriff had to pull me out of the woods when it started raining, said if I kept searching, I'd break my fool neck. But somehow I knew that if we didn't find him that night, we wouldn't find him at all. How could a little tiny boy like 'at survive out there alone? My wife, Nora, she was beside herself, convinced someone had stolen him. But stuff like that don't happen 'round here. At least, it didn't."

"That must have been so hard for you and your family," I tell him. "Especially your other son." The acidic, heavy taste of dread floods my mouth and sends a zing of awareness up my spine. There must be something he doesn't want to tell us. I ease into my next question. "You all went through so much. How did Wyatt handle it?"

"They'd been arguing that morning over cereal or something, I can't recall. They fought a lot, but I thought that was how boys were. Like puppies, always scrabblin'." He shifts in his chair. "When I got home that night, Wyatt was already asleep. He was just a little guy himself, only a few years older than his brother. His hair was all matted with sweat even though it wasn't hot that day, not like it has been lately. He startled awake and started to cry. Told me he didn't mean to make Elam leave. He must have been having a nightmare, because he'd wet the bed. He hadn't done that in years."

The taste of oily fish floods my mouth, and I nearly gag. Guilt. I clear my throat, trying to get rid of the taste. "What about later, after they called off the searches, what happened then?" I nudge.

"Not long after, people started talkin', you know, saying I'd killed him. My cousin used to live up in Rawbone, and he said he'd heard someone say I'd murdered him and fed my own son, my flesh and blood, to the pigs. We never even kept pigs." He rubs a gnarled hand across his mouth. "Nora couldn't handle living in this house and being reminded, each and every day, of what had happened. And she couldn't listen to the rumors anymore, neither."

"When did your wife move away?" Rowan asks.

He sighs and another strong wave of guilt washes down my throat. "She packed up Wyatt and went to her aunt's place up near Charleston after they called off the search. Told me in no uncertain terms that she didn't care where I went, and it could be straight to hell. I was supposed to be watching him, you see. I didn't feed him to no pigs, but it was my fault just the same. Soon enough I didn't want to hear any more rumors, neither. I don't much leave the house anymore. No point to it."

I press a hand to my mouth and swallow hard. Rowan touches my shoulder, and I reach up to squeeze her fingers, blinking away tears. Mr. McCoy's eyes are still unfocused, seeing instead a different place and time. I hope that this has been good for him, cathartic, rather than a reminder of all the pain he's tried so hard to forget.

"She died a few weeks ago. Cancer. Came home for the tail end of it. I hadn't seen her in years, but her family had a plot she wanted to be buried in down here. Didn't want a funeral, though. Too much bad blood still with the folks 'round here, I reckon. But it was important for her to pass at home. She never gave up hope that Elam would find his way back. But now that Nora's gone . . ." He shrugs as if he's accepted his fate to stay in this house, the oppressive pain and loneliness crushing him to dust until he dries up and blows away.

I realize that's the point. Living this way is his penance for not being able to save his son. And it's killing him, slowly, right before my eyes. I hesitate, thinking of the cake incident at Dahlia's funeral and the way my emotions sometimes seem contagious. Gran wouldn't approve of using my ability to interfere, but if it could help him, how can I stand by and do nothing?

If I can make myself feel something strongly enough, maybe I can bring him a little peace. A short respite in the midst of all his pain. I try to summon the feeling of comfort, to think calming thoughts: a cool mountain breeze, the smell of freshly turned earth, a nap in the sun.

It doesn't seem to be working, but then I realize my mistake. Comfort isn't just a feeling to me. It's a flavor. I imagine warm, buttery biscuits fresh from the oven, the taste of a warm hug, until my stomach growls. And after a long moment, his shoulders lift a bit and the crease between his eyebrows starts to ease. A little of the weight taken off, a moment to breathe.

I suck in a tiny breath. Had it really worked?

"We'd better get going," Rowan reminds me, standing before I can fully consider the results of my little experiment.

I follow, but rush to ask one last question. "Mr. McCoy, about your wife, Nora. Did she know Zephyrine James?"

"Oh, sure, sure," Amos says. "Zephyrine helped Nora start the Moth Queen scholarship."

"She what?" I blurt out. I glance over at Rowan, but she looks as surprised as I am. Maybe this is the explanation for the research notes in Zephyrine's journal, a project she helped with during her time at the library.

"Working at the school, Nora saw the boys getting scholarships through the football program, but the sports for girls never got the same sort of attention. She'd always been interested in the history of the town, and so was Zephyrine." He gestures to a wall in the kitchen where several old family photos hang. "Nora's family was one of the first here in Caball Hollow," he tells us proudly. "But after they got funding for the scholarship, Zephyrine took off."

"Did Zephyrine tell Nora why she was leaving?" I ask.

"No, I don't think so. But I'm pretty sure something happened while they were working together. Nora was pretty upset and didn't like to talk about it."

He wags a finger as a new thought occurs to him. "Now that you mention it, though, that was right around the time she stopped all her genealogy research." He shrugs. "I guess if you go digging up old bones, you might unearth a skeleton or two you wish you hadn't."

"What about your son Wyatt?" Rowan asks. "Where'd he end up?"

"I'm not rightly sure, tell you the truth. He hasn't wanted much to do with me neither. I know he got into some trouble a while back for playing with matches, ended up doing a stint in juvie. But I haven't seen him in a long time. Not even when his mother passed."

"Thank you for telling us about Elam," I say, aware the words are woefully inadequate.

He nods. "It's nice to have the company, if you want to know the truth. Most people go out of their way to avoid me, but you have a very soothing presence."

"One last thing," I tell him, pausing next to the door. "My friend Dahlia Calhoun talked to you about Elam's disappearance last year, do you remember?"

"She sure did." He shakes his head. "Cornered me at the Pub and Grub and asked if I ever saw the Moth-Winged Man, and I most certainly did not. But if he ever were to show his face 'round here, I'm liable to have a few choice words for him." Anger heats his words. "I got too riled up, and the bartender escorted me out."

Maybe that explains why Dahlia's interview had been so brief. We thank him for his time, and when we step out into the fresh air, it feels strange that it's still daylight. That it's even still the same day. I swallow hard, trying to wash away the taste of sadness, guilt, and despair that still coats the inside of my mouth.

"He's lying," Rowan says as she climbs into the driver's seat.

"What do you mean?" My head jerks up, and I look back at the dilapidated house as though I can see through the walls to the broken old man inside. "I thought he couldn't lie after you gave him your blood?"

"He's lying to himself," she clarifies. "He thinks the older son might have done it, killed his brother over some silly argument. Maybe it's better to think an accident or an animal took Elam than to have to try to come to terms with suspecting his own son."

"Well, that's a dark thought," I tell her. It's cook-an-egg-on-the-sidewalk hot again today, but the tips of my fingers feel frozen. I'm cold all the way through like somehow a chip of ice lodged in my chest. "Though I guess after eighteen years without any answers, you might start to suspect anyone."

But if Wyatt truly did have something to do with Elam's disappearance, could he also be responsible for Dahlia's murder? Had she found evidence of his involvement? Maybe the answer is in that missing interview.

"How could Dahlia have interviewed Wyatt McCoy if his own father doesn't even know where he is?" I ask.

Rowan shrugs as she pulls onto the road. "It's a small town. Maybe Dahlia's grandmother kept in touch with Nora McCoy after she moved away."

I tap my fingers against the door of the truck, thinking. Both Parlee Wilkins and Nora McCoy have passed on since Dahlia did her research, so I can't retrace her steps. But maybe I can figure out what she did another way. Amos McCoy said he called for help from the gas station on the edge of the Forest. It's a place I know well. I was there the night I disappeared, too.

After the argument reaches its boiling point, I hear the back door close and Daddy's footsteps, heavy on the porch, as he makes his way out to the cruiser. Once the crackle of the gravel driveway fades, Mama makes a cup of sleep-easy tea and locks herself in their bedroom. I'm lying in my bed, staring up at the ceiling, when my phone pings with a text from Dahlia.

Are you coming?? We're all meeting up at the Ick.

It occurs to me that if I were to sneak out now, no one would stop me. I weigh the idea, the trouble I'd be in for so blatantly disobeying my parents in a way I'd never even come close to before, and realize I don't care. I know I'll have to pay the price later, but tonight I'm acting on credit. This time, I creep right down the front staircase, ease open the door, and take off at a run.

I pick my way carefully along the side of the road. It's warm and cool at the same time in the way that summer nights sometimes are, the chill curling like smoke around my neck and nipping at my ankles. I wait to get caught, for my phone to ring or the farm truck to pull up alongside me. But the farther I get from home, the more invincible I feel.

When I reach the parking lot of Caball Hollow's only gas station, people are already milling around, the fluorescent lights casting harsh shadows that distort their familiar faces. I hang back, crossing my arms over my chest as the first whispers of doubt swirl through me. Maybe this was a bad idea.

"Linden, you coming?" a deep voice calls, and for a moment my traitor heart leaps.

But of course it isn't him. It's the TA from my English class, newly graduated like most of the others and taking his last chance to brave the Moth-Winged Man. I spot several members of the football team and even a few from student council.

"Come on, let's go," Bryson Ivers yells. He's always loud, but excitement cranks the volume up even more, his eyes gleaming in that way that could go from fun to dangerous in an instant. It's the third time my instincts prickle in warning and the third time I ignore them.

"I want to see how many beers it takes to convince Maude to call the Moth-Winged Man," Bryson jokes, playfully shoving the guy next to him, someone I don't recognize, with brown hair buzzed short and eyes so deeply set I can't make out their color.

"No way. There's not enough in the entire county," Maude answers, making her way closer to me. "Hey, Linden. I thought Cole was coming. Have you seen him?"

My body goes hot, then cold. "Uh, yeah, I think he changed his mind," I finally manage. My lips feel numb as the words pass through them.

"Who here is brave enough to summon the monster?" Bryson bellows, arms spread wide.

"I'll do it," I say, shrugging a shoulder like it's no big deal. I told myself I wanted to come tonight so I could have fun with my friends, but it isn't fun I'm feeling. It's something bitter and acidic that drives me on against my better judgment.

Bryson lets out a loud whoop and throws a heavy arm around my shoulders, jostling me a little too aggressively.

"You can ride with us," Dahlia offers, extracting me from Bryson's choke hold and pulling me toward a group of her student council friends.

"What are you kids playing at? Loitering and carrying on like a bunch of hooligans," Hillard Been complains as he makes his way through the crowd from his old white pickup truck toward the door of the Ick. "Get on out of here before you get yourselves in trouble. Go on, scat."

It's the push everyone needs to get moving, laughing in anticipation as we squeeze into a handful of vehicles. Engines growl to life and tires squeal out of the parking lot, turning toward the river and the strange allure of danger.

CHAPTER TWENTY

BEFORE LIGHTNING strikes, there are surefire signs: a sound like buzzing or crackling in your ear; a tingling sensation skittering down the back of your neck; all the hair on your arms standing on end; a metallic taste on your tongue; the sharp, crisp smell of ozone. There are signs as electricity builds up all around you. But by the time you realize, it could already be too late. A hundred million volts might be headed right for you.

There's not a cloud in the sky today, but all morning it's felt like lightning is about to strike.

The dining room is empty except for good ol' Hillard Been, who doesn't appear bothered by this in the least. He's sitting at the counter again, since it seems Buck won't be joining him anymore. I reach for the coffeepot and top off his cup. "Can I get you some dessert? I made a sweet tea pie today. You can have the first slice."

Hillard considers this. "Better not, too much overindulging lately. That lemon bar last week gave me some powerful strange indigestion. Just the bill, I think," he says.

I cringe knowing it might have been me, not the lemon bar, that caused his discomfort. Though, to be fair, it could have been the fourth or fifth lemon bar, not the first, that did it. I pull his check out of my apron pocket and set it down next to him, then turn back to finish wiping down the area around the coffee maker.

Rowan stomps in carrying the newly cleaned floor mat that goes behind the counter. She's in a foul temper because she spent the past hour elbow-deep in one of the chores Gran always saves for slow days: cleaning out the refrigerators. I exchange an amused look with Juniper, who is rolling silverware into napkins at the other end of the counter.

Rowan takes a step toward the kitchen door right as the diner's big front window implodes into a million tiny pieces, shooting glass across the room like sparkling shrapnel. She flinches as I throw myself at Juniper and pull her down to the floor. We huddle there, unsure of what might happen next. After what feels like forever, but is probably no more than a moment, the last shard of glass pings onto the floor and the diner falls silent.

Rowan is the first to move. She flies out the door, glass glittering in her hair.

"Holy shit," I breathe. "What the hell was that?" I stumble to my feet, then reach down to help Juniper up. "Are you okay?" I ask, my voice tight with fear.

"I . . . I think so." She lifts shaking hands to inspect them, and a small cut across the back of one drips blood down her arm.

"Mr. Been?" I turn to look over to where he sits at the counter when he doesn't answer right away.

"My entire mortal life just flashed before my eyes." Hillard lifts his coffee cup as if to take a sip, then thinks better of it and sets it back down. "You know, I think I will have some pie after all."

Mama, Gran, and Sorrel rush through the swinging door from the kitchen. "What happened? Juniper!" Mama jumps into action when she spots the blood, grabbing a clean towel from the wait station and wrapping Juniper's injured hand. Her eyes take in the destroyed front window. The glass that remains, held in place by the frame, is shattered. Cracks like lacework spread out in all directions from the gaping hole. Fragments of all sizes, from tiny splinters to viciously sharp shards, cover the dining room for what seems an impossible distance.

We all stare at the destruction for a moment, shocked silent by the sudden violence of what happened. Rowan bangs through the front door, and the clatter of the bell seems to break the spell, pushing us all into action.

"By the time I got out there, whoever did this was long gone," Rowan fumes, kicking a large piece of glass and sending it sliding across the room. The emotion that pours off her tastes like Gran's special moonshine hot sauce with the heat of anger and the sting of betrayal. Above her left eyebrow, a cut wells with blood.

I hand Rowan a napkin and move closer to the large rock sitting in the center of the dining room. Crouching down, I notice a small piece of paper tucked into a crevice. I pull it out and unroll it. *You're digging your own grave* is scrawled out in angry black slashes. The sight of the words makes my stomach twist, as if I can taste the hatred in them.

"Sorrel, honey, call the sheriff's department," Mama says, her voice small and a hand pressed over her heart. With the dark circles that have taken up permanent residence under her eyes, she looks like a shadow of her former self, diminished somehow.

I slide the paper into my pocket.

We close up the Harvest Moon for the rest of the day— not that anyone would notice—sending Hillard home with the entire sweet tea pie for his trouble. Then we spend what would normally be the lunch rush sweeping up glass and picking shards out from between the cushions of the booths. When Daddy arrives, he pulls each of us into a hug, one by one, then checks us over carefully for injury.

"It's just vandalism, Lyon," Mama murmurs after she's spread balm over the butterfly bandages he placed on Juniper's hand. "I didn't expect you to drop everything and rush over. Ethan could have handled this on his own."

"Of course I came," Daddy answers gruffly.

Deputy Ethan Miranda takes each of our statements separately. When I finish mine, I step into the kitchen. Mama and Gran are huddled near the box fan in the back corner, next to the dishwasher, their voices carrying more than they probably realize.

"We've had fewer sales in the past week than we normally do in a single day," Mama says, her voice weary. "With everything that's happened and now this, I'm not sure it's safe anymore. And you know the girls are worried, too, even if they don't say it."

"I know it. I had to throw out those lemon bars Linden baked because they made everyone who tasted them anxious," Gran says, a hint of worry in her tone.

"Do you think she realizes what she's doing?" Mama asks. "That she's capable of influencing how people feel?"

"It'll be a heavy burden once she does," Gran acknowledges.

"I know it's different because she's not using the diablerie," Mama says. "But I don't want her to go through something like what happened between you and Zephyrine. For her to think she's doing the right thing and then have to pay a horrible cost."

The words knock me over like a wave, not fully registering until they roll back across me, stealing my breath. Gran had used the diablerie to somehow influence Zephyrine—the one thing she always told us we must never do.

"Now, now," Gran chides. "What I did was plain hubris, thinking I knew better than everybody else about how to live their lives. Linden isn't that way."

"I'm afraid," Mama whispers. "I don't know what I'd do if we lost her again."

"That girl is stronger than you give her credit for, and so are you." Gran reaches out and gently squeezes Mama's arm.

"Well, I wish she didn't have to be strong," Mama argues. "I wish she could just be a kid."

Rowan calls my name from the dining room, and I scramble away before I'm caught eavesdropping. The concentrated flavors of fear, grief, and guilt are enough to leave me nauseous.

Mama sends us home in the Bronco while she and Gran stay to deal with the insurance company and get the window boarded up.

We've barely pulled out of the parking lot before Rowan turns to me. "What does it say?"

"What does what say?" I ask, confused.

She rolls her eyes. "That little piece of paper you pulled out of the rock and slipped into your pocket."

I take it out and pass it to her. "Do you think it's because we talked to Amos McCoy yesterday?"

Rowan lets out a low whistle. " 'You're digging your own grave,' " she reads.

"This was what was thrown through the window?" Sorrel asks, meeting my eyes in the mirror as she drives toward home. "If this is because you're asking questions about Dahlia, then it's getting too dangerous. We need to let Daddy know what's going on."

"And what exactly do we tell him?" Rowan asks. "We don't have anything other than a vague threat, and all the broken glass makes the same point."

"But does it mean we're onto something? Is Dahlia's murder really connected somehow to what happened to Elam McCoy?" Juniper asks.

"We don't know enough yet," I tell them, leaning forward in my seat. "That's why we can't give up. If we stop looking, it doesn't mean the threat goes away. It just means we won't know which direction the danger is coming from until it's too late."

What happened today at the diner proves we've gone too far to be able to give up and turn back now. I can see in Sorrel's face that she wants to argue against it, but she knows I have a point. "Then we're going to need some powerful protective magic," she concedes. "A stinging nettle rope bracelet isn't going to cut it."

"I may know of something," I say. It was the threat itself that reminded me of the spell I saw when Sissy was flipping through the pages of the diablerie. But I'm not sure I'd be brave enough to try it if I hadn't overheard what I did today. Gran might have forbidden us from using the book, but she clearly didn't always feel that way. And honestly, there isn't much I wouldn't do to protect my sisters.

Sissy asked me not to tell anyone, but it's a relief to no longer have to keep the secret. By the time we pull into the driveway at the farm, I've filled them in on what I learned about the diablerie. But when I stand in front of the little drawer in the summer kitchen, the key feels heavy in my hand.

"We don't have to do this," Sorrel says solemnly.

"Can you think of another way?" Rowan argues. "Sometimes there is no right path. There are only different paths, and you have to make a choice."

I slide the key into the lock.

We walk silently, two by two, toward the cemetery gates. The heat from the sun reflects back off the pavement, and it feels a little like I'm being baked alive.

A graveyard is a place of contradictions. Both a place of peaceful rest and strong emotion, it's a bridge between the world of the living and the world beyond. And according to the protection spell in the diablerie, the spirits of the dead can work magic on behalf of the living. If you're brave enough to ask.

"We're messing around with something we don't understand," Sorrel mutters.

"Let's get this over with," Rowan says, stepping through the gates, then looking back when she realizes I'm not following. "What is it?"

I hesitate, worried that my new propensity for being drawn toward death will take hold like it did the last time I was here, during Nora McCoy's internment. But after a long, tense moment, there's no strange buzzing. No pull.

And yet something still feels off. My gaze slides to the section of the cemetery where Nora is buried. Under the sweet gum tree is a huge rhododendron bush I've never seen before with heavy, dripping blossoms in a vibrant shade of blood red. With an uneasy gnawing in my stomach, I recall one of Gran's many plant lessons. In the language of flowers, rhododendron means *beware*.

"I don't think this was here before." I gesture toward the shrub.

"This is West Virginia. We have more rhododendrons than people," Rowan replies, unconcerned. "Let's find the grave so we can get out of here."

I walk up and down the rows with no luck. There's Homer and Hazel Shepherd, Innocent Quick, Myrtle and Clinton Garland, Wes and Kenna Gabbert, Lenora Pruitt, but all of the dates are older, the stone markers already worn.

"Maybe we're in the wrong area," Juniper suggests, scanning the horizon.

Finally, on the third pass, I spot a small metal tag on the ground, already partially overgrown with crabgrass. It says only N. G. MCCOY, but the date of death is right. I kneel and clear away the grass growing over the small marker so the name is more visible. Rowan sinks down on the ground next to me, opening her tote bag and pulling out the contents one by one: a trowel, a knife, a small muslin pouch, a bottle of Gran's dandelion wine. And the diablerie.

I open the book and flip through, but as I pass the section on the Moth-Winged Man, I notice a small, jagged edge, like pages have been torn out. I run my thumb across the remaining fringe, trying to remember if it was like this when Sissy showed it to me, but I can't recall.

"Something wrong?" Sorrel asks.

"No, everything's fine." I turn to the page for the spirit magic protection spell. It calls for dirt from a mother's grave, and like everything else in the diablerie, it starts with a little blood. "Here goes." I blow out a slow breath as I bring the knife to my finger.

"Try this." Rowan pulls the cork out of the half-full wine bottle with her teeth, takes a swig, and passes it to me. I take a long drink, letting the warm, earthy sweetness coat my tongue, then press the tip of the knife into the pad of my index finger and push until several drops of blood fall onto the ground.

"Why does it hurt so much more when you know it's coming?" I've cut my fingers dozens of times in the kitchen over the years, but it never hurt like this.

"Maybe it's because of what it is," Sorrel suggests. "Forcing your intention on the universe shouldn't be painless."

Juniper digs around in the bag and pulls out a tissue. "Here," she says as she passes it to me.

I wrap it around my finger, then take another quick drink from the bottle, before reading from the open pages of the book. "Next, we have to call the spirit." We all look at Juniper.

"This is powerful magic unlike anything I've done before." She bites her lip, unsure. "I guess let's make a circle."

We move to sit around the grave, joining hands. Juniper closes her eyes and slows her breathing until, at last, she's ready to begin. "Nora McCoy. We've come here to ask for your help. We want to find out what happened to your son Elam. Can you give us a sign if you're here with us?"

A sweet gum pod falls out of the tree above us, directly into the center of our circle. I jump and Rowan squeezes my hand. When I glance over, she's trying not to laugh at my overreaction. I squeeze back to tell her to take this seriously.

Juniper opens her eyes and nods to me. "Oh, um," I stumble. Talking to the dead is decidedly outside my comfort zone. "We've brought some homemade dandelion wine as a gesture of goodwill." According to the diablerie, it's best to offer a gift when you're asking a spirit for something.

Rowan sets a jam jar next to the grave marker, and I carefully fill it. "Someone out there doesn't want us to find the truth about what happened to my friend and to your son, and they're trying harder and harder to stop us. We'd respectfully like to ask for your protection while we search for answers."

I pause, looking to Juniper, but she shrugs. Apparently, Nora McCoy isn't the talkative type. Yet, if she really is here listening to us now, this might be my only chance to ask her about Zephyrine. After all, it was Nora's name on that note. "What secrets did you and Aunt Zephyrine uncover in your research that should have stayed buried?" I murmur, then wait, trying to be open to hearing whatever the response may be, but there's nothing.

Sorrel leans over to read the next step from where the diablerie is open on the ground in front of me. "'To the charm, add grave dirt that has been through at least one full cycle of the moon but no more than a full year.'"

I use the trowel to dig a tiny amount of the dirt from where I spilled my blood. Rowan holds open the muslin pouch so I can pour it in. Then Sorrel adds a drop of bay leaf honey to boost the power of the spell and bind it together. Next, Rowan passes the bag to Juniper, who adds a sprinkle of salt and ties it shut. We make enough so we'll each have one to keep with us, plus one to bury at the farm.

As I watch the process, with the warmth of the sun beating down on me, my eyes start to feel heavy. Everything seems to move more slowly. A bee circles the wispy white clusters of boneset blossoms growing nearby, but its flight is unnaturally slow and sluggish, like it's moving at half speed. I can barely keep my eyes open, each blink becoming longer. And longer. And . . . longer.

The dream unfolds in front of me. A woman sits in a darkened office on the lower floor of the library. She wears a black dress with a full skirt, and her hair tumbles in loose waves down her back. On the desk, a metal fountain pen and sharp-looking scissors gleam in the flickering light of a single candle. She holds a familiar book above the flame and leans forward to read.

"Zephyrine?" a woman's voice calls.

Zephyrine turns, surprised, as another woman steps into the doorway. She is tall with dark hair braided into an elegant crown on her head and green eyes that sparkle in the candlelight. Eyes I feel like I've seen before.

"Nora," Zephyrine says, closing her journal and blowing out the candle. "Sorry, I'm finishing up now. Have the scholarship donors arrived?"

"Yes, and that handsome Malcolm Spencer is asking for you."

Zephyrine moves toward the door, but Nora reaches out to stop her. "I got your note," Nora says, holding a piece of paper up between them. "But what does it mean?"

"Not here." Zephyrine grabs the paper and shoves it into her pocket, her eyes scanning the hall outside.

A hand lands on my shoulder. I open my eyes, and Rowan's face is a few inches from mine. She's shaking me, and I reach to push her hands off. "What's wrong?"

"What's wrong?" she repeats, leaning back. "You were sitting there and then you just . . . went blank."

"Sorry, I must have fallen asleep." I blink, trying to clear the languid, heavy feeling from my head.

"Uh, I don't think you were sleeping," Juniper says, her voice strange. "Linden, look down."

I glance at the ground in front of me. Scratched into the dirt in precise, narrow letters are the words *Carve the bones. Bake the bread.* The stick I must have used to write it is still in my hand, and I drop it like it's on fire.

"I knew this was a bad idea." Sorrel surges to her feet and starts pacing. "Messing with magic we don't understand is pure and utter foolishness."

"What does it mean?" Rowan asks.

"I have no idea." I shake my head. "I thought I was asleep. I dreamed about Aunt Zephyrine and Nora and the scholarship."

"Nora must be trying to tell you something," Juniper says.

"I wish I knew what it was," I murmur, rubbing a hand across my forehead, where a dull ache has bloomed.

"We'll have to figure it out later." Sorrel stops in front of me. "Unless you want to explain where we've been to Mama and Gran, we need to hurry home."

Rowan stands and stretches, then tugs at her shirt in an attempt to get air moving. "Good lord, if this heat doesn't let up, I'm going to resort to nudity."

"I think that might be a health code violation for the Harvest Moon." A deep, smoky voice trails out from the other side of a nearby mausoleum, followed by the man it belongs to, violin case in hand. "Not to mention the risk of uncomfortable sunburn at the farm."

I scramble to my feet as Hadrian moves closer, surreptitiously scuffing out the message in the dirt with the toe of my shoe.

"When I want your opinion, I'll ask for it," Rowan retorts. "Why don't you go ahead and hold your breath for me, sugar."

"Speaking of sugar, any idea why my bed was filled with Lucky Charms last night?" Hadrian asks.

"I'm not really interested in what gets your shamrocks off," Rowan replies.

"Lie," Hadrian says in a low voice, a susurrus like the gentle breeze right before a raging storm.

"What did you just say?" Rowan spins around to face him.

Hadrian goes completely still and stares back at her. "What happened to your face?" he asks, crossing his arms so the HELL tattooed across the knuckles of one hand and the BENT on the other are on prominent display.

And for maybe the first time ever, Rowan blinks first. "Some asshole sent a message through the window of the Harvest Moon this morning. I look forward to figuring out who so I can return the favor." She gestures to where the flying glass cut her.

He studies her for a long moment. Sorrel catches my eye and lifts her brows. I agree, it feels almost indecent to be watching this exchange. And it doesn't seem to be doing anything for Rowan's temperature. When she turns back to us, she's flushed.

"What are you doing out here, anyway?" Hadrian takes in the things still strewn across the ground, eyes landing on the wine bottle. "Day drinking in the cemetery?"

"Us?" Rowan glances back over her shoulder at him. "What about you? Shouldn't you be working?" She shoves the wine bottle into the bag. His eyes follow her movements, and when she stands, he looks down at the space I cleared in the grass earlier, cocking his head slightly.

"N. G. McCoy," he reads softly, mostly to himself.

My palms get sweaty, and I remind myself there's no way he can know what we've been doing. I just hope he doesn't think to mention we've been hanging around Nora McCoy's grave to Mama or Gran.

"Come on," Sorrel says. "We'd better scratch gravel."

Rowan casts one more withering look at Hadrian, bumping her shoulder into his as she passes. "Outta my way, slacker."

He shakes his head as he watches her go, then winks when he catches my eye. Very few people can pull off a wink, but Hadrian is a master. It's not at all flirtatious, which is where most people go wrong. Instead, it's like he and I are the only two people in on a joke. "She seems especially feisty today."

"Might want to start locking your doors," I tell him.

"Do you really think that would stop her?"

I wait until the others get farther away. Rowan suspects Hadrian of being the liar from Dahlia's message; maybe now is my chance to find out what he's really hiding. "You know she's convinced you're lying. Wouldn't it be easier to tell her the truth?"

His face goes tight for a moment before he puts on his usual teasing grin. "And let her win? Never."

"I know Gran wouldn't have hired you if she didn't trust you." I shake my head. "But it's not a game anymore."

The smile drops from his face. "Then that's a question for your gran."

It's clear he's not going to tell me anything else, so I turn to follow the others. "That's an unusual book you're reading. Learn anything interesting?" he calls after me.

My steps falter, and my eyes snap to his. "What are you doing out here in the cemetery, anyhow? You never said."

He shrugs a shoulder and lifts the violin case. "I like to practice out here where it's peaceful." His eyes drift back to the small metal grave marker in the grass. "Makes me feel more at home." But the taste of his words is more hunger than flavor, the yearning and longing like the pangs of an empty stomach.

I don't know if Hadrian was telling the truth, or if he followed us out to the cemetery. But what I do know is that he's hiding something. Rowan has certainly said as much enough times over the past year. I just never really thought that it was any of my business. Yet after the warning at the diner and Nora's cryptic message, something about the graveside encounter has left me unsettled enough that, when we get back to the farm that evening, I don't return the diablerie to its drawer in the summer kitchen. Instead, I stash it with the journal under the loose floorboard in my bedroom.

That night, I work up the courage to tap on Gran's door. When I push it open, she's sitting up in bed with her reading glasses on and a paperback romance novel in her hands. "Gran, can I talk to you about something?" I ask, hesitant in a way I've never been with her before.

Her eyebrows draw together in concern, and she pats the quilt next to her. "Of course, darling girl."

"I heard you and Mama talking today, in the diner," I admit. "Did you really use the diablerie to keep Zephyrine and Malcolm Spencer apart?"

She takes off her glasses and closes her eyes, pinching the bridge of her nose. "I'm sorry you found out that way. I never meant it to be a secret, but it's hard to admit something so shameful." She shakes her head and shrugs. "I know there's no excuse for what I did, but I thought if Malcolm Spencer moved on, Zephyrine could too. And in a way, I guess she did. She moved right on out of Caball Hollow."

"This is why you believe we should never do anything that could change the lives of others, isn't it?" I ask.

"I never wanted you girls to have to learn that lesson the hard way like I did." A single tear starts to roll down her cheek before she brushes it away impatiently. "I tucked the note she wrote to me in the back of the diablerie as a reminder before I locked it away for good. The cost of that kind of magic is too high. All these years later, I'm still paying the price. And there's no telling how much time we have left to make it right, neither. I realized when you went missing that it wasn't enough any longer to just wait for Zephyrine to come home."

The pieces click together, and I'm struck with a sudden realization. I had thought Hadrian meant I'd have to ask Gran why she'd hired him, but maybe he'd been saying the secret itself wasn't his to tell. "Hadrian is helping you look for her, isn't he?"

She nods. "We got to talking about his search for his brother one day, and I was impressed by how much he knew about methods and resources, so I asked him to help me find Zephyrine."

"Have you found any clues about where she might have gone?"

Gran presses her lips together and shakes her head. "Not yet, but I knew it wouldn't be easy. Zephyrine never did anything halfway. And every false lead we can eliminate brings us one step closer to the truth."

CHAPTER TWENTY-ONE

IT'S A little more than a mile to the gas station, but the humidity is so thick it sits in a haze over the road. It feels like riding my bike through a hot tub. I'm not even sure exactly what I'm hoping to find, but the note on the rock someone sent through the diner window is a pretty clear sign we're onto something. When I finally coast into the parking lot, my shirt sticks damply to my skin and my hair has grown to twice its normal size. I prop my bike up against the side of the old cement block building.

Officially known as the QuickStop, all but three of the letters on the sign out front have burned out and never been replaced, so everyone in Caball Hollow calls it the Ick. An electronic chime sounds when I push open the door, and I lift a hand in a half-hearted wave to Dreama Kinnaird, who's been a clerk here for as long as I can remember. Because of its location on the opposite side of town from the Piggly Wiggly, the selection in the gas station convenience store is more eclectic than most.

"I've got a fresh batch of boiled peanuts," Dreama offers from her stool at the checkout counter as I approach. A tinge of fennel hits my tongue. I'm making her nervous.

I shake my head, about to explain the reason I've come, but something on the bulletin board behind her catches my eye. A sheet of paper, yellowed with age, the edges curling in. I must have seen it a hundred times and never really noticed it. But there, in big, bold letters across the top, is stamped MISSING, and beneath it is the smiling photo of a young boy with dark hair. I move closer, squinting up at the poster, trying to discern any recognizable features from the poorly copied black-and-white photograph.

"That's Elam McCoy, isn't it?" I ask.

She nods. "I won't take it down until he comes home. I was here that day, you know, when Amos McCoy came in to call for help."

"You spoke to Amos McCoy on the day Elam disappeared?" My heartbeat kicks up.

"His hands were shaking so bad I had to dial 911 for him." She plays with the crucifix on her necklace, running it back and forth along the chain over her bright blue smock. "He was covered in mud, too, scratched all up from searching for Elam. It felt like it took forever for them to get here, though it couldn't have been long. Your daddy was the first one to respond. Course he was only a deputy then."

"My father was the first on the scene?" I repeat, surprised. Why hadn't he mentioned that when I asked him about the disappearance?

"Oh, yes, he was so diligent." She nods, her white hair floating around her head like a cloud. "After my shift, I went down to join the search party. He stayed out there the whole time. But then it set in to rain, a real gully washer, and they made us give up for the night."

"What were they like, the search parties?" I ask.

"I recollect it was bitter cold, dropping down to freezing overnight. The weather report said it was the fall equinox, so the days got shorter fast, but the search parties kept going back out for more than a week, sunup to sundown, lookin' for that baby. They turned the Methodist church on the corner into search headquarters, and Apollonia kept everybody fed with pans of cornbread and sawmill gravy and pots and pots of hot coffee." Dreama sighs so deeply she seems to shrink in front of me. "But it didn't matter one bit, not in the end. That poor little baby all alone out there in that great big wilderness."

I reach out to squeeze Dreama's hand before I realize what I'm doing. Her eyes focus back in on me, and she smiles sadly. "I haven't given up hope. Something tells me he's still out there. Somewhere."

"I hope you're right," I tell her, though with what I know now, my hope is in finding closure for his family. "Did Dahlia Calhoun ever come in, asking about the disappearance?"

"No, at least not during any of my shifts. So terrible what happened to that poor girl." She shakes her head, mouth turned down in distaste. "She deserved better, especially after everything she'd been through lately."

"Lately?" I knew Dahlia's family history had some dark spots, like her mother's overdose, but this is the first I've heard about more recent troubles. "What do you mean?"

"Oh, maybe I shouldn't speak on it," she demurs, then leans forward on her stool and lowers her voice. "She came in once, a while back, to buy one of those phones." She gestures toward a rack of prepaid phones near the counter. "But she had tears just a-streaming down her face the entire time. I swear, if she lay down, she woulda drowned. It was shortly after her grandmother's death, so I tried to console her, but then the whole sordid tale poured out. Apparently they'd had a family phone plan in Parlee's name, and when Dahlia went to change it, they denied her. Cut 'er service clean off. Turns out that good-for-nothing father of hers had been opening fraudulent accounts in her name for years and had completely ruined her credit."

"That's awful," I agree. Could this be the reason Dahlia had been in contact with her father recently? But why? It's not like he could undo the damage to her credit if he'd even be willing to try. He hadn't bothered to come to his own daughter's funeral, after all. But if she'd confronted him about it, could that be motive for murder?

Dreama pats my hand where it sits on top of hers. "You know, your aunt was the first one to volunteer the day Elam disappeared. Showed up here not long after your daddy, offering to help. Her and Vivian Spencer, back when those two were thick as thieves. Your family did everything they could to help during that awful time, and I don't believe all the things everyone is saying about you now."

I'm saved from trying to formulate a coherent response by three men in their twenties entering the shop. There's a restless, eager sort of energy about them that Dreama must pick up on too, because her posture gets stiffer and her eyes sharper.

One heads for the snack aisle and loads up with several bags of chips and beef jerky. The other two grab drinks out of the refrigerator case.

"You fellas headed out on a road trip or somethin'?" Dreama asks.

"Huntin' trip, more like," says the one with brown hair curling around the collar of his camo shirt advertising beer. "A bunch of us are going out to the National Forest, see if we can get rid of the Moth-Winged Man once and for all."

"And what good are you supposing that'll do?" Dreama asks. "Can't stop a tornado by getting rid of the warning siren."

"Hey, you're that girl." The second guy dumps his snack selections onto the counter next to the register, and I get a better look at him. It's the assistant football coach, Hammond, Cole called him, from the night we discovered Dahlia. "You're the one who found the body in the woods."

There's something familiar about him now that I didn't see that night. He can't be more than a handful of years older than the guys on the team, with closely cropped brown hair, deep-set eyes, and the beginnings of a beard. Maybe it's being back at the Ick with the same fizzy feeling that might be fear in my blood, but I'm almost positive he was here with Bryson last summer before we all went out to the Forest.

"I recognize you, too," I blurt out, surprised. "You were there that night, after the festival last year."

"You must be confused," he asserts, a tick in his jaw.

"Wait, I heard about you," the third guy chimes in, pointing at me. "You're the witch."

An uncomfortable silence fills the small store as all the attention settles heavily on me. Dreama shifts on her stool and clears her throat. "Did y'all see these ones are buy one, get one free?" She points to some energy drinks, and the men's gazes shift to the refrigerator case.

I use the distraction to slip out the door, nearly running into a dirty white pickup parked out front. For a moment, my feet stop, images of that day outside the cemetery when a white pickup nearly ran me over playing in my head. Could it be the same truck? I glance over my shoulder.

Here in the parking lot isn't the only place I remember seeing Coach Hammond. He was at the diner the day Dahlia arrived in town. He was wearing his Caball Hollow High School polo shirt and held the door open for her. Did they know each other?

I ditch my bike to cut across the footpath up the hill where their truck can't follow. A tingle of fear skitters down my neck, and I squeeze the grave dirt charm in my pocket for reassurance. I'm halfway to town when the sound of gravel crunching and brakes squeaking has me whirling around.

"Hey!" Rowan leans out the window of the farm truck, one arm draped over the driver-side door as she idles in the dirt road. "Fancy meeting you here."

Despite the fact that I'm looking right at her, she honks the horn.

I jump. I always jump. "Rowan!"

"Come on, I'll give you a lift." She shoves her sunglasses up on her head and grins at me.

"What's got you in such a chipper mood?" I grumble as I move toward the truck.

"I have an excellent plan for a prank," she tells me. "Hadrian will hate it."

I roll my eyes at her. When my fingers touch the passenger-side door handle, Rowan hits the horn again, then laughs when I nearly come out of my skin.

"What is wrong with you?" I climb in and buckle my seat belt. "As if we need to give people any more reason to think we're strange."

"Oh, please." She pulls her sunglasses out of her hair and slides them on. "There's not a soul for miles."

"I wouldn't be too sure about that. I'm starting to think that there are eyes everywhere. And you might be right about the kind of secrets Hadrian is hiding," I tell her. "Or maybe it's that he seems a little too interested in what secrets we might be."

She shakes her head slowly without taking her eyes off the road. "Like I've been saying, he's trouble."

"Trouble? When have you ever stayed away from trouble?"

"Well, there's a first time for everything, now, isn't there?" She sticks her tongue out at me as she flips on the blinker and turns onto the road toward town. "Where are you headed this early in the morning, anyhow?"

"To see Daddy."

Rowan drives with one finger hooked through the bottom of the steering wheel, her left foot up on the seat, knee pressed against the door as I fill her in on what I learned from Dreama Kinnaird.

"Elam went missing on the fall equinox. That's a liminal day, like the solstice," I tell her.

"What do you think it means?"

"I wish I knew." I let out a long breath. "But there's too many coincidences for everything not to be connected."

Rowan drops me off and heads to the hardware store. When I reach for the handle of the front door, a quick whoop and chirp of a siren splits the thick air, accompanied by a bright flash of blue light. The official greeting of the Eldritch County Sheriff's Department. I turn to see Daddy's Suburban pull up, the street underneath it wavy in the heat, and retrace my steps to meet him.

"Dadgum, girl, it's hotter than the hinges on the gates of hell out here today," he calls out the open window. "Hop in before you melt."

I pull open the passenger door, taking a moment to inspect him before I climb up. He looks drawn, a roll of antacids sits in the cup holder next to a coffee cup, and the circles under his eyes are so dark they're nearly purple, but the wide grin he gives me is the same as it always is.

"You must have inherited some of your gran's perfect timing. I just got back," he says as he checks his mirrors and pulls away from the curb. "No bike today?"

"I left it at the Ick earlier. Where were you?" I prod, despite knowing he won't answer. "Is there a new lead in Dahlia's case?"

"What did I tell you about playing investigator?" he chides, but his voice is gentle. "Sergeant Markin is under the impression you might be working on a project for the Moth Queen scholarship."

"Why didn't you tell me you were first on the scene of Elam McCoy's disappearance?" I ask, twisting in the seat so I can face him.

He doesn't say anything for a long time, looking intently out the windshield instead. "Because I screwed up." His throat clenches as he swallows hard. I freeze, startled by the revelation and afraid that if he notices, he'll stop talking.

He blows out a long breath. "Spencer and I were the only two on duty that day. He and Vivian had just gotten some devastating news about their son. I told him to go home, to mourn, to be with his wife. But it wasn't my call to make. I was the senior officer only because I had a couple weeks' seniority. And when the call came in . . ." He pauses, swallows, still looking straight ahead. "If I hadn't been covering two patrols, I would have been there sooner." He shakes his head. "Maybe I could have found him before the rain hit." The earthy flavor of deep-rooted regret coats his words.

"You couldn't have known," I offer quietly.

"There's not a day goes by I don't think about it." He lets out a low sigh and rubs a hand against his chest, just over his badge. "It destroyed his family."

The way people treated Amos McCoy after the worst day of his life makes my blood go hot. "How can people live with themselves when they spread the most vile awful gossip with no evidence whatsoever?" My words come out more vehemently than I intend, and Daddy looks at me for the first time since we started this conversation, sympathy in his eyes and heartache on my tongue.

"Tragedy brings out the truth in people, Linden. There are those in this world who will lift up and support people who are hurting, and there are those who will gleefully tear them down. That's the hardest part of this job, to see the worst of people."

It's my turn to look away, leaning my head against the window, a swirling mess of hurt and sadness. And an anger inside me growing ever hotter because it isn't only me these rumors harm; it's my family.

"Anyone giving you any more trouble?" Daddy asks, studying my face.

"Nothing like the rock through the window." I shrug. "But . . . I was at the Ick and ran into the assistant football coach from the night we found Dahlia." I swallow hard, pushing back the memories.

"Did he say something to you?"

"Not really," I admit, replaying the conversation in my mind. "But I remembered seeing him before. I think Dahlia might have known him. Maybe he met up with her at the field house. I mean, why was he there so late that night, anyhow?"

"Linden, I know how to run an investigation. Trust me to handle it. I want you to be careful." He waits for me to meet his eyes so he can be sure I'm listening. "People are scared, and scared people are dangerous people. You don't need to be getting more mixed up in this."

I nod. I'll be careful, but I'm no longer naive enough to think that means bad things won't happen.

"I can't get into the particulars of why, but Parker Hammond was at the field house that night because he is currently responsible for washing the team's laundry." Daddy reaches to shift the truck into drive. "Now, let's go pick up your bike."

We pass by the diner on the way to the Ick, the memory of the day Dahlia arrived back in town fresh in my mind. She made a special point of coming into the Harvest Moon when she got to town, not even to eat, just to reminisce about the time we spent at her grandmother's house. Was it her way of trying to reconnect after a rift grown too long? Was she missing the grandmother she'd lost? Or was she trying to tell me something?

I sit up straighter in my seat. Could that be why she wrote my name in the candle smoke? Not because of something she thought I'd seen last summer, but because she'd already told me exactly where to look. What if she'd hidden the answer at her grandmother's house?

CHAPTER TWENTY-TWO

AFTER DADDY drops me off at the farm, I text Cole about my theory. His response this time is almost immediate but predictable: *Shed*.

When I get there, he's pulling the cover off of the Triumph. "Wait, we're not getting on that, are we?" I ask as I instinctively grab the helmet he pushes into my hands.

"Quick riding lesson: hold on to me and don't let go." He shoots me a wicked grin, and I know, without a doubt, I'm getting on the bike.

Straddling the motorcycle, he pulls on his own helmet, then jumps on the kick-starter. I watch, wide-eyed. When I don't move, he reaches back and pats the tiny space left behind him. There's really no room for two. My entire body is going to be pressed up against him. I swallow, my throat gone suddenly dry, then buckle my helmet and get on.

The bike roars, and I flinch, clutching at his shirt. Cole reaches down and takes my hands, pulling until my arms wrap around his middle. I lean my head against his back and then we're flying.

We avoid the roads when we can, riding along dirt paths and hunting trails until we come to a stop in the woods down the street from where Parlee Wilkerson lived. It's a small house that was in her family for generations but has been sitting empty since she passed.

Mrs. Wilkerson took great pride in the flower beds out front, filling them with foxgloves and delphiniums and poppies, but they're all overgrown now, choked out by jimsonweed and finger grass.

"Careful," Cole murmurs as I step up on the neglected front porch.

The doorknob turns easily in my hand, but the door is swollen tight from the humidity. "Can you try to force it?" I ask, moving back to give him space. But my eye catches on something familiar. Above the doorframe is a round medallion with a clover carved in the center, just like the one at the McCoy house.

"Wait." I catch his arm. "Give me a boost?"

He braces himself against the wall and helps me step up onto his thigh. I stretch and brush my fingers against the clover. My skin prickles hot and cold as everything seems to shift sideways. Cole's arms clamp around me, and he shouts something, but it all feels slower and muffled, like we're moving through water. I yank my hand away like the carved wood is a hot stove. I know this feeling, like reality shifts and time moves differently. It's the Bone Tree.

"Carve the bones," I whisper, thinking back to the words scratched into the dirt next to Nora McCoy's grave.

"What the hell was that?" Cole sets me carefully on my feet.

"You have one of these above your door, too," I tell him. "What does it mean?"

Cole shrugs, watching me like he's ready to catch me if I pass out. "It's been there since the house was built. All the original houses have them. That's why the Caball Hollow historical society uses the clover as their logo. I think it's an old protection symbol or something."

I look up at the carving again. Was it some old superstition the town founders brought over with them from their homeland? Or was it meant to protect them from something much more local? Something connected to the Bone Tree?

"Do you still want to go in?" Cole asks.

I nod and he puts a shoulder to the door, popping it free. When we step inside, the only light is the late-afternoon sun that shines around the edges of the thick drapes and illuminates clouds of dust swirling in the air.

I flick the switch on the wall up and down, but nothing happens.

Cole takes out his phone and switches on the flashlight, and my hope deflates. Dahlia's aunt, Nettie Hinkle, must have already cleared out the house. All that remains is a floral sofa with crocheted doilies on the arms to cover the worn-out places, a table with one broken leg, a lamp with no shade.

The house is one story, made up of a front room that opens to a small dining room and kitchen, with a laundry room and bathroom tacked on the back. A short hall off to the right leads to two small bedrooms. We start our search in Dahlia's old room. I run my fingers along the seams of the hardwood floor, checking for loose boards, while Cole looks inside the vents and behind the trim. But despite our best efforts, we turn up nothing.

By the time we reach the kitchen, the disappointment feels like a hot pit in my stomach. Even the refrigerator is gone. The house is airless and close, and I'm coated in sweat and dust. I wipe the perspiration from my forehead with the inside of my arm because my hands feel coated with grime.

"I really thought there would be something here." I look over at Cole. A smile tugs at the corners of his mouth, and he drops his head. "Are you laughing at me again, Cole Spencer?"

"You just smeared dirt all over your face," he says, lifting the hem of his shirt to wipe my cheek. It's Cole's nature to take care of people, but as he stands there with his shirt pulled up, inches between his skin and mine, I lose my breath.

I try to distract myself with thoughts of the last time I was in this kitchen, at the stove with Dahlia and Mrs. Wilkerson, laughing at her old stories. And I remember then what Dahlia said at the festival, how we'd reminisced about cinnamon apple moonshine cake.

"Moonshine," I whisper, pulling away from Cole and dropping to my knees in front of the cupboard under the sink. All the way at the back is a hook where a dish brush still hangs, long forgotten. I pull it to the left and a false panel slides open. A zing of anticipation flashes through me.

Cole passes me his phone, and I shine the light inside. There's something there, at the bottom. I reach in as far as I can and pull it out.

It's an old green metal lunch box. I pass Cole back the phone and flip the latch. Inside is one of those cheap, disposable pay-as-you-go phones from the Ick. Why would Dahlia hide this? I hold the power button down, and miraculously it turns on. There are no calls in the log or saved contacts, but there are a few text messages, all from the same number:

I can help you

I can protect you

I'm the only one who can

My heartbeat kicks up. If they were about her research into Elam McCoy's disappearance, who could have sent them? Or had Dahlia been mixed up in something else? The messages promise help and safety but feel increasingly ominous. Could they be from her killer?

"There's more in there." Cole points the light into the box. "Maybe the missing interview transcript?"

I set Dahlia's phone on the floor and pull out the papers stuffed at the bottom. But when I unfold them, my blood flashes hot, then turns to ice. They're from the diablerie. The torn-out pages. Why would Dahlia have these?

The first one is about the power of the Bone Tree, and handwriting that matches Zephyrine's journal entries is scribbled in the margins. Some of the notes have been crossed out, arrows sketched in to point to a new thought. It looks like my notebooks when I'm testing new recipes, switching out ingredients and adjusting measurements.

"What is this?" I whisper, working to decipher the notes.

I hear the front door creak open just on the other side of the wall next to me a second before a voice calls out, "Eldritch County Sheriff's Department."

My head snaps up, but Cole is faster. He hooks an arm around my waist, pulling me into the laundry room and then the tiny closet inside as I hurriedly shove the papers into my pocket.

"It's Ethan," I whisper, and almost can't hear myself over the galloping of my heartbeat. He can't find us here.

With the two of us pressed together in the dark, stifling closet, it's like an oven, but adrenaline makes me shiver. Cole wraps both arms around me, pulling me against him to keep me still.

I can hear Ethan move through the house, clearing it room by room. His radio crackles to life, and a voice on the other end squawks something I can't understand.

"Responding to a suspicious activity call," Ethan answers. "Neighbor across the river saw a couple of kids running this way through the woods."

His footsteps come closer—he must be in the dining room now—and I stop breathing. Cole's body goes rigid behind me.

"It's probably nothing, but when I heard the address, I thought I'd better check. Never can be too careful with this case." Ethan pauses, listening to whoever is on the other end. "Yeah, we're checking into other suspicious deaths where items not belonging to the victim were found near the body. Maybe the necklace is some sort of calling card."

His footsteps move in the other direction, down the back hall toward the bedrooms and away from our hiding spot. At least for now. Ethan may be new, but he's diligent. He won't stop until he's searched every inch of the house.

"When he gets to Dahlia's room, we run for the door," Cole whispers against my ear. "Put this on." He presses something into my hand. A knit hat. It sounds like torture in this heat, but it's better than being identified.

Slowly, careful not to make any noise, Cole pulls an old, moth-eaten jacket from a hanger in the closet and puts it on, pulling the hood down low, while I tuck my hair up inside the hat. It's like playing Twister inside a sardine can.

When Ethan's footsteps reach the far end of the house, we make a run for it, trying to move as quickly and quietly as possible. Cole pushes me in front of him as we round the corner into the living room, using his larger frame to block me from Ethan's line of sight.

The front door is wide open, and I break into a sprint.

"Hey!" Ethan shouts. "Stop!"

I hear him thundering down the hall behind us as I burst through the front door. Without pausing to take the stairs, I leap off the front porch and land hard. Cole hits the ground beside me seconds later and grabs my hand, pulling me toward the woods.

"Go," I yell to Cole once we're in the trees, and he knows what I mean. He nods once, then takes off, his longer legs eating up the distance.

I can hear Ethan racing through the trees behind me. We had the element of surprise, and twenty pounds or so of gear weighs him down, but he's not giving up.

I hear the growl of an engine and push myself to run even faster as Cole's motorcycle cuts through the trees in front of me. When he gets close, Cole drops a foot to the ground and spins the bike around. I jump on behind him, and we take off.

When we hit the deer path, I slump against Cole in relief. Ethan would have to race back to the house and get his patrol car to even have a prayer of catching us now.

But just as I start to breathe easy, I realize I left Dahlia's phone sitting in the middle of the kitchen floor.

We curl our way around the mountains like smoke, snaking up and down hills, zigzagging along switchbacks. After a while, the trees and grass and mountains alongside us run together like watercolors. And when I'm not listening for the distant sound of sirens, I can admit it's truly breathtaking. With the wind in our faces, not even summer's oppressive heat can catch us.

Cole turns onto a dirt two-track up on the hill, and we rumble down the road a ways until he stops the bike in a wide-open meadow.

"That was intense." I pull off my helmet, then flop down into the grass, my heart still racing from our narrow escape.

He fiddles with something on the bike, and I watch the muscles of his back undulate under his sweat-dampened shirt.

"I remembered something else," I tell him, finding the words easier while his attention is elsewhere. "From last summer." I swallow as he stills but doesn't turn. "I think I saw that assistant coach, Hammond, with Bryson when we all met up to go to the Forest. But why would he have been there?"

The last time I spoke to Dahlia, she'd alluded to the possibility there was someone else there the night I went missing. Maybe this is what she'd meant.

"There was a rumor last season that Parker Hammond had been reprimanded for fraternizing with some of the players," he says over his shoulder. "He's Bryson's cousin, and he knew a few of the other guys from when he played for Mud River, two or three years back. Apparently he wasn't keeping what the athletic director considered a professional distance."

"So that's why he's doing the team's laundry. It's some kind of punishment. But if he was hanging out with the players, it's possible he knew Dahlia," I suggest.

Cole straightens, turning to face me as he realizes what I'm implying. "Sure, but lots of people knew her. It doesn't mean he killed her."

"It would have been quite a scandal if the town found out an employee of the school district was there that night. Maybe he was paying for her silence."

"She isn't the only one who would have seen him there," Cole objects. "And to be real honest, I don't think anyone wants to keep a crappy assistant coaching job in Caball Hollow that badly."

I agree with his reasoning, but there's still something about Hammond that makes me uneasy.

Now that my heart rate is approaching normal, I glance around at what appears to be the middle of nowhere. "Is this where you always run off to on that thing?" I ask, gesturing toward the motorcycle. "Why here?"

Cole lies down next to me. "Give it a second." He looks to the horizon as the sun dips behind the mountains.

When the bottom of the field fills with shadows, I spot the first one. A brief prick of light against the darkness. Another one flashes a few feet away. Then we're surrounded by blinking lights, what seems like hundreds of them, flashing in unison like a synchronized dance.

I turn to Cole and find his eyes already on me. "Fireflies," I gasp, falling hard under their spell. They flicker around us as stars begin to appear in the darkening sky.

"Cole," I whisper as his fingers find mine and the nocturnal chorus of crickets and frogs takes over from their daytime counterparts, the birds and cicadas. "Thank you."

His eyes melt into golden pools as he tucks a strand of hair behind my ear, setting tingles skittering across my skin. He's so beautiful it makes my chest ache. I don't remember leaning in, but we're so close I can feel his soft exhale brush against my lips.

"You have no idea how much I've missed you," he whispers.

I erase what little distance remains between us. "Oh, but I do," I murmur against his lips. It's barely a peck, but it tastes like belonging, like peace, sweet and gentle as vanilla sugar. I pull away to look at him. He makes a sound of protest in his throat and buries his fingers in my hair, pulling me back to his mouth.

If the first kiss was a sweet spark, this is a forging fire. A crucible, molten and caramelizing. Then I forget all about the fireflies and stars, except the ones blazing beneath my skin.

When I get home, I push open the door to my room, only to find Juniper crouched on the floor, the old hooked tapestry rug folded over and the loose floorboard underneath set aside.

"Juniper!" I check that the hallway is clear, then firmly close the door behind me. "What are you *doing*?"

"I wanted to take another look at that graveyard spell," she whispers. "I still can't figure out how the connection between you and the spirit world was so strong, even accounting for the blood." She flips through the diablerie, shaking her head.

"Wait until you see this." I kneel beside her and unfold the pages I found hidden at Parlee Wilkerson's house. "Dahlia had these stashed."

"How did she get pages from a book Gran has kept locked away since before we were born?"

"Maybe Zephyrine took them." I consider out loud. "Those are her notes. They could have gotten mixed in with the Moth Queen scholarship project somehow. Or maybe she gave them to Nora for safekeeping, then Wyatt McCoy might have passed them along to Dahlia when she came around asking questions about the Moth-Winged Man." I push my hands into my hair. It's a theory, but one I have no way to prove.

Juniper reaches for the papers just as the bedroom door flies open, and we both jump. Rowan marches in, tugging Sorrel along behind her.

"Whispering behind a closed door is a surefire way to make people suspicious in this house," Rowan says. "Have I taught you nothing?"

"What's got you so ornery?" I jump up to shut the door.

"I found something." She pulls some papers out from under her shirt and passes them to me.

It only takes a moment for me to realize what they are. "This is the missing transcript from Dahlia's interview with Wyatt McCoy. Where did you find it?" I ask, stunned.

"Hadrian's room," she answers with a lift of her eyebrows.

"You were snooping in his room?" Juniper asks, quick to jump to the defense of anyone she feels has been wronged.

"What do you think all the ridiculous pranks have been about all this time?" Rowan folds her arms. "It's a hell of a lot easier to create an overt reason for being somewhere than to make it look as though you've never been there at all. I go in, look around, then set up some childish trick as a diversion."

"You're an evil genius," I tell her, only half paying attention as I scan the pages.

"I only use my powers for good."

"Based on your own unique definition of 'good,'" Juniper argues.

"Doesn't everyone?" Rowan shoots back.

"If you've been searching his room every time, how come it's taken you so long to find this?" Sorrel asks.

"It was underneath the lining of his violin case. I realized after seeing him with it at the cemetery that I hadn't checked there in a while."

"You don't really believe Hadrian had something to do with Dahlia's death, do you? He didn't even know her," Juniper says.

"Maybe he did know her," I say. "He could have met her somewhere else, like up in Rawbone. Her ex-boyfriend lived there, maybe they knew some of the same people." I warm to my theory as the dots start to line up. "And Amos McCoy told us that his son Wyatt was taken away by his mother when he was young. How many people could know about the existence of this interview?" I wave the papers. "But the person who gave it certainly would. What if Hadrian *is* Wyatt McCoy?"

"Holy shit," Rowan breathes as her eyes go wide.

"Maybe he said something that he didn't want to get out," I continue. "Or maybe he knew Dahlia was getting closer to the truth about what happened."

"I just don't believe Wyatt McCoy could have been involved in his own brother's murder. He was just a kid," Juniper protests.

"We know Amos McCoy suspected him. Maybe it was an accident and then he covered it up," I suggest.

But when I read the transcript, it's not the damning evidence of Wyatt McCoy's guilt that I thought it might be.

Dahlia: Take me back to the beginning of that day, did anything unusual happen?

Wyatt: Unusual, no. (long breath) We fought over a stupid cereal box prize. That's what I remember the most. The last day I spent with my brother, and I was furious that he got the stupid little toy badge instead of me. He wore it fishing that day, and it made me so mad. I can still picture it like it was yesterday. It said Deputy Crunch (short chuckle), so ridiculous.

Dahlia: You were the last person to see Elam. What happened while your dad was fishing?

Wyatt: I didn't want him following me around like he always did.

Dahlia: What did you do?

Wyatt: I didn't mean to. (loud sniffle) I didn't mean to leave him all alone. I just wanted to play by myself. (throat clears) It's my fault. I told him to go away. I was his big brother. I was supposed to be watching him.

Dahlia: You were a child.

Wyatt: Yeah, well, so was he.

"This doesn't sound like a person covering up his brother's murder," I say. "And definitely not someone who would kill again to keep it hidden, not with the amount of guilt he clearly feels about what happened to Elam."

Rowan exhales, barely loud enough for me to hear, but her relief is strong enough to taste. "So then, why would someone take it? And why did Hadrian have it?"

"If Hadrian is Wyatt, maybe he didn't want his real identity uncovered and connected with Dahlia after she was murdered," I tell them, folding the transcript pages.

"But why the secrecy?" Rowan asks. "Why sneak into town under a fake name?"

"I mean, think about it," Juniper says. "For his entire life, he's been the brother of the boy who disappeared. Can you imagine coming home to discover that the worst day of your life has become an urban legend kids use to scare each other?"

She's right, and her words sting. I'm ashamed I was ever part of something that brought Elam McCoy's family pain, that I never even took the time to learn the truth.

"Or maybe he's doing exactly what we are," I say. "Trying to find his brother's killer."

"So now what do we do?" Juniper asks. "Do we confront Hadrian about this? Ask him directly if he's Wyatt and have Rowan tell if he's lying?"

"Well, we can't for a few days," Rowan says. "Gran sent him up to Mud River to sell some sheep at the livestock auction. That's how I had time to find this." She waves a hand at the transcript.

"In the meantime, we need to talk about Dahlia." I fill them in on the hidden phone and the strange texts on it.

"Dahlia's father ruined her credit, so student loans would be near impossible, especially with no family who could cosign."

"Yeah, her mother and grandmother are both dead, and Mr. and Mrs. Hinkle are barely scraping by with all his medical bills," Sorrel agrees.

"But Mrs. Hinkle told me that Dahlia had figured out her money problems," I tell them. "What if Dahlia had resorted to alternative means? If she had discovered something about Elam's disappearance, she could have used it to blackmail someone."

"Would she really be willing to risk her life to go to college?" Rowan asks.

"She wanted to get out of this town more than anything in the world," I answer. "Who knows what lengths someone might go to if they're desperate enough."

"Wait," Sorrel says, looking pensive. "Did it say Elam had a Deputy Crunch badge the day he went missing?"

I skim the transcript again to check. "Yeah, why?"

"Linden." She grabs my arm, her gaze intense. "The night after you disappeared, you were in the bathtub, and I was putting away your things. I saw something in the bag from the hospital, and I asked you what it was. Do you remember?"

I think back to what I've recovered from that night. In my distraction, I'd thought she'd spotted the shine of my necklace in the bag. But the scar on my neck is proof enough that it was ripped away somewhere in the Forest, not tucked into a pocket to be forgotten. "I didn't see it."

"It was a Deputy Crunch badge. I'm sure of it."

My stomach drops. Could Elam's badge somehow have ended up in my possession, like my necklace had with Dahlia? I throw open the closet door and dig through everything on the floor, smearing my hand with dirt from a pair of boots I don't remember wearing, until I reach the very back of the closet. But there's nothing here.

"It's gone," I tell the others over my shoulder.

Sorrel drops down next to me, and we go through everything again, but the plastic bag from the hospital is nowhere to be found.

August

➤➤ Red Sturgeon Moon ◄◄

When the sturgeon in the river are plentiful, unavoidable truths rise to the surface. The sultry fever of late summer casts a red haze. It is a time to prepare for future hardships, difficult lessons, and important endings as what we've sown begins to bear fruit. On the cusp of transformation, we can never go back. The only way forward is through.

➤➤ In Season ◄◄

Garden: apples, blueberries, broccoli, cantaloupes, cauliflower, celery, honey, garlic, greens, onions, pears, peas, peppers, plums, sweet corn, turnips, watermelon

Forage: crab apples, hazelnuts, elderberries, mint, dandelion, huckleberries, hedgehog mushrooms, muscadine grapes, pawpaws

➤➤ Elderberry Soothers to ◄◄ Ward Off Illness and Ill Will

Gently simmer water, a pinch of lemon zest, a dash of lemon juice, a good amount of elderberries, and a touch of marshmallow root. Strain out solids and discard. Add honey to taste. Bring to a gentle boil and watch closely until molten, then pour into molds. Cool until set and use at the first sign of irritation.

The salt under our mountains is the same as the salt within us. Our blood, our sweat, our tears, even the water of our wombs, a cycle ever connecting us back to this land as it is reborn forever within us and through us. And thus, wherever we go, we will always be home.

—*Eustacia James, 1814*

CHAPTER TWENTY-THREE

NOTHING GOOD comes from a phone call before dawn. When the old kitchen phone blares to life well before the rooster crows, I break into a cold sweat. Like a knife stuck in the floorboards, this feels like trouble coming.

"Oh, god, no," Mama cries out a moment later.

We race to the Harvest Moon, where police cars line the street. Deputy Ethan Miranda stands beside the back door, phone pressed to his ear. He grabs my arm as I pass, and for a moment, I think he's recognized me from Parlee Wilkerson's house. Only instead of anger, it's sympathy I taste. "It's bad," he warns, his expression wary.

But when I step inside, it's so much worse than bad. I can't take it in all at once. Instead I see it in bursts, like the flash of a camera. Our commercial-sized bags of flour and sugar from the storeroom lie empty in a corner, the kitchen now coated in white powder like a snowstorm ripped through. Dozens and dozens of eggs are smashed all over the floor, the counters, the shelves; they're splattered against the walls, and yellow yolk runs down the fronts of the ovens. The doors of the refrigerators and freezers all hang open. Everything inside will need to be thrown out. Plates and glasses lie in shattered fragments. Entire drawers have been pulled out and overturned.

"Why would someone do this?" Juniper asks in a stunned whisper. But we all know the answer.

Gran stands with Daddy next to the prep counter. "How'd they get in?" she asks.

His jaw clenches and releases before he answers. "Pried the plywood off the front window. Looks like they were more interested in vandalism than burglary, but let me know if anything is missing."

I make my way, around deputies taking notes and photos, into the dining room. The broken window hangs open like a gaping maw. Our large four-pot coffee maker lies smashed on the floor behind the counter, grounds scattered around it. The fabric of several booths was sliced open with knives from the kitchen, one still sticking straight up from where it was stabbed into a cushion. Whoever did this was intent on inflicting maximum damage.

Nowhere is the hatred that drove the actions of the vandals more evident than on the dining room wall, where dripping letters are written in blood from a slab of beef left to rot on the floor: *WITCHES BURN*.

They've left an indelible mark in their wake, a stain on all the memories everywhere that made this place as much our home as the farm. There is where I learned to make a piecrust, my hands almost too small to hold the rolling pin, now covered in broken glass. And that booth, cut open and spilling out stuffing, is where Daddy sat the first time he laid eyes on Mama. Over there, along the doorframe of the pantry, is the record of our heights over the years from the time we could each stand, now smeared and defiled.

Mama moves around the diner, pausing now and then to pick up a piece of broken plate or the ripped-out page of a cookbook, tears rolling down her cheeks.

When the deputies finish gathering evidence, Daddy has them board up the broken window again before they leave. "Fat lot of good it did last time," Gran mutters under her breath. She sees me watching her and gives me a small, sad smile.

Mama starts crying again. "With business so slow lately, we won't be able to afford the mortgage payment and the insurance deductible, let alone replace all the food and equipment they've destroyed." She shakes her head in disbelief as the burnt taste of hopelessness sticks to the roof of my mouth.

I walk outside and lean against the wall. Closing my eyes and letting my head fall back against the bricks, I take a few deep breaths to try and cleanse all the powerful, unpleasant emotions filling my mouth and roiling my stomach.

"Well, I sure am disappointed to see this."

My eyes fly open to see Hillard Been looking through the open front door at the destruction of the Harvest Moon.

"Seems like you're about the only one in town who is. No one else even comes in anymore, Mr. Been," I tell him, too worn out to be anything but blunt.

"I'm sure that's not true," he says.

"How can you say that? You sit in that empty dining room every single day. Even Buck Garland stopped coming with you," I argue, pushing off the wall and gesturing widely toward the rest of the town.

"Well, now, I can't speak for everyone, but Buck stopped coming in on account of this being a difficult time for him."

"What do you mean?" I ask, my anger and grief ebbing a bit as something in his tone tells me to pay close attention.

"He don't like to speak on it, what with all the busybodies, but I think he'd want me to set your mind at ease." He drops his chin to give me a long look over the top of his glasses. "With the understanding that you'll keep it under your hat, of course." He waits for me to nod before he continues. "The last time the Moth-Winged Man made an appearance in Caball Hollow was when Buck's brother disappeared."

All the puzzle pieces slide around, rearranging to create a very different picture.

"Buck is Wyatt McCoy," I breathe.

"You didn't think his birth certificate said Buck, now, did ya?" He chuckles. "I reckon that nickname is owing to his energetic disposition."

"But what about his last name?" I ask.

"Ah." Hillard nods. "Garland was his mother's name. They changed it back when his brother's disappearance was still on the news all over the state. Kids can be cruel, as I'm sure you know."

"Why come back to Caball Hollow at all?" I ask.

"His mother asked him to." Hillard slides his hands into his pockets and leans back on his heels. "She was dying and worried about Wyatt being alone, so she wanted him to try to mend fences with his father. He applied for the post office job about six months ago to reassure her, but he hasn't worked up the courage to speak to ol' Amos yet. It's a hard thing, I imagine."

"Linden!" Someone calls my name, and I turn to see Cole getting out of his Jeep where it's parked on the side street. He crosses the distance in a few long strides, cupping my face in his hands. "Are you all right?" His eyes scan me, the taste of his concern so strong it overwhelms me for a moment.

"Someone destroyed the diner last night." My voice hitches, stumbling over the words.

"I saw the flashing lights and my heart stopped." He drops his hands from my face to pull me tightly into him as the passenger door of his car opens and Mayor Spencer steps out, slipping his cell phone into his pocket and rubbing his temple. He's looking a bit drawn, mouth tight and face pale.

"Now, this is a surprise," Mr. Spencer says as he reaches us, with a small smile that doesn't quite erase the strain from his eyes. "It's good to see you two reconnecting." He pats Cole on the back as he passes us to step into the Harvest Moon, and I watch as he shakes Daddy's hand, then gives Mama a hug.

"Is your father feeling poorly?" I ask Cole.

"Dahlia's murder and everything, it's getting to him. He

hasn't been sleeping much lately, so I took him to see his doctor this morning. He'll be fine once this is all over."

I nod, thinking of the strain my own parents have been under lately.

"Well, I'll leave you to it," Hillard announces from behind me. I had forgotten he was even here. "Let me know when y'all reopen."

He ambles down the sidewalk toward the Pub and Grub, leaving me with more questions than answers in the wake of his revelation. If Buck is Wyatt, then who is Hadrian, and why did he have those transcripts? Was I seeing what I wanted to, making connections that weren't there?

"So this is what Caball Hollow has become," says Cole, shaking his head in disgust as he takes in the damage. He turns back to me with a concerned look. "Has anyone bothered you out at the farm?"

"Nothing like this." I hesitate, thinking of the missing hospital bag. "But there was something strange." I tell him about finding the missing transcript in Hadrian's room and the toy badge that disappeared from my room. His eyebrows draw down while he listens, color blooming high on his cheeks.

"Someone was in your house?" Cole asks, voice low and carefully controlled.

Before I have a chance to answer, his dad steps out of the Harvest Moon and hooks an arm around his shoulders.

"I'm afraid I need to get to work," Mayor Spencer says. "But I told your parents to let me know if there is anything I can do to help, and that goes for you too, Linden."

"Thank you, Mayor Spencer," I tell him as he heads for the Jeep.

"Promise me you'll be careful," Cole murmurs, squeezing my hand. "No wandering off alone, all right?"

I nod, but the only way I'll truly be safe is by finding the killer.

That night, Mama, Gran, and Sissy retreat to the porch with a bottle of Gran's medicinal apple pie moonshine, but I catch a few of their words through the open kitchen window.

"These slow weeks have eaten away all our savings," Mama says. "Without some kind of miracle, I don't see a way out of this. And if we lose the Harvest Moon, how do we afford to keep the farm?"

The stark, metallic taste of her fear is stronger than the volume of her words, and I cover my mouth, stepping back.

"Don't go borrowing trouble," Gran tells her as I turn away. "We've faced hard times before."

The sounds of the crickets and frogs outside are incongruently calm and cheerful. As I pass Sorrel and Rowan's room on the way to my own, I peek in and see Sorrel's side already filling up with the boxes she plans to take back to college in a few short weeks. I squeeze my eyes shut, fervently hoping she'll still be able to go. But Mama's right. If we lose the Harvest Moon, we lose everything.

I empty the nook under the floorboards next to my bed, spreading the diablerie, Zephyrine's notebook, and the loose pages from Parlee Wilkerson's kitchen across the rug, determined to find some answers. Stuck between the very last pages of the diablerie, I find the note Zephyrine wrote for Gran on the day she left, the top jagged like she ripped it away from the pad too aggressively.

My life is MINE. I don't owe it to you or anyone.
Stay away from me. I NEVER want to see you again!
—Z

But it's the diablerie pages that were behind the sink with Dahlia's phone that intrigue me the most. I pick them up, reading through Zephyrine's scribbled notes about the Bone Tree again. Gran said she had become obsessive about the diablerie in the months before she left, and Amos McCoy speculated that something had happened when she and Nora were working on the Moth Queen scholarship. After which Nora stopped her own family genealogy project. And the McCoy home had a piece of wood, carved from the Bone Tree, over the door like the houses of the other founding families of Caball Hollow.

Bryson said Dahlia knew the old stories about my family. Could these pages be why? Or did the rumors start even before then, all the way back to when those protective clovers were cut from the Bone Tree? *Carve the bones. Bake the bread.* That was the message I scratched into the dirt at Nora's grave while we were trying to communicate with her.

A spark of awareness goes through me. Dahlia's family was one of the last to keep up the labor-intensive tradition of salt-rising bread. Could that be the bread she'd meant?

But how had the pages ended up in Dahlia's possession in the first place? Had she found them, or had someone given them to her? She'd been able to find Wyatt McCoy when his own father couldn't, so maybe she'd been able to find Zephyrine, too.

Just because Zephyrine didn't come home doesn't mean she never came back. Could those text messages on Dahlia's phone have been from her? The hidden journal, the stolen pages, her obsession with the diablerie that holds the spell to summon the creature seen before both murders—what if it was Aunt Zephyrine who had something to hide?

I could spin a thousand colorful explanations for everything, but without evidence they're only stories. Rubbing a hand over my face, I toss the pages back onto the floor. But then something in the diablerie catches my eye: Spell for Illuminating Secrets.

The instructions reference a drop of blood and a candle flame to reveal hidden messages. In the strange vision I had when we were trying to communicate with Nora McCoy, Zephyrine had held her journal above a candle flame. A strange thing to do in an office with a ceiling light.

I grab a candle, a pack of matches, and a needle from my sewing kit, then scramble back to the rug. Folding my legs underneath me, I strike a match and light the candle. Quickly, I prick my finger with the needle and squeeze a single drop of blood into the flame. It flares up, pure white, and I jerk back. When the flame settles, I lift the open journal above the candle.

"Flickering fire, flame undo. Cast off shadows, the blood speaks true." I whisper the incantation over the pages, and as my breath skims across them, words begin to appear in brownish ink along the margins.

I rush to read them all as quickly as I can, gobbling them up before they disappear again. At first, I'm not sure why Zephyrine hid these notes and not the others she wrote on the torn-out pages. It's clear she was trying to figure something out because, page after page, the hidden notes move from topic to topic, only tangentially related. She seems to have been researching the past, both the history of Caball Hollow and that of our family.

She wrote about Caorunn James and the legends that were passed down through other local families, not only that Caorunn had come out of the Forest alone, but that there was something peculiar about her. When others were around her, they would feel calmer or happier, even if they had reason to be upset. Some found it pleasant and would seek her out, but others felt it was unsettling and profane.

A scribbled line about the good folk catches my eye, and I remember reading the same phrase in the diablerie. I turn its pages until I reach the one about the Moth-Winged Man. It calls him "one of the good folk." In Zephyrine's notes, she wrote *Blessing or curse?* followed by another line I read out loud.

"'Salt to salt, blood to blood, bone to bone, a life for a life—what if it were a trade?'" I read it again, but I'm still not sure what it means. The writing feels frantic, like she was desperate to find the answer. But why? What was so urgent about a centuries-old mystery?

After hours of tossing and turning, I wake up standing in the middle of the road. Slowly, I spin in a circle, the moon casting just enough light to see the driveway that leads down to the farm behind me. My breath comes in raspy bursts, and my heart races.

"Enough!" I yell into the night. "What do you want from me?"

A low whistle comes from my right, and I spin to see Hadrian Fitch leaning against a tree trunk.

"Hadrian." My cheeks heat with embarrassment at the same time a frisson of fear goes through me. There's something off about him, a careful stillness like a coiled spring, that sets my deepest instincts on alert. "I didn't realize you were back from Mud River," I say as I take a slow step backward.

"I know Rowan found the transcript, Linden." His voice is strange, low and dangerous.

"Why did you have it?" I glance toward the farmhouse. The light over the barn glows like a beacon, but it might as well be miles away. "At first, I thought you might be Wyatt McCoy, but now I know you're not."

"No." He shakes his head almost imperceptibly, but he's standing in the shadows, and it's too dark to see his expression.

Then, with a flash of clarity, I realize all the clues I'd thought pointed to him being Wyatt could also point to someone else.

"Elam," I breathe as all the blood in my veins starts to fizz.

"Maybe once," he says. "But I haven't been him for quite some time."

He steps away from the tree, but the shadows seem to cling to him. Darkness moves around him differently than it should, slipping and slithering like a living thing. His green eyes turn red-tinged, like a nocturnal animal, reflecting the moonlight back as he tracks my every breath. He moves closer. And then two sets of wings unfurl behind him, taller than his six-foot height and just as wide, coated in an array of powdery scales.

I stumble backward. My heart races so fast, I feel light-headed. The reaction is instinctual, like prey under the eye of a predator, but I push it down, refusing to let fear stop me from finally getting answers. Leaning forward, I brace my hands on my knees and try not to pass out. Knowing something exists in the abstract and coming face-to-face with it in the real world are two very different things.

"Holy hell," I whisper, my mind racing as quickly as my heart. "How?"

"Holy hell is sort of my wheelhouse." He grins, but it's a baring of teeth, feral.

"It's you, isn't it? You're the reason I've been sleepwalking." I think of what Juniper said about our subconscious being more susceptible to messages from the other side. I guess that applies to the death-adjacent, too. "Something pulls me to you, but only when I'm asleep."

"I'm not sure you can blame me for the sleepwalking," he says. "But certainly the destination. The dead are drawn to me, and I to them. You came close enough for death to leave its mark, but you lived. Now you are pulled to both the dead and to me."

The diablerie said the Moth-Winged Man was responsible for leading the souls of those who met a tragic end from this life to the next. And that he himself had once been such a soul. Yet, even with Hadrian standing in front of me, wings unfurled, it doesn't make sense.

"Elam McCoy was only four years old when he went missing. How is this even possible?" I demand, gesturing toward him.

He lifts one shoulder, a lazy shrug that sets the wings on that side fluttering and sends another shock wave through me. "How much has your family told you about the grave-yard watch?"

I shake my head. "Not much."

"When the former watcher's term is up, he trains the new one. It didn't matter how old I was, it was time. I was taken to the Otherworld, beyond this one, and trained until I could assume the role."

"But why are you here now?" I push. "You've been working on our farm for almost a year, and you never said a word."

"I'm searching for answers, just like you," he says. "Last summer, when I came for you in the Forest, was my first time back in Caball Hollow. I have very few memories of my short life and even fewer of my death. This is the first chance I've had to figure out who I am and what happened to me. But I'm running out of time. I'm not meant to walk among the living indefinitely, and the pull back to the Otherworld grows ever stronger."

He's right. Wanting answers is something I can relate to. "Why didn't you tell us who you really were?" I ask, but then I realize he had no reason to trust us. If he is investigating his own death, he likely doesn't trust anyone.

"You really don't remember what happened last summer, do you?" he asks.

I shake my head. "Only some. I haven't been able to piece it all together."

"If you want to remember, then remember."

"It's not that simple," I grind out through my teeth, sick to death of hearing every possible variation of those words. Of trying to force myself to remember the worst night of my life.

"Isn't it?" he murmurs. "Take my hand."

He reaches out into the space between us, and I look down at the calluses across his palm. Ones he earned here, working on our farm for so many months. But fear drops like a stone in my belly. Because every time I try to remember that night, it feels like jerking back from a hot stove. I don't need to be burned again to know it's going to hurt.

And yet one thing I know for sure is that hiding from danger won't make you safe. So I reach out and press my hand into his.

*It's brighter near the river, the light of the moon no longer blocked
by branches, and its glow reflected by the water. A laugh rings out
from where the others are sitting around the campfire, and I
glance back over my shoulder, even though I know they're too far
away to see, before sitting on a large rock near the river's edge.*

*"Moth-Winged Man!" I call out, hoping it's loud enough for
them to hear, to prove I've done what I said I would. That I
belong here, with everyone else.*

*As I look around, the trees lining the riverbank feel like
they're pressing closer, all manner of things concealed within
their unrelenting darkness, and the skin on the back of my neck
starts to tingle.*

*"Moth-Winged Man." Quieter the second time as I start to
feel just how alone I am. No one at the fire can see me all the way
down here. I can't even hear them anymore.*

*"Moth-Winged Man." By the end, my voice fades to barely a
whisper. I glance over my shoulder again, searching for the eyes
I can feel watching me.*

*I stand, turning toward the top of the hill where the others wait,
far behind the trees. But exposing my back is a mistake. Strong
hands come out of the darkness, knocking me to my knees and
shoving my face into the cold mountain water flowing downriver.*

*Not the Moth-Winged Man I had called out to; this monster
is all too human.*

*Water rushes into my nose and mouth. I struggle for breath
as the hands hold me down, pushing my head farther beneath
the current. Fighting to get my hands under me, I slip again*

and again in the mud of the riverbank, until finally I claw my fingers in deep and push back as hard as I can.

I break the surface and come up sputtering, coughing up water and gulping down air. I open my mouth to scream for help, but someone shoves me from behind. My head hits something, hard, and everything goes blank.

I float several feet down the river before my mind clears enough for me to try to get to my feet. Something large splashes behind me. I turn, blinking water out of my eyes, and the moonlight shines on a terrified face hiding in the woods. A face I recognize.

Dahlia Calhoun.

A huge dark form rushes toward me. I slip on the rocks below the surface and fall back into the water once more as the man grabs for me. He's wearing a hood, and in the dark, his face is a mass of shadow. The pull of the current is stronger on his larger form, and it knocks him off his feet. I scuttle on all fours to the riverbank, pushing to my feet as soon as I touch mud.

Once I'm out of the river, I run for the trees at the edge of the Forest, desperate for somewhere to hide. Something warm drips down my forehead into my eyes and tints my vision red.

My shirt is wet and sticky, and my thoughts feel sluggish. I lose track of how long I've been running. I crouch down in a small cluster of trees to catch my breath. It's full dark, made darker still by the clouds that have filled the night sky, roiling over the face of the moon.

The Forest is holding its breath, waiting. The sudden hoot of an owl sends prickles across my skin.

I sense some sort of movement at the edge of my vision and look over my shoulder, but I can't make out anything in the dark. A crack of lightning zips across the sky, near scaring me to death and sending up a lick of brightness.

The flare of light illuminates a pair of glowing red eyes between the trees, and my heart squeezes in my chest with fear as my brain switches over to static.

At the next flash of lightning, nothing is there but tree bark.

But as my racing heart starts to settle, the trees blow apart with a sound like ripping paper. I rise to my feet, using the tree trunk behind me to steady myself. What I had mistaken for bark unfurls into a set of camouflaged wings, mothlike, revealing the shadowed form of a man beneath. He blinks open those red eyes, and when he narrows them at me, I run.

And then I fly.

My stomach drops as my feet leave the ground. And as I'm lifted into the starry sky, the Moth-Winged Man adjusts his hold, putting one arm around my shoulders, the other behind my knees. His wings spread out above us, covered in a million tiny scales, all in shades of brown and green and gold and twilight.

"Don't be afraid," his voice rumbles in his chest against my ear. But I'm not. I'm too numb to feel anything.

We soar across the dark blot of the Forest, covering ground impossibly fast. Until he lands and sets me gently on my feet in front of the Bone Tree, then bends to pull a knife from his boot. He slices open his palm and steps closer to the tree, whispering something I can't make out before pressing his bloodied hand against the bark.

A light begins to shine around his hand, slowly growing larger until an opening big enough for him to pass through appears. He takes my hand and pulls me forward, through the door.

And then everything goes black.

When I wake the next morning, I'm lying next to the remains of the campfire, shivering uncontrollably and dizzy from the pain in my head. I hear a man's voice shout somewhere in the distance and push myself up on my hands and knees, then slowly stand. Is it someone who could help me, or the man who attacked me last night, still searching so he can finish the job?

Stumbling and exhausted, I don't make it far before I fall to the ground, my stomach lurching. I throw up until the muscles of my abdomen are sore and there's nothing left in me.

Slowly, I crawl beneath the overgrown branches of a rhododendron. My instinct is to hide like a wounded animal. I must pass out again, because the next time I open my eyes, it's to Ethan Miranda's face, gone paler than the khaki of his uniform.

"She's over here!" he calls out, waving an arm over his head. "It's going to be okay, Linden, you're safe now."

CHAPTER TWENTY-FOUR

WHAT DOES it mean to go missing? To become lost, to disappear. None of the tales we're told as children are useful instruction. We don't hike with pockets full of bread crumbs to leave a trail, and no fairy godmother will appear to point the way. Sometimes, no matter how good and righteous we are, we may never find our way home.

Being lost is as existential as it is physical. The loss of your spatial orientation, an unmooring of your place in the world. The disorienting sensation that nothing is as it was before.

When I open my eyes, still clinging desperately to Hadrian's outstretched hand, my stomach pitches with that same sort of slip-sliding feeling, as though the earth under my feet has shifted just enough to change everything. I barely make it to the grassy ditch along the side of the gravel road before I throw up the entire contents of my stomach.

"It's a door." My voice is barely a whisper, awed by the memory of what I saw. "Where did you take me? What's on the other side?"

"I'm afraid those aren't memories you get to keep," he answers. "No mortal can touch the Otherworld and remain unchanged."

Yet that's not what I read in the diablerie. "But how can the Bone Tree be a door? I thought it was the burial place of the first person in Caball Hollow to become the Moth-Winged Man."

"Is that what they told you?" Hadrian smirks. "It isn't a door, it's a bridge. And no one is graveyard watch until *after* they die a violent and tragic death. The founding families needed a connection between this place and the Otherworld, so they planted him like a seed to grow it."

I try to remember the words my ancestors wrote in the diablerie about the legend of the graveyard watch, those like the Moth-Winged Man who had once been members of the community, then took on the role of guiding others into the afterlife. It was old Celtic folklore, part of the good folk, that catchall name for the uncanny.

"Are you saying what I think you're saying?" My stomach roils again. "They killed him?"

He crosses his arms. "Murder is nothing new in Caball Hollow, Linden. And then, once they had the clarity of mind to fear what they'd unleashed, they tried to fend off the influence of the good folk with salt-rising bread and carved clovers."

"What do you mean, unleashed?" But I think I already know. My heartbeat stutters, and my mind flashes to Zephyrine's note to Nora: *what are we*, she'd written.

"The Bone Tree responds to my blood, but it responds to yours too. Why do you think that is, hmm?" He leans closer. "A life for a life. Those first settlers sacrificed one of their own to create the area's first graveyard watch. Caorunn James didn't walk out of the Forest unbidden one afternoon. They welcomed her and then couldn't decide if she was a blessing or a curse."

This is the reason for the strange talents that manifest in the James family, I realize. Our ancestor was one of the good folk.

"A life for a life, literally? As in someone must die when a bargain is made?" If someone else knew the Moth-Winged Man really could grant their deepest wish, might it have been motive for murder?

"Sometimes, but not always. The bargain must balance the scales. Whatever it is, both sides must be equal. For something as valuable as a life, the cost must be truly dear. It must mean something to the bargainer."

"Then why did you save me last summer?"

"You're asking the wrong questions," he tells me with a sharp shake of his head. His wings fold back and disappear as his eyes fade back to normal. "We have similar stories, you and I. When someone becomes part of the watch, they're no longer who they were before. You must leave your old life, your old name behind. I was so young, I have few memories of my life as Elam. But when I came for you, when I came back here, I remembered that Forest, that river. The place where I was killed, it was the same place where you nearly were."

He says the words so directly that the shock of them takes a moment to set in. He's here, flesh and blood, but also not. A murdered boy, dead longer than he was alive.

"There was a man fishing and an older boy. I followed him." His brow furrows as he concentrates on grasping those few threads of memory. "I remember there was so much water, and something shiny—a star, I think."

"The Deputy Crunch badge," I realize.

"When I hit the water, it was so cold I forgot how to breathe. And then I couldn't." He focuses on me again, his gaze intense. "I came to find the person who murdered me, Linden," he says. "And after watching you this summer, I believe my goal and yours align."

I take a deep breath, recalling the conversation I over-heard at Parlee Wilkerson's house when Deputy Miranda was hypothesizing about the necklace found around Dahlia's neck. Elam's toy badge could link us all together: Elam, me, and Dahlia.

"I need to go," I tell Hadrian over my shoulder as I start for the house.

"Linden, wait. Until I know for certain who was involved in my death, I would appreciate it if you kept the truth of my identity to yourself," Hadrian says. The words are nice enough, but his tone is a warning.

I nod once, and then I'm gone.

When I get to my room, Juniper is sleeping peacefully in her bed. Mine looks like a tornado hit it, sheets twisted and crumpled, pillows on the floor. I tap the flashlight on my phone and kneel next to the rug, pulling everything out from under the floorboard again.

If Dahlia saw someone try to kill me, why had she never come forward? I'd considered she might be blackmailing someone with information she'd uncovered while investigating what happened to Elam McCoy. But maybe it had never been about him at all. Whoever had tried to kill me would likely pay a pretty penny for her silence. Until maybe the price got too high. Coach Hammond might not have killed for his assistant coach job, but he might to keep her silent. And yet I didn't even know him. What motive could he have for harming me?

My eyes grow heavier as I try to understand. It feels like the answer is right in front of me, but I can't quite make it out.

I blink, once, and when I open my eyes, Juniper is shaking me awake, sunlight streaming in through the window behind her.

"Did you sleep on the floor all night?" she asks.

"Hmm" is all I manage, pushing myself up into a sitting position and rubbing my eyes. Exhaustion has sunk down into my bones after the intense revelations of last night. Revelations I can't even tell anyone about because of my promise to Hadrian.

I fell asleep with the flashlight on, and now my phone is completely dead. I plug it in next to my bed after I tuck all

319

the papers away. Then I head downstairs and find Mama and Gran in the kitchen, drinking hot coffee despite the heat that's settling into the valley.

"Morning, Linden," Mama says. "After we finish cleaning up the Harvest Moon today, I think we should stay close to home for a while. Work in the garden, maybe get some projects done around the farm that we've been putting off."

"Odette," Gran says in a gentle but chiding tone. "You can't keep everybody swaddled in tissue paper."

"I know it, Mama, I just want us all to lie low for a bit."

"I understand the impulse, but the girls didn't do anything wrong. We aren't the sort to hang our heads in shame because of a few small-minded people. As you well know."

"It's more than that, Mama. I don't want them to hang their heads, but I don't want them to risk their necks to prove how high we can hold them, either." Mama sets her mug down hard enough to slosh coffee on the table, then dashes upstairs. A few seconds later, her bedroom door shuts with an uncharacteristic bang.

"She's a bit keyed up with everything. She'll be fine." Gran sighs as she takes their mugs to the sink.

I don't answer, I just slip out the screen door and onto the porch, dragging my fingertips through the pollen along the railing as I make my way toward the front of the house. For three generations now, we James women have been serving up fried chicken, biscuits, grits, and cornbread at the Harvest Moon. Mama learned to cook at her own mother's apron strings, and then so did we. In that kitchen, working a new recipe or learning when dough is perfect by touch alone at Gran's elbow, I can be my whole self.

We spend the next several hours scrubbing every inch of the diner, piling up everything that was destroyed and needs to be hauled away, and making lists of everything that will need to be replaced. It's a lot.

Mama keeps shaking her head as she adds more items to the list, and she's pulled the calculator out more than once.

"Of all the hateful, no-good . . ." Juniper mutters as she attempts the impossible task of scrubbing flour out from between the cracks in the hardwood floors.

But it's the blood on the wall that seems to have sunk in like indelible ink. No amount of scrubbing will completely remove the words, and when we try to paint over it, the letters rise like ghosts through the coat of white.

By the time we get home late that afternoon, we're all exhausted and defeated. The taste of ash is heavy in my mouth as I drop onto the porch swing, too hollowed out to make it all the way inside.

I'm not sure how long I've been sitting there when an unholy racket blares from inside the house. Gran pushes open the screen door, beating a pan with a wooden spoon and creating such a clamorous cacophony it's liable to split my eardrums in half.

"Good lord, Gran!" I push myself up and cover my ears.

"It's time for a family meeting," Gran says briskly. "Everyone in the kitchen in five minutes," she orders as she sets off to rouse the others.

I slide into a seat at the kitchen table next to Juniper as Gran herds Mama down the back stairs.

"I called this meeting because I can't stand to see you all like this," Gran starts. "We're not ones to hide from trouble down in this holler like a pack of timid little mice. We're not going to let these rumormongers and busybodies cow us."

"It's not just gossip. Someone destroyed the Harvest Moon," Mama objects, her voice breaking.

"We can't let the actions of a few hate-filled cowards change us. If we hide who we are to make others comfortable, we lose everything we're fighting for anyway. A mother's instinct is to keep safe her young, but she also needs to teach them how to fly."

Tears start to roll silently down Mama's face, and Sissy reaches over to hold her hand.

"So if you've forgotten, I'm going to remind you. And I'll keep on reminding you until you remember," Gran says, punctuating her statement by jabbing a finger against the surface of the table. "We are strong mountain women. We're going to stop believing the lies the world tells us about who we are and letting them make us small. Because I know who you are, each one of you, and I didn't raise you to be small."

Gran takes Sissy's other hand and looks her in the eye. "Salome, you are not damaged, you are not broken, the beauty you see in the world is a reflection of what is in you." She looks to Mama next. "Odette, you are a force of nature, and a volcano does not fear a little rain. Sorrel, your roots are deep, so go and spread your branches, but don't forget what it is that makes you strong. Rowan, you are not a sin eater, their lies do not define you, follow your own truth. Juniper, when you look into the darkness, know you are a multitude of stars. You have fire in your veins.

"And, Linden." She turns so she can look me in the eyes. "You believe in everyone else so strongly, have the courage to believe in yourself that way too. It's empathy that has the power to change the world." She stands and grabs her work gloves from the sideboard. "If living in West Virginia has taught us anything, it's that difficult roads lead to beautiful places. Now, I'm going down to the garden to get my hands in the dirt for a while. When I come back, we'll sit down and we'll make a plan."

The screen door closes with a slap behind Gran, and we all turn to look at each other. Gran has always been the pragmatic one. The one who patiently taught me the same recipe over and over, until I knew the rhythm by heart, but had no time for exaggerated tears over skinned knees or playground insults.

"Well." Sissy dabs a tear from the corner of her eye with the hem of her shirt. "Y'all heard the woman. I'm going to go get cleaned up."

I run up to my bedroom to retrieve my phone. When I check my texts, there's a video message from Cole. I click play.

"You know how I feel about texting and one word wasn't enough this time, so I thought I'd give this a try." A tiny smile tips up one end of his mouth as he leans against the side of his Jeep. "Practice just ended, and I'm heading over to the Harvest Moon to help, but I remembered something about last summer. It might be nothing, but I'm going to check it out. I'll see you soon."

There's a faint noise in the background, and he glances away right as the video cuts off, just long enough for me to catch sight of something on the side of his neck, right below his jaw.

A red moth.

CHAPTER TWENTY-FIVE

FRANTIC, I try to call him, my fingers clumsy with fear, but it goes straight to voicemail. I check the time stamp on his message. It was sent more than two hours ago.

"Hadrian," I realize. The red moth is a sign of coming death, but the Moth-Winged Man is the one who guides the souls of the dead to the other side. Now that I know who he is, maybe I can stop it.

Shoving my phone into my pocket, I race across the grass to the carriage house and pound on the door of Hadrian's apartment. I jiggle the knob, and it turns in my hand, the door cracking open. It's a small, open space, and I can take it all in with a glance: a kitchenette, the living area, a bed, and a tiny bathroom. Empty.

I run back to the house, bare feet crunching across the dry

summer grass. As soon as I reach the porch, the old landline phone on the kitchen wall begins to ring.

"It's Vivian," Sissy says as I burst into the kitchen, followed closely by Gran.

"I know," I tell her. She passes me the phone. "What's wrong? What's happened?" I ask without preamble, before Vivian has a chance to say anything.

"There was an accident." Her voice wobbles with emotion, and I almost can't hear her over the ringing in my ears. "The Jeep ran off the road into that big elm tree outside the old Miller place."

I squeeze my eyes shut, clinging to the moment that hangs in between before and after as I gather the courage to ask. "Cole?" It's barely a whisper, but she hears me.

"He's missing."

I let out a slow breath, losing my grip on the phone as I sink to the floor. It's not too late. Not yet, anyway. Sissy picks up the call, talking to Vivian in low tones as Mama helps me to my feet. Her lips are moving, but I can't make out the words. Slowly, my hearing comes back like a picture coming into focus. I need to do something, anything, to find him and bring him back. Alive.

"We need to do a finding spell, right?" I ask the room at large. The words are ragged, scratching at my throat, as I dig through every single drawer in the kitchen, but I don't miss the look that passes between Mama and Sissy.

"Oh, honey, it's not that simple," Sissy says.

"What are you looking for?" Mama asks, closing the drawers I leave open in my wake.

"A map! I need a map for the finding spell." I turn to her, pleading now. "Why won't you help me find Cole?" Hot tears drip off my chin, and I swipe at them angrily.

"Because, darling girl," Mama says, "he's not a misplaced key."

"I have to find him before it's too late." Abandoning the drawers, I press my hands flat against the table in frustration. "I saw the red moth," I growl.

"Oh, god, it's happening." Sissy sits down hard in the chair next to me.

"What do you mean?" My eyes snap to hers.

Aunt Zephyrine wasn't the only one with access to the diablerie. Just because she'd written the notes on those pages didn't mean she'd been the one to remove them. It was Sissy who had shown me where to find the hidden key, the one who already knew the contents of the book. I rub a finger along the cut on my index finger, where I'd given drops of myself over to power spells, and remember the larger scar I'd seen on Sissy's arm.

"Sissy, what do you know?" I demand. The screen door slaps closed somewhere behind me, but I'm too focused on her answer to bother looking to see which one of my sisters just came in.

She's quiet for a moment, staring down at her hands. Then she shakes her head and leans forward. "When Vivian was pregnant and the doctors told her that Cole likely wouldn't live more than a few days, she came to me. I tried everything I could think of and every spell I knew, but nothing worked." Sissy sighs, and it's a heavy thing. "And as she became more desperate, I became more willing to do any-thing, until finally I took out the diablerie . . ." She trails off.

"What did you do?" I push. Gran stands behind me with one hand gripping the back of my chair and the other pressed against her mouth.

"We made a deal with the devil," a new voice interrupts from the doorway, and I turn to see Vivian Spencer, looking fragile enough that a strong breeze might shatter her into a million pieces. Sissy moves to pull her into a gentle hug.

"Care to elaborate on that?" I ask as Gran puts the kettle on and gestures for everyone to take a seat.

"I like to think I might not have done it if I knew that other people would get hurt, but I'm not sure that's true. I was willing to do just about anything to save my son. But someone who offers to grant your deepest desire is always going to want something in return. Maybe something you're not equipped to give," Vivian continues.

"The summoning spell calls for James blood at the Bone Tree." Sissy reaches out and gently takes Vivian's hand. "When the Moth-Winged Man stepped out of the woods, I expected a monster, but he looked almost human. Almost. There was something terrifying about the way the shad-ows clung to him, moving with him and keeping him hidden."

Gran sets a teacup in front of Vivian, and she startles, shaking off the long tendrils of memory.

"He told us we were foolish to summon him and warned we would come to regret it, but I still didn't listen. I told him I would do anything. Pay any price." Vivian takes a sip of tea and swallows hard, then keeps her eyes focused on the table in front of her. When she continues, her voice is barely a whisper. "He said my son would live. But when we left the Forest and stopped for gas, we heard about the missing boy.

"Even then, I didn't start to connect the dots until the FBI brought in those special search dogs and they couldn't track little Elam past the edge of the trees. No one had ever seen anything like it. But I knew the truth." Vivian nods as her eyes fill with tears. "The Moth-Winged Man had taken him."

"A life for a life," Sissy whispers, echoing what Hadrian told me last night.

A sob escapes Vivian's throat, and Mama passes her a tissue. She takes it and buries her face in her hands. Sissy slowly rubs circles along her back.

"Cole lived," Vivian continues. "The doctors called him a miracle. The best thing I've ever done born of the worst. Yet, even now, every time I look at him, all I see is guilt for what I did. And when I discovered he saw red moths before someone died . . ." She trails off, then swallows hard, steeling her nerve. "I knew that somehow he was still connected to that monster, and I started to fear that one day it'd come for him."

"Death always gets its due," Gran murmurs, shaking her head sadly.

I'm hit with a physical pain at the idea of what it must have been like for Cole growing up that way. But something else in what she said strikes me. Cole told me his mother supplied him with those little pink candies. Clove has a lot of folk uses, including protection, banishing hostile forces, psychic masking. And more mundanely, repelling moths.

"That's what the cloves were for," I realize. "You basically cloaked Cole to hide him from the Moth-Winged Man."

Vivian nods, dabbing at her eyes. "I made sure he always had them on him, I asked Salome to put protections around the house, I did everything I could to keep him safe, but it wasn't enough." She turns to Sissy. "And now I'm here, begging for your help again."

"There must be something we can do to find Cole. You found me last summer. How did you do it?" I can't sit still anymore, and I push to my feet. Mama won't meet my eyes.

"Linden, you know how." Sissy reaches over and squeezes my hand. "Now that you've seen the diablerie."

Mama sucks in a sharp breath. "Salome, tell me you didn't show her that book."

"Hellfire and apple butter," Gran mutters. "That damned book has brought this family nothing but trouble. I should have destroyed it as soon as Zephyrine rode off on that silly little Bonneville."

"Fine." I spin on my heel and head for the door, bound and determined to do whatever it takes to save Cole. And if summoning the Moth-Winged Man with James blood at the Bone Tree worked eighteen years ago, it could work again. All I have to do is venture back into the Forest that nearly killed me.

"He won't help you unless you can give him something he wants," Sissy says.

"Well, you would know." I spin around and grab her arm, pulling her sleeve up to show a row of thin, shimmering scars.

"Salome! How many bargains have you made?" Mama cries.

"It wasn't like that. Every spell in that book requires blood, big or small. I've only summoned him once," Sissy argues. "And you don't really have the moral high ground here, Odette." Sissy slaps a hand over her mouth as though trying to catch the words. "Oh god, I didn't mean to—"

"Odette?" Gran says sharply.

I glance down at Mama's arms before she crosses them against her chest. One thin white scar sits halfway up her left forearm.

My eyes shoot to hers, and she takes a bracing breath. "I started having premonitions about you girls when Sorrel was a baby. They were always right. Like a strong feeling not to take a certain road right before a bad accident, or waking up suddenly in the middle of the night to find Rowan out of her crib and about to tumble down the stairs."

She stands and cups my face with her hands, willing me to understand. "That day last summer was the worst one I've ever had. I already knew before Cole showed up that something was very wrong, and I would have done any-thing to save you."

A sick feeling goes through me as the events from last year start to line up. "What did you trade for me?" I press my hands over hers on my cheeks. "Mama, what did you trade?"

"A life for a life," she whispers. "I gave up my life with your father. I gave up our love, our family."

I flinch like I've been slapped. Pushing out of her hands, I race for the stairs. Mama calls out to me, and Gran tells her to let me be. But I don't intend to lock myself in my room and cry. I pry up the loose floorboard and take out the diablerie, stuffing it into my backpack, then cross the hall to Rowan and Sorrel's room and open the window.

I step out onto the roof and leap, catching the branch of the big hawthorn tree and scurrying down. The minute my feet touch the ground, I'm running full tilt. A stitch pierces my side and I can't catch my breath, but I don't even notice the tears until my vision blurs too much to be able to see where I'm going. I swipe at my eyes, angry I have to slow down to do it.

And then I see the flares.

CHAPTER TWENTY-SIX

THE BRIGHT flames of emergency flares line the side of the road, warning other drivers of the accident ahead. As I round the curve, I see where Cole's truck crashed through the underbrush and went over the side of the embankment before it smashed into a wide oak tree.

The back of the Jeep sticks up at an unnatural angle, and even though I know he isn't in there, I can't help but run toward it. Before I make it more than a few yards, Deputy Miranda comes out of nowhere, catching me around the waist and pulling me to a stop.

"Linden, I can't let you down there."

"Let me go, Ethan. I need to see," I yell, struggling to break free.

"Just calm down, okay? Calm down, and I'll let you go."

I take a deep breath, then another, and will my muscles to unclench.

"Linden?" another voice calls from across the street. I turn to see Daddy climbing out of his Suburban. "What are you doing out here?"

"Sir." Ethan releases me, and I stumble. "She was passing by and offered assistance at the site of an accident."

"I need to see it for myself," I tell him, willing my voice not to shake. If he knows how upset I am, there's no way he'll let me down there.

Daddy pulls me into a fierce hug, and I cling to him, Mama's confession still hot in my ears. When he pushes me away, he holds on to my shoulders so I have to look up and meet his eyes. "I know you won't go home unless I take you there myself, but if you're going to be here, you stay behind me, you don't touch anything, and if I tell you to leave, you go. Understand?"

I nod, my throat too tight to speak. Daddy turns to Ethan and gestures for him to begin.

"Let me show you what we know so far," Ethan says as he leads the way down the embankment, shining his heavy flashlight in front of us. "Watch your step. This rock is loose."

Daddy follows with a backward glance, warning me to stay behind him. It's that hazy time before dusk when the bugs are most active, and they're buzzing around, attracted by my sweat. When we reach the truck, the driver-side door is open, the interior light on. Cole's clove candies are still nestled in their bag in the cup holder, but the front of the truck is crumpled around the tree like it's made of paper.

The taste of fear hits me as I get closer, rolling out of the Jeep like a wave, but there's an undercurrent of something else, too, something complex like deception or betrayal and anger.

"The cell phone was busted in the crash, so he wouldn't have been able to call for help," Ethan says, shining the light onto the floor on the driver's side. The phone is pressed behind the arm of the gas pedal, screen shattered. "He was obviously injured. It's possible he was disoriented and took off." Ethan shines the light on a splatter of red blood against the cracks in the windshield, then on little pools and droplets along the console, driver's seat, and the inside of the door.

"Any sign of what caused the collision?" Daddy asks.

"A few. Take a look." Ethan leads us back up to the road. He points to some dark skid marks that end where Cole's truck left the road. "It looks like he slammed on his brakes and swerved to avoid hitting something. But here's the strange thing." He points his flashlight toward the side of the road. "There's another set of tracks in the softer dirt on the edge of the road, like somebody pulled over to check on him."

"But no reports matching his description at local hospitals?" Daddy asks.

"Not yet, but we'll keep checking in case he turns up there later."

Daddy squats down next to the second set of tracks, then pulls a pen out of his pocket and carefully holds it in the groove in several places without disturbing the soil. "Hmm" is all he says, glancing in my direction.

"What is it, sir?" Ethan asks.

"Linden, why don't you go wait in my truck," Daddy tells me. "You've seen everything you need to see here."

"I'll find out anyway, just say it." I cross my arms tightly over my chest.

He studies me, considering, before he finally nods. "We'll need to verify with the field techs, but based on the starting point, ending point, lack of curving, and depth of the tracks, I'd say this wasn't a passerby stopping to help. It looks to me like this car was driving the wrong way in this lane and forced the Jeep off the road, which suggests one of two scenarios. Either this car was in the wrong lane by mistake, stopped to see what happened, then drove off to avoid getting in trouble for whatever caused them to be driving carelessly in the first place . . ."

"Or this car intentionally ran the Jeep off the road, then stopped while Cole was disoriented or unconscious," Ethan finishes.

"I'll call in a request for techs so we can dust for prints and take impressions," says Daddy. He strides back to the Suburban and reaches for the radio.

"You think someone took him, don't you?" I ask Ethan.

"Judging by the evidence, I think that's the most likely scenario, yeah. I'm sorry, Linden."

Tears threaten, but I shove them back down. They won't help Cole. When I have my voice under control, I ask the one question I'm not sure I want answered. "Do you think it's the same person who killed Dahlia?"

Ethan takes off his hat to rub a hand over his dark hair. "I can't answer that, Linden. Anything's possible, but there aren't really any similarities between that case and this one. Dahlia was killed in the Teays River."

"Stillhouse Creek," I correct him automatically.

"No." He draws it out like he's realized he ventured into unsafe territory. "Sorry, I assumed your father had told you. I'm probably not supposed to say." He stops, but I give him a look, and he relents with a glance toward the Suburban. "We were able to determine that she was killed in the Teays, then floated loose off the rocks and ended up down where you found her near the high school."

He gives me a sympathetic look before he continues. "The analysis of the tread can help us figure out what sort of vehicle was involved here. But statistically, the perpetrator in abduction cases is far more likely to be a family member or an acquaintance of the victim. And, Linden." Ethan pauses again; he seems to be carefully choosing his words. "Cole is eighteen, he's over six feet tall, he's been running two-a-days for the football team all summer. That's not the typical victim of an abduction. I'm thinking this feels a lot more like a robbery gone wrong."

I add up what he's not saying, and the result staggers me. "You think he's already dead."

He lifts a shoulder in a half shrug. "All I'm saying is he wouldn't be easy to abduct."

I turn away as my mind flashes to the amount of blood in the Jeep. My gaze slides to where the front end is wrapped around the tree, and I squeeze my eyes shut. I won't believe it. I refuse.

"Linden," Daddy calls, hooking a thumb toward the Suburban. "Come on, you can come in to the station with me to wait for news."

I climb into the truck, glancing back at Ethan as I shut the door; his expression is stark, but he tries to give me a small smile when our eyes meet. I don't want to think about what a smile from Ethan Miranda means about his estimate for Cole's chances of survival.

When we get to the station a few minutes later, Daddy is pulled into the meeting room that's now the hub of the search. Despite the hour, it's buzzing with more people than I've ever seen at the station at one time. But if everyone is here, who is out looking for Cole?

Sergeant Markin brings me a cup of tea and two butterscotch candies from her drawer while I wait in the break room. "Here you go, baby, a little something sweet for the shock." She pats my hand.

"Thank you." I pull the mug toward me. "Any news?"

"Nothing yet." The warm, yeasty taste of sympathy fills my mouth as she closes the door behind her.

Despite what Ethan said, it's too much of a coincidence that Cole sent me a message about remembering something from last summer right before he was forced off the road.

I squeeze the charm of graveyard dirt in my pocket, wishing I'd thought to make one for Cole, and replay his message, searching for some hint of where he was going. But there's nothing. I drop my phone onto the table and shove my hands into my hair, growling in frustration. Then I pick it back up and watch the short video again and again until I lose count of the number of times. Until, at last, I notice a tiny reflection in the bottom corner of the Jeep's window behind Cole.

Coach Hammond.

Cole said he was leaving practice, and I kick myself for not immediately thinking of Hammond. A loud bang from the other side of the wall behind me makes me jump, and the sound of an intense debate leaks out of the meeting room next door.

"I don't care. Get out there and find my son!" a voice roars above all the other noise.

The station goes quiet, and I tiptoe to the door of the break room, peeking out. Mayor Spencer stands in the hall, hands on his hips as he faces off with the people in the meeting room. His eyes meet mine, and my mouth floods with the hot metal taste of anger, fear, and something else, something earthier. Then Daddy steps out and puts a hand on his shoulder, murmuring something too quiet for me to hear. Mayor Spencer nods and heads back into the room.

"Daddy," I call out to him before he can follow.

"I'm a little busy right now, Linden," he objects in a weary tone.

"It's important." I hold up my phone, playing the video message for him and pointing out the blurry figure of Coach Hammond.

"Linden, it was football practice, of course he was there." He can't keep the exasperation out of his voice as he glances toward the meeting room, and I know I only have a few moments to convince him that this is a lead worth investigating.

"I remembered something from last summer," I begin, and his gaze snaps to mine. "Coach Hammond was there that night in the Forest. Dahlia witnessed someone attack me in the river. I didn't see his face, but she might have."

"Did Hammond have a reason to want to harm you?" His voice is carefully neutral.

"I'm not sure," I admit. "His cousin, Bryson Ivers, alluded to the fact that their family may hold some old grudges against ours after he shoved me into the creek at Dahlia's vigil."

He gives me another hard look, then rubs a hand across his face. "There's a lead the mayor wants us to follow up, but I can spare a couple deputies to check on Hammond."

"What can I do?" I grab his arm before he can turn away.

"Stay here. Hopefully this'll all be over soon." He pats my hand, the bright fluorescent lights catching on the badge pinned to his chest, and then he's gone.

I drop back into my chair in the break room and take a sip of the tea, now long cold, but still sweet with too much sugar. The shuffling of deputies packing up and heading out from the meeting room ratchets up the anticipation already heavy in the air.

When the station goes quiet, it's even worse. There's no way I can stay here, doing nothing. My body feels buzzy with fear and adrenaline, but I force myself to sit and count out five minutes to make sure I won't run into Daddy in the parking lot and get delivered home instead.

Just as I grab my backpack and rush toward the door, Mayor Spencer steps into the room, and we nearly collide. He's carrying a cup of hot tea in each hand and moves his arms wide to keep from spilling them.

"Oh, Linden, are you leaving? I thought we might wait together in case there's news," he says, lifting the cups like an offering. As he moves to the small table where I've been biding my time, I eye the door, but my manners win out. Mayor Spencer slides one of the cups across the table. He looks terrible, drawn and sallow.

"Thank you." I sit and take a sip of the tea. He made it with considerably less sugar than Sergeant Markin, and it tastes bitter.

"You kids used to play together in this room. And run around begging everyone for change for the vending machine." Mayor Spencer gives me a watery smile, spinning his cup out of nervous energy.

A phone rings, and he pats his pockets until he finds it. "Oh, it's Vivian. Excuse me a moment." He pushes away from the table and heads for the door on the other side of the break room that leads out to the parking lot.

It's supposed to be shut and locked at all times, but it's perpetually propped open for the department's many smokers.

I hear Mayor Spencer answer as he steps outside, his voice becoming too muffled to make out anything.

But I've already stopped listening by then, my mind snagging on one word. *Vivian*. She told me only a few hours ago that she and Sissy had been at the Bone Tree the day Elam McCoy went missing, but Daddy said he'd let Mayor Spencer leave work early so he could be with her after getting news about Cole's fatal heart defect. It's why Daddy took longer to get to the scene when Elam went missing. But if Mayor Spencer wasn't at work and he wasn't with Vivian, where was he?

The way the light hit the star on Daddy's uniform flashes in my mind, like one of Hadrian's only memories from the day he was killed. Did it catch the sunlight off the water? Did it shine in his eyes, blinding him as he reached for help? What if the memory wasn't of the Deputy Crunch badge that he'd fought over with Wyatt, but one pinned to the front of a uniform? A uniform like the one Mayor Spencer used to wear.

I start to sweat, my palms already clammy as I push myself out of my chair and stumble toward the door. My thoughts feel like bumblebees thrumming in my head, loud and frantic. Mayor Spencer is halfway across the small parking lot behind the building, leaning against his car with the phone pressed to his ear. He must see something in my face, because he quickly hangs up and turns to me.

"Why?" is all I can croak out at him, my throat thick with emotion and the sheriff's department at my back making me bold. But, with a feeling like a tuning fork somewhere deep inside me, I realize I know the answer to this, too. "You were dating Aunt Zephyrine when she was working on the Moth Queen scholarship. She told you about her research, didn't she? She'd discovered the truth about the Bone Tree—a life for a life, and your son was dying."

"I heard the call go out on the radio on my way home." He rubs a hand across his mouth, not even trying to deny it. "I wasn't far, so I took the old mine access road and went up the back way. It didn't take me long to find him. He'd climbed a tree and gone too high, got stuck. When he slipped, he dropped into the water without making a sound. No scream, barely a splash. I waded in after him. And then it occurred to me that I didn't *need* to save him. I'd already tried to summon the Moth-Winged Man the way Zephyrine had told me, at the Bone Tree, but it didn't work."

I shake my head. "James blood," I whisper. Hadrian had said our blood could summon the Moth-Winged Man because whatever he was, we were partly the same. "But you thought of another way."

Mayor Spencer nods. "When my outstretched hand touched his hair, instead of pulling him out, I pushed him under. It hardly took any time at all."

Bile rises in my throat. "You were a deputy. He thought you were there to save him, and you killed him. All to summon the Moth-Winged Man?"

"I didn't even see the Moth-Winged Man." He shakes his head. "The current pulled the boy downriver, and I lost him.

I thought it was all for nothing, but then the doctors told us that the hole in Cole's heart had somehow closed on its own. A miracle."

He moves toward me, and I take a step back. "Don't come any closer." I gesture behind me. "I'll scream and have every deputy in that building out here in seconds."

"Now, Linden, calm down." He lifts his hands in a placating gesture as he takes another small step in my direction. "There are no deputies here. They're all out chasing down false leads."

A chill rolls down the back of my spine like a drop from a mountain spring. My thoughts feel heavy, my mind sluggish. I stumble, and he catches me. "I really wish you would have finished the tea," he murmurs. "It would have made this much quicker."

I want to scream for help, but my mouth won't open, and no matter how hard I fight to stay awake, each blink becomes longer. And longer.

And . . . longer.

CHAPTER TWENTY-SEVEN

MY MIND feels foggy and my body sluggish. I blink hard until my vision clears and try to take in my surroundings. I'm propped up in the passenger seat of a car, leather seats sticking to clammy skin, the taste of metal in my mouth. As we move along a bumpy dirt road, the car rattles and shakes over deep ruts, and everything comes rushing back. I swallow hard and slowly turn my head toward the driver.

Malcolm Spencer is already watching me. "You weren't supposed to wake up so fast," he observes flatly.

No longer the charming mayor from the election signs. His eyes are hard, sunken and shadowed. It's not worry over Cole, I realize. His clothes are loose, and his skin is sallow. The headaches, the nausea at Dahlia's funeral, the sleeping problems, and the doctor's appointment yesterday.

"You're sick." My voice is salt against my raw throat, and the sting brings tears to my eyes.

"Brain tumor," he agrees with a short nod. "They found the first one after my motorcycle accident." He chuckles darkly. "I survived a potentially fatal crash only to learn an inoperable time bomb was growing deep inside my head."

My mind whirs at the revelation. Gran said Zephyrine used to ride with Malcolm, I'd assumed together on his bike. But tonight Gran had said she left town on a Bonneville, the same kind of bike that Cole had found hidden away in his great-uncle's garage. Her notes about our family origins had been frantic, like she was racing against the clock. *A life for a life . . . what if it were a trade*, she'd written. Had the breakup been a ruse? Had Zephyrine used the example of Caorunn James to save Malcolm's life?

"Zephyrine never left town, did she?" I whisper. "She was the first."

His throat bobs as he swallows. "She chose to walk into the Bone Tree and give up her life to save mine," he insists. "But now the tumor is back and growing twice as fast."

"Is that why you tried to kill me last summer, to trade my life for yours, too?" I shift in my seat, my body starting to slough off the heavy, drugged feeling. "Tell me one thing, though. Why me? You were friends with my parents, you watched me grow up."

"No! I never planned to kill you, Linden," he argues, eyes flashing as he looks at me. "I only needed you to open the door and walk through, like Zephyrine."

"And Dahlia? Did you plan to kill her?"

His expression goes dark. "Dahlia wasn't supposed to die. She was helping me."

The betrayal sits heavy on my chest, making it hard to breathe. "But she was there that night. She saw you try to drown me in the river. Why would she ever agree to help you?"

"No," Malcolm insists with a dark chuckle. "She saw *it*. Again."

And then I see it all unfold in front of me. Dahlia had been there when her mother died of an overdose, a tragic and untimely death. What if she'd seen the Moth-Winged Man come for her mother? What if that memory, sparked by what she saw last summer, made her believe the stories others told about making a trade for your deepest desire? She'd been desperate for the money she needed for college with no way to get it. And those text messages on her phone. She'd turned to the same person who helped her when she'd needed to file a restraining order.

"She came to you for help, and you gave her the pages Zephyrine took from the diablerie."

"At first, I only wanted to make sure she hadn't seen anything last summer that could connect me to what happened, but then I realized we could help each other. Those pages were enough to convince her that all the rumors and old stories she'd heard about your family were true."

"That's why she wanted to meet up with me at the festival, to lure me out to the Forest so you could make your bargains with the Moth-Winged Man."

"Then she got cold feet. Told me she wouldn't force you to cross over." His voice goes harder, and he tightens his grip on the steering wheel. "But Zephyrine had told me about liminal days, and I didn't have any more time to wait."

"So you tried what you'd done with Elam. You killed her to bargain her life for yours with the Moth-Winged Man. And I'm sure the realization that she knew too much didn't factor into your decision at all." And I know he's wrong. Cole survived because of the bargain Vivian and Sissy had made, not anything Malcolm had done that day.

"I'm not a monster!" He hits the steering wheel with the palm of his hand. "I was trying to protect my family. But it didn't work. The doctor said there's no change."

"So what makes you think it'll work now? Today isn't liminal." I desperately try to use his own misconceptions to talk him out of whatever he's planning.

He gives me a look. "I heard you the other day at the sheriff's department. You're starting to remember what happened last summer. And now, with Cole . . . Time is running out."

"Just tell me one thing. Is Cole still alive?" My voice breaks, adrenaline and emotion flooding my system.

"He was never supposed to be involved!" Malcolm Spencer roars, his voice filling the car and pushing me back toward the door. That earthy flavor I'd tasted a hint of earlier, the one I couldn't quite put my finger on, comes over me now like a wave. *Desperation.* "But whether or not he remains alive is up to you. All you have to do is summon the Moth-Winged Man, make the bargain, and walk into the Bone Tree."

He wouldn't be telling me all of this if he had any intention of ever letting me go home again. Sliding across the gravel shoulder at forty miles an hour suddenly seems preferable to whatever he has planned. My heart rabbiting in my chest, I spin and reach for the door handle.

But he's faster. Before I can even get my hand on it, the lock flips and holds no matter how hard I pull. With no time to waste, I do the only other thing I can think of; I work at the knot of the graveyard dirt charm bag in my pocket until it comes untied. Bundling it in my hand, I throw it in his face.

"Bitch!" he yells, but he doesn't take his foot off the gas while he's temporarily blinded and struggling to keep me in the car.

We swerve wildly across the road, into the other lane and then back toward the trees on the opposite side. A scream spills out of me, filling the car. I think of Cole and what he must have experienced when he was forced off the road and into that tree. My stomach clenches, and I fight back with renewed vigor, swinging my fists and kicking as hard as I can in the small, enclosed space. I turn into a snarling animal, all claws and teeth, aiming for any soft bits, like Daddy taught us. Eyes, nose, throat, anywhere I can reach.

But he's still stronger and his reach is longer than mine and there's nowhere to get away from him. His fist nails me hard right in the cheekbone as he jerks the steering wheel with the other hand. I feel the car leave the road as my head bounces off the passenger-side window in a blaze of stars.

The screech of an owl overhead startles me awake. I reach up a hand that feels too heavy and rub my eyes, disoriented.

Somewhere something drips, then sizzles, and the smell of burning rubber is heavy in the air. Slowly, I turn my head, careful not to jolt the tender lump on the right side.

Malcolm Spencer is slumped in his seat, the air bag hanging limp between him and the steering wheel. There's a red smear on his window. I move too fast, causing my head to throb so hard it nearly turns my stomach inside out. My feet hit something, and it makes a crinkling sound. Leaning forward, I reach under the seat, and my fingers skim plastic. I grab on to it and pull it the rest of the way out. It's the bag the hospital sent home with me, my name written in black ink on the front. I squeeze my eyes shut at the sight of the clothes I wore that night, stiff with river water, and a tiny metal star with the words *Deputy Crunch* across the front. A set of keys on a ring from the library that I've never seen before, thrown in on top.

So there had been someone in the house that day. It was Malcolm Spencer, stealing this from my closet so I wouldn't find Elam's badge and connect the dots between what happened to him and what happened to me that night in the Forest. No matter what excuses and pretty lies he tells himself, a person who takes trophies or leaves calling cards on his victims isn't protecting his family. He's a monster.

I need to get out of here before he comes to. Wrenching open the car door, I stumble out, only making it a few steps before I gag and my dinner makes a reappearance. My head feels like it's being split apart, and my vision swims. I brace my hands on my knees and will the dizziness and nausea to pass.

Somewhere, Cole's still out there.

The sky is already going deep blue along the tops of the mountains. There isn't much light left. I look around, trying to get my bearings, but this could be any number of wooded back roads. Malcolm Spencer wanted to take me to the Bone Tree to summon the Moth-Winged Man, and if Cole was the means by which he intended to make me do it, I can only assume he'd have stashed him somewhere nearby. That narrows down the possibilities of where I am considerably, but I know all too well how easy it is to get turned around amongst all these trees.

I move toward higher ground. The words Hadrian told me last night pound in my head to the same beat as the pulsing knot from where I hit the window. I was drawn to the dead and to the Moth-Winged Man because I'd brushed against death but lived. Now I know it's because my mother made a bargain, like Cole's mother did all those years before. The pull was strongest when it led me to Dahlia shortly after her murder, but I'd felt it anytime I was near death. And Cole felt it too. He was connected to it like I was. So maybe we were also connected to each other.

I find a small clearing among the trees and sink to the ground, folding my legs underneath me. As I close my eyes, I try to push beyond the pain in my body, quieting my mind so I can tune in to even the slightest tug. It takes longer than I'd like, the threat of Malcolm and fear for Cole like a ticking clock in my head. Until at last, there, underneath my rib cage, a tiny pull. I latch on to it and scramble to my feet, taking my first steps into the Forest since last summer.

Somewhere nearby, water drips slowly onto stone and a stream gurgles. Darkness has settled in between the trees, spreading out and thickening. Farther away, like a whisper, I can hear the rush of the river. I must be getting close.

Moving deeper, I push through a dense copse of trees, branches interlocked like a maze, into a small clearing. And there, just before the edge of the cliff, is the Bone Tree, its white bark glowing above the creek and five thick branches clinging tightly to the earth.

A large dark shape on the ground moves to my left, and a low moan cuts through the silence. I freeze, but when the distinct smell of cloves hits me, I cry out in relief.

"Cole," I whisper. He's lying a few feet away, his skin ashen in the moonlight. When I reach him, he's clammy to the touch. Blood coats the side of his face from a gash on his forehead. I run my hands over him as gently as I can to check for signs of internal injuries from the crash. There's so much blood, he's sticky with it. His breath and heartbeat are too fast, and a worrying line of dried and foamy pink blood trails out of one side of his mouth. He needs to get to a hospital. Now.

"Cole, wake up. Come on, open your eyes for me."

He doesn't, but he grunts and catches my hand. "Linden, I remembered . . . the badge was in his office last spring . . ." He trails off, and his grip goes slack.

"Cole?" I sit up, wiping the tears off my cheeks as determination sets my jaw. "I'm going to get you out of here."

"I'm afraid not." Malcolm Spencer steps into the clearing, blood in his hair and a knife in his hand. "It's too late for that, Linden. I know you care for him. I've seen it with my own eyes. Open the Bone Tree so you can save his life."

"Why bring him into this at all?" I push up to my feet, throat thick with rage.

"You did that!" Malcolm roars back, surging toward me. "You encouraged him to dig into things he had no business messing with. He was never supposed to be part of this!"

Cole's eyes crack open, and he coughs, more pink and foamy blood running from the side of his mouth. He struggles to sit up, and I rush to help him. "Careful," I caution.

"He's running out of time," Malcolm observes solemnly. He points the knife at the Bone Tree. "If you want to save him, open it and summon the Moth-Winged Man so we can make a deal."

"There's only one of me, you can't trade my life for both of yours." I rise slowly to my feet and move toward the Bone Tree. "Would you save his life if it cost yours?"

Malcolm reaches for my arm, pressing the knife against my skin hard enough that a drop of blood rolls into my palm. "Quit stalling."

But I don't know the words that unlock the tree.

Malcolm is so focused on me, he doesn't see Cole moving until it's too late. Cole lunges and takes him to the ground hard, the knife biting deep into my arm as they fall.

"Run," Cole grunts, struggling to hold back his father.

I hesitate for a split second, not wanting to leave him injured and alone, but this could be our only chance to get help. I push off from the Bone Tree and run as fast as I can.

I've only made it a few yards when I hear the pound of heavy footsteps behind me, closing in fast. The thick canopy of branches blocks what little light there is from the moon. I run as fast as I dare through the trees, but when the dark closes in completely, I have to slow to a walk or risk giving myself another concussion.

"You won't get away, Linden," Malcolm's voice calls out, too close for comfort. "No one is coming to save you. By the time anyone thinks to look out here, it'll be too late. You'll die in these woods, one way or another."

I bite my lip, knowing better than to respond to his taunts and give away my location. Focusing on moving as quickly and quietly as I can, I don't notice at first that he has stopped talking. I pause for a moment, listening for the sound of his footsteps.

An owl shrieks and swoops down through the night sky. I duck, just as a fist smashes into a tree trunk right where my head was.

"Shit!" Malcolm shouts, cradling his hand.

I take off, racing through the Forest, but panic makes me clumsy, and I stumble in the twilight. Branches and brambles pull at my hair and tear at my skin, but the thrum of terror racing through my veins numbs me to the pain. My steps move from soft dirt to the crunch of pine needles. All I hear now is the rush of my own blood in my ears.

This is my nightmare bled into waking life. These are the endless trees I see every night, the darker blackness that marks the cliff's edge, the same feeling of panic in my chest as someone chases me. It becomes harder and harder to breathe.

A white moth flutters between the trees in front of me, then another and another, until there's at least a dozen spots of light against the darkness. *Moth of white, loved one in flight.* Maybe it was never a nightmare. Maybe it was a warning.

Before I can follow the moths, Malcolm tackles me from behind. Pebbles and twigs dig in and scrape the skin of my face as my momentum pushes me across the ground. The sharp, copper tang of my own blood fills my mouth. I spit it out into the dirt.

"Is this how Zephyrine *chose* to walk into the Bone Tree, too?" I struggle to get away, but he's too heavy. "Did you wear your uniform, like with Elam? Did you use your service revolver, hold her at gunpoint? Is that how she made her choice to save your life?"

"She wouldn't have figured out how to make the trade if she wasn't willing to do it." He shoves me over onto my back, trapping my arms between his knees. "It's not my fault I fell out of love with her. That she caught me with Vivian. It was too late to back out."

"Her note was for you, wasn't it? You ripped your name off the top and used her keys to get into the farmhouse and leave it for Gran so no one would ever suspect what you'd done."

The ice of his cold detachment freezes in my throat and I choke. He slaps me so hard my head bounces off the ground.

I must black out for a second because, when I come to, his hands are wrapped around my throat.

"You stupid, stupid bitch," he says in a voice low and deadly. "I think I might actually enjoy killing you."

My vision goes black around the edges, and I can barely muster the strength to fight him. His grip loosens for a moment, and I feel him slide something into my pocket. "Dahlia's four-leaf clover," he says, as if from a long distance. "It has a nice symmetry."

As my lungs scream for air, my oxygen-deprived brain offers up an idea. If I could give Amos McCoy a little peace by calling up the taste of the emotion, then maybe I can make Malcolm Spencer feel something too.

I squeeze my eyes shut, struggling to focus when my entire body is screaming to fight. Calm. Calm is the taste of freshly whipped cream, light and airy on the tongue.

Malcolm's hands loosen on my neck, and the smallest sip of air makes its way into my lungs. But he doesn't let go. I need to make him feel something stronger than calm.

Guilt. He should feel guilty for everything he's done. Guilt is the taste of oily fish. It coats the mouth and the conscience with its pungent flavor. Malcolm lets go of my neck and scurries backward across the forest floor away from me. He stares down at his hands as if he can't believe they're his.

I struggle to get my feet underneath me, crouching as I gasp for breath and clear the fog in my head. Malcolm looks around, checking over his shoulder. He focuses his attention back on me and advances, jaw set in grim determination, and I realize my mistake. People hate to feel guilty, and they'll do almost anything to keep others from discovering the source of their shame. He'd kill me just to keep it secret. I scramble backward on my hands and feet in an awkward crabwalk.

When he grabs my ankle, he goes flying backward.

"Hello, Malcolm Spencer." A voice echoes through the shadows around us. "I've been waiting for this day for a long time."

"Who the hell are you?" Malcolm growls from where he landed, his back against the forest floor.

"Don't recognize me? I'm not surprised. After all, I was only four years old when you held my head underwater and watched me drown."

"That's not possible," Malcolm whispers. "You're dead."

"Turns out it's a bit more complicated than that." Hadrian's wings unfurl behind him and his eyes go red. "Do you have anything to say for yourself?"

Remorse, I realize. Remorse is the feeling Malcolm Spencer has never shown, not once. Not when confronted with everything he's done, not even when he was willing to sacrifice his son in order to extend his own life. Every life he stole never added up to what he thought he was owed.

Remorse is the taste of licorice root. Bitter, salty, and earthy with a hint of cloying sweetness. I know the exact moment he feels it. His entire face seems to slide downward, and he stumbles backward with the force of it.

I push myself up and move toward him, the taste of the licorice root building in my mouth as I think of all the people he's hurt: Zephyrine, Elam, Dahlia, Cole. And all those harmed in the aftermath of what he's done: Gran; Amos, Nora, and Wyatt McCoy; the Hinkles. Hell, the entire town, divided by fear and poisoned by his lies.

"Linden." Hadrian's tone is warning, but I ignore him and step closer to Malcolm.

The taste of the remorse is pouring out of my mouth, seeping from my pores, overwhelming all my senses.

"I'm so sorry. All those people. My god, what have I done?" He clutches his head and backs away from me, trying to escape the power of the emotion.

At least that's what I think, until I realize his true intent.

"No!" I scream, releasing the feeling and rushing forward to try to stop him, but it's too late.

Malcolm disappears from sight, plunging over the cliff and into the shadowy blackness of the water below.

Hadrian hooks an arm around my waist, pulling me from the edge before I follow Malcolm over. "It's too late. There's nothing we can do now."

"Oh god, it's my fault." I press my hands over my face, trying to block out the image of him tumbling over the edge.

"You couldn't have made him feel that way if he didn't warrant it. People aren't gardens where you can plant whatever you want. You can only grow what's already there."

"What are you doing here, anyway?" I ask, sniffling. "How did you find me?"

"James blood spilled at the Bone Tree," Hadrian reminds me, pointing to the gash Malcolm opened in my arm.

"Cole," I gasp, turning on my heel and retracing my steps back through the Forest as quickly as I dare.

When I reach the Bone Tree, my stomach drops at the sight of him, lying there on his back, one arm draped across his chest, the other over his face.

"Do you want me to check?" Hadrian offers softly as he comes up behind me.

"No." I shake my head, and it flares with pain. "I need to do it."

I drop to my knees beside Cole and gently move his arm. The knife his father used to cut me is planted deep in his side. His skin is cool to the touch. I slide my fingers up his neck to find his pulse. It's barely there and much too fast, like the flutter of a hummingbird's wing. He's not going to make it. A sob, just one, escapes my throat, but I'm not ready to give up.

Not yet.

"Hadrian?"

"Linden, don't." His voice is solemn but firm.

"I'd like to make a bargain."

He shakes his head as if he can't believe my foolishness. "Have you learned nothing from the mistakes of others?" He breathes a heavy sigh and meets my eyes. "What price are you willing to pay?"

CHAPTER TWENTY-EIGHT

THE WAIL of sirens cuts through the silence of the night as red and blue lights flash between the trees. When I reach the edge of the Forest, the glare from the headlights of all the squad cars lined up and pointed at me is blinding.

"Step out of the trees with your hands up," a voice commands through a bullhorn.

I lift my arms above my head and step forward. My bottom lip trembles, and I pull it between my teeth.

"You're safe now, kiddo," a very familiar voice says from my left.

I turn and spot him amongst the sea of brown uniforms. I'm covered in dirt and sweat, blood and tears, but when Daddy opens his arms, I fling myself against him, sobbing with everything I can't hold back anymore. He hugs me as tight as he dares, then ushers me into the back of a waiting ambulance.

At the hospital, Ethan sits next to me, explaining how they were able to find me in what I'm pretty sure is a thinly veiled attempt to distract me from the pain as a doctor stitches up my arm. Or maybe he does it for himself, since anytime he accidentally glances down, he goes a little green.

"As much as I'd like to say it was my stellar police work, it was actually Hillard Been," Ethan says.

"I'm sorry, the pain meds must be kicking in. Can you repeat that?"

He grins at me, showing off the dimple in his left cheek that I know he must get mercilessly teased about at the station. "He's taken to sitting out in front of the Harvest Moon most nights. But on his way there, he said the strangest thing happened. A whole gust of red flower petals blew across the road in front of him, and when he turned to look, he saw Malcolm Spencer's car headed toward the Forest with you asleep in the passenger seat. It struck him as odd, so he called it in. We found Spencer's car wrecked on the old mine road, and your dad tracked you up the mountain."

The best tracker in the whole county, together with a simple finding spell, powered by the magic of six James witches, led them right to us.

Daddy pushes aside the curtain and leads Mama inside as the doctor finishes up. She swoops in and pulls me into a fierce hug. "We're going to have a nice long talk when we get home," she whispers in my ear, then squeezes me again. "Don't you ever do anything like this to me again."

When Mama is busy with the discharge nurse, I sneak away to a room at the far end of the hall. The door is open, and I lean against the frame, taking comfort in the steady beep of the heart monitor while Cole sleeps peacefully in his hospital bed. His color is better already, and I watch the blanket rise and fall in time with his strong breathing.

"The doctors say it's another miracle," Vivian tells me as she walks up, a cup of vending machine coffee in her hand. She turns to look at me, tears in her eyes. "Whatever deal you had to make, I hope it's one you can live with." Her voice breaks, and the last words are barely a whisper: "Thank you."

When we get back to the farm, I take the hottest shower I can handle, standing under the stream until the water heater groans and gives up. I pull on clean pajamas and drag myself down to the kitchen, where Mama and Gran wait to give me what I expect will be the greatest and most terrifying lecture of my life.

When I sit down at the table, Gran presses a teacup into my hands. I take a sip and nearly choke. "Gran, this is moonshine."

"I know good and well what it is, child. Some things call for tea. Some things call for 'shine. A true mountain woman always knows the difference."

"Linden, first of all," Mama starts, "I'm sorry."

"Excuse me?" I ask, thrown by the very last thing I ever expected her to say.

"We're all sorry." She nods toward Sissy and Gran. "I was furious with you for running off and nearly getting yourself killed." Mama chokes up and has to pause for a second to regain her composure. "But then I realized you were doing what we taught you. Keeping secrets and trying to handle everything all by yourself. A lesson that could have cost you your life, and for that I am sorrier than you'll ever know."

"Girls, come in here, please," Gran calls out.

Sorrel, Rowan, and Juniper come down the back stairs so quickly they could only have been already there, eavesdropping.

"This concerns all of us, so take a seat and grab a cup. We James women have faced innumerable adversities through the years. The kind that would crush most people. But the only way we made it through is together. We're stronger that way. So no more secrets."

"And no more hanging our heads in shame." Mama smiles at Gran.

I cringe and clear my throat. "Speaking of secrets," I begin, then fill them in on Hadrian's true identity.

Everyone starts talking at once, and it's too much to pick out any one voice, except Rowan, who crows, "Told you he

was a liar!" before topping off her teacup of apple pie moonshine while no one is looking.

In the morning, we find Hillard Been sitting on the steps of
the front porch, hat in his hands.

"Mornin', ladies," he greets us, standing up. "I know y'all
have been through a lot, but I was wondering when you
might be reopening the Harvest Moon."

Mama and Gran exchange a look. "The thing is, Hillard.
We probably won't be reopening," Gran tells him, her voice
low and toneless.

"Not to pry, but do you mind my asking why not?"

"We can't afford to, Hillard," Mama tells him flatly.

"Well, now, I thought that might be the case, and I'd like
to help," he says, rocking back on his heels bashfully.

"Oh, Hillard, that's mighty kind of you," Gran says. "But
I'm afraid the amount we'd need to reopen is quite a bit of
money."

"Apollonia." Hillard lowers his voice. "I figured that, too.
The thing is, I'm frugal. I have no children, never married. I
live in the same house I was born in. My one extravagance
in life is eating at your diner every day."

"Hillard, what exactly are you saying?" Gran asks. She
looks like she's afraid to get her hopes up.

"I'm saying, I've *got* quite a bit of money," Hillard insists.
"And I'd like to invest it in you and the Harvest Moon."

CHAPTER TWENTY-NINE

A COUPLE weeks later, I stop at the cemetery on the way to the Harvest Moon's grand reopening and make my way to the small metal grave marker for Nora McCoy. The violently red rhododendron that had grown up out of nowhere over her final resting place had dropped all its blossoms and is now growing back in a creamy shade of white.

I can't help but wonder about that strange, discordant breeze that blew through town on the day she passed. Was it a curse on those who couldn't or wouldn't bring back her younger son? Or was it a warning that his killer was about to strike again? Either way, I hope she's at peace now.

I place the bouquet I cut from the farm this morning next to the marker, rosemary for remembrance and honeysuckle for letting go.

"They found Malcolm's body a few miles downstream," I say. "When they pulled him from the water, it looked as though he had already been dead for twenty years. No one can explain it."

Hadrian moves around the sweet gum tree and comes to stand next to me. "Stolen time." He shoves his hands in his pockets.

"I wanted to give you this." He holds up a key monogrammed with a *J*, the perfect match to the one Gran keeps in the secret cupboard. "This was the only thing I had with me after I died. I can almost remember grabbing it, trying to hold on. I think Malcolm must have been wearing it around his neck."

"It would have been helpful to know you had this a few weeks ago." I wrap my hand around it and meet his eyes.

"It was the only clue I had in my murder, and it pointed directly to your family," he tells me. "I am sorry, though, for what it's worth."

"Is she really gone, then?" The legend tells us that white moths are the spirits of our lost loved ones, and I've considered more than once that those moths I saw were sent by Aunt Zephyrine, guiding me along, but I've been holding on to Gran's hope. Maybe we'll go to bed one night and she'll be home by morning.

"Not everything can be clearly defined as either one way or the other."

I nod. He's evidence of that himself.

"I went out to the Bone Tree this morning." He shifts to look at me. "There's a crack through the center, so big it's nearly split in two."

"What does it mean?" I ask. "Is it a bridge no one can cross or a door no one can lock?"

He shrugs. "Only time will tell."

We stand next to each other for a while, both lost in our own thoughts. "Come by the diner later," I say at last. "I made a batch of soothing lemon lavender shortbread. You can take some to Amos."

"I'm sure he'd like that," Hadrian says. The words are simple enough, but the emotion that rolls off of them is gristle in the mouth, tasteless and uncomfortable, and something I know well myself. Loneliness.

I finally ask the question that's been bothering me for weeks. "How could Elam's life—your life—have been traded for Cole's? It wasn't Vivian's to give."

"It wasn't," he says simply. "The life Vivian traded for Cole's wasn't Elam's. It was her own. She stopped living after that night, closing herself off and losing who she was to her guilt."

"So you didn't need to die." My throat goes tight, choked by the unfairness of it all.

"No one did."

"Do you think you'll tell Amos who you really are someday?" I ask.

He studies the grave marker before he answers. "I don't know how to be Elam McCoy anymore. I think to try would be unfair to both of us. And I can't stay here. What I can do is help him with some of the work around his place and make sure he eats a good meal once in a while." He bumps his shoulder into mine, and then, with a farewell wink, Hadrian walks on, and I make my way to the diner.

Every single person in Caball Hollow and their brother have descended on the Harvest Moon today. Every booth is full. Every stool at the counter is occupied. There's a line out the door waiting for tables, and the phone has been ringing off the hook all day with to-go orders.

"What do they taste like, feelings?" Juniper asks in a soft voice as we look out at the crowded dining room.

"All sorts of things," I tell her. "Like lemon is the taste of fresh starts and new beginnings. And happiness is sweet and crisp like biting into a fresh apple. Grief is earthy and bitter like chicory root. Sadness is potent and sour like buttermilk." I rub at the bandage on my arm. My stitches have been itching all morning.

"Boy, something smells delicious," Hillard says as he squeezes in at his usual table across from Buck Garland. "I sure have missed your cooking, Apollonia."

Some of our most popular new menu items are the special baked goods I developed. We've already sold out of the calming chamomile tea cakes that help soothe nervous dispositions, the cardamom rose petal shortbread to soften hearts, and the chocolate chess happiness pie.

I glance toward the new front window, where Sissy painted a logo for the Harvest Moon. A circular image, all in white, of the Forest with a stag leaping between curving trees, the full moon framed by his antlers. Beyond the glass, two figures catch my attention.

Sissy faces Vivian Spencer, with one hand cupping her cheek. She leans forward and presses her mouth to Vivian's in a kiss that looks like love but tastes like goodbye. Then Vivian climbs into the passenger seat of a dark sedan, and Sissy watches as it drives away before she steps back into the diner.

When she gets to the counter, I toss her an apron. "Everything okay?" I ask under the din of the packed dining room.

"She's going away for a while to get the help she needs. She's finally ready to move on with her life."

"What about you?" I ask. "Are you okay?"

"I'm ready to move on with my life, too." She smiles, only a little sadly.

"Order up." Rowan slides a to-go order into the window from the kitchen side.

I pull it down and check the ticket. "There's no name on it," I call to her through the window.

Her face reappears, but she just shrugs.

"Tomato and mayo on white for pickup?" I read off the order as I turn back to the dining room.

"That's me."

My head jerks up, and there's Cole, looking as perfect as ever. One new scar bisects his right eyebrow now, and somehow it makes him even more handsome.

"Hello, Cole," Sissy says. "I heard you were out of the hospital."

"Yeah, the doctors said they should study my healing abilities." He rubs the back of his neck. "How have you been, Linden?"

Malcolm Spencer's betrayal and death hit the whole town hard, but it sent a shock wave through Cole. He deferred his acceptance to Georgetown, and he's planning to leave Caball Hollow for a while. Last week, he told me he understands if I want to see other people. I haven't spoken to him since.

"Good, but busy. Really busy with reopening and everything. And we're taking Sorrel back to college tomorrow," I ramble, feeling like my heart is trying to crawl out of my throat and across the counter to him.

"Right, well, that's good to hear. I guess I'll see you around." He drops some cash next to the register and turns toward the door.

"A miraculous recovery, hmm?" Sissy asks from behind me as Cole heads out of the diner. "Are you ready to tell me what you traded yet?"

"A life for a life," I tell her without taking my eyes off him.

She grabs my arm and forces me to look at her. "Care to explain that?"

"I gave Hadrian the diablerie. No future generation of James witches will ever be able to summon him again. No more bargains. No more favors. His life for Cole's."

Sissy's eyes widen, then slowly she nods and squeezes my arm.

When I turn back, Cole is already gone and I drop my eyes, straightening my apron to give myself a moment to blink away tears.

"What do Cole's feelings taste like?" Juniper asks from behind me. "When it's just the two of you?"

Her words bring back that night in the field, surrounded by fireflies. Cole and me, together. "Like the first peaches of the summer, fresh off the tree and still warm from the sun," I tell her, my voice watery. "But it doesn't matter, he's leaving."

"Oh, it matters," Sissy says. "What is love if not the most powerful magic of all?"

"What would you do, Sissy?" I ask her.

"For love?" She turns so she can look me right in the eye. "What wouldn't I do?"

I glance over at Juniper and spot Rowan and Sorrel grinning at me from the order window.

"Well, what are you waiting for? Go get your boy," Rowan tells me.

I whip off my apron and throw it at her, then rush for the door.

"Cole!" I call out as he opens the door of his new truck. He sets the takeout box inside and turns to watch me approach, his expression giving nothing away.

"Is something wrong?" he asks when I reach him.

"No. Well, yes," I say. "I know you're leaving town soon."

"Yeah, tomorrow, actually." He scratches his arm under his sleeve, like he's a little embarrassed.

"Tomorrow?" I squeak.

"I've watched the sun set in these hills my whole life, Linden. I thought it might be nice to maybe get a little lost for a while, see what it looks like from the other side."

"Well, before you go, I just wanted to tell you." I pause to clear my throat. My cheeks heat up as he watches me try to be brave one more time. "That is, I wanted you to know that I think I might be a little bit in love with you. And I understand if you don't feel the same way, but I wanted to tell you in case maybe you thought that someday you might."

A slow smile lifts the side of his mouth. "Well, it's about damn time." He pulls me into his arms. "I love you, too, Linden James. I love the way you buzz when you're working on a new recipe, how you'd move heaven and earth to help anyone who needs it and how you don't even realize how uncommon that is, and how you're sweet as sugar and strong as hell." He leans in closer until I can feel his breath against my cheekbone. "And I love how when I kiss you, you make this little humming sound in the back of your throat."

He takes my hand and presses it over his heart, and when I lift up on my tiptoes, there, on the back of my tongue, is the taste of peaches and sunshine. As he puts his mouth on mine, right in the middle of the street, the skies open up and rain drenches us, crisp and cool. Steam rises up from the hot pavement, and a cold front moves in with an audible snap, breaking the heat wave.

I realize, at the end of this long, hot summer, that I can add a few more hard-won lessons to the list of things I know for sure: There's always room for another seat at the table. Love is worth fighting for. And if not for the bitter, we'd miss the magic of the sweet.

ACKNOWLEDGMENTS

FIRST, THANK you, dear reader, for spending some time among these pages. While writing can often be a solitary endeavor, turning my words into the book you hold in your hands was the work of many. I don't know how to fully convey the depths of my gratitude to all the amazing people who helped make this dream come true, but I'm sure going to try.

Pete Knapp, the best agent in the whole wide world, thank you for being such a fierce champion and tireless advocate. You saw the potential in this story and in me, and for that I'm forever grateful. It's an immense relief to know you've always got my back. I couldn't navigate this industry without you and I wouldn't want to try. My heartfelt thanks as well to the members of #TeamPete for so warmly welcoming me, especially Ayana Gray and Amélie Wen Zhao.

Polo Orozco, my extraordinary editor, I'm so grateful this story found its way to you. You guided it through the publication process with the utmost care and helped me shape it into the very best version of itself. Thank you for your patient counsel and unwavering encouragement. I am a much better writer because of you.

To the incredible teams at Penguin Young Readers and G. P. Putnam's Sons Books for Young Readers, I am in awe of the work you do. Thank you for turning my words into the book of my dreams, Jennifer Loja, Amanda Close, Shanta Newlin, Elyse Marshall, Emily Romero, Christina Colangelo, Alex Garber, Carmela Iaria, Helen Boomer, Kim Ryan, Cindy Howle, Misha Kydd, Jacqueline Hornberger, Ana Deboo, Miranda Shulman, Nicole Rheingans, Shannon Spann, Felicity Vallence, James Akinaka, Liz Vaughan, and Natalie Vielkind. My sincerest thanks as well to Jessica Jenkins for designing a gorgeous cover that beautifully captures the essence of this story and to Imogen Oh for bringing it to life in the most breathtaking way.

And a very special thank-you to my publisher, Jennifer Klonsky, for believing in this little story about sisters from the very beginning. I hope it makes you proud.

My unending gratitude to the extraordinary team at Park & Fine Literary and Media. Abigail Koons, Kathryn Toolan, and Ben Kaslow-Zieve, thank you for working so diligently to get this story into the hands of readers throughout the world. Stuti Telidevara, thank you for always keeping everything running smoothly and being altogether amazing.

Isabel Ibañez, you are the fairy godmother of this book.

Thank you for reading so many messy drafts, for sharing your creative brilliance, and for your unerring counsel in navigating the publishing world. And, of course, thank you for giving Cole his motorcycle. You are a gift, and I'm thankful I can call you friend.

Kristin Dwyer, I'm so glad we found each other and could walk part of this journey together. Thank you for always answering my questions, no matter how ridiculous, even when I forgot how time zones worked.

Thank you to Adrienne Young, Stephanie Garber, Erin Bowman, Alexandra Bracken, Sara Raasch, Siobhan Vivian, Andrea Hannah, Lindsay Eager, and Shea Ernshaw for sharing your advice and insight at some of the most pivotal moments in this journey. You may not have even realized how much your words meant, but to me they were signposts that led me to this moment.

To the 2019 Pitch Wars mentees and mentors, thank you for your friendship and support. I'm so grateful to be part of this community.

Martin Vecchio, thank you for your vast stores of patience, perhaps matched only by your immeasurable skill as a photographer. Nick Katsarelas and Julie Bitely, thank you for your steadfast encouragement and support. Let's never stop meeting up for lunch. Amy Kukla Duwe, Erika Vecchio, and Jessica Holmgren, I love you all so much. I'm so grateful that, no matter how much time has passed, we can still pick up right where we left off.

Publishing a first book is a rather lengthy process, so if you've been around since this book was little more than a scramble of ideas on my computer, thank you. Each encouraging word meant the world to me.

To my family, thank you for a lifetime of love and encouragement. This novel grew from a seed that was planted long before I even realized, all the way back to when my sisters and I would beg our mother for bedtime stories from her childhood, growing up in rural West Virginia. There was a special cadence to those tales, a rhythm that wove a spell of mist-covered mountains and coal-dusted shadows. It never left me. Which is why, at its heart, this is a story about family.

Ava and Ellie, this world is beautiful because you are in it. Thank you for being my most ardent supporters. David, thanks for keeping the home fires burning on the nights I was up writing with the moths. To my parents, thank you for filling our home with books and showing me that each one was made of magic. To Grandma Ann and Mamaw Joyce, thank you for everything you've taught me. You have inspired me greatly and, in turn, have inspired the women in this book. I hope you can feel my love for you on every page. And to my sisters, Liberty Pearsall and Josie Castro, who were my very first readers back before I knew about things like plot and spelling, I can't imagine life without you. Thank you for always accepting me for who I am and also never letting me get away with anything.

A new beast prowls the Forest.
A new mystery haunts the Hollow.
Can Rowan James smoke out the
secrets of this town?

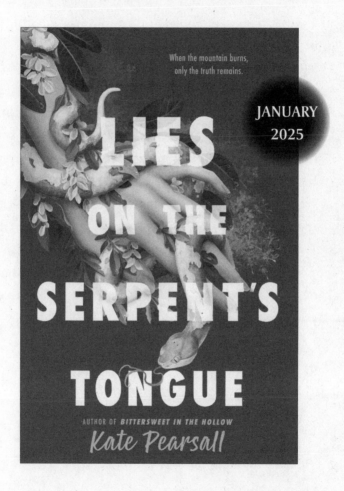

Turn the page to start reading.

CHAPTER ONE

THE SMELL of a lie is a potent thing, burnt around the edges and foul all the way through. Sometimes it's so strong I imagine it must singe the mouth of the teller like a hot coal. But not even that would stop them. Everybody lies, and that's the honest truth.

Some are chronic liars, almost like they've developed a taste for it, and the stench lingers like smokers' breath, a pungent reminder they're not to be trusted. Others dabble in the practice, a few choice fibs they keep around, like bits of charred meat stuck between their teeth. And then there are the ones who lie like they're doing you a favor. They fill the air with putrescence and expect you to be grateful for the experience. As if the truth could ever be more shameful than their falsehoods.

"I shouldn't have let myself get roped into this," I mutter as Gran parks the old Bronco in front of Caball Hollow's town hall, a squat brick box built in the 1980s generic corporate style of so many insurance agencies or orthodontic practices dotted throughout Appalachia.

"We'll be in and out in an hour," Gran says. "Two tops. And you know good and well we woulda been here anyhow. This way, at least we get paid for it. Now, quit your bellyaching and get a move on."

The first public meeting of the town council following the sudden death of the mayor last month is likely not the best place for someone with my particular ability, but Gran isn't wrong. When she got the call at the diner this morning asking us to cater, I knew I couldn't miss it. Not after everything my family has been through.

The first of the maples and poplars have already started to drop their leaves, and they crunch beneath my feet as I make my way to the tailgate, where I collect trays of lavender shortbread to ease conversation and chess cake for softening hearts.

For as long as anyone can remember, we James women have been born with certain talents. Sorrel, my older sister, can charm bees to do her bidding, making honey with special properties that enhance any spell. Linden, younger than me by only eleven months, can taste the emotions of others. And my youngest sister, Juniper, sees beyond this world to the next. Yet, since our earliest ancestor, Caorunn James, first stepped out of the Forest and into Caball Hollow more than two hundred years ago, those

4

gifts have meant we've been treated with an air of suspicion, if not downright contempt, by our neighbors. Even when we use them for their benefit, like Gran's healing tinctures. Or the baked goods Linden made for this very meeting. It's more than I would have done after what this town put her through.

When I reach the wide front door of the hall, I press my back against it to push it open while balancing the trays in my arms, nearly plowing into council member Gayle Anne Gerlach. She casts me an annoyed glance, then puts a perfectly manicured hand on the shoulder of a tired-looking woman I'm pretty sure is the town clerk, leading her away to continue their conversation with a saccharine smile.

My eye catches on the black-and-white photograph of the original town hall, prominently displayed in the fluorescent-lit lobby. The ornate, neoclassical structure was struck by lightning and burnt down decades ago, its image a sharp contrast to the yellowed walls and generic industrial carpet of the current building. The only room with any ounce of grandeur now is also the only one filmed by the local public access station—the city council meeting room, with its raised dais for the council members, dark wood-paneled walls, and the large gold medallion with the Caball Hollow town crest, front and center, behind the empty chair reserved for the mayor.

One of the staffers points me to a folding table at the back of the space, and by the time Gran and I have finished laying out the refreshments, the room is thick with too many bodies and too little circulation. The smell of strong coffee wafting from the carafe next to me isn't enough to cover the stench in the air as the council members scramble to impress voters ahead of the election in a couple months. Even local politicians are prone to stretch the truth with empty promises.

Okey Spurgeon, president of the town council, ends a call on his cell phone and steps up to the seat on the dais behind his nameplate before attempting to quiet the crowd and call the meeting to order. Gran eyes me from the other side of the table when I drop down into a hard plastic chair, but she holds her tongue for once. I prop my elbows against my knees to cover my nose without drawing attention. Beulah Fordham Hayes from the school board cuts me an irritated look anyway, her steely gaze matching the steel-gray hair that ripples in reproach as she turns away. I pull the collar of my sweater up over the lower half of my face. Not that it matters. I've always been able to sniff out a lie, even when I'd rather not.

"All right, y'all, let's get down to our first order of business," Okey begins. His perpetually rosy cheeks are extra sanguine this evening. It's standing room only now. Big entertainment for such a small town. "And the reason I'm sure most of you are here. We're only a couple weeks into ginseng season, and already we have some grave concerns. Preliminary evidence shows the recent car accident near the National Forest that killed one young man may have been related to ginseng poaching."

"Ginseng numbers are at an all-time low, and the National Forests in North Carolina and Tennessee aren't allowing harvesting this year, which means the prices per pound are higher than ever as dealers struggle to fill orders from their international buyers," Gayle Anne Gerlach chimes in from his right. "It's driving an unsavory crowd straight into Caball Hollow."

"There ain't much ginseng here no more, neither," Hillard Been mutters from the row in front of me in that old-man way that means the whole room hears it.

"It sure is getting smaller and harder to find," someone else agrees. "Large root, old 'sang is a thing of the past."

Okey looks annoyed as he brushes a hand over his receding hairline, but ignores the interruption. "As I was saying, in light of recent events, we've asked a representative from the Forest Service to come and address the issue of how we can work together to keep our community safe during the rest of ginseng season."

He gestures for someone in the audience to come forward. A woman in a dark green Forest Service uniform stands and makes her way to the lectern stationed at the front of the room. Frances Vernon, known to all and sundry as Vernie, has been a fixture of the National Forest for as long as I've been alive and probably a lot longer.

"We have just the right elevation, rainfall, and mineral-rich soil to produce some of the best wild ginseng in the world," she says, inciting murmurs of agreement. "But wild ginseng is threatened from centuries of overharvesting.

Taking the root ends the plant's ability to replace itself for new generations. That's why it's only legal to dig the roots from the end of summer to the first frost, September through November, and only those at least five years old and with seed-bearing, bright red berries. All diggers must have a current permit from the Forest Service to remove ginseng from the National Forest and are required, by law, to plant the seeds where they dug the root."

"And what happens if someone violates those rules?" Gayle Anne demands, her arched eyebrows shooting up over her glasses. "Laws are only as good as their enforcement, and I believe in being tough on crime." She nods decisively, like she's making a campaign promise.

"We've certainly seen an increase in violations over the last decade or so," Vernie admits. "Which is why we now have harsher penalties. A first violation may be a one-thousand-dollar fine, but subsequent offenses can mean much higher fines and jail time. A man over in Mud River just pleaded guilty to five Lacey Act violations for illegally trafficking in ginseng. Each of those could mean up to a hundred-thousand-dollar fine and one year in prison."

A rumble runs through the crowd as this statement sparks dozens of side conversations, and Vernie is forced to raise her hands for silence before she can continue. "We take this very seriously because illegal harvesting puts ginseng at risk of disappearing, an important part of our culture and heritage. But the potential for a big payday means some are willing to take that risk."

"Ranger Vernon, what can we all do to help keep poachers out of Caball Hollow?" Okey asks, gesturing toward the audience.

"If you see signs of possible illegal activity, like vehicles parked in remote areas for long periods of time; possession of sharpened sticks, trowels, or even hoes that have been altered to avoid damaging the skin of the root, which would drop its value; and disturbed soil where ginseng is known or likely to grow, please report it. We'll also be increasing the number of patrols within the National Forest itself," Vernie explains.

"Poachers better stay away from my spot, or the law will be the least of their worries," someone to my left mutters.

"Please do not attempt to confront suspected poachers," Vernie stresses, holding up her hands for emphasis. "There's no need to put yourself in danger. Notify the Forest Service or local law enforcement, and we'll handle it."

"I'm sure we'll all keep a lookout for anything suspicious," Okey says. "Thank you, Vernie." He gestures for the forest ranger to take her seat.

I roll my eyes. The National Forest is nearly a million acres, with the Appalachian mountain range running right through its center. It surrounds Caball Hollow like a massive jaw waiting to snap. With its rocky crevices, deep rivers, murky bogs, dense woods, and laurel hells so dense and twisted that if you wander in you're liable to never make it out, the National Forest is made up of some of the most ecologically diverse land in the nation. The idea that Okey

Spurgeon, sitting in a lawn chair inside his open garage with binoculars and a beer, might catch a poacher is so laughable, I have to bite my tongue.

"All right, y'all, let's come to order." Okey Spurgeon tries to get the meeting back on track. "We still have a lot to cover this evening, including the recent uptick in petty theft."

"I'll just say what we're all thinking." Gayle Anne Gerlach taps her ink pen against the notepad on the table in front of her. "I don't think the increase in crime and the increase in unfamiliar faces around town is a coincidence. And I'm not just talking about ginseng hunters coming in and causing problems. We've also got people like those internet folks. They may not be breaking the law, but they've been sticking their noses where they don't belong, stirring up trouble that's better left to lie."

I scoff, earning myself another glare from Beulah Fordham Hayes. No, it's not strangers we need to fear most—they're the ones we keep at a distance. It's the people you trust who are close enough to stab you in the back. Because everybody lies. And in knowing their lies, I become the keeper of their secrets.

Caball Hollow is a one-stoplight town stuck so far out in the middle of nowhere that rarely even does a strong cell signal find its way to us. For generations, our only claim to fame was the folklore of a monster that haunted our Forest. The legend of the Moth-Winged Man, a creature with the body of a man and the wings of a moth said to be a sure sign of impending misfortune, was a tale told by old men to prove their mettle or young mothers to keep their children from wandering too far. Completely fictional. Until it wasn't.

When sightings of the Moth-Winged Man were reported just before Caball Hollow's first official murder a few months ago, it made the news and drew all kinds of morbid curiosity seekers. Most of them gave up once the scandal died down, but the crew of so-called monster hunters with a YouTube channel that rolled into town last week doesn't seem in any hurry to leave and is clearly ruffling a few feathers. I'm certainly no fan, but the idea that crime only happens in Caball Hollow because of outsiders isn't just delusional, it's downright dangerous. The empty chair on the dais is proof enough of that. After all, the murderer was born and bred right here.

"It's true. Crime is becoming a real problem," Beulah informs me. "Just the other day, Roy Bivens couldn't find his keys, and when he went outside, his car was gone. Disappeared right out of his driveway."

"It was in front of the Pub 'n' Grub, where he left it the night before." Hillard Been turns around in his chair. "Fool was probably still so pickled he didn't recognize it. Whoever took his keys did the whole town a favor."

Beulah huffs and picks an invisible piece of lint from her jacket, but Hillard isn't done. "Course, on the other hand, he's not the only one who's lost something lately." He lets the sentence hang, and there's clearly some context I'm missing, but I don't have to wait long for the answer to present itself.

"I already done told you once," Buck Garland growls at Hillard Been from somewhere behind me. He must have come in late, like the others standing in the back of the room. "I got no earthly idea what you're talking about."

"You've got to have it, Buck," Hillard argues back, undeterred. "I gave it to you when I retired. It was my most prized possession, and you promised you'd take care of it."

Buck shakes his head in frustration. "You must have me confused with someone else at the post office, old man."

Hillard stares at him, bug-eyed and whompyjawed. "You fall on your head recently, son?"

"I take it y'all lost something?" I interrupt, partly because they're getting louder and others are starting to notice, and partly just to needle them for my own amusement.

"*We* didn't lose nothing," Hillard insists. "This damn fool claims he never had my granddaddy's pocket watch when the entire Caball Hollow postal service saw me give it to him."

I remember the day he's talking about. The two of them came into the Harvest Moon diner for lunch afterward, like they do every day, and Buck was showing the watch off to everybody who'd listen.

"And I told you, you're confused," Buck insists, then turns to me. I brace for the lie I know is coming. "It happens sometimes with the elderly," he says in a voice Hillard is clearly meant to hear. "But I ain't never had that dang watch."

12

I know the words are false, but no stench accompanies them. He shows none of the outward signs of dishonesty I've learned to identify over the years. No shifts in the tone or volume of his voice, no fidgeting, no changes in the level of eye contact. And yet I know he's lying, so how can that be?

"I had your name added to the engraving!" Hillard loudly objects.

The rest of the meeting hall goes silent, and those closest to us aren't even trying to pretend they're not watching. I inhale deeply through my nose, trying to catch the scent that should be so strong by now it'd make my eyes water.

"I don't need this." Buck pushes off the back wall. "Call me when you recover your senses," he tells Hillard, pulling his hat down over his eyes as he stomps toward the exit.

Hillard slowly shakes his head. "My apologies, folks," he tells the crowd. "He's not been acting like hisself lately. Buck isn't usually one for confrontation. Most days I'm not even sure he's completely awake."

Slowly, I get to my feet, following the path Buck took. When Gayle Anne Gerlach told the town council clerk that her expenses were work related, a puff of papery smoke wafted through the air. When Okey Spurgeon called his wife to tell her he had to work late tomorrow, a smell like burnt meat slid across the room in a greasy swirl. Or even at home, when my sister Linden says she's fine, despite being bad-mouthed, shunned, then nearly killed less than a month ago, her breath is scented with coal—and it makes me want to burn this whole town to the ground. But now, after Buck had so clearly lied and the air should be thick with the stink of it, there's not so much as a hint of ash. Nothing.

And maybe the only thing worse than knowing every single lie is not knowing.